Bridgehead

Eden Chronicles – Book Four

S.M. Anderson

Other Books by S.M Anderson - and reading order:
All titles are available on Amazon and for Amazon's Kindle Unlimited. Audio versions for both series are available on Audible and have been released by Podium Audio.

The Eden Chronicles:
Book One: "A Bright Shore"
Book Two: "Come and Take It"
Book Three: "New Shores"
Book Four: "Bridgehead"

The Seasons of Man:
Book One: "End of Summer"
Book Two: "Reap What You Sow"
Book Three: forthcoming 2021

Chapter 1

Kaerus, Kaerin Capital, Chandra

Hundreds of spans below ground, the portal chamber was not at all what he had expected. Darnas' Moijan had always known the underground labyrinth beneath the Council Hall had its beginnings as a natural cave system that ran for kamarks beneath the city. He had not realized, nor been told, how much of it had been created or expanded by his people. Carved out of living rock, the gate chamber was massive. The air at its edges shimmered like black stone under the sun. Hints of orange fire reminding him of a sunrise danced within. Whether it was a reflection of the sky in the world to which they would be sent, or some effect of the gate itself, it mattered not; he was ready.

As a younger man, he had served in the Council Hall as one of the honor guard to the current prelate's father. For nearly forty years, he had served the S'kaeda family faithfully. It was time to step down and let a younger, more fit man lead Lord Noka's warriors. He did not dispute the tradition that would see him removed, and he was honored that he'd been chosen to lead this last mission. It was a trip from which he would not return; he knew that. They all did. Dying in the service of the Kaerin and the S'kaeda family appealed to him far more than watching an endless succession of sunsets from his estate while younger men fought for the Kaerin's survival.

Lord Noka had taken him into his confidence and told him what they were up against. A fight for their survival; their first in a very long time. The Kaerin prelate was preparing for an invasion he was certain would come. Those lords on the council who had been told of the threat were doing the same. Every holding on the planet was preparing, and getting stronger by the day. Subject war hosts were being mustered and equipped, standing ready to do their bidding. None of this would be his fight. Lord Noka had issued him only one command; "Attack until you cannot, then sell your lives dearly for our people. Let them have a true measure of what awaits them here."

Simple orders; the best kind. He looked through the barrier of shimmering light and could just make out the rough forms of his men waiting on the other side. There were only High Bloods within the gate, volunteers from each of the houses Lord Noka had felt he could trust with the truth. They were all veterans who had spent a lifetime carrying the sword. This was a death for which they had spent a lifetime preparing. Darnas stepped through the shimmering wall of air and came face to face with his men, standing in tight ranks before him. Further back in the massive chamber, hidden behind the supporting columns of stone, were other warriors who had their own mission. They'd entered the chamber hours ago, unseen.

Nothing more needed to be said. They had trained and planned as a group for two moons, waiting for the gate to become active. He turned in place and readied himself for a journey straight out of his people's legends. The Gemendi who had been standing next to him but a moment ago were now barely visible, as if they were on the far side of thick, dark glass. He could see them hovering over their arcane machinery like children at a puzzle, harnessing and controlling the natural power that grew out of this place and the impetus their generators added to the phenomena. As much as he despised the Gemendi as a group, now was not the time to be thinking ill of them.

A loud humming filled his head as the hair on his bare arms stood on end. The noise went from sound to something else felt in his bones, and then . . . nothing. The next moment, he was in an open field, surrounded by his ranks of men and forest. The echo of thunder rolling around him.

New Seattle, Eden (April 2033)

The morning shift in the Seattle operations center wasn't what it had been in terms of excitement six months ago. It was quiet, too quiet; all the action was on Chandra, at the Jema settlements and forts that were being planted across what they had labeled Caledonia. In Jeremy Ocheltree's mind, it was just Scotland and Northern England, albeit on another planet. Back on Earth, his father's family had emigrated from Scotland in the early 1800's. Nine years ago, the Ocheltrees had been among the early immigrants to Eden, early enough that their status as founders was secure. He was more than ready to bring the family name full circle and return. He had two months until his eighteenth birthday, and then he was formally signing on with the Eden Volunteers on Chandra.

He was already a militia member; everyone who had pitched in during the Strema invasion could say that. He hadn't just been part of the auxiliary army of teenagers that handled a lot of the logistics and supply; he'd flown actual missions delivering strike teams, including the first one that had located the now allied Jema. His father, a captain in the Eden Defense Force, had put an end to that as soon as the invasion had been defeated. "It's not our fight" encompassed pretty much everything that his father felt about Chandra, and until he turned eighteen, it was all that mattered. The volunteers, or the EDF for that matter, *would* take a seventeen-year-old if they could pass the physical, but only with both parents' permission.

Jeremy looked up at his shift partner, Roda'lis. The Jema woman's face pulled back from a high school physics book as she rubbed at her eyes, a pad of scratch paper balanced on her knee. Roda'lis was one of the thousands of new mothers among the Jema who had remained on

Eden. "They aren't putting *their* children at risk. Why should we?" was another of his father's standard arguments. That argument actually made some sense to him—except the part where his parents still considered him a child.

"This makes me angry . . ." "Roda" never said much at all. But when she did, she used her broken English rather than Chandrian, which he spoke quite well. English was just one of the things that the Jema who had been left behind had been asked to learn. Jomra and his council were adamant that the Jema were going to be the center of learning and advancement on Chandra. As a people, they were as hungry for knowledge on Eden as they were for justice on Chandra. The knowledge they were taking on went hand in hand with letting go of a culture that had been forced upon them. The Chandrian language itself was now often referred to as "Kaerin" by the Jema. It was just one of the many things they were forcibly letting go of.

"Is it the math?" he grinned, glancing at the textbook. "Makes me angry too."

"No, those are simple rules building on one another. It is not difficult. It is fact that your people learned of these things hundreds of years ago. Some of the math? Thousands of years ago! We have been robbed of all this."

He couldn't argue with that. "You'll catch up quick," he offered. "You already know more than the Kaerin." *And you're already better at math than I'll ever be . . .*

"Our children will perhaps have your knowledge. We will fight."

"We'll help you with that, on both fronts."

Roda pushed the book farther away. "You still wish to go to Chandra? When your parents allow it?"

"In seven weeks and three days, my parents won't have a say."

Roda shook her head in admonishment. "You would go against your father?"

He'd complained enough about his dad that Roda'lis was familiar with his problem. This was the first time she'd really done anything besides listen. Not exactly a sign of sympathy, but he would take what he could get.

"At eighteen, I'm a legal adult. I can do what I want."

"I thought this rule applied to your vote."

"That, too, but it gives us status as adults. From then on, we can make our own decisions."

"And you have decided you will go to Chandra with the volunteers? To fight the Kaerin?"

"I will."

"You can have a life here, raise a family. Join your Defense Force, like your father."

"Have you been speaking to him?"

Roda'lis gave him a strange look as she scooped up the textbook. "I have not met your father."

An hour later, he looked up at the line of clocks on the wall. As usual, it was the one labeled "Caledonia" that caught his attention. It was 10:30 a.m. in New Seattle; it would be close to dinnertime for some of his friends whose parents had given their consent. The first and main volunteer base was on the north coast of Solway Firth, near what would have been the small town of Kirkcudbright, Scotland back on Earth. With the growing movement among the Jema to eschew all things Kaerin; the base, the surrounding town, and everyplace they went in Caledonia or across Chandra proper, the Jema seemed to adopt the place's traditional English name.

The Jema and the volunteer force didn't have GPS on Chandra, but they would as soon as they built the satellites. Launching them into orbit was easy, just load them into the portal and enter the coords. Putting something into orbit around Chandra was no more difficult than sending a load of supplies to Caledonia. In the meantime, every Jema carried a compad with an exhaustive library of world maps. When they got to someplace new, they looked at what the map labeled the location and the name stuck, usually. Jeremy smiled to himself, thinking of his own people's opposing pressure on the language to shorten

5

everything. Scottish or Welsh place names could hardly be given an acronym, but Kirkcudbright had become Kirkton very quickly.

"Have you been to Kirkton yet?"

Roda stuck out a finger to mark her place in the passage she was reading and looked up at him with one of her eyebrows starting to arch. He realized he was about to be told to leave her alone when the computer terminal behind him went apeshit with an overlapping series of alarms.

"Translation detected," the computerized voice spit out and then repeated before he could turn around to disable the alert system. He reached over and flipped back the cover over a red button next to the keyboard and mashed it. Instantly, a new alarm sounded throughout the building and select structures across the city. Similar alerts would take a second or more to activate in every settlement across Eden.

Jeremy glanced at the large monitor dominating most of one wall and saw the red blob covering the center of North America. The blob was rapidly shrinking as the circular error probability algorithm was fed data from additional translation sensors scattered across the globe. The circle continued to tighten until it stopped; a fifteen-mile-wide area of probability. The easternmost edges of the circle encompassed the city of New St. Louis.

"Oh, shit."

The Jema's expedition to Chandra last fall had been able to confirm that some Strema had escaped to make it back to Chandra and report what they'd seen. In response, every settlement along the suspected path of the survivor's flight south, from the battle of the Mississippi to the Gulf of Mexico, had been put on notice that the Kaerin might know of their location. They'd all prepared, drilled, and readied themselves for an attack that hadn't come—until now.

He glanced up at Roda'lis, who was standing, looking at the monitor. "May their defenses hold."

*

6

Outskirts, New St. Louis

Gabby Martins was enjoying the laughter of her three children around the table. What started as good-natured bickering between the two older boys needed only a snide comment from their younger sister until the three of them were howling and trying to outshout each other. If there was anything better in life than the laughter of your own children, she hadn't heard of it.

Then it happened: the first biscuit was cocked back in the best throwing motion a seven-year-old girl could muster. The boys ducked, and Merlin, their three-year-old rottweiler, always alert for mayhem, readied himself to collect the thrown ordnance. She needed to put an end to the hilarity before a mess was made. She slapped the table with her palm. "Cassie! Don't you dare."

The world exploded around them as if God agreed. The heavens opened up with a massive clap of thunder that spiderwebbed the large pane of safety glass behind her, and shook the house hard enough that the table jumped and pictures came off the wall. Most of Eden had lived in fear of that sound for the better part of a year. Samuel, the oldest boy, ran to the window. She watched as the twelve-year-old turned back around to her, his face drained of color, even as Cassie's startled cry reached her ears.

"Mom . . .?"

She made it to the window and looked out at her worst nightmare. Hundreds of men with long rifles and long swords strapped to their backs standing in even ranks, in the field that Roger and some of the neighbors had cleared. The nearest ranks were less than thirty yards away. She took in the forest-green uniforms, some decorated with what looked like gold piping and red sashes. Long swords, some strapped to their backs, others in hand, made her blood run cold. Her brain struggled to catch up. Those weren't Strema; photos of the Kaerin collected by the Jema Expedition had been widely distributed in the last six months.

She grabbed Samuel by the shoulders as some of the men in the nearest edge of the formation start to turn towards their house. "Get them to the safe room!"

"You too, Mom!" Samuel tugged at her hand as she turned back to the window.

"Go! Now!" she screamed.

Three dozen heavy rifle rounds blew through the window.

"There were two of them; find the other." Teark Le'om looked down at the bullet- riddled body inside the strange dwelling. A woman, dark of hair, looked no different than the people of Chandra. They'd all been briefed that they would see much they would not understand. He glanced at a strange painting that had fallen from, the wall. A representation of the family that lived here. Not a painting, something . . . different. A man, a woman; the same that lay at his feet, and three offspring. He couldn't help but squat down in the broken glass and reach out to touch the strange painting that lay within a clear, glass-like frame. He was so mesmerized by the realism of the image; he did not hear the movement behind him until it was too late.

A boy, not yet of age, had popped up from behind the low cabinet separating the room from the one adjacent. He held a strange, short-bodied weapon in both hands. The child yelled something he could not understand but was raising the weapon as he did so. His own rifle was still coming around on his hip with a practiced efficiency when the room was filled with the staccato firing of the hummingbird gun. Teark Le'om, veteran of a dozen campaigns, had already been hit twice when his mind shouted at the injustice of his death at the hands of a child.

Several more bullets ripped into him as he crashed to the floor. He was dimly aware of the pounding of boots and then the firing of several Kaerin rifles. The last thing he saw was the face of the dead Shareki woman staring back at him.

Dadus Conid led three more warriors out of the dwelling carrying the weapon that the young boy had used to kill Teark Le'om. Such power in the hands of a child; what kind of cursed planet was this? The rest of the warriors were streaming past the house. They were all moving fast towards the line of taller structures they could see in the distance.

"Where is your teark?" Another scarred veteran stopped him and glanced at the Shareki weapon he carried.

"He has fallen," Conid reported. "To this."

"Did you find more of the ammunition cases that go inside it?" The teark's only concern was for the weapon.

They'd all been shown the weapons the Strema had managed to bring back from this world. The Gemendi had even been able to show them how they functioned. They'd been different than the one he now held, yet similar in form and function. The ammunition, molded brass, was all self-contained in slender boxes made of some strange material. It was those boxes he'd looked for, and not found in the house.

"Keep the weapon; there will be other opportunities to collect ammunition." The teark gripped him by the shoulder and glanced at the men behind him. "I am Teark As'tim. Your finger will now attach to me."

"Yes, Teark." The four of them spoke in unison. Conid didn't like this but knew that was unimportant. Le'om had served Lord Madral just as he and his men had. Teark As'tim's shoulder patch bore the symbol of Lord Atan'tal. If their new teark thought it strange to command men of his lord's rival, it did not show in his face.

"We are only Kaerin here," As'tim emphasized as if he could read his mind. Maybe tearks were the same everywhere. "Now move!" Other warriors streamed out of the two other adjacent dwellings; rifles and, in a couple of cases, reddened swords were raised in victory, signaling that the enemy within had been eradicated. Their entire "host" was three hundred volunteers; three meager "arms" of Kaerin warriors in the face of an entire world. There would be no victory for them; none of them expected anything but death. Conid could see the forwardmost edge of the leading arm approaching a series of two-story buildings ahead as the sounds of Kaerin rifles reached him. He ran a little faster, promising himself that his would be a better death than that which had greeted teark Le'om.

*

"Where are they?" Susan Park did her best not to shout over the bedlam of her operations center. She had begun her life on Eden as the settlement coordinator for New St. Louis. Following the influx of new arrivals to the small city and surrounding settlements, elections had been held. She'd won the position of city manager in a landslide; something she was regretting at the moment. Everyone in the room was looking to her for answers.

"Translation sensors have them on the outskirts of New Clayton." Bob Akers looked to be the only one who wasn't totally freaking out. "Alarms were sent from three homes, and the Clayton School just tripped theirs."

"Thank God it's a Saturday." Angela Levetti gave voice to what she'd been thinking.

"School's full of community training classes at the moment." Bob was shaking his head.

Shit . . . New arrivals learning new skills. They usually made it a family affair. "Alright, we've practiced this." She flicked out her hand and started ticking off her action plan on her fingers. "Get aircars up, get the count and photos to our ready response team, and make sure Seattle and Fort Appalachia get the report as well; start the evacuation plan for all noncombatants in the city to the other side of the river— ferry's only, for the moment. Any aircars not being used by the alert force will help evac Richmond and Wellston community centers, get those people out of there."

"Bob, how long before the EDF can get here?"

"Best case? An hour and a half." The taciturn industrial planner gave his head a shake and turned to go.

"Where are you going?"

"I'm on ready response this week. I'll radio back in as soon as we're on the ground."

"Good luck," she shouted at his back as he headed for the door. "Now, people!" She kept it under a shout, just barely.

*

Giroja and Want'ala were among the Jema who had elected to stay on Eden and raise a family. Giroja had every intention of joining the forces on Chandra next month, but only after he and his handfast had finished the building of their own house. They'd decided to attend the training classes in nearby Clayton; there was to have been a class in basic home wiring that he desperately needed. Electricity was one of the hundreds of things on Eden that a year ago had seemed like magic to him. Now it seemed like a necessity.

What was happening outside the Clayton community schoolhouse was something he understood very well. He'd taken one look at the advancing enemy from the window of a classroom and darted back to the main hallway. The Kaerin had come. Frantic Edenites were spilling out of the classrooms. Some were running for the outside doors, and he shouted for them to stop. There was no safety to be found outside these walls. Within, the safety would last only as long as they held the entrances. His voice went unheard amid the tumult. He found Want'ala standing against the far wall.

"Our child is safe." She smiled at him. She knew how this was going to end as well as he. They'd left their five-and-a-half-month-old daughter in the care of their neighbors to attend the training.

"She will live," he agreed. She might grow up speaking German in the care of the Schwebels, but she would grow up. His life's desire was complete. All that remained was what he had spent a lifetime doing. He saw the same determination set in his handfast's eyes.

He caught sight of one of the teachers rushing past; he reached out, grabbed the man by the arm, and swung him to the wall. He pointed up at the ceiling as the man stared back at him in fear. "The roof! How to get to roof?"

"The roof?!"

"Can we go to the roof? Outside?" He wished his English was better than it was.

The Edenite just looked at both of them, confused for a moment before his eyes seemed to clear. The man nodded once and pointed up at the ceiling. Outside the next classroom down the hall, was a recessed panel with a thin rope hanging out of it.

"Pull the ladder down; it goes to the attic. There is another ladder to the roof."

Giroja nodded his thanks, aware that Want'ala was already headed in that direction. He patted the gun holstered to the teacher's thigh. They could all be thankful that it was rare an Edenite went unarmed. "Collect all with weapons, guard the entrances, direct some to the roof. Do not let anyone go outside."

As if to emphasize the last, enemy long guns rippled their fire into the heavy doors at the end of the hall. Half a dozen Edenites and two children were killed outright when the heavy door nearly came apart under fire. The teacher's face went gray at the sight. They called it shock; he'd seen it in Edenite militia during the fighting with the Strema. These were a people, by and large, unused to war. He slapped the man's face.

"Guard the doors, from the rooms! Make them come to you."

The teacher nodded once in understanding and seemed to come back to himself as more Kaerin rifle fire blew through the windows of a nearby classroom.

"Go! Now."

He went up the strange folding staircase into the attic and saw the portal of sunlight ahead. Want'ala's feet were just disappearing through small square hatchway. He gripped his new 6.5mm assault rifle that the EDF and volunteer forces had been issuing over the last few months and knew he had only the one magazine already inserted. He might be a Jema, but he had been planning on learning how to wire the receptacles in his new kitchen this morning, not fighting Kaerin. Thirty rounds with which to make the Kaerin pay for his life—plus the single magazine he knew Want'ala had for her older 5.56. After that, they' would be be down to their sidearms and blades.

"Are you ready?" Want'ala asked, as he approached where she stood, fifteen feet back from the low wall running around the roof.

"They are Kaerin." He smiled at her. "We have been ready our entire lives."

*

"Good God . . ." Bob Akers crossed himself as he spotted the trail of bodies leading away from the school. From an altitude of two hundred feet, it looked like a mass of people penned up inside had made a break for it, or been driven out the back door. The Kaerin had been waiting for them. Their bodies lay atop each other where they'd been hit. The asphalt of the school's basketball courts was slick with pooled blood that glinted back at him as the sun's angle hit it during their circuit of the school.

There was no doubt the invaders were Kaerin. He saw a group of dead enemy warriors, their characteristic long swords, some in hand, lying where they'd been killed.

"Back up!" James Gorman, seated in the front next to the driver, shouted. "Let's find them!"

It shouldn't be difficult. There was a path of bodies to follow, leading away from the school towards the city. As they arched over the school, he saw the remains of another battle on the roof. A pile of dead Kaerin lay at the entrance to the attic door; a path of three more dead warriors led to two defenders who had been hacked apart by swords. Jema, from the looks of their clothing. He found himself wishing that the former, small "Jema town" area of New St. Louis was still a thing. In the last three months, most of the clan had followed Jomra back to Chandra.

*

Chapter 2

New Seattle

"How many?" Colonel Hank Pretty asked. He'd been made the formal commander of the EDF three months earlier, in what had been an unpopular move among some of the Edenite population. His "approval" of the Jema expedition to Chandra had been a damning indictment in the eyes of those who felt Eden had no business going to war on another planet.

David Jensen was not among that contingent, and the lead program scientist gave his head a slow shake. "We've got reports ranging from a platoon to over five hundred. They are Kaerin, though; that's been confirmed."

"At least it's not another host." One of Jensen's minions spoke up from where his face was buried in a keyboard. "And no other translation alarms. So far, this is isolated."

Hank knew that would be zero comfort for the people in the path of the Kaerin.

"Appalachia has scrambled their ready company; Captain Nagy is in command." Jensen finished updating him. "They are airborne and an hour out."

"Do we have a current location on the enemy force?" Hank asked. "Specifically, where are they? Where are they headed?"

"Beelining to the city so far, from small settlements to the west. The last report had them following the new road that is being built, on foot, but moving fast." The minion didn't look up from his computer.

"Where exactly on that road?"

The young man turned his computer around. "Here, sir, at the intersection of this north-south road. It's not exactly a road, more of a cleared track used by the settlers that have pushed out of the city."

Hank looked up at Jensen and nodded. "Get me the portal coordinates of a clear space, somewhere on that route into the city. No closer than five miles from their last reported area. Get St. Louis to try and slow them down."

Jensen knew where Hank's head was at. There was a ready force that could get to St. Louis a lot faster than Captain Nagy's Ospreys. They'd discussed the operational concept in rough terms, and right now, Hank had the right people in place to pull it off. It was time to demonstrate what a permanent presence on Chandra could do to protect Eden.

"I'll be in the portal room."

Kirkton Base, Chandra

The sound of rain, turning to sleet, then back to rain had been near-continuous over the last three days. It pounded on the roof, and the only time the deafening racket subsided, was when it was replaced by the howling moan of the wind coming off the Irish Sea, trying to uproot the carbon-plastic Quonset hut.

"Pot's good." Jake ran a finger around the table.

"I'm sorry," Kyle yelled, with a hand cocked behind his ear. "I can't hear you over the rain."

"You should have been here over the winter," Lupe Flores kicked in. "This is nothing."

"Seriously," Carlos grumbled as he started dealing the next card. "What asshole talked the Jema into coming here? We've been here four days, and I haven't seen the sun once."

"At least the fishing is good." Audy finished the circuit of comments.

"Bite me." Jake slowly gave the entire table his middle finger. "All of you."

Jeff sat at the end of his cot behind Jake, reassembling his rifle. "Speaking of fish, you do know they swim around in their own pee, right? When are we going to get some real meat around here? I'm about to dive into my pack for an MRE pouch of dog biscuit with cream sauce."

"I thought we ported some cows over?" Kyle was certain he'd read that in a report.

"You did," Lupe confirmed.

"A fine bull," Audy confirmed, "and nearly a dozen cows to breed. We butchered one that very day, to celebrate the New Year."

"I'm for celebrating again tonight." Jeff made it sound like a decision.

Kyle noticed Lupe and Audy were smiling at Jake in expectation of an answer.

"Jake? Where are the cows?" Kyle asked.

"I gave the cattle to the Creight tribe to the north of us. It's not like we can't ship more over, and I've already put in the request. They were hungry and needed them a lot more than we did." Jake sat back in his camp chair and dared anyone to challenge him. "What? We got a friendly Creight tribe out of the bargain, one that can watch our back as we move south."

"This is true," Audy agreed, looking at him. "They are friendly, and have been helpful."

Kyle had read the reports of the fledgling alliance with the scattered Creight to the north. Disparate bands of people living at the edge of survival, hunting and gathering for subsistence while hiding from annual summer Kaerin hunting parties. Jake's face was a mask of inscrutable calm. There was something here that hadn't made the reports.

"But?" Kyle asked.

"Rai'nor," Lupe kicked in. "We call him Ray; he's the Krathik of the northern Creight. He was so happy with the gift, in addition to the fact we weren't Kaerin come to slaughter his people, he offered up his youngest sister to Jake in exchange." Lupe shrugged and smiled. "But only because he didn't have a daughter of his own."

As much as he was enjoying the look of pain on Jake's face, he also knew Jake was an avowed man-whore. "You didn't . . ."

"Of course not." Jake threw his hand of cards down on the table in disgust. "I've never paid for it in my life, and I wasn't going to start with trading cows."

"So, she was ugly?" Jeff spoke up.

Jake turned in his chair and just stared at Jeff.

"I have to admit, I was thinking it too." Carlos laughed, breaking the tension.

"Noooo." Audy shook his head. "Quite the opposite, in fact."

"So . . . ?" Carlos didn't get a response from Jake and turned to Audy.

"Rai'nor was offended at the refusal of his . . . gift," Audy explained. "Though I think he may be . . . you have a word for this, preparing the ground for future negotiations."

"Posturing?" Kyle asked.

"Yes," Audy agreed. "I think he is only posturing. We thought Arsolis was difficult. Rai'nor is cut from an even rougher cloth. His people remain friendly. The woman, though, Dere'dala, she was unhappy."

"She tried to castrate Jake," Lupe corrected.

Audy waived off Lupe's comment. "Not truly. She was angry, embarrassed perhaps. She holds no authority with her people, so it will not be a problem for us or our presence." Audy smiled at him and then looked across the table at Jake. "Except for him."

It took Kyle a moment to figure out what he was seeing in Jake's face; it clicked in place with a surprise that bordered on shock.

"Holy shit . . . You've fallen for the girl! Haven't you?"

Jake pushed the pile cards in front of him across the table. "I fold."

"Dude!" Jeff got up and placed a hand on Jake's shoulder. "Every legend has to die. Go get the girl."

"What I was saying." Lupe grinned. "He tried—that's when she tried to castrate him."

"Maybe some more cows?" Carlos deadpanned. The room, even Jake, exploded in laughter.

An hour later, their barracks hut was quiet. Or would have been without the incessant rain on the roof. Kyle was reading up on the reports from the scouting teams Audy and Jake had been sending south from Kirkton for the last two months. He was amazed at how empty Chandra's version of the British Isles was. They could only assume it had everything to do with the Kaerin's distrust of indigenous island populations. Islands were harder to control. For the original Kaerin who had been marooned on Chandra, it had been much easier to subjugate the entire Eurasian landmass with their subject armies than it had been to develop the maritime capacity or traditions necessary to manage populations in far-flung locales across water. At least it was their working theory.

Piecing together what they'd learned from the Creight to the north of them and from Arsolis, their Hatwa fishermen turned pirate; it appeared that original populations of what he thought of as England, Scotland, Wales, and Ireland had been transplanted to the continent centuries ago. No one knew where they'd wound up. The story was akin to that of Audy's people, who had been indigenous to Scandinavia and the Baltics. Too much water, too many islands. Once defeated, the Jema had been uprooted and forced- marched across Europe to the Iberian Peninsula. All of the British Isles were "owned" by the Kaerin lord Atan'tal, who controlled the BENELUX countries and the northern half of what they thought of as France. The nation-state references in the report were of course meaningless on Chandra, but it was by far the easiest way for all of them, Edenite and Jema alike to build out their mental map of the world created by the Kaerin.

Jeff turned around from where he'd been standing at the door, watching the rain in the early-evening darkness. "I think the deluge is lightening up to just a downpour."

Rain or not, he was getting out of camp tomorrow. He hadn't made the trip to sit inside waiting for good weather. He wanted to see what the Jema and the EDF were building here. Hank had kept him busy on Eden, as had Elisabeth and their daughter, Sophie. He was ready to stretch his legs. He was about to reply when their radios blared to life.

"This is Colonel Pretty. We have a Kaerin landing west of New St. Louis. Gear up. Train leaves in five mikes. I'm at the Kirkton portal; report to me as soon as possible."

"Several hundred at least, maybe more." Hank answered the question he'd been about to ask the moment he entered the brand-new portal complex. Hank kept talking as he shook Kyle's hand. "Moving directly east towards the city. How many troops are we going to be able to move?"

Kyle smiled back. Kirkton's portal chamber could hold two hundred fully armed soldiers. A snap-kick like this was going to be just weapons and ammo; he'd seen the numbers gathering outside where Audy and Jake were organizing them. "It'll be standing room only, two hundred thirty, maybe two hundred fifty."

Kyle turned to the young technician running the portal's programming just outside the massive doorway. It was Augustine, who had helped carry his ass through Idaho not very long ago. "August? How long before you can send a second transmission after us?"

"The solar array hasn't seen the sun in a week. It'll be several hours before the generators can recharge the capacitors, sir."

"Nagy's troops are already in transit by air," Hank cut in. "He'll be on-site in about forty-five minutes with two companies, but it will be too late for a lot of people."

"How bad is it?"

"Ugly." Hank shook his head. "If there hasn't been another translation, I'd have to guess it's a raid designed for terror. They can't expect to accomplish much else."

Outside New St. Louis, Eden

"War Leader, the enemy has taken a position blocking this road. Half a kamark ahead." Hala'mos, the bastelta reporting to him, was as old as he was. With the blood of this world splattered on the side of his face and staining his tunic, the man looked half his age.

"They do not attack?"

"They wait."

"They think we fight like Strema slaves. Send a fist to either flank, signal when you are in position to attack, and I will get their attention for you here, in the middle."

Hala'mos nodded once. "The order was already given. They should be in position."

Darnas' gave the veteran bastelta a nod of appreciation.

This was the second time the sparse defenders had set up defenses as though the Shareki expected them to walk into their guns. No doubt, it was what the Strema and Koryna had done. The Kaerin had trained their subjects to fight that way. By Kaerin design, wars between subject clans were bloody, violent affairs that could be decided in a matter of days while limiting the destruction to surrounding infrastructure and productive land. The goal was twofold; first, to cull the subjects to keep them more manageable in terms of numbers; and second, to instill in them an honor-based system of warfare that would make them that much easier to defeat should the need arise.

Darnas' had read closely the reports supplied by Lord Noka. The Jema, according to the few Strema survivors, had adopted a more flexible way of fighting against the Strema. He' had been a warrior all his life, and seen more than one subject war leader try to adopt better tactics. Such efforts had always been punished to the point the leader's entire clan suffered. Indeed, the Jema insurrection and the subsequent culling of those wretched people had begun in just such a manner. Lord Noka had shared his concerns that sound tactical measures may need to be disseminated to the subject clans to fight the war they feared were coming. He understood the concern, but so far had seen little in the Shareki world's fighting ability that would seem to necessitate a move so laden with risk.

Their superior weapons aside, these people did not seem to rely on warriors. Still, his numbers had been significantly reduced by an enemy that he had yet to see. There had been exceptions; the two Jema warriors at the first large structure they had encountered, and the damaged airboat that had purposely steered itself into a group of his warriors. To a large extent it was an enemy that they never saw; he'd lost many warriors to unseen weapons fired from the woods or the buildings they passed by in their headlong rush to reach the city ahead.

Darnas' looked down one of the aisles of the strange building he was in, a large structure for the collection and dissemination of food, as near as he could tell. Ten or more Shareki lay dead in the aisle he could see. Women and children for the most part, though some of them had managed to take a warrior with them before they had been put down. Even the women of this place seemed to have weapons. Where were the vaunted Shareki warriors they had been warned of?

It was time to move. He walked out of the building, and was immediately tackled to the ground and pulled behind one of the hundreds of mechanical ground vehicles that seemed to grow more numerous the closer they got to the city ahead.

"They have marksmen, War Leader!" His warrior pulled himself off and helped him sit up behind the vehicle. "They are firing from their positions ahead."

He nodded his thanks as he brushed himself off. "From where they block the road?"

"Yes, some of them have weapons that reach the distance. We lost another teark and two more warriors.

He took a position on one knee, glanced around the back of the vehicle. If anything, the line of defense was farther away than half a kamark. It was impossible to be accurate at that distance. An angry whine buzzed past his ear, and he flinched at the sound made by the projectile slamming into the building behind him.

High blood of the ancients! What his people could do with such weapons. He glanced at the teark who had just saved his life and offered a nod of thanks. "Bastelta Hala'mos will soon be in position to attack. We must be ready." No sooner had he turned back around, when warriors across the street began flashing hand signals to those around them. Hala'mos's men were in position.

Some of the surrounding buildings were made of materials he couldn't recognize; others were of wood and stone. They had left the graveled paths and reached roads that were covered in a remarkable material that he did not recognize. All of it, though, he could tell was new. The whole area they were in and had already moved through, had the look of having been recently carved out of the surrounding forest. The buildings were new as well. All of it was evidence that this world was a colony of some sort. What else could explain the lack of coordinated resistance?

He added his own hand signals and waited for his warriors, hunched down behind cover in all directions, to acknowledge him. His men knew what they had to do; focus the enemy's attention. Let the Shareki think they were Strema slaves who would assault a defended position out of honor. Meanwhile, the warriors hidden on their flanks would move in and catch them unawares.

"Now!" He rose up over the side of the vehicle and fired his rifle at the first head he spotted. Rifle fire exploded around him as he remained up and worked the bolt on his rifle. One of his men from a position fifty spans ahead, cut loose with one of the captured Shareki guns; he crouched down to watch the gun in action. The rapid staccato fire stopped as suddenly as it had started. He watched as his warrior worked the bolt on the strange weapon before dropping it to the ground and swinging his own long rifle around off his back. Miraculous or not, the enemy's guns needed ammunition just as their own did.

He rose back up and fired just as the Shareki position up the road was taken under fire from both flanks. The sound of the gunfire took on a different quality as a mass of Kaerin rifle fire in the distance joined that of the defenders. He heard the screams over the distance and saw a long blade rise and cut downward on an enemy behind the makeshift barricade of vehicles. He stood. "Forward!" The center of the Shareki town stood less than three kamarks away.

Darnas' had taken three steps when an enemy airboat, the one the Strema had named a "Dragonfly" for its ability to hover, swung out over the road behind them. He was amazed to see the strange blades whirling above it. The craft fired a rocket of some sort that streaked over his head, and slammed into a 'hand' of his warriors that had been sheltering behind a line of vehicles. The blast blew him off his feet. He rolled to a stop and watched in amazement as the airboat's nose seemed to flash with sparks.

The fireball, from whatever had been shot at his men, was still rising when the hummingbird gun in the airboat's nose blazed with rifle fire so rapid, he could not fathom how it was done. Chunks of road material exploded upward with dark puffs in a line that marched across the road, towards a pile of cut trees that had hid a hand's worth of his warriors from the Shareki defenders.

The warriors scrambled to get around the pile to reach the safety of the other side. The airboat's fire reached the log pile and went silent just before another rocket streaked out from under its body. He almost had time to curl into a ball before the world went white behind his eyelids and something hammered into his hip.

He forced his eyes to open and saw the log pile had been reduced to a cloud of fire and wood shrapnel, even as the man next to him grabbed him by the shoulders and pulled him back across the road, behind a vehicle.

"War Leader! You are hit."

There was a handspan's worth of wood sticking out of him just below his hip bone.

"Leave it!" He pushed the man away. "Where is the airboat?"

"It flew away."

"Move, everyone move now." He pulled himself up against the vehicle and did his best to ignore the pain of shredded muscles in his leg. He pulled a small vial from his waist bag and ripped the waxed cork free with his teeth. The bitter Gemendi concoction tasted of earth and moss, but he felt his heart answer in thanks. His warriors streamed forward past him, far fewer than there had been a moment ago. His pain receded behind a tide of energy as the elixir worked its magic. He pushed the warrior away. "Go!" He had work to do before he bled to death.

The pain was gone by the time he reached the defender's skirmish line a few minutes later. There was only the taste of dirt in his mouth and a growing chill in his fingers. Bastelta Hala'mos ran back to him, and he waved off the concern he could see in the man's eyes.

"How many are we?" he asked.

"We have a full Arm left, perhaps another fist of injured that can still fight."

He appreciated Hala'mos including him in that number, but the chemicals were wearing off. He would follow until he could not. A hundred healthy warriors left, a third of what they had come with.

"You will lead them. I will follow as I can."

Hala'mos glanced down at the piece of timber sticking out of his commander's hip and jerked his head once in understanding. They both flinched in reflex as a massive wave front of sound washed over them. The echo was still bouncing around when they looked at each other in surprise.

"It sounds like when we arrived." Hala'mos was smiling at him. "Lord Noka has sent reinforcements."

Darnas knew that was not the case, and the only other alternative

24

sent chills through him. "Those are not our reinforcements." He pointed towards the city. "Send scouts to locate them. I think their warriors have arrived."

Hank's radio, programmed for the local St. Louis EDF channel, fired to life before the echoes of their arrival had faded. Kyle shook his head, trying to remind his brain that it had made the trip, and was no longer in the "nowhere" it had just passed through. Audy's team of Jema scrambled outward to set up a defensive perimeter, even as Jake's squad sprinted forward with claymores.

Hank was busy plugging in an earpiece so he could coordinate with the local militia when a burst of gunfire erupted in the woods west of them. "They've moved fast," Hank announced. "We're almost on top of them." Several pillars of dark smoke were prominent on the western horizon above the trees. The enemy had headed straight for the city. Hank stared at his compad that had linked to the local net and was updating his map.

"There." He pointed up the road. "They are in the woods, either side of the road a half mile out."

"We should pull apart," Audy suggested, "let them come on, and then catch them." Audy pulled his hands apart and then brought them back together.

"No time for much else," Jeff agreed.

They all turned to look behind them as a dozen vehicles screeched to a stop, coming out from the town behind their backs. The cars and trucks had barely stopped before the occupants, men and women of the local militia, unloaded and came running forward. "Kyle and I will get these people in a line here." He turned to Jake, Jeff, and Audy. "As soon as the perimeter is set, take your teams to the flanks. Leave Kyle and me a platoon here and a couple of the SAWs. We'll hold them by the nose; you guys move in."

"Going roof," Carlos called out and led Lupe and four Jema snipers away.

At the last intersection before the main east-west road entered the city, they had just gotten into position and set up across the road. The SAW teams and the snipers were on the second and third floor of a line of new apartment buildings overlooking the approach, when they spotted the lead elements of the Kaerin moving up. And they were Kaerin, of that there was no doubt. From the second-floor balcony, Kyle could see the long swords strapped to the backs of the Kaerin. He even spotted two of the enemy carrying captured EDF rifles. The tactics the enemy used to move from cover to cover and advance in a leapfrog manner between the individual homes, vehicles, and terrain features was a long way from how the Strema operated. It was a significant and very unwelcome improvement.

"Never thought I'd wish to see more Strema," Hank said from behind his field binoculars.

"There's about to be a lot fewer of these." Kyle palmed the trigger to the first line of daisy-chained claymores they'd emplaced across the road and just inside the defile of a small stream paralleling their crossroad. He watched as more Kaerin warriors moved forward to mass out of sight in the creek's depression.

"EDF One, for all—hold fire. Flanking teams advise when you are in position." Hank sat his radio aside and glanced at him as he scooped up his assault rifle. "Tell the SAW teams to wait until I fire."

They didn't have time to do anything of the sort. A line of Kaerin surged up and out of the streambed onto the road and moved towards them. The Kaerin moved fast in a controlled wave, and Hank opened up a split second before the three squad automatic weapons (SAWs) fired. In an instant, there were more Kaerin almost to the crossroad than Kyle had guessed had been using the streambed for cover. He slammed the clacker for the nearest line of claymores and managed to keep his eyes open as three large gaps were torn open in the enemy line as the Kaerin on the road were shredded by the expanding wall of steel projectiles. The gunners on the SAWs had more distinct groups to target, and the machine guns chewed up those still on their feet at the edge of the road before starting to rake across the lip of the small gully.

Kyle saw more movement in and beyond the streambed. He scooped up the second clacker and lit off the remaining line of antipersonnel claymores they'd placed across the road in the shallow ravine. He shut out the screams of men dying that he could hear between bursts from the SAWs, even as their friendly flanking forces gave up on trying to get in position and added their firepower to the mix. Jeff, Jake, and Audy directed their teams to move in. The heavy-caliber rifle fire from Carlos's sniper teams on the roof above them was continuous. The fire from the St. Louis militia on either side of him was running out of targets. The enemy had utilized the terrain on their approach to good effect, but now they were caught in a pocket, surrounded on three sides. The only way out, was back the way they'd come. Not a single one of the Kaerin chose that option.

*

Four young warriors who counted themselves among the most elite of Lord Noka's personal host, had hidden in the back of the massive translation chamber as the elder volunteers had filed in. They had made the jump between worlds along with Darnas' Moijan and "landed" two hundred spans from the meadow that had been the site of the main group. The same distance that had separated them within the chamber itself.

They were only three now. Kilnas had the bad fortune to "appear" in this world inside a large tree. The portion of the tree that had lived in that same space had disappeared, and Kilnas had laughed in surprise for a half second before the rest of the tree collapsed straight down under its own weight and crushed him. The tree had nearly killed him as it toppled. They'd left their brother where he lay and followed the volunteers at a distance, staying in the woods and seeking the high ground south and west of the city. As much as it had pained them to just watch the ill-fated attack, they had their orders.

"That was impressive." Gurl'ansa let the captured looking glass fall against his chest. They had just watched the remaining Kaerin force be slaughtered like weaponless Creight.

Manoma sighed. "Everyone here is armed, even the women and some of the older children. Darnas Moijan was at half strength for that fight."

It would have made no difference. They were all experienced enough to know that. Which was what made their mission so critical. Gurl'ansa clapped Hanlas' on the shoulder. The quiet warrior's face was set in determination. His father had been among the veterans who had just died.

"Which is why we will avoid them all. We will not waste the sacrifice that delivered us. Lead off, Hanlas."

*

Chapter 3

New Seattle, Eden

It had taken nearly a week to gather the elected leaders from all of Eden's settlements for the first in-person gathering of the Eden Council. Seattle had more people in it than Kyle could remember seeing since right before the Strema had invaded. In what he took as a sign that they were doing something right, this time around, the visitors couldn't wait to leave and get back to wherever they'd come from.

He knew it was a sentiment he shared with Theo Giabretti. The former cruise ship bartender and Marine had been elected as the settlement chief in Chief Joseph against his will. He'd voted for the man himself, and didn't know anybody in Joseph who didn't like the man.

"Hey, how come I had to fly in?" Theo as usual was talking with his hands. "Some of my more esteemed colleagues were saying how they got here via Chandra. Two quick portal jumps, in something they called the phone booth, and no air sickness." Theo looked like a big, bearded teddy bear, and his time on Eden hadn't done a thing to dilute his Bronx accent.

"I'm guessing they had a lot farther to come than you did?" Jason Morales answered for him. The three of them were standing outside the program headquarters building, enjoying the momentary sunshine that none of them expected to last long in a typical Seattle spring. Jason and Theo were headed into the big council session, and Kyle was headed out, having just finished two hours of an emotionally charged military council meeting that he knew wouldn't hold a candle to the meeting that his two friends were about to endure.

At one point in the morning's meeting, an aide to General Majeski, who commanded Fort Appalachia, had asked Kyle "whether or not he should have to decide between keeping a role in the EDF or involving himself in the Jema jihad on Chandra." Hank had saved him from having to answer and settled the issue for the EDF.

"As I've been discussing all morning, they are one and the same," Hank had answered. "And that will be the official stance of the EDF going forward, or you can find someone else to wear my hat. The Kaerin will not stop. They cannot stop and maintain their power on Chandra. I shouldn't have to point out that during recent events in St. Louis, a combined unit of EDF volunteers and Jema troops were able to get to St. Louis from Chandra long before the ready force from Fort Appalachia arrived, on the fly, with zero prep. Captain Nagy would have been just as effective as we were, probably more so, as it is the exact scenario his unit trains for—but the EDF cannot garrison this planet."

Hank had laid out the cold military logic that not a single person in the room could argue with. "Going forward, with the EDF focused on Chandra and specifically at our bases on the British Isles, we are quite literally a split second away from anywhere on Eden." Hank held up a hand. "And yes . . . the Kaerin will discover us there. It's something we need to come to terms with as a group. They are at war with us and the Jema, with anyone not directly digging ditches for them. We fight them on their territory, on a world full of potential allies—or here, playing a game of whack-a-mole that we will eventually lose."

"If anybody has an issue with anything that I've laid out, speak up now." Hank had waited a long moment, searching the faces in the room before he carried on with a more jovial tone. "As we all know, a logical, coherent military policy is one thing, but in an hour, I will present this same strategy to our civilian leadership. They are good people and reliable partners, but let's not forget that two hundred sixty-seven of our civilians have just been massacred. Prayer, burnt offerings, small animal sacrifice—whatever you think might help with our civilian oversight would be much appreciated. They'll deliberate for the next day or so, I'm sure, so stay in town and talk to them. They have to understand we fight there or here, but we are at war."

"And please," Kyle had added his own voice, "our people have to understand that the Kaerin are coming for us because we beat the Strema, because they know there are people within reach that could challenge them. It's not because of the Jema. The Jema have asked for our help, yes. But I think some of our people need to be reminded that we recently asked for theirs as well."

Kyle had walked out into the crowd gathered in front of the headquarters building, prepared to do the first lobbying of his life, when he'd spotted Theo and Jason. He smiled at Jason's response, and then leaned in to Theo, "Some of your colleagues might have needed a personal demonstration of how fast we could get to anywhere on Eden via Chandra. Doc Jensen's phone booth was the perfect marketing tool."

"I get it." Theo shrugged in mock offense. "My support is taken for granted."

"Exactly." Kyle smiled.

"I could have sworn I mentioned getting airsick on the way in?"

They all shared a laugh, and he turned to Jason, who, as the program's economic policy director had more contact with the settlement leaders than anyone. "How do you see this going from your optic?"

Jason smiled and shook his head. "I'll be forced to negotiate a few promises of additional development with some of the settlements. It's no different than what I do every day."

"You'll bribe them?" Theo grunted. "I should learn how to play this game better. Did I mention that Chief Joe has requested another nano bed?"

"Everyone needs more nano-production." Jason shrugged. "Demand is a good thing."

"Besides," Kyle added, "I thought we'd already determined your support is a given?"

"I'm rethinking it." Theo rubbed at his beard. "In fact, if I stand in opposition to helping out the Jema, I'll piss off most of my constituents and be voted out of office. That would be a win as far as I'm concerned."

And a real loss for Chief Joseph. He knew Theo was only half joking; the man hated politics. Which was one reason he'd run unopposed after being nominated by Kyle's father. "Seriously." Kyle shook his head. "Don't let anyone paint this as helping the Jema or leaving them to their own fate. This is about our long-term security, maybe survival. Which is exactly how the Kaerin must see the issue."

"You're good at this." Theo clapped him on the shoulder. "You should—"

He was interrupted by a young woman with a bullhorn. The session was about to begin, and the crowd started flowing inside.

"I got it." Theo gave him a nod of confidence and indicated the civilian leaders around them. He leaned in close. "These people are probably smarter than you give them credit for. They know the score."

*

"You would not believe the stupidity of some of these... ASSCLOWNS!" Elisabeth was growling as she stormed through the door of her Seattle apartment. They'd kept her original apartment besides their home outside of Chief Joseph because it seemed like one or both of them were always in town. Little Sophie jerked at the sound of her mother's voice as Kyle was attempting to complete a diaper change with a particularly high degree of difficulty. How anything so cute could produce what he'd just had to deal with, he did not know. His mother, his own flesh and blood, who had been helping out with their daughter, had offered no assistance and sat at the kitchen table enjoying his torment.

"Hey." He looked over his shoulder. "What if she'd been asleep?"

Elisabeth kicked off her shoes, shared a smile with his mom, and came up to peek around him at their daughter. "Somebody sent me a video of your efforts here."

"Seriously, what are you feeding her?"

"Kyle, you are the last person in the world, two worlds," his mom crowed, "to be complaining about radioactive diaper loads."

Kyle leaned in over his daughter, whose eyes seemed to follow the voices. "Don't listen to the mean old lady." He gave Elisabeth a kiss on the cheek. "How bad was it?"

Elisabeth had just finished her second ten-hour day of deliberations being held by the settlement committee and looked like she needed to hit something. She checked his work on the diaper and then scooped Sophie up. "Four hours into the session, it was the first time I've been thankful I had to excuse myself to go pump."

"That bad?"

He watched as Elisabeth starting feeding the baby and turned towards his mom.

"Did you know your son is one of the ringleaders of an effort to get Eden involved in—and I quote, 'an endless cycle of warfare and defense spending in line with what the United States has done since the end of World War Two'? OR—my personal favorite, 'The program is walking Eden into a cold war that guarantees their continued control.'"

"Wow. . ." His mom shook her head. "I'll be the first to admit history isn't my strong suit, but I don't ever remember the Soviets or Al Qaeda invading us."

Kyle just shook his head; last night's report from Elisabeth had been much the same. "How strong is that sentiment?"

"Tough to tell." Elisabeth shrugged. "First vote is tomorrow at noon. I do think Jason had it right. A lot of the settlements see the need to be present on Chandra. They're just bitching to get more resources and plant allotments."

"That's just politicians being assholes," his mom said. "You can't expect them not to stick their noses into the trough and slurp up everything they can."

Elisabeth laughed at that. "Christine, I know—it's just that part of me, naively I guess, expected we could have left that BS behind. Not everyone is just playing lip service to the arguments." Elisabeth gave her head a shake. "There are some true believers that seem to think the Kaerin will leave us alone if we could only convince the Jema to cool their jets."

"Might as well hope for no more rain in Seattle," he commented.

"Speaking of Jema," his mother said, "where is Audy? And for that matter, Jake? I thought they'd all be here."

"Chandra." He smiled to himself. "Audy is helping Jake work out some issues with the some of the locals we've managed to contact."

"What'd Jake do?" Elisabeth looked at him with knowing expectation that only someone who had spent a good portion of her childhood with Jake could understand.

"In this case, it's something he didn't do . . ." The memory of the look of anguished frustration on Jake's face was still with him. "If I didn't know better, I think Jake thinks . . . he's in love." The look of shock on Elisabeth's face was priceless, and he explained what had happened, cows and all.

"I knew when he fell, he'd fall hard." Elisabeth was shaking her head. "He's going to be worthless until he sorts it out; you know that, right?"

Yeah, he knew that.

"I think it sounds romantic, in a . . . medieval, I guess, sort of way." His mom had clapped her hands together. "He's such a nice man; it'd be good for him to settle down."

"Mom, this is Jake," he reminded her. "He has a girlfriend in every town he's ever visited on three different planets, and the girl's tribe is more Bronze Age, hunter-gatherer than anything we'd recognize as medieval. You did hear me say that she was offered up in trade for some cattle."

"Well, I'm still happy for him."

Elisabeth had a strange look on her face. "What are you thinking?" he asked.

"I'd give a finger or two to get there and study these societies on Chandra. It's like being an astronaut and having to watch everyone else hop aboard a rocket and go to Mars while I sit here talking to them on the radio." She looked down and smiled at their daughter. "Not that I'm complaining."

He understood where she was coming from. Most of the background reports from Audy and Jake's foray to Hatwa lands during the last fall had been destined for her desk. Elisabeth had written the protocols for making contact with the Creight on Caledonia that the Jema had utilized.

"Well then, you'll just have to convince the council to go forward with our plan." He reached out and put his hand atop Sophie's tiny head. "To do this right, Kirkton Base or Dumfries is going to be as safe as anyplace on Eden." Maybe safer, he thought. At least on Chandra, they'd be able to see the enemy coming. He doubted if the attack on St. Louis was the last they'd see. The strategy made too much sense from the Kaerin's point of view.

"You can't be serious?" His mom panicked.

"Are you?" Elisabeth asked him.

"Yeah," he admitted. "There's not enough housing at the moment, but there will be soon. Maybe I'm being a little selfish, but I'd love to have you both there with me."

"Christine." Elisabeth shook her head. "I won't be going anywhere for a while yet. Sophie's still too young." She turned and faced him. "But give us a few months." Elisabeth leaned her head down and nuzzled their baby girl. "I think we'd both like that."

*

Caledonia, Chandra

"You weren't kidding, were you?" Jeff was looking through binoculars down at the Creight village that lay thirty miles inland, northeast of Kirkton Base. It had taken them two full days to negotiate the distance on foot through near-trackless heavy forest separating Dumfries, which lay roughly halfway between Kirkton and Rai'nor's village. They would have flown, but Jake wanted to give Jeff and Carlos an appreciation for the terrain they were going to be dealing with, and map familiarization was a poor cousin to the real thing. "Village" was an exaggeration; "camp" would have been more accurate. In this case, it was the winter camp belonging to Rai'nor's personal band. "I thought Detroit was bad," Jeff added.

"How long have they lived like this?" Carlos asked.

"They do not know," Audy answered. "This is Rai'nor's camp; his own band has other camps to the north of us. Creight stay to the far north in the summer, and his band is making preparations to move again. The Kaerin hunt them in summer for training and for sport."

"Not this summer," Jeff countered, pulling the binoculars away and taking a moment to spit out a stream of tobacco juice. "This year is going to be different."

"These are the Kaerin out of Portsmouth?" Carlos asked.

"Yes," Audy said. "All the British Isles to include Ireland are part of Lord Atan'tal's holding. Portsmouth on the south coast faces his primary lands across the channel in what you and we are now referring to as France. Portsmouth is his only settlement on Britain, or Caledonia as we call it. It is not as big as Legrasi in the Hatwa lands, but it is substantial and has a large garrison force. Elisabeth wrote in her report that it is in effect a large latifundium. I had to look up the word."

Carlos and Jeff shared a look of confusion. "Don't keep us in suspense, Audy. What's it mean?" Carlos asked.

"It's basically a large armed plantation," Jake answered, shaking his head at both of them. "About the size of Maryland. It has agriculture, mining, some industry, and a big naval base. The Kaerin fort there is big, lots of High Blood assholes running around polishing their long swords. The high lord Atan'tal makes his home across the channel near what we'd have called Rouen."

"How many Kaerin?" Jeff asked.

"A war fist," Audy answered. "Five thousand warriors in and around Portsmouth, with many others as well."

"What do you mean, others?" Carlos asked.

"Lots of sailors." Jake shrugged. "Sailors, Marines, I guess. There's a shit ton of them, too, but they come and go with their toy boats."

"And the slave labor?" Jeff asked. "How many of those poor bastards?"

"Tens of thousands," Audy answered. "They have been brought from the mainland over the centuries. They work the farms within the interior, near what your maps would have called Winchester or Sale . . . berry?"

"Salisbury," Jake corrected without taking his eyes off the village below. It was apparent Jake was only half listening to their conversation, his attention focused on what or who lay below.

"Salis-berry," Audy tried again. "Rai'nor's ancestors are descended from these same subjects brought over as labor. He says that his people were of the Junata, but I do not think even he knows for certain. It would make sense; the Junata people are part of Lord Atan'tal's holding on the continent."

"So, the plan is to take Portsmouth." Jeff nodded to himself. "Before they realize we're here and reinforce from the mainland."

"In a nutshell," Jake shrugged. "Yeah."

"Is a tough nut," Audy offered. "This island has a lot of coastline to watch."

"Which is why we are here." Jake nodded down to the Creight village of hide tents and a few rock structures with thatch roofs. "We need the Creight's help."

Carlos laughed and slapped Jake on the back. "Not the only reason we're here, right? I mean, who better than us to offer up a solid character reference for you?"

"More cattle would have been better." Audy smiled.

Jake made a point of brushing off Carlos's hand. "You can all kiss my ass."

"We should make our way down," Audy interrupted their laughter. "We have been seen." Activity in the village had ceased. Every person they could see looked like they were getting ready to run. Jake bent over to grab the heavy duffel bag of supplies he'd brought as a peace offering.

"You should not be the one to carry that." Audy waved. "Your status would be . . . further diminished."

Jake dropped the heavy bag at Audy's feet. "Now you're making sense."

Audy looked at the bag for a moment and then back up at Carlos and Jeff in apology. "I'm negotiating on behalf of the Jema today. As Jomra's representative, my status is . . ."

"For fuck's sake." Carlos grabbed the bag and grunted as he lifted it onto his shoulders. "Aren't we lucky there's a Marine to help you ladies out."

They knew they were being tracked as they made their way down the hillside to where a small stream, nearly hidden by thick underbrush, ran at the bottom of a grassy meadow. They were met by two spear-and-bow-wielding warriors and a single middle-aged woman, standing like sentinels on the far side of the small stream. All three carried a long knife at the waist, wrapped in a hide scabbard.

Jeff shared a look of surprise with Carlos; the Creight's clothing were a couple of steps below what they had seen among the small number of Hatwa who now made Kirkton Base their home. They'd both seen poverty up close during their careers and were no strangers to cultures living a hardscrabble existence. Outside of the new boots worn by the warriors, evidence of previous contact with the Jema and Kirkton, the Creight looked like they belonged to the Iron Age civilization they had devolved to.

"Greetings, Mat'isa," Audy intoned. "These are warriors from Eden that I have spoken about. Jeff and Carlos." Audy turned to them. "This is Mat'isa, handfast to Rai'nor, the Krathik."

Jeff bowed his head slightly as Audy had instructed them. "We are pleased to meet you, in peace and friendship."

"In peace and friendship," Carlos followed suit.

The woman bowed her head in return and eyed the bag Carlos was holding. "Well met, though we have nothing of value to trade." Mat'isa's eyes swept past Jake, ignoring him, and settled back on Audy. "Rai'nor is in the woods to the east, hunting. He should return by midday."

To Jeff, whose Chandrian was as good as any Edenite's, the Creight woman's speech carried the slightest accent, which caused him to think of a New Englander back on Earth. The connection was meaningless, but the accent was a sharp contrast from the Jema and the Hatwa living in Kirkton; it was just one more indication of how long these people had lived in the wilds of a nearly empty British Isles, separate from the rest of Chandra and on the run.

They'd put up a small recon drone that morning and spotted Rai'nor's hunting party several miles away. Audy didn't feel the need to say, "We know." "We would wait for him," Audy explained. "We have brought our own food and drink; we will not impose upon you."

Jeff saw what could only be relief wash over the woman's face. Audy had warned them that the Creight might believe they were expected to sacrifice one of their precious cattle for a feast every time someone from Kirkton came to visit. Mat'isa, Jeff figured, was technically the "queen" of the village. She looked at all of them in turn, except Jake. "Be welcome among us."

"Mat'isa," Audy called out, stopping her in mid-stride back towards the village at the top of the hill. "I also would like to speak with you and Dere'dala concerning my friend, the warrior, Jake. There has been a misunderstanding that lies heavy upon him. On all of us." Audy indicated the four of them. "And on all of our peoples at Kirkton, Jema and Edenite alike. Jake is a leader among us, and we count his name among the Jema."

"You may speak for him." She nodded after a moment. "Your people have helped us greatly. Our pots will be full next spring, and that is a time of great trial for our people. Even now, we have the milk from the cattle. It is the first such gift to us, and perhaps we knew not how to respond in showing our gratitude. For that, friend Audrin'ochal, I will listen. My handfast sister, though, I warn you, is of her own mind."

"Thank you," Jake spoke up for the first time.

Mat'isa acted as if she did not hear him and continued looking at Audy. Jeff wanted to smile at Jake's discomfort, but he figured there was a lot more at stake here than his friend's social life.

The woman pointed at Audy. "I will listen to you. Your friend should wait here. I do not want Dere'dala's shame and anger to risk our people's peace."

"A wise choice." Audy accepted the conditions with a bow of his head.

They watched as the woman led her two bodyguards up the trail to the village.

"You will wait here." Audy smiled at Jake. "Like a hunting dog, waiting to be called. I only hope my English is good enough to convey your stated intentions to the woman."

"Seriously?" Jake whined. "Come on! What about my status?"

"I think the lady was pretty clear on that." Carlos clapped Jake on the back and dropped the bag at his feet.

Audy was trying not to laugh as he turned up the path. "You will be sent for when it is safe."

"I really can't wait to meet these people." Jeff punched Jake in the arm as he passed, following Audy and Carlos.

"Shouldn't somebody stay with me?" Jake called after them. "Guys?"

*

40

The inside of the hide tent was as dark as it was smoky. Fillets of dried and smoked fish hung from the tent poles. A bow, a spear, and a long knife of crude hammered iron lay in a neat pile by the door. Audy wondered if Kyle had looked at the Jema and their low technology during those first meetings with the same amazement that he felt now. In a moment of reflection, he realized that whatever their way of life and harsh conditions, these Creight were free. His own people could not have said that a short time ago.

Introductions and small talk past, Audy was as struck by Dere'dala's beauty as he assumed Jake was. The young woman's dark hair was braided into a rope and sat on her shoulder in a fashion recognizable to anyone who had grown up with women warriors. Rai'nor, he knew, was offended in the "official" sense, and stood ready to milk the situation with Jake for every advantage his people could get. Audy could only assume Mat'isa was prepared to play that same game. He understood their position. Had the roles been reversed and the Jema were the ones who had found a strange, friendly, and advanced people in their midst, they might have acted in a similar fashion.

Dere'dala, though, was a different matter. For her, this was personal. The young woman had clearly been embarrassed by Jake's rejection.

"He is here?" Dere'dala directed the question at her much-older sister-in-law.

"I left him waiting down the hill, by the stream."

Dere'dala seemed to take some satisfaction from that and turned to him. "He would have you speak for him?"

"Yes, until he is given leave to speak to you directly."

The young woman grinned back at him. "Until he is certain I won't collect his sack and hang it above my fire? I have doubt that he has stones."

Audy struggled not to laugh. "My friend has shortcomings, as do we all. I assure you that is not one of them." It was the wrong thing to say, he could see that immediately. He cursed his mouth and wished Kemi'sfrota or even Elisabeth were here to do this. The Edenites had a saying of "walking on eggshells," and he was certain someone else could do it far better than he.

"I can see from your face," he pleaded, "that my answer was misunderstood."

"Perhaps you can better explain." Mat'isa was suddenly offended, and he didn't think it had anything to do with bargaining for trade goods. "Is my sister not worthy of him?"

Jake was going to pay for this. He wasn't sure how, but it would be slow and painful. "I know Jake as well as any Jema. He is a great warrior, a man of honor and deep feeling, and is quick to laugh. He. . . takes as much joy from life as anyone I have known. But I have never seen him as interested in *a single* woman, as he is at this time."

"His actions say otherwise," the older woman deadpanned.

"His people's ways are strange even to us, and we have lived among them for more than a year. We have spilled Kaerin blood together, and our own. Many of them, including Jake, are now Jema." He leaned back and regarded Dere'dala. The girl was at least listening.

"They choose their handfasts over a longer period of time than what you or we are accustomed to. Jake refused the offer of your hand, because he takes such things to be a matter of the heart. He would not allow himself to take you in return for a gift that was given in friendship by his people. In his heart, it would be no different than buying you."

"Her hand was meant to seal the friendship between our peoples!" Mat'isa was getting angrier as the younger woman's face softened.

"Their people's friendship is in their words, and the fact they stand behind those words." He let that sink in, before turning to face Dere'dala. "A herd of cattle is nothing to them. Jake places far more value on your happiness."

The young woman's eyes opened in surprise. "My happiness?"

He shrugged, not having to pretend. "As I said, their ways are strange, but I think in these matters they have it right. My own handfast believes it so."

"How much more value?" Mat'isa asked suddenly.

"I will discuss that with Rai'nor," he said as formally as he could. He had no doubt the wily Krathik would come away happy.

Dere'dala looked in annoyance at her sister-in-law and then faced him. "He would speak to me?"

If he was any judge at all, Jake's stones were safe. "Yes, I think he would like that."

Mat'isa took that moment to exercise whatever authority being the wife of a Krathik held with these people. "You will not speak to that man until Rai'nor has met with him."

Some battles weren't worth fighting. He had no doubt Rai'nor would sell his own teeth for what Jake had brought this time. He was about to agree with the older woman when Dere'dala stood up and took a step towards the tent's flap door before spinning back.

"Rai'nor is your handfast, Mat'isa; you have to listen to him. He is my brother, and it will not be the first time I've given him reason to be angry."

Audy almost went after the young woman. She had taken the time to grab her bow and knife before storming out of the tent. He looked back at Mat'isa, whose jaw was working furiously as she rubbed her forehead. "Your friend has no idea the trouble he is tying himself to."

Audy felt himself smile. "Nor does Dere'dala."

*

Chapter 4

When Rai'nor and his hunting party hadn't returned by midday, Jeff and Carlos had been put to work by Mat'isa, splitting wood for the camp, while Audy went around carrying a foldout map of northern England and Scotland and talking to every Creight adult he could. Jeff knew Audy was trying to gather more intel on the other bands of Creight and where they might be located or headed as the spring wore on and the Kaerin Creight "hunting season" grew closer.

Carlos buried the axe, one with a fiberglass handle and made in Wisconsin back on Earth, into the chopping block. It was just one of several gifts from Audy's and Jake's previous visits. Besides new footwear that most of the Creight seemed to be wearing, he and Jeff had noted the water filters sitting atop large insulated jugs of drinking water and small paperback-sized solar panels that powered lights inside many of the tents. These people's world was close to getting irretrievably altered, but they seemed to have rapidly adapted to the gifts.

He leaned over, stretching his back with a loud groan. "Something isn't right here," he announced loudly. "That idiot is out there picking flowers with a local hottie, Audy's walking around playing diplomat, and we get stuck working."

Jeff pulled up a log from the pile they had created over the last hour and sat down. There was no question who the "idiot" was; no one had seen Jake since Dere'dala had stormed out of her tent, weapons in hand. They hadn't heard any screams or shouting, so they'd figured Jake had things well in hand.

"You think he closed the deal, or settled for the layaway plan?" Jeff asked as they both eyed three young children approaching, carrying a plastic bottle of water. Carlos figured that it would have been an animal skin or a gourd not very long ago.

"This *is* Jake we're talking about," he answered, flashing the kids an expansive smile. Two young girls and an even younger boy who carried a long branch like a spear, protecting his sisters. The first time the children had brought them water, they'd dropped the bottle and taken off running, giggling with fright from the strangers who both had skin far darker than any they'd probably seen. This time, they stood their ground until Jeff waved them closer.

"What are your names?" he asked as he accepted the water bottle.

The two girls both took a quick step back, mouths open in surprise. "You speak our tongue?" one of them asked. The young boy stood his ground, terrified, just watching them, with the stick held out in front like it was a shield.

Jeff nodded. "We both do. Thank you for the water." He pointed at Carlos, saying, "Carlos," and then at himself. "Jeff."

The oldest of the girls, who might have been seven or eight, pointed at herself. "I am Ver'asa." She placed a hand atop the younger girl's head. "My sister is called Din'asa. This is Tardem." She pointed at the young boy. "But we call him 'Veet.'"

He glanced at the boy, who was now squinting at him with a five-year-old's idea of bravery. Give the kid another decade, and he'd probably be able to feed a family with one of the bows his people he carried. Right now, he was just practicing.

"What does 'Veet' mean?" he asked the boy. "I don't know this word." His best guess was rodent; that couldn't be right.

"The small tree creature, the one that is very fast," the older girl explained. "It has a bushy tail, and makes a lot of noise in the forest— like him."

"A squirrel?" he wondered in English and glanced at Carlos, who had moved off towards the duffel bag they'd brought. "The one that collects nuts?" he asked the boy.

The young boy nodded once but otherwise didn't budge.

"It is nice to meet you." He turned and caught the bag of lollipops Carlos tossed to him. They were both grinning at the kids' reactions as he slowly unwrapped one and popped it into his mouth. "Mmmm," he said rubbing his belly with a big smile. He handed one out to each of them. "Don't bite it, just enjoy it."

Carlos started laughing at the look of surprise on their faces. "Now you've done it, another world ruined by sugar."

The oldest girl pulled it out of her mouth and gazed at the sucker like it was magical. "*What* is this?!"

"Lollipop," he answered with a grin and turned to Carlos. "We won't tell them these are fortified with vitamin C."

"Why ruin it?" Carlos agreed.

"Lawl-pop," the boy repeated.

"Lollipop," Jeff corrected as the kids all took a step back, gazing past his shoulder. He turned to see Mat'isa and Audy approaching. Rai'nor's wife didn't look happy, but then again, they hadn't seen her smile yet. He wondered if the woman knew how.

"Another gift?" Mat'isa shooed the children away, and fired the question at Audy.

"Just a treat," Audy answered. "Try one."

Jeff handed one up to Audy, as the young boy shouted, "Lawl-pop," over his shoulder.

Audy unwrapped the sucker and handed it to Mat'isà. "Don't bite it."

After a tentative lick, the woman's eyes opened wide in surprise. "What do you call this?"

"It's called candy." Audy gave the two of them a sly look.

"It's called diplomacy," Carlos said in English. He nodded to Mat'isa. "We have some for all the children. As Audrin'ochal said, they are just treats. We expect nothing in return."

Audy gave Carlos a nod of appreciation. "It is just a kindness," he explained to the woman. "They are not trade goods."

Mat'isa shook her head as she pulled the sucker out. "Your kindness is strange to us. We have done nothing to earn these gifts. But I warn you, whatever it is you want from Rai'nor will have a price."

Jeff thought the look on Audy's face screamed, "No shit." But the Jema bowed his head and nodded once in what he thought was very diplomatic acceptance. "As I have said, I will discuss that with Rai'nor. We do have the best interests and the safety of your people in mind."

Mat'isa worked on the lollipop with an unreadable look on her face as Audy turned to them. "Rai'nor's scouts have just returned ahead of his main party. Could you two find Jake and Dere'dala before he arrives?"

"Where'd they go?" Carlos asked in English.

"I do not know." Audy's eyebrow twitched upward as he answered in kind. "Neither does this woman, and we do not need another diplomatic insult before this evening."

Jeff stood and clapped Audy on the shoulder. "I'm sure he's being very diplomatic."

"I'm sure he is," Audy deadpanned.

*

"Your friends are watching us." Dere'dala glanced past him over his shoulder, into the woods.

"I know," Jake answered. He'd heard them coming through the woods for some time. Carlos would cough "politely" every minute or so, and Jeff had been making a point of talking loudly enough that Jake would have had to have been dead not to hear them coming.

"They move through the forest like the cattle you gave us."

"They were, uh, being . . . polite."

"What does that word mean?"

"It means they didn't want to surprise us. It must be time to head back to your camp."

Jake cocked his head over his shoulder and yelled into the dense wall of forest. "Is it safe for me to go back?"

"You tell us, amigo," Carlos yelled back through the trees. "You still a whole man?"

Dere'dala bounced to her feet atop the tree that had fallen over the stream, with a grace and agility that Jake couldn't have matched in his youth. It had taken her half an hour of threats and promises to do him irreparable harm in his sleep before she had sat down on the tree next to him. Whatever worries her family had regarding her virtue had been entirely unnecessary. They'd just talked; she'd needed to vent, and he needed to explain why he'd shunned Rai'nor's offer. The longer they'd talked, the more worried he became. She was the one; he was sure of it. He'd never been more scared in his life.

"All good here," he shouted as he came to his feet and followed Dere'dala across the log to the bank. She stopped and spun back towards him and jabbed him in the chest with the end of her bow.

"Did they think we would be rutting like animals in the forest?"

He could feel his face redden. "Nooo, of course not." She looked back at him with a face that called his bullshit. "They were just . . . I'm not sure what they thought. In truth, neither one of them is very bright."

"I'm thinking they know you well." She gave him a smile that had him hoping Audy's conversations had gone well.

Three hours later, the entire village had turned out to watch the demonstration of the "gifts" Jake had brought Rai'nor. Carlos and Jake had walked off a hundred yards from the target that Jeff had set up in the middle of the village. Audy had made certain everyone was standing well off to the side but had a good view of the strange-looking, knot-covered squash set atop a pole in the village's courtyard.

"No pressure or anything.' Carlos laughed. "If you miss, you lose the girl, and we probably don't get the allies we need."

"Thanks, anything else I need to know?"

"Scope's zeroed in at two hundred." Carlos glanced at the trees surrounding the clearing. "No wind to speak of. You miss this shot, I wouldn't do you either."

Jake couldn't help but laugh as he hefted the new assault rifle. The 6.5mm, 147 grain bullet's drop would be meaningless at his range. Carlos's point was valid; the squash was the size of a basketball, and it was a shot he should be able to make in his sleep.

The program had used up a lot of its considerable stockpile of 5.56 during the fight with the Strema. The use of the older weapon system had been a product of what the program could easily get their hands on in large quantities during the years they were stockpiling supplies. Throughout the fight, they'd been producing the new 6.5mm assault weapon and its ammunition, and waiting for a good time to introduce the weapon to the EDF and their Jema allies. Given a relative breather in open hostilities, the transition was nearly complete.

"You look a little nervous, Jake. You want the Marine to do it?"

"Fuck off." Jake looped the sling around his left arm, pulled the gun tight, and went to a knee. He sighted and fired before he could think about it.

He pulled his head back from the scope as Carlos clapped him on the shoulder. "Sounds like wedding bells! You two going to do a gift registry somewhere? I never know what to get as a gift."

*

Audy was watching Rai'nor's face as the rifle boomed and the target squash flew apart. He recognized the look on the man's face all too well. He could remember the promise he had attached in his own mind to the tools of the Edenites. He had come to learn that it was their honor that was much more valuable. To the Jema, it had been all-important. He had to remind himself that these were Creight. They had not been, as Kyle said, brainwashed by the systems of control the Kaerin had put in place over the centuries since their arrival. They were game animals to the Kaerin, and they knew it.

Rai'nor looked over at him and shook his head in what might have been disappointment. "What do we have to offer that you could value as highly as a weapon like that?"

"We would ask for your friendship and trust. There is nothing we value more," Audy responded and gave the man a nod. He smiled to himself, thinking that revenge would be his. "Jake will talk to you about the weapons; they belong to him."

*

Rai'nor looked into the fire between them for a long moment as the celebration continued outside the Krathik's hut. The village leader's abode was a step above the hide tents, in that it had a low rock wall upon which hide walls and a thatch roof had been erected. Following the demonstration, the whole village was excited at the prospect of gaining access to the weapons. They might not have slaughtered a cow, but they had fresh venison from Rai'nor's hunt, and to augment the celebration, they'd continued to hand out the candy and chocolate.

Jake recognized it for the genuine "beads to the natives" moment that it was, and knew it would have been offensive to anyone not so very long ago. As things stood with the Creight, the "beads" were akin to magic. The village people seemed to be coming around to the idea that their lives were going to be vastly different from the run-and-hide mentality that had ruled them for centuries.

Part of their glee was due, Jake knew, to the fact he had walked back into the village accompanied by Dere'dala. Whatever their relationship was, and he wasn't certain he was going to get a say in the matter, it seemed to be a cause for celebration—a symbol of the friendship that now existed between Rai'nor's people and the new arrivals with the magical tools. Everybody seemed to be of the same good cheer except Rai'nor himself, who sat across the small fire from him and Audy.

"All of the weapons?" Rai'nor looked at both of them. "And the . . . things which go inside them? For which you only wish us to help you locate other Creight bands, and keep an eye out for Kaerin ships putting warriors ashore?" Jake had been worried over the way Rai'nor had been looking at them. What he had taken for suspicion, might have been confusion.

"As a first step," Jake confirmed. "We'd also like your band to remain here or come to live in our town we call Dumfries. There is no reason to run from the Kaerin, not with us and the Jema here. Our people would continue to help you."

"To begin," Audy explained. "Then we will end their rule across this entire world."

"We are saying that the Kaerin will not threaten you," Jake agreed. "They are going to be worrying about us. We will stop them and kick them off this entire island." From the look on Rai'nor's face, he might as well have promised to stop the sun from rising the next morning. Though, given the recent weather, how would anyone know he hadn't?

Rai'nor smiled knowingly and nodded himself. Jake was starting to agree with Audy, who had maintained throughout the winter that Rai'nor might be friendlier than Arsolis, their first Chandrian ally, but he was far smarter and would be more difficult to convince to help. Jake had no problem believing the first; he had boots that could give Arsolis a run for the money in the brains department. It was more difficult for him to imagine Rai'nor, or any Creight for that matter, wouldn't want payback for centuries of living in abject fear. The Creight weren't like any other Chandrian clan they were going to come across. They had no internal ruling class that derived their authority from the Kaerin.

Rai'nor pointed at the opening in the roof that was doing a passable job in drawing out the fire's smoke. "We always move from our winter camp when it begins to warm. This year will be no different. With or without your gifts, we will soon leave for the great forest and mountains in the north."

"Would your people not prefer to stay and live in one place?" Audy asked.

"They would prefer to live. Some of our bands will be caught in the hunt." Rai'nor's acceptance of the Kaerin hunt seemed no different than his belief in the fact it would probably rain during the night. "One time, before I was born, I have heard it said there was a year they did not come. Anyone who remembers that has passed long ago."

Jake made a point to indicate the duffle bag of assault rifles. "We are asking you to help us, so that they will never hunt your people again. Our war, our struggle with them will not be over in a season, or a year. I speak of a future where year after year, your people could live where they wish, have children, and grow without living in fear."

Rai'nor listened carefully, seeming to weigh each word. At the mention of children, his eyes flickered to the tent flap that acted as a door. Groups of children squealing with sugar-fueled excitement passed by the tent every few minutes.

Rai'nor looked at him for a long moment before raising a single finger. "Why would you need us to remain here? In this place?" Another finger popped up. "If your people are so powerful, why would you need us?" A third finger joined its brothers. "You would not be so certain of victory if you had seen the Kaerin appear at the edge of the forest and run through one of our camps, slaughtering everyone."

Rai'nor rubbed his knees and shook his head. "At some point in our lives, we are too old to run to safety . . . or as often happens, too young. Those moments will come. I will not invite them." Rai'nor's gaze drifted over to Audy, as if he would understand.

"Yes, the Jema invited our own destruction," Audy admitted. "We would not live as slaves any longer."

"And you lost." Rai'nor's eyebrows crawled up his forehead. "The Hatwa, Arsolis, has told me of your people's story."

"He spoke true," Audy admitted. "Yet he does not know the whole story. There was a time when our people admired the Creight. Different bands of Free People that lived far to the north of where Arsolis's people now live. A land of rock, ice, and deep snows. We thought they lived in freedom that was denied us. But we now know that they were as hunted as you are. They are not slaves to the Kaerin, but to their own fear."

"You say I am a slave to my fears?" Rai'nor bristled, his hand going to his waist in reflex. They'd all stripped themselves of weapons at the door of the tent upon entering.

"No." Audy held out a hand. "I do not. But I ask you, what drives your people to the far north in the summer? I will not believe it is the shorter growing season. Why do your women try to bear children in the late summer? I know this is so that you will not have newborns with you as you have to flee north every summer, denying your people the warmth, food, and crops that could more easily be grown here. We know why your people do not stop moving, why your movements are no different than those of the game you yourselves hunt. We do not fault your ways; given your situation, we understand them. You and the Krathik's who came before you, have done what it took for *some* of your people to survive. I do not call you a slave to anything other than your traditions. You are what our Edenite friends call creatures of habit."

Rai'nor looked at Jake and then back at Audy. "Yet we survive."

"Yeah, you survive." Jake said. "But you aren't living. First off, we will defeat the Kaerin; we don't have a choice. We've got a magic box around here somewhere that can show you how we fight. More important, let me tell you what will happen to your people if you remain apart from us and our struggle. It's a story that has played itself out on my own world a hundred times. We will be victorious with or without your help. Those Creight alive now will continue living as you do, but every year, more and more of your young people will come to live among the Jema and ourselves. They'll do it for a better life and the opportunity to live in safety, in one place where they can raise children. Over time, you will be left with old people or those unwilling to better their lives. And to be honest, they probably won't have to work, or hunt and fish to feed themselves."

"How would they survive?"

"There will be enough of my own people who will take pity on you for the change our civilization and tools have made to your way of life.

They will give you what you need to survive. Not so much to live well, but to survive. In that future, your children's children will be on the way to becoming slaves to my people's guilt. It's not pretty, but one thing I've figured out between living on three different worlds is that people are people. Our nature isn't any different." Jake looked at Audy, who nodded back at him in agreement.

"Doesn't matter if you are a Jema, an Edenite, or Creight." Jake paused, and thought back on his own family's small percentage of Native American roots. "Over time, the dominant culture, the way of life of those who win, will swallow up those who lose or try to stand apart."

Rai'nor tilted his head to one shoulder and looked at both of them almost sideways. "You seek to change Chandra to your ways?"

Jake almost laughed to himself, thinking how much the Jema had changed Eden. Technology and freedom would have a lasting effect on the Jema, but the cultural shift in both parties—the intermarrying, the friendships, and the joint military—had already changed both in a process that could only continue.

"Rai'nor." Audy leaned forward. "There are no such things as Chandrian ways. There hasn't been anything of the sort for centuries. Everything we have been left with, even the language we are now speaking, came from the Kaerin. They won; our people's cultures, our different ways of life across this world have over the centuries been altered, grown like a field of crops to help the Kaerin maintain their control. Your . . ." Audy paused and pointed at the perimeter of the tent indicating the entire village. "Existence has its own ways, and yes you live free. But your way of life is driven by the Kaerin, as much as any clan on this world."

Rai'nor took a moment, staring into the flames of the small fire. "Your words have the sound of truth in them. What you are asking of me will weigh on all the Creight living on this island."

Audy leaned forward towards the fire. "What we are going to do to the Kaerin will weigh on every person on this world." He threw the remaining contents of his cup at the fire. The jasaka he himself had distilled flared into a bright blue flame.

"We understand." Jake nodded. "We ask only that you ask yourself what your people could become if they didn't have to hide."

*

Chapter 5

Holding of Landing, Chandra

To someone who had been born and lived his entire life on the island of Landing, the changes wrought upon the desert island over the winter were unimaginable. Lord Tima's changes had turned the dusty archive of forgotten knowledge into a center of research and learning that was further growing into an industrial center that threatened to outgrow the island's ability to sustain the workforce. The new factories and forges were producing weapons for the Kaerin. Amona knew the weapons being produced were patterned after what had been collected by the Strema on the Shareki world and were not the result of any breakthrough with the ancient Kaerin tools.

He, of course, had shared this knowledge with Breda and the Hatwa Gemendi, A'tor. The rest of the subject Gemendi on the island had been told they were Kaerin weapons of an old design. He doubted if Lord Tima's cover story was widely believed among the Gemendi, but actual belief and the willingness to question the origins of the new weapon models were two very different things. As it was, he'd just come from a meeting with Lord Tima where his input had been sought on how best to construct replicas of the new production lines elsewhere on the mainland.

It was the reason he was late for his meeting with A'tor and Breda. Hopefully, the two other members of his Hijala cell had managed not to kill each other and leave him alone with his worries. He' had become accustomed to Breda's temper and general surliness; with time, he had accepted it was just the man's way. When A'tor Bendera had first arrived from the Hatwa lands to the far north, identified himself as a Hijala, and told his incredible story of having shared a meal with two of the Free People, Amona had felt vindicated.

Till that moment, he had lived with the constant need to reassure Breda that he was not touched in the head. Until A'tor's arrival, it had been only his own tale of an overheard conversation wherein the Kaerin prelate, Lord S'kaeda himself, stated that he was concerned with the threat represented by these off-worlders. A'tor's story had added details they could hardly believe.

He assumed Breda would have welcomed the confirmation of what they both already believed. Instead, Breda treated A'tor's arrival like a threat. A potential plant by the Kaerin Gemendi. It was only in the last few 'ten-days' that the younger Jehavian had warmed up at all to the older Gemendi. Everything was a process with Breda, a demanded upon routine, that he alone seemed to know the rules for. When to meet, where to meet, what to do were all determined by the angriest man he had ever met. It was a wonder that any of them were still alive.

It was late, and he approached the old city's crossroad tavern on foot. Gone were the days where he and Breda would meet in storage closets behind closed doors in the depths of the pavilion. Breda insisted that they always have a reason to be seen together. It made sense to him, to A'tor as well, and at their last meeting, they had both formally let Breda know that he was in charge of their group. The man's response should not have surprised either of them; "Have either of you assumed otherwise? My family has been smuggling goods in and out of Kaerus for generations; you two don't know the first thing about how they really operate." Assured that his authority wasn't going to be questioned, Breda had slowly begun treating them better than something he had accidently stepped in.

The tavern, like all such dens on the island, was doing more business in a ten-day than an entire year had produced not very long ago. The machinists and artisans shipped in to work the manufactories were fighting for table space with the army of Gemendi working within the pavilion itself. The logistical nightmare involved in keeping both workforces fed, happy, and productive was still his primary job per Lord Tima's orders.

A fleet of supply ships kept the island running, and of late, was beginning to ship off its products to points back on the mainland. A'tor, recognizable by his bulky, sloped shoulders, stood next to the diminutive Breda outside the tavern, leaning against the side of the building. Both Gemendi had their heads bowed in conversation, until Breda spotted him approaching and dragged A'tor off the wall by his tunic.

"Amona!" Breda shouted. "Friend, you look like a man who is going by coach back to the pavilion. Could we share a ride? My friend is in his cups."

"Who is he?" Amona played his expected role.

"Gemendi A'tor, of the Hatwa, you've met him."

"Of course, of course. Well met." He directed them both across the street, realizing that A'tor wasn't playing a role. The man was past drunk. A trio of coaches, each hitched to a pair of plodding farm horses, waited to transport Gemendi to and from the pavilion. One of the coachmen saw them coming, stood up on his seat, and looked both ways and across the street. Satisfied there were no Kaerin waiting for a ride, the man relaxed and waved them forward.

"Gemendi Amona," the coachman acknowledged him. Prior to Lord Tima's arrival, the entire island had boasted perhaps seven thousand souls; it was now ten times that, and he couldn't recall the name attached to the coachman's familiar face. Something like that would have bothered him not long ago. As it was, the three Hijala members riding in a coach together had his heart beating in terror.

"Take the old coast road, if you would," Amona spoke as he watched with genuine concern as Breda levered the bulkier A'tor up the step into the coach. "Our friend could use some time to sober up."

"Same to me." The coachman shrugged. "Not my horses."

"How drunk is he?" Amona asked as the coach jerked into motion. Between the horse's hooves and the creaking of the coach's springs, there was no danger that their conversation would be overheard.

"He's not having to act," Breda responded. "He received a message from his Hijala brother in Legrasi." Breda elbowed A'tor in the ribs. "Tell him."

A'tor's face screwed up for a moment as he forced his eyes to stay open. "The Kaerin, it seems, have no idea where the 'Free People' have gone." Amona was glad the coast road was smoother than the more often used new road that cut across the island to the pavilion. He doubted if A'tor's gut could have handled the rougher ride.

Breda shook his head at his drunk colleague and leaned forward. "The message he received was written nearly six ten-days ago. It would be dangerous to assume anything with regards to what the Kaerin may or may not know."

A'tor rubbed at his cheeks and leaned forward with a groan. "Are you going to be sick?" Amona asked.

"Get it over with," Breda goaded. "You will feel better."

A'tor held a hand above his bowed head and waved off the question before leaning slowly back into the seat and lolling his head at the ceiling of the carriage. "I am used to beer, or spirits. This wine you southerners drink leaves my mouth feeling like an old boot."

"To say nothing about your head in the morning." Breda sounded almost sympathetic as he gave A'tor's arm a squeeze. "Tell him the rest."

A'tor's eyes met his own across the carriage. "My son is still missing. There's been no word. His absence has been recorded but has not raised an alarm. There are many warriors missing from around Lord Madral's estate, and Hatwa villagers have vanished from the offshore islands. No one is talking about it, and the High Bloods don't seem to be seeking answers."

"Which means the Kaerin are hiding what happened," Breda explained to him unnecessarily. He might have lived a life of servitude on this island, but Amona was very familiar with the first law of Kaerin rule; nothing painting the Kaerin in a bad light ever happened.

"I can only hope that Lord Madral's High Bloods believe he was among the fallen at the hands of the Free People." A'tor rubbed at his face and then shook his head. "He may very well be dead."

"Did we not just agree that it was dangerous to make assumptions? Your son could just as easily be alive." Breda had a way of hissing when he was trying to make a point. Even in trying to comfort A'tor, it came across as a rebuke. Amona had only to glance at A'tor; even drunk, it was clear to see the man had about all he could take from Breda.

"What of our circle?" Amona had long past accepted he needed to play peacemaker between these two. "Do we still bide our time?"

"Circle?" Breda snorted. "It's just us; we're a fucking triangle."

For a moment, Amona considered admonishing Breda, not that it would do anything but set the man off, when he noticed A'tor, eyes closed and nodding with a wide smile cracking his face. "A three-legged stool," A'tor slurred, opening his eyes. The Hatwa Gemendi pointed at himself and then across the coach. "With two tired old legs and one much shorter than the others." He grinned and looked at Breda as he said the last. Amona watched in relief as Breda's face lit up in appreciation of the insult. Soon they were all sharing a much-needed laugh.

"So, what does this stool do for now?" he tried again.

"We stay alive," Breda answered. "And hope that no one figures out the ancient batteries. If they do—"

"When they do," A'tor interrupted. "We are getting closer."

A'tor was a member of that particular research team, along with their erstwhile Hijala member Barrisimo. In the height of irony, the most successful researcher on the island to date was technically a member of the Hijala. What should have been a four-legged chair was the lopsided three-legged stool, which lived in fear that Barrisimo would provide the Kaerin what they were after.

"You refer to the work with the power crystals?" Amona asked. He was responsible for collating the disparate reports from the research teams into something manageable for Lord Tima on a daily basis. He had not seen any report that suggested a breakthrough was imminent.

"I do." The Hatwa Gemendi paused and covered his mouth for a moment that passed slowly for all of them. "The ancient batteries do not contain crystals; it is some sort of metal framework that merely resembles a crystal lattice, if you will. Our colleague Barrisimo's early assumption was wrong. The label has staying power."

"Doesn't matter what label that old fool attaches to them," Breda clarified. "How close is your team to being able to charge the things?"

"You sound like Lord Tima," Amona chided the younger man, who ignored him and maintained his focus on A'tor.

"A month." A'tor shrugged. "A year, five years—I am only pointing out it is merely a matter of time. The people that created them were no more intelligent than we are. They simply had centuries of uninterrupted technical progress that we, and the Kaerin for that matter, cannot boast of."

Amona watched as Breda's cheek twitched in irritation. "Time *is* critical to us," Breda growled. "Either the traitor Barrisimo figures out how to charge the batteries, or he doesn't. If he does . . . we all know what has to be done."

"No, we don't." Frustrated, Amona raised his voice to the point that he surprised himself. "First, you say we need to keep him alive. Allow him time to figure out the technology and the manner of charging the devices, if indeed they can be charged. Are you saying we now have to . . . remove him? After he makes a discovery? What possible good will come of that? The Kaerin will have what they want, and his death would just endanger all of us."

Breda slapped A'tor on the knee as if to ensure the man was still conscious and listening. "Any real chance someone else on your team can do what Barrisimo can?"

A'tor's waxen face looked back at him for just a moment, before the man shot forward and thrust his head and shoulders out the open top half of the door. Breda moved just as quick, and managed a two-handed grip on the back of the man's belt, keeping him in the coach as the Hatwa's body convulsed, painting the coast road in Tarnesian red.

Breda smiled at him over A'tor's backside, and jerked his chin out the door. "Finest mind the Hatwa have ever produced, heard it from Barrisimo himself."

He couldn't help but smile. Until a moment ago, he had been craving a strong drink himself. They were all under a great deal of stress; A'tor, whose son was unaccounted for, was doubly invested in their treachery. The man's whole family, perhaps his entire clan, was at risk. If anyone could be forgiven for over imbibing, it was A'tor.

Breda clapped him on the back as A'tor pulled himself back into the carriage. "Feel better?"

"Much better." A'tor dragged his sleeve across his face and tried to smile. "A horrible waste of even shitty wine."

"The only kind they serve us," Amona agreed. Working a decade in the manor house of Lord Tima's predecessor had taught him the difference between good wine and bad. Another measure in which the Kaerin ruled them. "We can stop, if it would help."

"I will be fine." The Hatwa waved off his concern and regarded Breda with a sidelong glance. "To answer your question, Barrisimo is an insufferable, boot-kissing wisp of a man. He has no backbone or honor to speak of. He is also without peer on this wretched island. The man is undeniably brilliant, as good at currying favor with our Kaerin masters as he is at running circles around them."

"That sounds like the man I know," Amona agreed. "He cares for nothing but the knowledge itself, and the credit, of course. I suspect he would manage to get the credit even if someone else on your team managed to find a breakthrough."

"That will not happen," A'tor grunted. "We are all following his lead. He loves that fact as much as the Kaerin detest him for it.

Especially Haws'molk; as the Kaerin lead for our section, he should be leading it. Everyone knows he isn't and has to pretend to protect his pride."

"There it is." Breda opened up his hands and smiled at both of them. "Time arises to put the old man down, we have Haws'molk do the deed for us."

"You mean take the blame?" A'tor asked.

"Same thing to the Kaerin." Breda grinned.

"That could work." Amona was thinking back on an overheard conversation in the dining hall at Lord Tima's table. One of the Kaerin Gemendi had made a comment that it was unseemly that Barrisimo had been given so much authority. Lord Tima, ever the paragon of calm, had explained that he didn't care if good ideas came from kitchen slaves; he would use them. The Kaerin who had taken offense at Barrisimo's role was no longer working on the island. "Lord Tima is already aware that some friction exists due to Barrisimo's success."

"When the time comes," Breda started and then stopped himself. "No, don't wait. When the opportunity presents itself, make a comment to Lord Tima. Something that will have him aware of the tension. Not so much that he would replace Haw'smolk, right?"

"I will try." Lord Tima spent most of his time overseeing the investigatory digs outside the pavilion itself. The operation of the Gemendi effort within was a well-oiled machine at this point. Lord Tima was more focused on discovering additional lost Kaerin writings from the old ruins. What little progress they had to date, had come from recovered records, and not technological breakthroughs.

"Don't try, Amona." Breda's hiss showed itself again. "It needs to be done."

"It will be," he said, as he noted the look of sympathy coming from A'tor. The two of them took their lead from Breda as much as A'tor's team was led by Barrisimo.

"What of the new firearms?" Amona changed the subject. "The Kaerin aren't waiting for a miracle from the Gemendi. They are producing the things right now." He'd briefed them both earlier on the massive scope of the effort the Kaerin were putting into the production of the new weapons and ammunition.

"The more the better." Breda smiled. "Who do you think is going to be producing these new weapons? Kaerin women and children? Our people will. Subject clans will learn to make them even while we wear their chains."

Amona shook his head. "Our people have known how to make Kaerin rifles for centuries. It hasn't served us at all."

Breda just grinned back at him. "There's a small difference in quality between a High Blood's rifle and those allowed to our subject war hosts during battle. There is an ocean's difference between those rifles and the new weapons. One man with a fully loaded new weapon could slay a dozen Kaerin before they take him."

"Or until it jams," A'tor pointed out with a grin. They all laughed at that. The precision machining of parts required by the new weapons, and the minimal tolerances allowed in creating the vast volumes of ammunition needed, were proving difficult. The new hummingbird guns jammed more often than they worked.

"Is not the reverse true as well?" he asked. "The Kaerin could kill us in numbers that before would have been difficult even for them."

"Certainly," Breda agreed. "But that side of the equation has long been true. They've always been able to kill us at will." The veins in Breda's forehead and neck stood out as he struggled not to scream. "By the prelate's hairy balls, we do their bidding for them. Remember, it was the Strema that hacked the Jema to pieces; the Kaerin didn't fire a shot after the fighting was over. It was slaves killing slaves. These new weapons, like any rifle, don't care which direction they are pointed— and there are a lot more of us than them."

"And the Free People?" A'tor asked. "What advantage will they still have if the Kaerin have the same weapons? They may not bother with this world if they have a real fight on their hands."

"Fuck the Free People," Breda growled. "At some point, we do this ourselves, or we will just trade one master for another."

"You did not speak to them," A'tor responded, his anger sobering him up. "It did not seem their way. The Jema are their allies, not subjects."

"Where are they?" Breda opened both hands, leaning back into his couch. "Are they waiting for the Kaerin to finish preparing for them?" The youngest of their trio looked at Amona and then at A'tor. In a gesture that almost shocked Amona, Breda put a hand on A'tor's shoulder and gave it a friendly squeeze. "Your son may be with them still, and you may be right, perhaps they *will* help. I'm thinking we need to do all we can to help ourselves."

*

Kaerus, Chandra

"Where have they gone?" Noka S'kaeda wasn't one to spend hours talking to himself. Having spent the last hour staring at a map of the Hatwa lands and the Frozen Sea, he had summed up the question that haunted him, out loud.

"My Lord?"

He glanced up at his honor guard across the room, standing just inside the door of his office. He waved the question off. "I'm just thinking out loud, Seb'as. I'm not losing my mind."

It was past time to brief his guards. There had been too many meetings, with too many lords who had been summoned in the dead of night, for them not to know that something was afoot. Warriors talked; if he wasn't careful, rumors of threats of a coup or some internal political machinations might grow into something real. At the moment, he could wish for a run-of-the-mill power play by one of his rivals. That, he would have no problem in deciding how to handle.

"Seb'as, this evening, I wish to dine with the guard. Inform Kareel Oront'as that he, his bastelta, and tearks are all expected. Nothing formal. I will join you in the barracks."

"We would be honored, my Lord."

No, the honor would be his. Those warriors would learn their world was at risk, and they wouldn't flinch at the news. They would welcome the fight. He understood the mentality; he felt it too. But this new enemy wouldn't march in ranks to a chosen place of battle. He never seen or met one of these people the Strema had labeled Edenites, a name taken from Jema they had captured during their failed invasion of the Shareki world. Yet, as he tried to construct the minds he was working against, the enemy seemed far too Kaerin in their way of thinking for comfort. It was so unlike the conditioned subjects under their sway. Not since the time of their ill-fated landing on this world, and the bloody two centuries that followed, had a Kaerin leader been forced to make war on an opponent that wasn't made up of conquered peoples.

Beyond their weapons, and the gaps in his knowledge about his foe, his biggest worry was that he was somehow not up to the task. Would he be remembered as the prelate who had preserved his people or as the failure who had led them to their doom?

As prelate, he had only had one writ to adhere to; protect Kaerin power and authority. Keep this world for the Kaerin until such time as their home world found them. The dream of rejoining Kaerus proper had died a slow, inevitable death over the centuries. No one knew what had become of their people, or their original home. For most, there were only fables remaining, passed down through word of mouth. He dismissed the old stories for what they were; Chandra was the only home the Kaerin had, and it was up to him to preserve it.

*

Chapter 6

New Seattle, Eden

"Just promise me you'll talk to him."

Kyle would have to have been deaf and stupid to miss the tone in Elisabeth's voice. It was the *I can keep this up all day* tone. He was smart enough to know that he wasn't nearly as smart as his wife, not about stuff like this—not about most things that didn't involve soldiering or blowing shit up.

"I'll do my best," he promised. It was as far as he could go. Everybody wanted his ear before he jumped to Chandra, and there were several ears he needed to bend before he left. To make matters worse, it appeared as if the Kaerin might have left "stay behind" troops during their attack on New St. Louis. If it was true, they'd all missed it, and he was already mentally kicking himself.

"It's all I'm asking."

He wrapped Elisabeth in a hug and kissed the top of her head. "I'll write as often as I can." He grinned. Eden had almost continuous e-mail exchanges via the portal at Kirkton Base, but he wasn't going to be hanging around the base much. E-mail communication between the two planets was a simple matter of jumping a hard drive back and forth, but until they had a microsatellite network up on Chandra to match the one over Eden, he was going to be worlds apart as soon as he got a few miles away from the base.

"And be sure to tell Jake that if he dares to get hitched without me there, I'll never speak to him again. My mom and I are the only family he has left."

"Will do."

"I'll send pictures of Sophie; let you know what you're missing. Make sure you get us there, as soon as it's safe." Elisabeth pulled back and stared at him. "I mean for Sophie. I'd be going right now . . ."

"I know you would," he said. "And I will; it all depends on how fast we can get the Dumfries settlement going for real. Keep the pressure on here, for resources," he added. "The Jema have families, too, now. They'll get it built quick."

She pulled him tight again. "Just be safe. I know how stupid that sounds, but you have a daughter now."

Everyone had kids now; most Edenites, and nearly all the Jema. He gave his wife a kiss. "You know that's why we have to do this."

She nodded. "I know." She broke off the embrace and nudged him. "Jomra's waiting at the door, glaring at your back."

"He can wait a second longer."

As he appoached, he noticed Jomra was almost smiling, or as close to it as he could ever remember. He liked Jomra and respected what the man had accomplished. He couldn't imagine anyone having done a better job of leading the Jema as they were yanked, nearly overnight, several centuries forward in terms of technology. That aside, he wasn't ever going to be a "close" friend of Jomra. He doubted if anyone outside of Audy and perhaps Colonel Pretty would make that claim. Jomra held himself apart, and Kyle knew there was a good reason for that. No one had been more sorely used than the Jema; in Jomra's position, he might hold himself a little apart as well.

"You are a fortunate man, Kyle Lassiter." Jomra held out a hand and lifted a chin in Elisabeth's direction. "Punching above your weight—is that the correct wording?"

Kyle laughed. "Yes, it is, and yes, I most definitely am."

"I listened to her speak to your council for three days. The Jema have no better voice than hers."

He knew Jomra had attended the council sessions and had to sit there and listen while many Edenites argued that the struggle on Chandra was of no concern to Eden. Jomra would have taken it in stride. The guy was so even-keeled and stoic that if asked to, Jomra would be able to argue the other side's points just as easily as his own.

"Don't put too much weight on what you heard," he said. "You have our support. Most of the bullshit you heard arguing against our involvement was from politicians maneuvering for advantage."

Jomra nodded slowly. "Politicians; it is amazing how fast they can change their minds when they get what they want. Makes you wonder what they are truly willing to fight for."

"Don't get me started, Jomra." He clapped him on the back and pulled the door open to see Hank Pretty standing across the lobby next to an open elevator, waving them on.

"Paul's tech team just confirmed it." Hank started the briefing the moment the door slid shut with a chime. "A comp-board issued to a Jema"—his boss glanced at his own device—"one Rhum'skal, has been active on and off since the attack on New St. Louis. Rhum'skal was reported missing after one of the early skirmishes along the Mississippi River last year. Audy believes he was one of the Jema who was captured, but he's still working on confirming that with the Jema at Kirkton Base. We know for certain that the man's comp-board hadn't connected with the net for more than a year."

"Could a Kaerin operate it?" Jomra asked.

"Operate is a moving target," Hank answered, pointing at his own device. "You only have to sign in to use the messaging system and any documents you might have downloaded. The other apps, the language programs we loaded on your people's devices, and more critically, the maps can be accessed just by turning it on." Hank led them out the elevator, still talking over his shoulder.

"Thankfully, the map application only works if the device is connected to the net. If they'd been able to access the device's map library from Chandra, I doubt they would have bothered with an attack on New St. Louis."

Kyle let out a breath in relief. No doubt, whoever was accessing the map application here on Eden was copying everything they could, while using it to get wherever they were going. It meant whoever had the comp-board now, needed to be found and stopped.

"Where are they?" Kyle asked as Hank pulled up outside the door to the operations center.

"Last connection had them about a hundred eighty miles southwest of New St. Louis; they aren't following the river this time."

"That region is empty, yes?" Kyle was reminded just how smart Jomra was; the man had made a quick study of their geography. "It was one of the areas we considered for our primary settlement here," Jomra explained.

"For the most part, yes," Hank agreed. "With the exception of a few scattered homesteaders who have all been alerted to keep an eye out and stay hunkered down until our team arrives."

"Who'd you send?" Kyle asked. He knew it hadn't been him; Hank would have had him in motion hours ago.

"Tom Souza and his team, with two quick reaction teams from Appalachia standing ready. The rest of Nagy's ready force has already ported to Chandra and is standing by if needed." Hank smiled at both of them. "You both already have your hands full on Chandra; we've got this."

"Let me know if we can help. A prisoner might be useful."

"They will not be taken prisoner easily." Jomra was shaking his head.

Kyle couldn't argue that point. Nothing he'd heard from Audy or even Jake regarding the Kaerin lent itself to a belief that a Kaerin warrior would ever surrender.

"We don't plan on asking them." Hank lifted his chin. "I've got Jomra for the next hour or so. You've got your dirty-tricks meeting with Doc Jensen, and I'm holding you up." Hank held out his hand. "I'll get out there to catch up within the week. In the meantime, slow and steady. Don't write checks we can't cash. Our whole campaign there depends on infrastructure and staying below their radar until we are strong enough to take the punch we know will come."

"Copy that." Kyle shook the offered hand, knowing Hank's comments were meant for Jomra far more than him. He and Hank had come up with the strategy together, with input from Audy and even Sir Geoff, who was still holding on to life in the hospital across town. Jomra settled for a fist bump that the Jema had adopted. One without the thumb in the up position, which seemed reserved for soldiers in the field. It was just one of a million ways the two cultures were changing. He doubted if any of them would recognize their own joint society by the time they were grandparents, if they survived that long.

He headed off down the hall, thinking of Tom Souza. The two of them and Jake had promised each other that they would go goat hunting in Alaska when this was all over. He silently wished the man luck with his present hunt and caught himself smiling as he remembered who else was on Souza's assault team.

*

Missouri, Eden

"I suppose this makes us astronauts." Josh Carlisle was grinning ear to ear. The thunder of their translation from Chandra back to Eden was still echoing around them.

"Whaaaa! What do you . . . mean!" Danny's eyes were big as saucers as he flailed about, hitting his own limbs like he was on fire. "Not again! Make it STOP!"

"The spiders? Again?" Tom Souza watched Josh scratch his head and look from his brother over to him. "Sir, it looks like the transporter thing gave him spiders again."

Tom shook his head. He'd known what he was in for when he'd

added the two brothers to his team. "I can see that, Private. Just give him a second." They'd just gone through what Danny referred to as "space spiders" thirty minutes ago on Chandra. Their translation "travel" had taken them from New Seattle on Eden, to Kirkton Base on Chandra, and then back to the Ozarks on Eden. They could have made the trip a lot faster, but he'd taken the time to catch up with Derek Mills, who he hadn't seen in a couple of months.

He struggled not to laugh as the eldest of the Carlisle brothers threw himself to the ground with a yelp and started a log roll back and forth, taking the time to slap at his face and neck. As much as he wanted to laugh at Danny's skunked-dog imitation, he took a moment to thank God that his own ears needed to pop. The psychosomatic symptoms the translation left some people with were all over the map. Being a confirmed "ear-popper" was a definite win compared to having space spiders.

Twenty seconds later, Danny was on one knee, looking at him, red faced and breathing hard. "Sorry, sir. I swear, I'd rather be kicked in the fruit bowl by a horse. I hate spiders."

"It's just in your head," Hans spoke up.

"Like hell, it was like they were all over me." Danny stood and brushed himself off, and rejoined his brother. "How you figure? I mean the astronaut thing?"

"We just came from a different planet, didn't we?" Josh Carlisle smiled as he spoke. "And Dad said we'd never amount to anything."

"Astronauts." Danny considered the logic, nodding. "I like that."

Tom Souza plugged his nose and blew out, popping his ears back open; or at least his brain recognized the action as the required fix. He regarded his two newest recruits with a shake of his head. They were both natural soldiers; as green as the trees that surrounded them, but possessing as solid natural talent as soldiers as he'd ever seen—even if they did seem to share a brain at times. The two of them had made it through the EDF's basic course with flying colors and pages of disciplinary notes in their files. Enough that other EDF units had passed them over.

"You two are so NOT the 'Right Stuff.'" Grant Ballard didn't bother trying not to laugh at his two brothers-in-law.

Tom looked around at the others. Dominik Majeski was on one knee, training his weapon outward. Hans Van Slyke was bent over at the waist, spitting as if he'd swallowed something awful. "You OK, Hans?"

Hans shook his head and coughed once. "I should not complain, but why couldn't I get the ear-popping thing or the numb fingers when I portal? It always tastes like I ate a bug."

"Probably one of my spiders."

Tom shook his head in amazement; Danny was probably trying to make light of his episode, but one could never be sure. He glanced over at Stant'ala. The famed Jema scout had been added to his team as their tracker. "Stant" stood in silence, rubbing at his closed eyes. Probably a headache, he figured. That or one of the more common side effects. He couldn't imagine what the stoic Jema thought of the Carlisle brothers. Stant was a legend among the Jema, and before leaving Kirkton Base, several Jema had approached him and offered their assurances that if anyone could the Kaerin's trail, it was Stant'ala.

They weren't strictly tactical at the moment, but he could foresee real issues with translation tactics that involved hitting the ground running. Somebody needed to develop an SOP to select for translation symptoms, especially the 'Space Spiders.' He thought about that for just a moment before adding it to his running to-do list, associated with his new position in the EDF.

He'd had six months to get his head square with the undeniable fact the Earth of his birth was no longer his home, and Eden was just one of many earths in the universe—or maybe it was the same Earth, just a different universe. It wasn't worth thinking on unless one spoke in math, and that wasn't him. His Pashto was pretty decent, better than his Urdu. His German and Russian were solid but very rusty and not likely to be used much going forward. His Chandrian was already much more fluent than that of many Edenites who had a lot more time being exposed to it than he had. But math? He'd given up trying to understand the explanation of how the translations actually worked.

He activated his compad and noted their transports were ten minutes out. Two aircars were flying out from New St. Louis and would carry them within hunting distance of their quarry. They could have translated a lot closer to the targets, but no one had figured out how to suddenly appear somewhere without the corresponding shock wave and thunderous echo that announced one's arrival.

"How long before our ride gets here, Captain?" Grant Ballard may have grown up with and been related to team "Wrong Stuff" by marriage, but he couldn't have been more different in temperament than the Carlisle brothers. Grant would never be the honed blade of a two-legged weapon that the Carlisle brothers could become, but he could easily see Grant becoming an officer, given some time and experience.

"Ten minutes . . . if nature calls, now's the time. We're going hunting, people, so game faces on." He glanced again at Stant'ala, who gave him a slow nod. He doubted if the Jema scout had another face.

*

That evening, as the sun dropped behind the forest-covered ridges of low mountains, Gurl'ansa adjusted the cooking sticks over their small fire. The forest they were in was thick with bushy-tailed veet, who seemed at times to be almost fearless in their presence. They had taken a handful of the creatures with nothing more than a throwing stick that Hanlas could wield with precision. The warrior was asleep on the far side of the fire, while Manoma was a half kamark back on their trail, keeping watch for pursuit of which they had seen none.

They had planned to have to move by night as they skirted their way around small towns and farms, but there had been nothing of the sort to slow them. They had ended up traveling by day, and had made close to thirty kamarks each day since leaving the city on the great river behind. The Shareki world was indeed empty, or as near as. On

Chandra, he had never been to this actual continent, but he knew that tens of millions of Kaerin and their subjects resided here on his home world. Even the strange Shareki map device, that now suddenly worked, showed a near-empty world.

There were large cities, marked on the map, but using the symbol for the city their brothers had attacked by the river as a reference, most were much smaller and spread far apart. Hundreds of tiny dots with strange writing beneath them covered the magical map, and they had been able to confirm the location of one such village from a ridgeline the day before. The small town, consisting of a handful of buildings, had sat next to a small river in the distance. It had been so small they would not have seen it without the Shareki looking glass. Yet, it had been right where the strange lighted map had indicated it would be. He glanced at the Shareki device with its dark glass, lying atop Hanlas's pack, and wondered why the map had not shown itself on Chandra.

The Gemendi who had shown them how to charge the thing in sunlight, and activate the device, had said nothing about the map. They had only been able to access the just-as-strange list of Kaerin words and the corresponding Shareki script next to them. The Gemendi had assumed the Shareki had used the Jema to learn Kaerin words. If one touched the Kaerin word shown in the window, the device would speak out loud as if there were a woman's spirit inside it. First in Kaerin, then again in some strange tongue that set his nerves on edge.

The Gemendi team that had helped prepare them for the mission had been proud of having figured out how the translation tool worked. The Gemendi who had instructed them in its use had just assumed he and his team would have the time to learn the Shareki tongue. How and when they were supposed to be able to do that remained a mystery to him. Or even why . . . he had orders to avoid all contact with the Shareki. If the Gemendi wanted to be of real use, they should have figured out how to access the map before Lord Noka's assault force had entered the portal.

Instead, the Gemendi and Lord Noka had been forced to rely on the word of Strema slaves who managed to survive their failed attack on this world. Just a glance at the glowing map in his hands, and he could see they should have attacked one of the larger cities lying on either coast. But the Gemendi, sackless wonders that they were, had as usual been close to useless.

Hanlas had gotten the map to work the first time they activated the machine on this world. For the first four days after their arrival, they had done nothing besides run south, away from the site of battle. Since then, they had turned it on every night to see where they were, and what villages lay close that they would need to avoid. His mission had been to find the locations of large Shareki populations; he now had that knowledge in his hands. It was as if the device knew it was home . . .

Gurl'ansa almost put his hand in the fire, reaching across to shake Hanlas. "Hanlas, wake up!"

The warrior came awake with a start, a Shareki rifle in his hands as he scanned the surrounding spill of light from the fire. "Bastelta?"

He walked on his knees around the campfire, holding the device out in front of him. "Show me! Show me exactly what you did when you first made the map appear."

Hanlas flashed a look of annoyance before running a hand over his face and slapping himself further awake.

"Apologies, but I just thought of something."

Hanlas took the device from him and powered it off. "It was like this," Hanlas waved it in front of him. "I held the impetus button as we had been taught." Gurl'ansa watched Hanlas's every movement carefully.

"I waited for the light behind the window to glow, like it is now. This is when the new things happen. Watch . . ."

There was a small symbol of a map globe with an arrow orbiting rapidly around it in the center of the screen. "The Gemendi did not show us this," he whispered.

"Before, it was not there to be seen." Hanlas shrugged. "When the arrow stops spinning, the map globe turns green, although only half of it is green now. Two days ago, more of it was filled with color."

"And now the map. Show me how you first made the map appear."

Hanlas's finger hovered over the small square symbol for a map. "You see how it has turned green? Before we arrived here, it was pale and did nothing when touched. Here, the first time I touched it, the map appeared. Should I?"

Gurl'ansa grabbed the device and did it himself. The device did nothing for a moment, and then the window changed to show the map. A small cross of red lines indicated where they were. What before he had found magical was starting to feel dangerous. "The Gemendi told us that the captured Jema had used these devices to communicate, like a long-talker, with each other, yes?"

"They did." Hanlas yawned and shook his head. "But many of the small squares are still pale; they do not work when we touch them. When we do, we only get some Shareki script and a different symbol, the one that looks like an upraised thumb."

"So, it can talk to the map . . . spirit, only here?"

"I don't believe in spirits." Hanlas shook his head. "Nor do you."

"I don't know what to call it. Why would it only function here? It's a . . . thing, Hanlas! How would it know where it is?"

Hanlas shrugged. "I'm no Gemendi, Gurl."

Gurl'ansa reached out and grasped his warrior's shoulder. "I thank the sun and stars for that, Hanlas. Besides a warrior, you have a gift for drawing. I will take your watch. I want you to copy this glowing map to your own map book. You already have the shape of the land on your pages; it's no different than Chandra. Start with the largest cities, but get all the strange symbols recorded and as many of the small settlements as you are able to before sunrise. When you finish, turn off its impetus."

Hanlas looked back at him for a moment and then down at the device. When his warrior's head came up, his eyes were wide. "You think the device speaks to something? Or someone?"

"I don't know what to think." He pointed at the small rectangle, thinking that the Gemendi's insistence that they bring the device along might have killed them. "The cursed thing knows it's back on its home world, and exactly where we are. Work quickly."

*

Tom read the message from the Seattle Ops Center. The missing compad was back up on the net. The location provided wasn't exact. He knew the eggheads back in Seattle were triangulating off of the satellite link and any nearby devices, but "rural" didn't begin to describe the area they were in. Homesteads in the area were widely scattered, but every one of them had an antenna. There just weren't many close by to get a clear picture of exactly where the Kaerin were. He didn't need "exact"; the feed from Seattle showed what hillside they were on.

The targets had covered nearly thirty miles the day before and since their compad had last accessed the mesh network. Tom couldn't help but admire the pace the Kaerin were setting. His team could load up in the aircars and get within five miles of them right now, without being heard. By then, the quarry would be off the net and on the move in a direction he could hopefully track. He made a decision; it was time to box them in and get them moving on his schedule.

"Seattle Base, Alpha Team."

"Go Alpha Team."

"Request FLIR recon units, overfly targets ASAP. Insert Bravo and Charlie teams ASAP to coordinates I will be sending. This contingency plan was approved by Colonel Pretty in advance." The Black Hawk helicopters, holding the two quick reaction forces helping them, were equipped with forward-looking infrared. They should be able to get them an actual count.

He listened to the read back as he glanced around the campsite at the sleeping forms, already stirring awake in their bags. He knew it was Dominik and Hans. He doubted the veterans were any more capable of deep sleep in the field than he was. Snores coming from where he knew team Wrong Stuff had bedded down made him smile. He was going to enjoy waking them up. It was the little things that got you through the day.

"Stant, return to camp," he whispered into his mic. "We're getting ready to move."

There was a one-click response from the Jema veteran who had set up two hundred yards farther up the day-old trail they had found.

*

Chapter 7

New Seattle

"You people are driving my team crazy." Doc Jensen had started his briefing with a complaint the moment his office door closed. Kyle knew it was entirely justified. He wasn't about to interrupt the man. One thing he'd learned about Jensen was that the man just needed to yell once in a while.

"I had a team working at Kirkton designing the dry docks where our shipbuilding effort is going to be centered; they were on-site getting shit done when they were pulled off to New Castle. Another base? You people keep adding to the to-do list, nothing is going to get done."

He grinned in response and decided to twist the knife a little. "Don't forget Dumfries, Doc. Bases come first, but we need to get our people out of tents and huts and sink some roots. It's going to need its own portal facility as well, and that means another small-scale reactor. Same set up in Newcastle, eventually."

David Jensen just stared back at him in silence. "You're killing me here, you know that, right?"

He knew it. He also knew Jensen had his own army of PhDs and engineers at his disposal. It had taken a lot of R & D to get Eden off the ground, and an army of engineers to make it a reality. They'd all made the trip, and they all worked for Jensen. Most of that army had been working nonstop for the last five months to make sure they could hold on to the beachhead they'd established on Chandra.

"I can't argue with Paul about everything." He shrugged and smiled. "You need to delegate more. You've got the people and the expertise."

"Is that why you're here? You could have sent an e-mail."

Kyle grinned back; getting David Jensen angry was the first step in ensuring something got done. Kyle started ticking things off on his fingers. "Let's see . . . Shipbuilding, housing, communications network, recon platforms. Power, portals, on-site nano-production . . ."

"I helped write the damned list!" Jensen yelled at him, waving both arms. "I don't need you here reading it back to me. I've got a team working every one of those projects. They're doing good work, too; some of them worked the same issues here, so it's not their first rodeo. You people need to remember that even with our small-scale nuclear plants and nano-production, a lot of infrastructure has to be put in place – physically! To put it in terms a troglodyte like yourself can understand, it means concrete! Literal shit tons of the stuff." Jensen stayed in place as he walked in a tight circle. When he stopped, he had a confused look on his face. "Why are you smiling?"

"Doc, you've got this shit handled. Everyone but you knows it. We need you focused on stuff to help us win the fight."

"You're right." Jensen held up his hand after a long moment. "Thanks for letting me vent. Half my team goes into apoplexy if somebody raises their voice at them. I wasn't joking, Kyle. You want this stuff in place? Right now, it all hinges on a two-thousand-year-old technology—concrete. We've got a lot of equipment wait-listed here, waiting for a place to install it on Caledonia." David Jensen took a deep breath and nodded to himself.

"Concrete . . . We have access to a great deposit of dolomite limestone that runs from Newcastle to Sherwood, and the cement plant just south of New Castle has been running for over a month. I've been told the Kaerin will be marching north in a couple of months. I can only imagine what they are going to think when they come across one of our backhoes, not to mention the limekiln."

Kyle would give anything to be able to see the look on some Kaerin High Blood lord's face when he was told the Shareki had set up shop on his land. "Now that you mention it, where are we with comms and recon?"

"Launching satellites is easy for us." Jensen shrugged. "We just translate them into space around Chandra. The problem is keeping them there. The micro satellites are ready to go, we're still outfitting their rocket packs. We should have them all up in three weeks, initial operability a week after that."

"Why do they need rockets if you just translate them into space?"

"Residual inertia."

"Umm . . . troglodyte, remember?"

"Sorry . . . Put it to you simple: How fast are you moving after you translate?"

"I'm not moving."

"Satellites won't be either." Jensen shrugged. "They'll have the same velocity they translated with. They'll just hang there in space for a moment until Chandra's gravity starts pulling them in. We could put them at a Lagrange point, but that's too far away for a communications network. We need a whole swarm of electronic suitcases orbiting in low earth orbit; they need to be doing close to sixteen thousand miles an hour to stay in orbit."

"The rocket packs . . ."

Jensen nodded in response. "We still let gravity handle most of the acceleration as they fall inward; the rockets just shift their trajectory into a stable orbit. Compared to having to lift something off the surface of a planet, it's an easy day. We'll have one photo-recon bird up, in a polar orbit, in ten days. That will give you three passes a day on any given ground location. Which reminds me, I've added a satellite ground station to your little finger-ticking to-do list."

"You are a miracle worker. How about air assets?"

"I'm working it." Jensen smiled. "For now, you'll have aircars, Ospreys and helos."

"What about—"

"Your special project?" Jensen cut him off and then smiled. "I think you're going to be a happy man. I haven't had so much fun in a long time." Jensen scrubbed his face with both hands. "The best update you can get on all the Chandra side issues is going to come from Derek Mills. Make sure you give him anything and everything he asks for out there. That man is an evil genius. On the science spectrum, he's a bit too software, Silicon Valley, wine-and-cheese focused for my taste, but he's a brilliant manager and doing a great job of keeping the tech team on Chandra focused. He's got some great ideas that we should have thought of."

"I'll do that." Kyle glanced at the clock on the wall; he'd jostled Jensen's elbow enough and would be able to tell Hank that the buildup was proceeding as quickly as possible. He needed to get going. "You have time for a personal question?"

"As long as it doesn't have anything to do with how much sleep I'm getting, or if I'm taking time to fucking exercise. I'm getting tired of people worrying over me. I work better this way."

Every time he started thinking of Jensen as some sort of modern-day da Vinci, the doc had a way of reminding him he was from New Jersey. "Not *that* personal, Doc, but now that you mention it—you're no use to anyone dead."

"Noted. What do you want?"

"I wanted to ask you about Daryl Ocheltree. Elisabeth is insisting I talk to him about his kid signing on with the volunteers on Chandra. I know the family has been with the program forever. I was hoping you knew why this was an issue, or more to the point, why it's any of my business."

"Damn . . . I *am* getting old." Jensen leaned back against his desk and crossed his arms. "I can't believe they have a kid that old."

"You know them well?"

"Not well, no. But given their history, I can guess what the issue might be. Back in the early days . . . the Carolina attack?"

"I've read the reports." Kyle nodded.

"Daryl's only sister and her entire family were among those killed by the Kaerin, or by whatever clan they'd sent. Darryl's wife, whose name I can't remember at the moment, she lost . . . I think it was both parents, and a brother. Between the two of them, I'd think he'd want some payback."

Kyle rubbed at the headache that was starting behind his eyes. The event in the Carolinas had been horrific by any measure. A sane person would do anything in their power to make certain it couldn't happen again. But people were different; where one would seek to remove the threat through vengeance, others would embrace anything to avoid it happening again. Two sides of the same coin minted out of tragedy. "Different strokes, Doc."

"Well, Daryl Ocheltree is a different kind of cat. He's a good guy, and I mean that. He's just always been a little crunchier than most of the founders, certainly more so than the traditional EDF types—not full-on tree-hugging, hair-shirt crunchy, just not a soldier by temperament or experience. He joined the EDF *after* the attack, probably out of some sort of guilt or something. He wants you to talk his kid out of joining?"

"I'm not sure." He shrugged. "Elisabeth just coerced a promise out of me that I would speak to him, the father—not the kid."

Jensen shook his head in disgust. "And you said, 'yes'?"

Kyle shrugged in defeat.

"Dumbass."

*

Kirkton Base, Chandra

Kyle had waited outside the translation chamber in New Seattle as two forklifts ran a relay, loading the chamber with pallets stacked with supplies. He took note of what was on the pallets. Clothing from New-New Orleans, which everybody had taken to calling "New New."

Javelin missiles in their hard-sided carry cases produced in Azteca, which had replaced New Mexico City. Bags of rice from the settlements in Japan, which meant they'd come by ship, fresh produce from all over, boots from El Paso, and ammo from his own home settlement of Chief Joe. The manifest was rounded out by crates of spare parts and building materials from the nano-pro factories on Whidbey Island. From the pile of gear and drums of fuel he could see in the loading bay, he could tell it was just one of several shipments going out today.

All of it was a good sign that Eden was solidly behind the effort to fortify their presence on Chandra. He wished it were all happening a year down the road; by then, every major settlement on Eden would have a translation facility, and they'd be able to ship materials and personnel directly to Chandra as well as translate anywhere they wanted to, point-to-point on Eden, albeit via a pit stop in Chandra. Much of that planned infrastructure had taken a back seat to building out the bases on Chandra.

The one shortage they couldn't fix was a shortage of people. Before the Strema invasion, underemployment had been a real issue. The problem had been replaced with a labor market so tight, people could pick and choose what they wanted to do, on what world, who they wanted to work for, and for how much. It was a good problem to have, and it didn't look like it was going to solve itself any time soon. Not unless Audy and Jake were having better success with Caledonia's Creight population than they had been before he'd left.

"Hey, buddy, you mind sitting on top? I can get another pallet in."

"Not a problem," he yelled back at the Heister driver, a woman a few years younger than him. The exhaust from the forklift's natural gas engine reminded him of his teenage years working in an onion-packing shed. "How many loads you send a day?"

"Lately, as many as we can load, twenty-four seven. Got to keep the Jema fed, and I'm married to one of them."

Kyle smiled and bowed out of the way to let her drive past him. She was probably pregnant, he figured. Otherwise, she'd be on Chandra with her husband. Everybody was pregnant. Elisabeth had warned him that huge families had been the norm even before he'd fully made Eden his home, and the two of them had already decided that Sophie needed a little brother or sister just as soon as the timing was right.

He crawled atop a pallet of uniforms and took in the scope of the shipment. Some quick math and he came up with forty-eight pallets; and he knew the really big stuff, like components for the ships they were building and industrial materials, would get translated directly from the facility on Whidbey Island. The caution lights outside the vault started spinning as the steel door dropped from its recess in the ceiling and cocooned him in silence. He hated this part. It was an expectation of something that didn't happen, or maybe it did; one could get lost in the quantum theory behind the ability to translate. He was half-convinced quantum theory was just a collection of best guesses made by people too smart to be comfortable with the idea they didn't have a fucking clue.

There was the slightest hum and a quick wave of nausea, and the door was opening inside the facility on Chandra. He hopped down into the space that had been occupied by the door, and came face to face with thirty or forty long-haired Creight, all of them in new boots and sweatpants. Half of them were shirtless, sporting crude tattoos as they ignored him and swarmed inside to start pulling boxes and bags off the pallets. It was clear it wasn't the first portal shipment they'd seen. By the time he made it into the loading area, they had a human conveyer belt set up, stretching out the open door on the far side of the facility, and the material began to flow.

From the look of the light spilling through the large garage door, the sun was shining. It was as welcome as the fact Jake and Audy seemed to have struck a bargain with the Creight. The supply depot outside was the size of a large parking lot, and it was full, with trucks and trailers working the far edge to reduce the pile. He figured most of this material would be staying here at Kirkton Base; otherwise, they'd just have ported it directly to Dumfries or New Castle.

"There's a sight for sore eyes!" Jake's voice brought his head around.

He grinned as Jake and Jeff came around the corner of the building. Jeff already had his hands out. "Hand it over."

"Good to see you guys too."

"Jackass dropped our last can of chew in the latrine last night." Jeff flashed a thumb in Jake's direction. "We can hug later."

He shrugged his bag off his shoulder and dug out a log of snuff tins. Some enterprising founder was going to be rich; many of the Jema had taken up the horrible habit that had been almost pro forma in the Army. He tossed the log to Jeff. "What's the plan?"

"Up to you," Jake answered. "We figured you'd want to check out New Castle. Nagy and his bunch are holding the fort there; we can get you up to speed on the way. Throw your shit in the hut. It's still home for the moment."

"For most of us, anyway," Jeff added. "Jake has a girlfriend."

"How many more cattle it take?"

Jake smiled as he gave his head a shake and flashed him a middle finger. "One dozen rifles."

"It worked." Jeff pointed through the door behind him. "The Creight have been coming out of the hills the last couple of days."

"Is this going to fall to shit when they figure out Jake's not a virgin bride?"

"Not going to be a problem." Jake waggled a finger. "Turns out, me bringing sexy back to this island is just what the situation called for."

"Shocker . . ." Jeff drawled.

New Castle Base, Chandra

"We aren't worried about being spotted from the ground?" Kyle asked when Jeff flew them in a straight line, hugging the northern edge of Solway Firth. He'd studied the maps enough to know New Castle lay just a few degrees south of due east from Kirkton, across the breadth of the island near its narrowest point. The line the two settlements, Kirkton and New Castle, made on the map wasn't too far off from where Hadrian had built his wall on Earth. Dumfries, the site of their first settlement, was almost twenty miles northeast of Kirkton—but the two bases, one on each coast, anchored the line they had drawn across the island. The plan was to take and hold the whole island, but they'd needed to have a secure jumping-off point, and safe harbors on both coasts.

"Hyrika has her scouts out," Jeff answered, pointing out the passenger-side window. "In an east-west line about fifty miles south of our flight path. They haven't seen any Kaerin activity yet, just bands of Creight pushing their luck staying that far south, for this long."

He'd read that report. Creight putting their lives at risk to get another week or two out of the short spring growing season. "It's a lot to risk for some turnips."

"They head north without enough food, they risk just as much." Jake shook his head. "Audy asked Rai'nor to send some people south to let those bands know there's a new neighbor. They should be close to Hyrika's forward line by now."

Kyle had been happy to read that as well. "So Rai'nor? He's going to help?"

"He'll help," Jeff answered. "But they aren't anywhere near as ready or capable as the Jema were."

"Juice isn't worth the squeeze," Jake blurted out and held up a hand in defense. "My opinion. They're as far behind the Jema, as the Jema were behind us when we first made contact. Near term, I think we're looking at scouts and lookouts."

"How about as bait?" Kyle asked. "You think they'd be willing?"

"That would be a lot for Rai'nor to take on faith."

"I was thinking when we are done at New Castle, the three of us take Rai'nor on a field trip south. We could pick up Audy, Carlos and his team, a few of Hyrika's Jema scouts, and do a little hunting of our own."

"Couldn't hurt," Jeff agreed. "Beats the hell out of this green zone duty, but what happened to keeping a low profile until we are ready?"

"I meant a lot further south," Kyle added with a smile. "We'll translate from Eden. We are going to keep the Kaerin guessing and make certain they are focused anywhere but here."

"It's better than beating the bushes in northern Scotland, looking for other Creight," Jake agreed.

The tour of the brand-new base in New Castle along the north shore of the River Tyne, a mile and a half upriver from where it dumped itself into the North Sea, didn't take long. There were a half dozen prefab Quonset huts, sitting behind a large concrete structure, that acted as the base headquarters. Farther back from the river's edge, the ground had been cleared and graded. Pads of concrete had been poured for what looked like several dozen more buildings. Kyle was most interested in the large patrol boat tied up at the adjacent dock, its bow pointed downriver towards the sea. He knew the assembly of its sister ship was almost complete at Kirkton Base.

"How was the trip around the tip of Scotland?"

"I got here via the portal," Captain Nagy commented with a grin. The former Green Beret had been a member of Colonel Pretty's unit on Earth, and had very nearly gotten himself killed getting to Eden. "The skipper was ready for a drink by the time she arrived. I take it the midway refueling, at night, from Arsolis's piece of shit sail boat was a bit of a show."

"I'll bet." What Kyle knew about the sea could fit inside a teacup, but it was enough to know that their patrol boat, patterned closely after the Mark VI Riverine, hadn't been specifically designed for blue water, especially the North Sea. It was what they had at the moment, and according to Jake, it far outclassed anything the Kaerin had afloat. For the moment, the two 25mm chain guns, fore and aft of the pilothouse, not to mention the anti-ship missiles and onboard Javelin team, guaranteed naval supremacy.

None of them had any doubt it would take the Kaerin a long time to adapt. It was why their plans for Portsmouth included a dry dock where larger ships could be constructed, or assembled as the case might be. Most of the larger components could be built on Eden and translated to where they were needed. That was the plan in the long term. First, they needed to take Portsmouth and secure "Caledonia."

"What do you need, that you don't have?" Kyle had come to hate asking that question. This time, he knew Nagy actually understood the meaning of the term "need."

Nagy rubbed at his bald head. "Another six months?"

Kyle couldn't disagree with the sentiment. "Three months, three and a half tops. That's if the Kaerin don't figure out we're here before then."

"'Bout what I figured. My main responsibility right now is providing security for the lime pit and concrete plant you overflew on the way in, and this naval base. I have it on good authority we need a road or rail connecting Newcastle to Dumfries and Kirkton soon. It's going to be at least six months before we have our own portal facility here."

"You get that from Jensen?"

"No, although I was told he agrees. It was Mr. Mills's idea; the guy keeps the hive humming here."

"*Mister* Mills? He didn't re-up?"

Nagy shook his head. "It would have been a waste. The guy is way too smart for Army, and I don't mean that in the way a couple of Navy pukes would think about it." They both turned to smile at Jake and Jeff, forestalling the comments both looked to have ready.

"Seriously smart," Nagy continued. "The guy used to be a Silicon Valley CEO? Sold his company for a ton of money and *then* joined the Army. Who the fuck does that?"

They all had a good laugh, shaking their heads at the thought. "Doc Jensen happens to agree with you; said he's the guy I need to listen to."

"I listen to him," Nagy agreed. "When he made the offhand

observation our miners and concrete plant employees would need to walk to Dumfries in the event this position became untenable, I took his desire for a roadway seriously. It's eighty-seven miles, flat as a pancake for most it. He thinks we can do two, maybe three miles of gravel road a day."

"We?"

"I can maintain and continue to improve our defenses here, and still free up two companies of troops for labor, until they are needed to do their real job. I get most of the newbies coming out of training on Eden. All I need is your OK."

"You have it." He shared a smile with Nagy. "Nothing worse than having bored soldiers hanging around the barracks. In fact, I might steal the idea and start from Kirkton. We could meet in the middle somewhere."

"Sounds good, just talk with Derrick. He's already had a route surveyed and has a list of specs for it, so we can turn it into a rail bed if the need or opportunity arises."

"He's in Kirkton?"

"Splits his time between there, Dumfries, and here," Jake answered. "I don't know where he sleeps, not sure he does."

"We're headed back to Dumfries next; you can look for him there." Jeff smiled at him as he spoke. "I'm betting you never thought you'd miss having a fully functional compad."

Kyle shook his head slowly. "You'd lose that bet. We need to make sure I'm in the field and operational by the time we get communications up and running. I don't ever want my day being planned by my inbox again."

"Well, let's go start some shit," Jake suggested.

"Don't you have a wedding to plan, Jake?" Nagy was looking at him sideways. "I was sure I'd heard something. Is there anything besides livestock the new couple will be needing?"

Kyle ignored Jake's muttered cursing going on behind him as he shook hands with New Castle's commander. "I'm glad you're here,

Rob. Keep training the new recruits. We'll be asking them to do a lot more than build a road all too soon."

"They know it."

Opposed to Kirkton and New Castle, Dumfries, at least from the air on their approach, looked like a town; or at least a very large armed camp trying to turn itself into a town. A basic network of roads was visible, framing a dozen or more prefab buildings. Many of the Jema must have gotten tired of waiting for building materials, as hundreds of small cabins had been built. He couldn't blame them; a very wet winter in England was a great incentive to get indoors. Patches of tilled earth next to most of the cabins spoke of gardens. Large tracts of fields had been cleared of lumber and turned over, readied for planting at the edges of the city.

"Welcome to Dodge City," Jeff commented. "If we don't let the Jema at the Kaerin soon, Audy and Jomra are going to have to turn a bunch of them into cops."

"How bad is it?"

"They're just anxious," Jeff answered. "They don't like sitting around, and they know this isn't going to be their long-term home."

"I think they want to get settled in the South as badly as they want at the Kaerin," Jake added. "They're taken with the idea of having a new permanent home here and everyone knowing about it."

"They aren't wrong," Kyle agreed. The Jema controlling a chunk of land in plain sight of the rest of this planet was the keystone to their entire plan. The cell phone towers were evidently in range of his compad as the device let out an impressive string of alert beeps that sounded like laughter to him.

"Shit! I knew it was too good to last." He read the message he was looking for. "Back to Kirkton, Jeff. I can check out Dodge City later. Mr. Mills and Audy are waiting for us."

The aircar was silent except for the whine of the fans as Jeff mashed the throttle and climbed. They'd just turned southwest for the short flight back to Kirkton when Jake leaned forward from the back seat.

"Hey, you two ever see that old movie, *Driving Miss Daisy?*"

Chapter 8

Eden, Central Missouri

"There are two trails now." Stant'ala sounded certain. Tom wasn't about to question the man everyone said was the Jema's best scout and tracker. "One track to the south, a single Kaerin," Stant'ala added a moment later. "The other trail. . . I think two Kaerin are moving to the southwest."

Shit . . . The overflights he'd ordered must have spooked the Kaerin. The reason didn't matter. The FLIR cameras had identified three individuals, and they'd all needed to know how big a Kaerin force they were dealing with. His tracker had just independently confirmed that number, as well as his ability to read the signs of the trail they'd followed up the hillside. The enemy's compad had shut down before dawn, and if the pattern held, they wouldn't come back up until the next night. Their quarry, regardless of which path the compad had taken, was headed into a zone with very few homesteads, and he doubted if the device would be able to connect to give them a fix.

They stood around the campsite the Kaerin had used the night before. Everyone, with the exception of Stant'ala, was breathing hard from the climb they had just made. The thick forested hills were tailor-made to set an ambush on a pursuing force, or to hide in. Spotting the Kaerin from the air would be next to impossible now that the enemy knew they were being pursued. The entire area was riddled with caves big and small, sinkholes and dens from the numerous black bears they'd already seen. It was the perfect place in which to hide.

"The single track is moving fast, long strides," Stant'ala added. Tom knew the Jema was more than ready to resume the pursuit.

"We'll follow both," Tom announced and pointed at his two veterans, Domenik and Han's. They were a mismatched pair; one a giant, the other a short, solid fireplug of muscle. Neither one was built for endurance, not to the degree he knew Stant was capable of. His veterans had been breathing as hard as he had while trying to keep up with the Jema all morning. He was going to have to split up his team. His first instinct was to have either Dom or Han's in command of the other half. Then again, Stant'ala had more experience than any of them, including himself.

"Either of you two think you can keep up with Stant'ala?"

The Jema spoke first. "Over distance. Any of you would slow me down. I should go alone."

"Easy there, amigo." Danny Carlisle grunted with laughter and jerked a thumb at himself and his brother. "No one is going to run the two of us into the ground." The elder of the two Carlisle brothers seemed to realize he'd spoken out loud. His head snapped around to focus on Tom. "I meant, no one is going to run us into the ground, sir."

Josh Carlisle, the younger of the two, looked at him in panic. "Sir, I don't think he meant—"

"Sounds good," Tom cut him off. If any of them had the ability to run with Stant'ala, it was his two cowboys, for the sole reason he knew they wouldn't quit. "You'll both go. Stant'ala, I'd appreciate it if you bring them both back. You're in command. Don't risk anything trying to make a capture. You understand?"

Stant'ala looked back at him, nodding gravely. Like many of the Jema, Stant had maintained the long tail of hair down his back, braided into a rope, but the sides of his head were almost bare. "The Kaerin will not allow himself to be captured."

"Fine, then make certain he doesn't take any of you with him. Report in if you get somewhere you have a signal. I'll do the same."

"As you command, Tom."

He was new to Eden, and still finding his way through the informal EDF structure and how the Jema fit in. The scout's acknowledgement struck him as a fair representation of how the Jema fit into the EDF's military. Ranks often went unacknowledged, but the authority they conveyed was followed with a strict discipline.

"Remember, the radios might be in range of the reaction teams. I'll have them up searching with infrared again tonight. They can run, but I don't plan to let these Kaerin get any sleep, and we'll box them in."

"We will not rest." Stant'ala flashed a grin in Danny Carlisle's direction.

Josh punched his older brother in the arm, hard enough that it sounded like a hammer connecting with a side of beef. "You're going to pay for this."

Danny rubbed his arm. "Feels like I just did."

"We go," Stant'ala announced before setting off at a quick pace down the hill into the forest.

"Well, shit," Danny muttered before taking off after him. His brother followed a second later, mumbling under his breath. The rest of them watched the trio disappear into the trees.

"Anybody else feel sorry for Stant'ala?" Grant was grinning from ear to ear.

"You don't think they'll keep up?" Hans asked.

"Oh, they'll keep up." Grant laughed. "He's just going to wish they didn't."

"Come on," Tom said, silently agreeing. "We've got our own trail to follow."

*

Hanlas had been running for half the day. His legs were beginning to tire. He'd fallen once, three hours into his run, having caught the toe of his boot on a half-buried tree root. He'd narrowly missed a repeat performance several times in the last hour. He pulled back on his pace and fell into a quick walk, letting his lungs catch up with what he was forcing his body to do. The forested rolling hills he passed though were spider-webbed with small creeks. The streambed he could see at the bottom of the latest hill was the largest he'd encountered so far, and was lined with a wide field of exposed, smooth river rock on either side.

He took a moment to stop and look behind him. His sight was limited to no more than thirty or forty spans before the deeply shadowed forest swallowed everything. The same would hold for anyone pursuing him. Despite the bright sun overhead, he'd run the entire morning in a shady gloom cast by the ancient, untouched forest. He was trying to use game trails where he could, to speed his progress. It was frustrating; the rough tracks rarely maintained the direction of travel he needed for long.

Gurl'ansa had become convinced the Shareki device was somehow "talking" to someone or something. Hanlas didn't know what to believe, but none of them had missed the beating of the spinning wings of the strange Shareki airboats during the night. If Gurl'ansa was correct, the bastelta and Manoma would use the device to lure their pursuers away from him and the treasure he now carried. Yet more sacrifice of others weighing on him. The death of the old warriors, his father included, and now his bastelta and a fellow warrior were sacrificing themselves so that he would survive.

The pressure of his map book, filled in with his hand-drawn symbols, felt heavy against the small of his back. The oiled-leather-wrapped book now held a value beyond words. Proof of how empty this world was, and more important, the locations of where the few Shareki cities and villages lay. It was knowledge that his father and hundreds of other High Blood warriors had given their lives for. He would return the map to Chandra if he had to crawl to the great gulf on his hands and knees.

He had half a year to survive on this world, before the world gate would open and facilitate his return. His intention was to get there as quickly as possible and hide within the swampland that ringed the area around the gate.

He pulled out a charred carcass of one of the veets they'd cooked the night before and bit into it as he walked. He didn't give the gamey charcoal taste a second thought; it would sustain him.

Kirkton Base, Chandra

Kyle felt a lot better after talking to Derek Mills - about almost everything. He'd met the guy very briefly in Idaho, on Earth, half a year ago. That meeting had lasted an hour before Derek had ported to Eden for the first time with his very pregnant wife, Denise. He hadn't seen the man since and had assumed that he'd rolled into the EDF along with Tom Souza and his wife, Brittany. Derek explained to him that both he and his wife were really science geeks at heart, and had been lured away by David Jensen soon after arriving on Eden.

Once a decision had been made to expand the footprint at Kirkton and Dumfries, Derek had been fingered to be Jensen's point man on Chandra. Kyle thought Jensen deserved a bottle of really good scotch for making that call. Every issue he brought up, Derek was already aware of, and if he wasn't working the problem, he had a plan and a schedule to get to it.

"Everybody I speak to thinks you are doing an amazing job," Kyle relayed. "Hank Pretty is going to be here in a week or so. We'll be finalizing the first steps of our campaign. He'll ask me what you need, so I'm asking you."

"Just more time," Derek answered. "A month ago, I would have said more hands. The recruitment effort the program has been running on Eden for equipment operators and foremen in the trades is paying off. Probably pissing off some businesses back home, but I try not to worry about that."

"Yeah . . . don't," Kyle agreed. "Most of them have realized we need to clean up the neighborhood, before they can get back to business as usual."

"With the Creight coming in, it's just a matter of training them up. In terms of bottlenecks, building materials are the critical shortage, but we're starting to see some improvement. It'll mean some folks on Eden are probably going to have to wait longer than they would have to get out of temp housing, but production is ramping up here and on Eden. The bottleneck is widening."

"Once we start operations in the summer," Kyle pointed out, "a lot of your workforce is going to disappear."

"Oh, I know, but so will the immediate impact on infrastructure. We'll be able to temporarily shut down the water treatment at Dumfries and complete the larger installation once they take the field. There're a dozen examples like that. One worry is the security situation going to shit, to the point we have to evac the Edenite workforce all at once. My personal nightmare is a logjam of civilians at the Kirkton portal, waiting for the capacitors to recharge while the Kaerin close in."

"Your family is here with you?"

"They are." Derek nodded. "So are those for most of my people. It's why the reactor expansion for the Kirkton portal and the one under construction at Dumfries are being overbuilt. Just in case we have to rapid fire the translations."

"That definitely remains priority one," Kyle agreed. He'd been stuck on Earth with no portal to access; repeating the experience on Chandra with Kaerin closing in would be a new circle of hell.

"Speaking of family." Derek smiled. "My wife told me to invite you for dinner this evening. I think it was a trick to get me to show up on time for once."

He had to laugh at that. It sounded all too familiar. "I will take you up on that, but it will have to be another night. Audy has convinced Rai'nor and his entourage to come to Eden; I'm headed back home directly. My wife is going to be more than surprised when I show up for dinner plus seven. I really hope the e-mail server translates before we do."

"Dinner with the Creight? That'll be interesting. Don't use the good silver," Derek joked. "Their pockets will likely be full when they leave."

Kyle had to think for a second before the realization struck that they didn't have any "good" silver. "Has it been an issue?"

"Early days." Derek nodded. "Take anybody living at a subsistence level and drop them into the open-air supply depot we have out there, there's going to be some issues. First day that we had a big group of them, there wasn't a single one that didn't leave the mess hall with their pockets stuffed." Derek gave a huge smile. "Mashed potatoes. . . not something you'd think people would try to filch. I think they thought they were in heaven when we served dinner that same evening. They're learning."

They were learning as well, he knew. Just as they had needed to do with the Jema. It would take time that he hoped they had. He stood up and offered Derek his hand. "You ever get tired of building our future and want to get your soldier back on, all you have to do is ask."

Derek gave his hand a shake. "I do actually miss it sometimes, and believe me, that surprises the hell out of me. I wasn't exactly cut out for that line of work."

Kyle didn't believe him for a second. He doubted if there was a line work that someone like Derek wouldn't figure out how to do well. "The offer will stand."

Derek waved back behind him as he left the broom closet that had been assigned to him. The small space had enough room for a small desk and two chairs. There was nothing on the walls, or the desk besides his day bag. His assault rifle leaned against the wall; everything about the space screamed temporary.

One more meeting to go, and then he was back to Eden for an unexpected dinner he'd rather miss. Before he could get up to call in the next victim, there was a knock at the door.

"Captain Ocheltree?"

"Please." The man stepped forward and offered his hand. "It's Daryl, and I should have made a point to meet you long ago. My wife and I have known Elisabeth for years."

"So she tells me." He gestured to the chair in front of his desk. "Yours was one of the founder families?"

"Arrived late in year one." He nodded. "Not exactly *Mayflower* status, but right after."

"I know there were some rough times in those early years. We all owe you people a debt."

"Nonsense." Ocheltree waved the comment off. "It was all done for a reason, and everyone that followed after, was the reason."

Kyle nodded politely, and just decided to jump in. He'd already had a very long day, and thanks to Audy, it wasn't close to being over. "I have to admit that my wife confused the hell out of me trying to explain why you needed to speak to me about your son. Your kid is your kid. I wouldn't presume to have a say."

"Jeremy." Daryl nodded. "He'll be eighteen very soon, and he's not speaking to me at the moment because I wouldn't let him sign on with the volunteers here at seventeen."

"You want me to try to talk him out of it?" Kyle asked. "I'm not sure I'm the guy to do that."

"Trust me, there's nothing you could say that would talk him out of it. He's joining up; in fact, I sent him the parental waiver form this morning. I just wanted to speak to you as a fellow soldier, and now a father—congrats on that, by the way. When I ran into Elisabeth, she had your daughter along. Very cute kid."

He gave a nod in appreciation. "I can't take much credit on that score."

A look of confusion tumbled across Ocheltree's face for a moment before he caught himself. Kyle was left with the impression of an individual who was very uncomfortable, socially speaking. Eden had its share of iconoclasts, people who had basically checked out of normal society and sought lives where they just didn't have to interact much with fellow humans. Daryl Ocheltree struck him as just that sort of animal.

"Yes, well, Elisabeth suggested I talk to you. I need to ask you, as a father, why you think it's the right thing to do; I mean taking this fight to the Kaerin." Kyle was taken aback by the question. The delivery left him with a sudden feeling that this whole conversation had been rehearsed. Technically, Ocheltree was his subordinate, and he half considered delivering an answer in those terms, but he'd promised Elisabeth he'd talk.

"I'm not sure I can add anything to the arguments that I know you've already heard." Kyle did his best to keep a straight face. "Surely you don't believe the Kaerin can or will just stop and let us be?"

"Has anyone asked them?" The genuine naïveté of Ocheltree's tone struck him like a hammer.

"No. No one has asked." *No one is going to.* "They've enslaved a planet; they've developed and enforced a culture that depends on regularly scheduled ethnic cleansing. We won't be negotiating with them on any level."

"And you don't expect them to reach out to you at some point?"

"How could they? We have it on very good authority that everyone who isn't a Kaerin is considered subhuman. I doubt they could afford to reach out to us and stay in power. The Jema's presence here is going to eat away at their authority. They can't afford to be anything other than the bullshit 'super-race' they've convinced the rest of Chandra that they are."

"So, you intend to kill them all? In their tens or hundreds of millions? Their women? Their children? Our own campaign of ethnic cleansing, forced on us by the Jema?"

Kyle felt heat bloom across his face and managed, barely, to keep his seat. He bit down on his gut reaction. "There's an ocean of difference between destroying someone's will to fight, and killing an entire race."

Ocheltree nodded slowly. "I agree with that, and I would never suggest that you or anyone in our leadership feels differently. But . . . I would posit that there is as wide an ocean between our understanding of that statement and how the Jema think this war ends. As to the other clans that may rise up against the Kaerin, who knows where their line is? How many people on this world are we going to be responsible for killing?"

There was a half-truth in Ocheltree's question that they'd all been aware of for some time. The Jema wouldn't shed a tear if the Kaerin, all of them, were suddenly gone. On the other side of the equation were the Kaerin themselves, a people who were willing and had shown the repeated ability to sacrifice entire peoples to stay in power.

"I can't argue with anything you just said, Daryl. It's not the first time I've heard those concerns. Hank Pretty feels much the same way. You might be surprised that Jomra Sendai, the leader of the Jema, does not want his people responsible for a genocide either. The difference is, none of us have the freedom to take responsibility for what becomes of the Kaerin. We can only worry about the billions, I repeat—*the billions*—living under the Kaerin yoke as slaves, not to mention the security of our own peoples on two different worlds. No one I know has ever framed the issue of the Kaerin using an argument based on some sort of moral equivalency."

"I'm not either."

The hell you aren't. It was clear that Ocheltree wanted to argue, or to convince him of something. He was starting to doubt if Ocheltree himself knew what that was. "I'm not sure what it is you want to hear, Daryl. We are going to *end* the Kaerin threat. We don't have a choice. We will try to engender popular Chandrian support to that end. If we are successful, which is by no means assured, it is the Kaerin who will have a choice to make. Because I do agree with you, Daryl. When we do get to that point, and God willing, we will, the issue of the Kaerin's future won't be in our hands but those of the peoples they have enslaved."

Ocheltree just looked back at him and gave his head a slow nod.

Kyle was certain his explanation had just confirmed something for Captain Ocheltree.

"My concerns must seem strange to you. I've never been a natural fit for a soldier."

"To some extent, none of us are," Kyle answered. "It's as necessary a role as it is unnatural. There's no avoiding this fight, Captain. We didn't make the ground rules, and we'd be fools to think we can change them."

Ocheltree chewed on the words for a moment that dragged on far too long before patting his own leg. "I understand, and I appreciate you taking the time to speak with me."

"Did it help?" he asked as he followed the EDF officer to his feet and shook the man's hand. "I think it was good for me to clarify, in my own mind, why we are here. I get pulled in so many directions the big picture can get fuzzy."

"I just realized that clarity doesn't always bring comfort." Ocheltree's tone matched the look of disappointment on his face.

It was a lid on the strangest conversation he'd had in a long while. Ocheltree was one of those people who needed to know why he was doing something. There was nothing wrong with that on the surface, but like a few others he'd met, the need to know was combined with a pedantic surety that they knew better. There'd been more people like that in the military than he would have credited.

"In my experience, it rarely does," Kyle added.

Kyle stood behind his desk, staring at the door Ocheltree had closed on his way out. Doc Jensen's comment had been spot-on, if a little weak-kneed. Ocheltree was a *very* odd duck. He knew he hadn't convinced the man of anything, and he still didn't know why the guy had felt it so important to reach out to him.

*

Chapter 9

New Seattle, Eden

A blessedly dry morning, with blue skies and a crisp breeze coming in off the cold Pacific waters, had welcomed their party to Elisabeth's mother's backyard overlooking Lake Washington. At nearly a decade old, it was one of the oldest homes on Eden, and his mother-in-law, Dr. Abraham, the senior, was a practiced gardener. It was the perfect setting to introduce the Creight to Eden. Kyle had been present months ago when Arsolis, the Hatwa village Krathik, and Cal'as, the Hatwa warrior, had arrived for their first visit to Eden. The strange buildings and the overhead aircar traffic had driven Arsolis to his knees in terror.

Elisabeth would tour Rai'nor and the Creight party around New Seattle later; the backyard brunch was a gentle first step and one that had already had its moments. Rai'nor's wife had been quite taken with the waffles and the magical machine that produced them. She wanted one for her village, and unless his Chandrian was failing him, she'd laid down the challenge to her husband to make certain they didn't leave without one of the miraculous machines.

For the moment, he watched as his own father and Randy Sykes, both of whom had been recruited as cooks, tried to explain the concept of electricity to Rai'nor. The Creight chieftain was on one knee with a confused look, running his hand over the small bundle of extension cords running across the patio's stone slabs to the cook's tables. Crawl, walk, run . . . it was the only way to get the Creight where they needed them.

The Creight's walk stage was going to be a longer road than the transformation the Jema had managed. In the latter's case, it had merely been a matter of getting accustomed to advanced technology and getting acquainted with new tools. For the Creight, the concept of technology itself was new. If they were going to be successful on Chandra over the long run, the Creight would only be the first group of many to have their horizons expanded.

He panned across the yard and took a moment to watch Jake work the Edenite crowd, introducing his girlfriend. He'd met Dere'dala just a few hours ago outside the portal building in Kirkton before they'd translated over. He'd known Jake was in love the second he saw his friend's face. It had been pure Jake, but it was as if someone else had been sharing his friend's brain and the new arrival behind his eyes was scared shitless.

Dere'dala had Mat'isa, Rai'nor's wife, in tow, and Jake was steadily working his way towards where Elisabeth stood holding Sophie. What he could see of his daughter in his wife's arms was limited to chubby cheeks and a set of green eyes as she was bundled up against the chill of the morning. He didn't want to miss Jake's torture at having to behave like a normal adult as he introduced Dere'dala to his stepsister. He'd made it halfway across the lawn before Arsolis stepped in front of him.

"We need to speak."

"I'd be happy to," he replied. He reached out and put a friendly hand on the man's shoulder. "But later, Arsolis. My wife needs me at the moment."

"Very well." Arsolis bowed his head. Kyle couldn't help but notice the Hatwa fell in close behind him, not put off in the least. He shouldn't have been surprised. Jeff and Carlos had heard the exchange and moved to rescue him but were too slow. They all arrived at the same time.

His own mother broke the sudden tension of the massed arrival. "Mat'isa." His mother looked at Dere'dala's sister-in-law. "Am I saying that correctly?"

"You are."

His mother offered him a smile. "Mat'isa just complemented you and Elisabeth on having such a plump baby."

He shared a knowing smile with Elisabeth. To the Creight, there probably wasn't a better predictor of infant survival than how well fed they were. Glancing at his daughter, he was reminded again why they were doing all of this.

"So healthy, and in the spring no less." Mat'isa reached out and let Sophie grab a finger. "May Jake and Dere'dala have such fat children. You are his sister, yes?"

"Yes," Elisabeth answered. They'd decided in advance, for Jake's sake, to leave the concept of step-relations out of it. Jake was firmly back in the Creight's good graces, and there was nothing to be gained by trying to confuse the issue. "I and my mother are what's left of Jake's family." Elisabeth reached out and touched Dere'dala's arm. "You are most welcome here, and we are very pleased someone has finally managed to capture Jake's heart." Elisabeth gave Jake a smile. "And it's easy to see that you have."

Dere'dala smiled up at Jake, who looked like he'd be happier anywhere else on three worlds. "Is this true?" Dere'dala asked him in a tone utterly devoid of sarcasm. Kyle had never been happier seeing a friend in genuine pain. From the looks on Elisabeth's, her mother's and even *his* mother's faces, he wasn't alone in his joy.

"Yes, it's true." Jake relented, surrendering to himself as much as to the small crowd reveling in his discomfort. "We are going to take it slow." Jake regained some composure. "Dere'dala needs to come to terms with being, uhh . . ."

"Married?" Elisabeth offered.

"Hitched?" he threw in.

"Joined for life?" Jeff suggested.

Kyle turned and winked at Jeff. "I like that one; it has *such* a ring of finality to it."

"We say handfasted." Dere'dala rescued Jake. "He wishes me to be certain. Jake has warned me that he can be . . . difficult. Is that the right word?"

"Yes." Elisabeth's mother, who had helped raise Jake, spoke up. "That one works as well as several others I could think of."

When the laughter died down, Jake took a deep breath and looked like he was doing a "one Mississippi, two Mississippi" slow count in his head.

"You are certain," Mat'isa announced to her sister-in-law. "It has been decided. This warrior sounds like he is as difficult as you. It is a good match."

"Speaking of matches." Arsolis spoke loudly enough that Kyle started at the man's voice behind him. "Do you forget me and my people? If it were not for me, you would not have found Rai'nor and his tribe. I've just now heard it said, 'Jakas' will marry into Rai'nor's family. My own daughter is yet to be joined with one of you."

"*Now* it's a party," Jake announced, thankful for the interruption.

Kyle had to rub the smile off his face. Lupe Vasquez stood at the edge of the crowd, looking like a deer in the headlights as nearly everyone turned to look at him. He was frozen with one of his sister's famous breakfast burritos almost to his mouth. Tama, Arsolis's daughter, stood next to him, visibly pregnant, and hanging off his arm. Tama had been fairly thrown at Lupe by her father after Arsolis had rejected Jake as a suitable candidate. The "joining" had irrefutably occurred months ago under Arsolis's own roof, and if Lupe didn't marry the girl soon, there was going to be a baby at the wedding.

"Next week," Lupe announced. "We will be getting handfasted next week, in Dumfries."

He turned round to look at Arsolis, who seemed to be pleased with the answer. "We will be the first to marry into the Eden clan?"

Kyle didn't think it would help to point out that there had already been hundreds, if not thousands of Jema/Edenite handfastings. "Sounds like you will," he answered.

"Very well." Arsolis relented with a satisfied jerk of his head as he moved off without another word.

Kyle turned to Jake. "He still calls you Jack Ass?"

"All that?! That's what you remembered?"

"Why does the Hatwa call you by a different name?" Dere'dala asked.

"It was just a misunderstanding," Jake explained. "But he's not going to stop, not after Lupe explained to him what a jackass is."

"So did I," Jeff admitted.

"Yeah, me too." Carlos smiled.

"Could someone tell me?" Dere'dala asked in the rough Creight version of Chandrian as she looked from face to face.

"I'm sure they will." Jake shook his head as he grabbed Dere'dala's hand and led her off. "Come with me; I have some *real* friends around here somewhere."

Kyle couldn't help but be happy for Jake. He was seeing a new facet in his friend and brother-in-law that he wouldn't have believed if he wasn't witnessing it himself. The man appeared absolutely besotted with his . . . his what? Jake had struggled to label it himself the night before: "Kind of like an engagement, I think. But she's free to dump my ass whenever she wants. No harm, no foul."

"That's familiar territory for you," Carlos had pointed out. "No problemo"

"Yeah," Jake had agreed. "But I don't *want* her to. *That's* what I'm trying to get my head around."

Aside from giving Jake a hard time at every opportunity, they could all understand where he was coming from. Besides being a knockout, Dere'dala seemed more than willing to call Jake out on his unending bullshit. Jake seemed to understand on a fundamental level that it was something he needed.

He was left standing there with Jeff and Carlos. Elisabeth had moved Mat'isa off, along with his daughter's two grandmothers. He knew his wife was "working" Mat'isa as much as Audy was working Rai'nor across the lawn.

"So, till tomorrow?" Carlos asked, yawning. His two friends were solidly on Caledonian time. Kyle's own body didn't know where it was; he was just tired.

"At least," he answered, "Audy and Elisabeth have a dog-and-pony tour planned for the Creight. As soon as they're done, we'll get Rai'nor and a couple of his bannermen and head back for the live fire show-and-tell."

"Where we headed?" Jeff asked.

"Portugal," he answered. "Audy and Jomra have a site in mind we can portal to without being swarmed on arrival. There's a Kaerin base relatively close. We'll hit it and run. Rinse and repeat somewhere else and keep them guessing until we are ready on Caledonia."

*

Ozark Mountains, Eden

Danny Carlisle garnered enough energy to look over at Josh. His younger brother was a hot mess. Josh was bent over, head bowed between his knees, spitting the tail end of whatever he'd just spray-painted the ground with. Josh swayed as if drunk. It seemed fair, Danny thought. He was pretty certain his own heart had exploded an hour or so ago. They'd been running nearly nonstop. When they hadn't been running, they'd been walking fast, crawling up steep inclines on all fours or wading across frigid streams.

"You gonna"—he sucked in another deep breath—"go tits up on me?"

A single hand lifted off of Josh's knee and flashed him a middle finger. "Hate . . . you."

"Yeah . . . I get that," he mumbled. He was hating himself and his big mouth at the moment. He'd known Stant'ala was tough and some sort of Kaerin killing hero for the Jema, but at several points during the last day and a half, he'd found himself wondering if the man was human. He risked a look around the tree trunk he was hiding behind to see if the Jema looked like he was settling in for an actual rest—a real one, one that involved not moving. And it *was* risky; he knew if the Jema thought the look was in any way a signal or sign that he was good to go . . . that would be a bad thing. He'd considered shooting Josh in the foot, accidently of course. His brother would probably thank him.

Stant'ala was kneeling just a few feet away, watching Josh. The man's head came around towards him. "We will rest here; drink all you can."

Danny mustered the strength to nod back in response. "OK, I mean . . . if you're sure you want to."

Stant'ala grinned back at him and stood up with an ease that laughed at him. "The Kaerin's stride is faltering; he will be forced to stop as well. We will eat and sleep, rest for tomorrow."

"What happens tomorrow?"

"I think we are five, maybe six hours behind. If it does not rain and wash his tracks away, we will cut that in half. *Tomorrow* will be hard."

Danny glanced up at the sky as the sun was beginning to set. There wasn't a cloud in sight. *Shit* . . .

*

Hanlas had run the day before until his vision began to narrow and his exhaustion caused him to grip nearby trees to keep from falling. He was confident that his effort had purchased significant distance between himself and anyone who could have followed him from their last campsite two days ago. He knew how much ground an airboat on Chandra could cover in the same time and had no expectation that he could outrun the Shareki version. That wasn't his goal; outrunning what the Shareki thought a warrior could do on foot was.

He awoke before dawn, hungry and sore. He'd eaten the last fresh meat he had with him the day before and would have to take the time to hunt today. He had a small supply of nuts and grains with him, and he looked around the clearing he was in as he slowly chewed. His body relished any activity that did not involve running.

He gazed south; the clearing he was in perched along the edge of a rocky drop-off some sixty spans above yet another rock-strewn stream. This whole area was an endless sea of forested low mountains laced with streams running between them. Hanlas used the Shareki eyeglasses that Gurl'ansa had gifted him to look at the stream below, and then started tracking his sight picture up the far bank and into the forested hills beyond. In the distance, a rock outcropping halfway up the largest hill seemed to poke out and above the surrounding hills.

It would suffice. He dropped the eyeglasses to his chest and picked up his chosen waypoint with his eyes. At a reasonable pace, that would give him time to hunt; he could make the rock outcropping in half a day. It would be a good location from which to watch behind him for pursuit.

With the eyeglasses, his current location should be easily visible from the outcropping. He'd run down the edge of the drop-off, working his way towards the stream for some time the day before. If he had pursuers on his trail, they would do the same, and he'd be able to spot them. He would know.

EDF Training Base, Olympic Peninsula, Eden

The last twenty-four hours had been a whirlwind for Jeremy Ocheltree. The e-mail from his father on Chandra, giving his consent for him to sign on with the EDF, had beat the official induction notice by a whole hour. His application had been submitted for six months. The system had just been waiting for his birthday; or as evidence now proved, his parent's permission.

His friends were already on Chandra, and he hadn't had anyone to see him off properly besides his mother. She'd personally flown him to the gates of the EDF's training camp on the Olympic Peninsula. His mom, having lost the "over my dead body" argument regarding him signing up before he turned eighteen, hadn't had much to say to him other than to give him a big hug. Standing at the gates of the facility, watching her aircar disappear behind the horizon of treetops, he felt free, truly free for the first time in his life. He could make a difference, contribute to keeping Eden secure, and help free the people of Chandra. He'd never been as certain about anything in his life.

The feeling had lasted a whole hour.

"Pick it up! We go again." The Jema teark, a sergeant by any other quality, twirled his own wooden bouma blade like it was an extension of his arm.

His left arm was numb, except where the teark's dull-edged blade had scored. That part felt as if it were on fire. He retrieved his own practice blade and readied himself.

"What are you doing?!" the Jema yelled at him in Chandrian. "You stand like you are preparing to get hit! Your job is to strike!"

This was stupid. He was going to be a pilot, for God's sake. He feinted once, twice, and slashed upward, aiming for the Jema's chin. The teark's upper body swayed back even as his sword arm slashed downward to block his strike. His own sword arm transmitted the impact up into his shoulder. He was aware for the briefest of moments of having lost the grip on his blade. The teark's blade seemed to rebound from the block and slash to the side with a speed that was blinding. This time, the teark struck his ribs.

His own sword was still clattering to a rest on the tarmac as he dropped to one knee, gasping for breath and trying to see through eyes watering in pain. He managed to look around him at the other four recruits who had been pulled out of his training platoon for this first round. Only one was still on his feet, but his hands were on his knees, and he looked like he was struggling to stay upright.

"Recover!" the Edenite sergeant yelled. He managed to grab his sword before falling back into line wondering where they'd found the

Edenite drill instructor. "Before I continue, is there any recruit who thinks he or she can do better than your four volunteers?"

Volunteer? He hadn't volunteered. Jeremy took a moment to take in the rest of his platoon. No one was stepping forward. He took some pride in the fact he wasn't bleeding; the same couldn't be said of the recruit standing next to him.

"Is there any one of you who can explain to me why we started with this exercise?"

Someone down the line raised their hand.

"It was a rhetorical question, recruit. Put your damned hand down." The sergeant was at least smiling when he said it. "This isn't preschool, and whatever you had to say was wrong." He had yet to provide his name and had only "Sergeant" emblazoned on his name patch, waved his hands to the ground. "Take a knee."

Jeremy hoped the nano booster they'd been given as they received their uniforms worked quick. He was starting to wonder if he had cracked a rib.

The sergeant kept his gaze on them. "Teark Nin? How long have you been training with your bouma blade?"

"Since childhood. I do not remember when it began." It was the Jema teark he'd been paired against.

"And other Chandrian subject nations, do they all train like that?" The sergeant asked, but kept his eyes floating across the recruits.

"It is law," the Jema teark confirmed. "All male subjects, if called upon, must be able to perform the duties of a warrior in their subject host."

"And the Kaerin High Bloods themselves?"

"They train in nothing but war from childhood. With a few exceptions, warrior is their sole profession. Their swords are more than twice as long as a bouma."

"Teark Nin? How close to your target do you need to be in order to employ your blade?"

The Jema flowed forward from where he stood behind the sergeant.

For a split second, it looked like he was going to brain the sergeant with the actual steel blade that had appeared in his hand. He let out an empty shout of air, and the blade sailed past the sergeant, over their heads, to bury itself in the foam arrow target affixed to a pole behind them.

"Not as close as one would think." The sergeant answered his own question, taking a moment to nod at the blade sunk six inches into the foam block before turning back to them. "The point of this demonstration is hopefully working its way into your thick, slow heads by now. You do NOT, I repeat . . . DO NOT want to get into a knife fight with any enemy you will meet on Chandra. We will bring guns to every fight. We will utilize the superior range and firepower of said weapons at every opportunity. Should you ever be faced with an enemy and you are out of ammunition, your one chance of surviving is to run, reload, and reengage. None of you are Jema. You will never be able to stand toe to toe with this enemy with anything other than a gun. If you hesitate to use your weapon, they'll carve out your heart."

"We do not have the numbers for our survivors to learn this lesson as they become veterans. Which is why you will take this knowledge with you to Chandra. It is a lesson that will be reinforced every morning by our Jema training cadre as you learn to service and utilize the weapons *you will* be issued. Does anyone fail to understand this very simple, very critical point? Our entire tactical mindset is to punish the enemy for having brought a knife or an inferior rate of fire to a modern gunfight."

Well, yeah . . . no shit, he was saying to himself as he realized he was nodding silently in agreement. The way the sergeant was staring them down, it seemed the right thing to do.

"Alright." The sergeant waved them all to their feet. "Which brings me to the second characteristic of our operations on Chandra. We don't yet have the air transport capacity there, that we are used to here. That has more to do with our desire not to be spotted flying around than it does with actual capacity. From your perspective, that particular distinction means dick. Point being . . ." The sergeant's face broke out into a sadistic grin. "We need to get you in shape for having to march the length of Caledonia, and quite possibly during that march, still be able to run, reload, and reengage."

The sergeant waved at a pile of packs to the side that Jeremy had assumed contained more of their issued training gear. "They are labeled by name, and weighted per an equitable ratio of your body weight. The trailhead is just to the left of that airbus across the field. You will stay on the trail until you come to the green flagpole. Not the yellow pole, not the white pole, not the silver metallic pole surrounded by green ferns— the green pole. If you happen to come across a black pole, you're either blind or too fucking stupid for the EDF because you'll have passed said green pole. Return on the same trail, after reaching the green pole. If you are not back by dinner this evening at seven p.m., you will be asked to drop until such a time when you can make the route in the allotted time. It's a little after one p.m. You may begin as soon as you're ready. I would not recommend any delay."

Jeremy looked around at the other faces as he slung his pack and cinched the waist strap tight. He didn't recognize any of them from the auxiliary pilot cadre he'd served with during the Strema War. Maybe there *had* been a mistake. He was supposed to be a pilot.

*

Chapter 10

"Doc, you are an evil genius." Kyle grinned at the name; *Door Knocker* painted on the flat hull of the ship.

"Nah, just a proud parent." Jensen waved off the compliment. "She may look like a heavyset badass, but she's got some delicate parts that are very important if you want to get home. Don't hurt her."

Kyle took in the converted river barge, which looked very out of place sitting in the middle of a graveled parking lot behind the Whidbey Island nano-plant. The massive flat deck, forward of the two-story pilot house sitting on the stern, had been refitted to hold three shipping containers. A single Black Hawk helicopter and two up-armored aircars were tied down to the flight deck forward of that with space left over. Two mini-guns, with six Gatling-style barrels locked into an upright position, had been emplaced amidships. He assumed there were two more on the opposite side of the ship.

Kyle noted the roll-on, roll-off ramp at the bow, and then pointed at the eight massive legs he could see attached to the hull. "What are . . ."

"Self-leveling jacks, four to a side," Jensen explained. "Finding flat parking lots where you'll be headed is a nonstarter. The quantum field will basically cut you a level landing area at the point of arrival, taking out whatever was there. But say it's an area of loose dirt or a sand dune: the ground is going to keep shifting after your arrival. The jacks are automated; within twenty seconds of arrival, if needed, you'll be level regardless of terrain, as long you don't land on a steep hill. They won't do anything that can stop a landslide from above. They can be fully retracted for water insertions."

"She's still a boat?"

"You're an ingrate. She's still a ship. We needed that massive space under the deck for the battery pile. But we haven't tested her in a water insertion yet. I have some concerns."

"Like?"

"You're familiar with the air displacement when you translate? That massive clap of displaced air would happen on a water insertion as well—except not just with the air above the surface. Loaded, even with the relatively shallow draft, it still displaces roughly a thousand tons of water."

"OK?"

"Water doesn't compress like air." Jensen clearly expected that was enough of an explanation.

Kyle just looked back, raising his eyebrows in question.

"A wave, Kyle. A good-sized one. We think it would propagate outward from the ship, but . . ."

"But it's a car ferry." Kyle could imagine getting swamped in heavy seas.

Jensen smiled and touched his nose. "It's a barge originally designed as a car carrier, converted into a floating crane and work platform we used while we were building out Seattle's waterfront. Now . . . I like to think of it as an assault carrier, but for land. We still have some modeling to do before we try a water insertion. It might entail extending the sides upward for added protection; it could mean reinforcing the hull to the point where it just isn't doable."

"Got it. For now, though? She's ready to dance?"

"If you mean, is she prepped for translation? Yes." Jensen bounced on his toes once. "But she's a big gal, Kyle. She doesn't dance. That said, she's definitely the turd in the punch bowl at any party you take her to."

"Speaking of which." Kyle pointed at the two dots he could see approaching in the distance. Two Osprey aircraft were inbound, carrying his assault team and Rai'nor.

*

Iberian Coast, Chandra

Kyle ignored the expected wave of nausea, and focused on the large bang that accompanied their translation. He really, really hoped it was the usual thunderclap heard through the thin walls of the shipping container and not something having to do with the *Door Knocker* itself.

A green light came on inside the container, and Carlos opened the door to a dark night a mile inland from the Atlantic, adjacent to what he thought of as the coast of Portugal. The first thing he noticed was the light mist of rain falling as he walked around the front of the container and looked up at the pilothouse. August Reverte, the Spanish engineer from Jensen's staff, was acting as the *Door Knocker's* captain. Darkened as the ship was, there was still enough light coming from the instrumentation in the pilothouse that he could see August flashing him a thumbs-up. So far, so good.

Kyle turned back to look into the container at Rai'nor and the two lieutenants he'd brought with him. Rai'nor had a hand over his mouth, Mala'nor was yawning, trying to pop his ears, and Garjen something-something was furiously scratching at his arms and chest. Jake was standing next to him, grinning. "The spiders? I've heard that's bad one; it'll pass."

"Every time, like this?" Garjen was almost frantic, slapping at his own limbs.

"Yep," Jake answered. "If it helps, it's just in your head."

Audy came up behind him, wearing an NOD headset strapped to his helmet and down over his eyes. "We appear to be alone."

"You know where we are?"

"Yes." Audy gripped him by the elbow and turned him around.

"That glow is from Lucit, the small town that supports the Kaerin base of the same name at the river's mouth."

He knew it was the Tagus River Audy referred to. The Kaerin name for the river was nearly unpronounceable. On Earth, the town would have been close to Cascais, and there was even a small settlement of Jema in that same location on Eden. Not very long ago, this area had been the Jema's assigned home. Chandra's version of where "Lisbon" should have been, ten miles further upriver, was open farmland.

He clicked the mic on his collar. "Lupe, get a drone up." He looked forward at the helicopter. Jiro Heyashi, their pilot, was already climbing in. They had no idea what they were getting into, and he wanted a pilot he trusted implicitly. Jiro had flown for the Japanese SDF before joining the program and was as experienced as any pilot they had.

"Hyrika's people know protecting Rai'nor and his people are the priority?"

Audy nodded. "They will keep him safe. We will follow in the aircar?"

Kyle looked at his friend and nodded. "I know you want in on this, but it's more important Rai'nor understands what he's seeing. No one can do that better than you."

"So long as you do not think playing diplomat is going to become a habit with me."

Kyle felt himself grunt in appreciation. "I know you better than that."

"Good. Tonight, I will be a very protective guide."

Kyle circled up his team, Jake, Jeff, Carlos, Lupe, and six Jema under the command of a mountainous teark named Care'pol. "OK, we've gone over this. Stick to the plan unless we can't. Jake, Jeff—we'll start the party, but not until I get an all-safe signal from you. You'll control your own party favors."

*

"How will you hurt them from up here?"

Audy was glad to hear Rai'nor's eyes were open behind his helmet-mounted goggles. During the first couple of flights in and around New Seattle, the man's eyes had been squeezed shut, and he'd been keening like a child in a fever dream.

Audy pointed out the front window of the aircar to the helicopter half a mile ahead of them, out over the river itself. Without the Black Hawk's infrared navigation lights and their goggles, they wouldn't have been able to see it at all.

"They will drop off two swimmers. They will jump from the helicopter and swim to where the Kaerin ships are anchored in the harbor."

"Swim? At night? This river is almost the ocean!"

Audy grunted to himself. Jema, by rule, weren't very good swimmers. He doubted if the Creight were any better. The thought of what Jake and Jeff were going to do would have seemed impossible to him not very long ago. He decided against mentioning the small detail that they'd be underwater for the last portion of their swim. Rai'nor was already in disbelief.

"They are very good swimmers," Audy explained. "Then we will follow the helicopter back to land. We will land somewhere safe and make our way closer to the fort on foot."

"Then you will attack them?"

"Yes," Audy answered.

"It is going down." Rai'nor pointed out the window.

Audy grunted in agreement and followed the helicopter. He wanted Rai'nor to see as much as he could.

"They jumped!" Rai'nor shouted. Audy could see the glow of the IR chem lights fall from the helicopter to the dark surface of the water below.

"Swimmers out." Jiro's voice came over the radio. "Lead the way, Audy; I'll follow you."

"Affirmative," Audy answered back. "Climbing and turning towards ocean, I will approach landing from the west."

Rai'nor was involved with a frenzied conversation with his two under-chieftains and spun back to him. "You are talking to the others? The helo . . . cawp."

"Helicopter," Audy explained. "This is an aircar." He slapped the wheel. "Helicopters have the spinning wing, and yes, I am talking to them. They use a device called a radio."

"And it would work for us, as well?"

Audy reached down and plugged his radio jack into the dashboard. "Kyle—Audy here, say something to our friends."

"Rai'nor, this is Kyle. How are you enjoying the flight?"

"I can hear him! It is Kyle."

Audy unclipped his radio and handed it to Rai'nor. "Press and hold this down when you speak to him. Let up when you are done speaking."

Rai'nor turned and faced the back seat, in the direction of the helicopter that was now following them. "I CAN HEAR YOU, KYLE!" he yelled at the top of his lungs, in the direction of the helo. "CAN YOU HEAR ME?"

Audy's ears took the brunt of the aural assault that nearly lifted him out of his seat. The laughter coming back from the helo was muted in comparison.

"I can hear you, Rai'nor; there is no need to yell."

"It is magic," Rai'nor exclaimed.

Audy took the radio back and plugged into the jack on his helmet. "Perhaps," he said in English, "next time, we do the radio demonstration on land."

"Copy that." Kyle's voice came back amid more laughter he could hear in the background. He was glad they were enjoying his pain. "Be advised, we are half a kamark behind and above you."

Audy glanced past Rai'nor and out the passenger-side window. The scattered lights of Lucit Base and the dimmer glow of numerous lanterns of the surrounding town were flashing in and out of sight behind the low clouds.

"Understood, turning north towards land, now. Descending."

"Copy." Jiro's clipped voice came back at once. "Turning north, descending."

Audy sat them down in the wide expanse of scrub brush that covered the headlands on the north shore of the Tagus River's mouth. He knew from experience, the constant wind and salt-heavy air from the ocean made growing anything here close to impossible. Nothing had changed since he'd last been here. The soft rain seemed to have stilled the worst of the wind.

He ran away from the aircar, tossed three infrared glow sticks as far as he could in three different directions, and walked back to the car where his passengers were unloading. "Landing zone marked," he announced to the helo above him. He could hear the incoming helo beating at the air above him, and he hoped the low-lying clouds and rain would dampen the sound of its blades before reaching the city.

The first indicator the helo was close overhead was when he saw Rai'nor point back behind him. A second later, the rotor wash cocooned them all in a storm of blowing sand and salt grass. He reached Rai'nor, who stood next to the aircar with his mouth open in shock. Audy turned back to look and was likewise amazed at the helicopter as seen through the NODs. It looked like a dragon out of the old fables, its rotor's IR lights creating a circle of fire over the top of the craft. Kyle and his team were on the ground and moving towards them even as the engines of the helicopter began winding down.

"Lead away, Audy." Kyle slapped him on the shoulder. "Nothing on IR all the way to the city except for some rabbits."

Audy nodded and looked back at Rai'nor. "We will run now; if you need to stop, say so."

"We are ready," Rai'nor acknowledged.

Both parties fell in behind him as he set off towards the lights of the Kaerin base, sitting at the western edge of Lucit's small harbor. It would take time for Jake and Jeff to approach their targets in the water and yet more time to get to safety. Audy realized a half mile into his run that he should not have been worried. Neither the Creight chieftain nor his men looked to be challenged in the least by his pace.

Twenty minutes later, he pulled up from the gentle incline they had been running up. He stopped the group with an upraised arm and reached out to stop Rai'nor. He motioned everyone down and went prone as he crawled to the lip of the hill. Below them was the walled city of Lucit. Jema had lived there not long ago, and he found himself wondering who the Kaerin had moved into the town. The fort itself was nestled into the adjacent southwest corner formed by the stone walls.

A barren, washed out boulder-strewn ravine lay between their perch and the base of the walls. There was no masking the pungent stench coming up from the small creek bed that doubled as the city's sewer outlet to the river. Two guards, close to their respective towers at either end of the facing wall, were slowly making their way towards one another.

He watched in silence as Carlos readied his sniper rifle, and Lupe laid his own rifle aside to implant his spotting scope's tripod in the mud. Rai'nor was up on his elbows, watching them.

"Top of the wall is four hundred thirty yards, straight away," Lupe intoned. "Wind is at your back, seven, gusting to twelve miles an hour."

"What is that?" Rai'nor asked.

"A device that tells him what the wind is doing, and how far away the target is." Audy answered.

"They can shoot so far?"

"Easily." Audy pointed at the sniper team. "They both can. Most of the things you will see tonight can be explained by their tools, what they call their technology. They are all very skilled warriors." He paused and pointed at Carlos. "But what that man can do with a rifle is truly magical."

Kyle was listening to Audy's show-and-tell; but most of his attention was taken up by the fort's wall across the ravine from him. Without a close examination, he couldn't tell through his night vision how thick the base of the wall was, or whether the stone was solid or just framework around loose fill. He'd half expected the same timber construction Audy and Jake had described from the experience on Gotland. It didn't matter; he had no intention of trying to take the fort. They just wanted to leave a calling card that no one was going to miss.

He looked behind him where Teark Care'pol and five Jema soldiers were all on one knee, breathing heavily. The Jema were all carrying heavy packs, loaded down with 81mm mortar shells.

"Teark, set it up. Aim for the center of the fort." Kyle turned back around to Lupe.

"Lupe! Range to that flagpole flying in the middle of the fort?"

"Nine hundred sixty-five yards," Lupe answered after a moment. "Nine six five yards."

"Nine six five yards," Care'pol repeated back. In the dark, the Jema teark looked a lot like Han's Van Slyke. He'd carried the baseplate and tube for the mortar himself. He watched as the Jema mounted the mortar tube to the base and began prepping the shells themselves, while Audy explained what was happening to Rai'nor and his lieutenants. He could hear the well-deserved pride in Audy's voice as he pointed out that the Jema had been new to these weapons a very short time ago.

Watching the mortar team, Kyle thought they moved as fast, and given the destructive power of the growing stack of shells next to them, as safely as any he'd ever seen in the US Army. The Jema approached military training with an almost religious focus, and it showed in everything they did.

He wasn't going to give the order to fire until he knew his two SEALs were out of the target box. The harbor they'd been aiming for cut directly into the fort itself, and the last thing his friends needed was a "friendly" mortar shell dropping in on them.

"Why do you wait?" This time, it was one of Rai'nor's chieftains, Mela'nor, who spoke up, pointing at the distant wall, "If they see you, they will send warriors."

Kyle listened for a moment as Audy began explaining the "swimmer's" role in the attack, and how vulnerable they were. He was two steps ahead, thinking of the next assault. Given what the *Door Knocker* could carry, and the number of troops it could transport, he had all sorts of options. He caught himself grinning; in another week, thanks to Jensen's satellite - he'd have photo-reconnaissance in advance of a target.

It was almost an hour later before Jake radioed in. Kyle hadn't started worrying, but the thought had begun to creep up on him.

"Kyle—Swim Team. We are feet dry, at downstream edge of fort. Small river inlet."

Kyle smiled into the radio. "Copy all. We are on the top of the hill, five hundred yards north of your position. Will mark with IR beacon. Be advised that stream is the city's sewer."

"I'd say 'no shit!'" Jake fired back. "But that would be a lie. Copy all; will move to you after we send."

"Copy." He was grinning as he spoke.

Carlos and Lupe were laughing quietly while Audy explained the communication.

"You good, Carlos?"

Carlos remained quiet, relying on Lupe to flash him a thumbs-up. "Ready."

He turned back to Care'pol. "One round now, let's see where we are."

The loud "ThwUMP!" of the mortar shell rocketing out of its tube couldn't be suppressed. By the time the enemy realized where it was coming from, they'd have other things to keep their attention. He knew what to look for and was able to follow the hot exhaust from the shell until it was swallowed by the low-hanging clouds.

"Did you miss?" Rai'nor asked Audy after a few moments. "You said there would be an explosion."

"There will . . ."

The mortar landed a hundred yards deeper into the fort than they'd been aiming, but as far as mortars were concerned, they were on target. The wet, soft earth on which the mortar's base was set would give them more than enough scatter effect for the following rounds. The explosion flashed a bloom of light that was hidden from them, but the pulse of light lit up the inside of the fort's walls.

"You're on target, fire away."

The second round left the tube just as Carlos' rifle fired. Kyle had seen where the sniper's gun had been pointed and watched the Kaerin warrior's body fall from sight a moment later. Carlos had fired again before the second mortar hit. By then, there was already another shell on its way.

He counted six impacts, knowing another was already in flight when he turned back to the mortar team. "Switch to antipersonnel." He didn't feel good about the order, but knew it was the right thing to do. The enemy had been blown out of their bunks and were probably stumbling around in shock or running for the walls or the harbor to see where the attack was coming from.

The first of the AP shells had left the tube when the harbor exploded with a fireball that turned the night hanging over the Lucit riverfront into day. The sound and shock waves rushed over them a second later as the fireball lit up half the expanse of the wide mouth of the Tagus. His SEALs must have found a powder store to rig; nothing they'd been carrying could have done that. A moment later, a second explosion lifted a gout of water right through the middle of a large paddle wheeler tied to the quay.

Everything in the small harbor looked to be burning. There was more than enough light to see the two halves of the steamship settle separately. The mortar team kept up their fire into the fort until Care'pol shouted they were out of AP rounds. "Three HE, two incendiary rounds remaining."

"Fire it all," he ordered, registering the fact that he could hear the light rain flashing to steam as it fell on the nickel-ceramic mortar tube. By the time the last round had fallen into the fort, the light from the interior fires was probably enough that they could be seen if anybody lived long enough to stand on the nearby wall and look for them. Carlos and Lupe both had been firing as soon as figures appeared on the wall, backlit by the conflagration below.

"Jake, where are you?"

"Two hundred yards behind you. We have your beacon in sight."

He turned around to see an IR illuminator hanging in the distance. "Hang tight; we are coming to you."

"Copy."

"All right, let's go, people."

He was watching as Audy got the Creight moving. He had to physically turn Rai'nor away from the burning fort. "Come," Audy was saying. "We do not wish to be seen."

"Why would they fight you? Your weapons fall from the sky."

"For the same reason they hunt your people. They are Kaerin," Audy explained. "They know nothing else."

Chapter 11

Ozark Mountains, Eden

"We will rest here." Stant'ala, the evil bastard, announced with a puff a breath as he flowed smoothly from a steady jog to a quick walk, before pulling up to run in place for a moment. The deer trail they'd been following broke out onto a wide bench of stone, overlooking a ravine with a stream flowing at the bottom of it. After running in the shade all morning, the warmth coming off the sun-soaked stone was too much for Danny. The minute he stopped, his hands went to his knees and he felt his whole body sway on its own accord as he struggled to keep his feet.

The sound of Josh collapsing behind him brought his head around. Josh's chest was still heaving up and down, and his brother was incoherently whispering something between ragged attempts to pull oxygen into his lungs. If his brother had the strength to bitch, he'd live. Danny struggled to stand up straight against a diaphragm that wasn't having any part of it. He'd fought a stitch in his side all morning and lost horribly. Right now, his gut was announcing it was done. . . finito. . . no mas. Stant'ala, whom he had imagined having liked pulling the wings off of butterfly's as a youth, had moved to the edge of the drop-off and looked like he was enjoying a post card moment.

"Sure thing. . .if you . . . need to . . . rest." Danny struggled to catch enough breath to speak. "Sounds . . . good." The act of standing upright was too much; a wave of nausea doubled him over. He threw up what little he had in his stomach. The cramping in his gut was painful enough that he stretched out on the warm stone, face down. Of all the stupid shit his mouth had gotten him into over the years, this was the most painful.

He could sense Stant'ala was standing over him. When he forced his eyes open, he could see the man's feet inches from his head. "I'm good. . . catching. . . my second wind."

"I can see that." He figured Stant was grinning that knowing, 'Fuck You' smile. He'd never heard the man curse, but with that grin – words weren't really needed. The Jema had been grinning a lot for the last day and a half.

"I must go on alone."

Danny already knew that. The man wasn't human; and they were slowing him down. He'd known it yesterday afternoon, again last night, and this morning before dawn, when Stant'ala had woken them and spoken the words he'd come to fear: "It is time." It hurt to admit, but the Jema scout had literally run them into the ground. Danny managed to lever up onto his elbows and twist his head to where he could see the Jema.

"Catch the bastard."

"I will." Stant'ala nodded. "The Kaerin chose this place for his trail. He is tired of running and may be watching us, even now."

The fact that the Kaerin bastard to blame for his blood-soaked feet, and the embarrassing fact that he was lying in his own vomit, was watching, gave him a surge of energy that he didn't think he had. "Where?"

"Out there somewhere." Stant'ala pointed out to the hills that rose from the far side of the ravine. "We've made up more distance on him. You and your brother should rest here, and report in. Follow when you can. From here, I must move fast and quiet. The Kaerin is as tired as you are and hungry. You have done well."

"We'll catch up," Josh said from somewhere behind him. Danny wanted to agree with his brother. He also wanted to toss him over the cliff, but he didn't think he could move just now. Besides, it wasn't Josh's fault they were here.

"Go get him."

An hour later, maybe two, Danny wasn't certain because lifting his arm to look at his watch would have taken energy he didn't think he had. He *was* certain the sun had moved and was closer to being directly overhead.

"You awake?"

"Am now," Josh answered, unseen.

"How you doing? I mean really."

"My boots are filled with blood," Josh answered. "It squishes between my toes when I move."

"Mine been doing that since yesterday," he answered. "Your legs doing that weird twitchy quivering thing?"

"They were; I think they've stopped. I'm trying to ignore everything from the neck down."

"Does that work?"

"Not really."

Danny was quiet for a long time. He managed to roll over onto his back. The sun felt good on his face as he took in the blue sky. He thought if he closed his eyes, he'd sleep for a week. He couldn't do it. His mind's eye kept imagining Stant'ala climbing the hills to the south of them, alone.

"Josh?" He looked over at his brother, who had managed to sit up with his legs out in front of him. Josh was already looking at him.

"Yeah . . . I know."

They both were wincing in pain as they levered themselves upright. Josh managed to do a slow deep knee bend and make it back up even more slowly. "I suppose we'll loosen up once we get moving."

"Sounds right," Danny agreed as he watched with envy. There was no freaking way he was going to try doing that. "Let's get some food in us, and radio in. There's water below us."

*

Gurl'ansa had been surprised to again see some green on the Shareki device's map button that morning. It had been just a sliver of color, but it had been there. Two nights without any color, and then it had been back. He no longer wondered if the device was somehow talking to something or someone. Within an hour of switching on the device, there were Shareki airboats in the air around them. The noisy ones with the whirling blades atop had been buzzing around the peak of the next hill over, and one of the smaller carriage-sized ones, which were much quieter, had flown directly over them, just as he and Manoma had found cover.

Let them come, he thought. The only issue that weighed here was that the Shareki continued to pursue him and Manoma, and not Hanlas. The map book carried by Hanlas could direct the next Kaerin attack. With luck, that hammer could fall against something other than a minor city. That was IF this world even held large cities. He was of half a mind that the strange Shareki might not be numerous enough to have real cities. All they'd seen were widely separated farms or small villages, from which the Shareki warriors seemed able to travel from with far too much speed for his liking.

Darnas' Moijan's strike force had been stopped at the river by a Shareki force that seemed to have been transported there by a gate. The only explanation he could think of was that this empty world was somehow in communication with its parent world, from whence the Shareki had come. His observations of that arrival and his assessment of their apparent skill were with Hanlas. It would be up to the Kaerin Council and Lord Noka himself to decide what to make of the information.

A low whistle brought his head and rifle around. Manoma was approaching, hunched over and taking care to move quietly. That told him everything he needed to know. Manoma had spotted the enemy, and they were close.

"It is as you thought." Manoma dropped behind the fallen tree next to him and handed him back their remaining set of far-seeing glasses. "There are Shareki on our trail; I saw two. They wear uniforms like the ones of those that stopped Moijan and our warriors." Gurl'ansa could see the decision in Manoma's eyes, the same one he had already made.

"I'm tired of running."

Manoma nodded once in agreement. "As am I. I saw the large airboat again . . . it hung in the air, as it dropped four warriors ahead of us in the saddle formed between these two hills."

"Dropped?"

"I saw them slide down ropes from the airboat to the ground as it hung in the air. It looked well practiced."

That was new information and did not make him feel any better about their chances of survival. He had assumed the enemy's flying craft needed a landing strip to operate from, just as their own did. What had been airboats looking for them, was suddenly something able to drop warriors on top of them.

"It no doubt was. These are warriors that hunt us. There is no shame in what we must do."

Manoma grinned back at him, and looked up at the sky between the treetops. "I would have liked it to end at home. With my sword buried in something."

"Which sword?" Gurl'ansa questioned with a smile.

"Either one, now that you mention it." They shared a much-needed laugh.

"We will separate," he ordered. "You have what you need?"

Manoma clapped his belt pouch and nodded. "I do."

His own pouch held two vials of heartfire. One vial of the Gemendi-produced battle augment would let a warrior forget any injury and fight with the strength of two men for a short period of time. Both vials would do the same, until it stopped their hearts. Gemendi gifts always came with a price.

Gurl'ansa held out his arm. "For Hanlas."

Manoma gripped him back. "For the Kaerin."

Ed Tapply had joined the Eden militia during the Strema invasion for what he had thought was the duration of the war, win or lose. He'd discovered something about himself during the struggle; he liked being a soldier. For a recent college graduate with a business degree from the University of Maryland, that had been surprising enough. His father's involvement with the program had come as a surprise to him as well, and a welcome one. There hadn't been any jobs available after graduation, and he'd jumped at the chance to join his family on Eden. The Strema invasion had put a damper on that enthusiasm, but he'd found what he thought of as a calling during the fighting.

He'd surprised everyone who knew him when he signed on with the EDF, especially his dad, who had figured his son would try to build a business on their new world. He couldn't wait to get to Chandra and discover a third planet Earth for himself, but his unit was one of the few that had remained on Eden, assigned to Fort Appalachia. His squad had been flitting from one mountaintop to the next for the last three days in pursuit of Kaerin warriors. Captain Souza and his team had been tracking the Kaerin on foot and were somewhere on this mountain above them. So were the Kaerin, which was why his short squad had deployed to the ground beneath them.

As the most junior member of his team, he was walking point, though climbing would have been more accurate. A storm, some years ago, had clearly taken down all the large trees in the area they were walking through. They were having to climb over, under, and around a scattered matchstick pile of logs that seemed to have no end. New growth, thick and verdant, blocked what clear space he could see between the jumbled pile of rotting logs.

"Tapply, hold up. You see a way around this shit?" Sergeant Cain's voice in his ear brought him to a stop. He had been atop the pile of fallen logs a moment ago and had gotten a good look at what they were facing.

"Another hundred yards or so before it looks to clear," he reported, turning out of reflex to look back in the direction he'd just come from, towards Sergeant Cain, who was somewhere behind him. "From there, it's just normal forest. Looks steeper though."

"Of course it does." Cain almost sounded like he was laughing. "OK, keep your head on a swivel; we're following."

"Copy that."

Tapply turned back around in time to see a flash of shining metal that impacted his neck. For a split second, he was aware of looking almost straight up at a patch of blue sky.

Gurl'ansa caught the body and eased it to the ground. The Shareki warrior had been speaking to someone he couldn't see. The ability was well known to him; the Gemendi had briefed them on this, but it had been a strange thing to witness. The Shareki's rifle looked to be an exact replica for his own captured weapon. He pulled the ingenious boxes of ammunition from the Shareki's battle harness and placed them in his pouch hanging off his own hip, before crawling away underneath a log and moving away. He only had one of the ingenious ammunition boxes with him, brought from Chandra and already inserted into his rifle. He'd witnessed how fast these weapons could fire, but they needed ammunition just as his old rifle did.

He'd moved no more than thirty spans through the child's puzzle of fallen logs when the enemy discovered the warrior he had taken. He heard the explosion of voices before their teark or bastelta seemed to regain control of his warriors and the forest went quiet. He belly crawled a few feet to the side and came up slowly against a fallen log. A curved sheet of bark sloughed off as he brushed against it. He cringed at the noise as it flopped to the ground and waited for a sign it had been heard.

He rose up further and looked back the way he had come, through the tangle of wood. A movement of green amid the gaps allowed by the weather-bleached logs grabbed his attention. His "window" wasn't big enough to determine whether the patch of uniform held a limb or a torso, but he took it as the target it was.

He slowly brought his Shareki weapon up and laid it atop the log. The Gemendi had "wasted" a box of Shareki ammunition, showing them how the weapons functioned, and he had dry fired it a thousand times in preparation for this. He chose the single bullet setting and fired. He was certain he had hit what he had been aiming at.

The warriors returning fire did not seem to be concerned with conserving ammunition nor with actually seeing a target to shoot at. Some bullets struck around him, spitting up chunks of freshly colored yellow wood on impact, but most seemed not to be aimed in his direction. He was already moving at the sound of the first shot, taking advantage of the noise to move further away. He had surprised them, yes. But these Shareki did not seem particularly skilled. He was moving as quickly as he could when a new sound, "THWUMP," caught his attention. It sounded somewhat like a fowling gun, but deeper and somehow heavier.

Gurl'ansa had not lived this long out of an abundance of curiosity and he threw himself to the ground. "THWUMP" the strange gun sounded again just as an explosion showered him in wood chips and branches. Somehow, they were *shooting* hand bombs at him. The noise from the explosion faded, and he moved again, choosing wherever he could to stay low and go under, rather than over, the next log. Sounds of breaking branches let him know that his pursuers did not have the same concerns. He couldn't fault their courage. With their weapons, he would be attacking as well.

His path blocked by a wall of trees, he angled back downhill, having to step over a log and maneuver around a large root pile that looked to have been yanked from the ground. Two Shareki warriors, their backs to him, were spinning around as he thumbed his rifle to the hummingbird setting. He moved as he fired, holding the trigger down.

One Shareki went down with a cry of pain at being hit, but Gurl'ansa attention was focused on where he was running.

He almost made it to cover when his right leg was hit in the thigh, and it collapsed underneath him. He lunged with one leg and half fell behind a log as he was hit again, grazed across the forearm. It felt like a red-hot fire poker had been laid against his skin as he rolled back up against the log. He didn't have to look at his leg to know the bone was broken and he was done running. The pain was blinding. He fumbled at his belt pouch and came up with the two thick clay vials the size of his thumb. The thick wax seals popped off easily, and he drank both of them before he could change his mind.

Nothing happened beyond a desire to retch the foul elixir back up. He was about to curse all Gemendi when the warmth in his stomach bloomed outward in an explosion of warm sunshine. The pain was forgotten as his entire body seemed to float for the shortest of moments until everything fell back in on itself to become very clear and distinct. He sucked in a deep breath of air, his lungs struggling to feed his racing heart.

Training took over, and he moved further down the log before popping up on his knees to look; one of the Shareki was on his stomach, pulling at the arm of the other. He had hit them both. He fired again, two bullets marching up the back of the one who had been moving. The bolt on his rifle locked back; his ammunition box was empty. He hit the release and let the empty box fall out. He grabbed one of the replacements that he had taken off his first kill as he pushed himself higher against the log with his good leg. The light in his eyes pulsed with his heartbeat as his tingling hands struggled with inserting the ammunition box.

The wounded Shareki saw him now and was less than ten spans away, on his back and fumbling with something at his belt. Gurl'ansa wanted to finish all of them before the heartfire took him. He pushed himself upright on his one good leg and looked down at the ammunition box. His drugged mind recognized the issue immediately.

The bullets inside the slim spring-fed box were bigger and longer than the ones his gun used. The ammunition box would not fit in his rifle.

"They are new." The Shareki lying on the ground spoke slowly, in passable Chandrian, and gave a short laugh. Whether it was the information imparted or the fact the Shareki was laughing at him, his own anger added fuel to the final fire burning through his chest.

He dropped the rifle and drew his long sword even as he hopped towards his enemy, dragging a shattered, forgotten leg behind him. The Shareki pulled a handgun from his waist and started firing. The first two impacts felt like someone had punched him lightly in the chest, and he managed to laugh himself, as he took another hop. The third shot he didn't feel at all.

Sergeant Cain looked down at the .45 caliber 1911 smoking in his hand and then at the Kaerin warrior dead at his feet. What the hell?! If his last shot hadn't hit the Kaerin in the head, he'd be skewered by now. These assholes weren't human.

"Ground Actual—Recon One, copy?"

"Copy, Recon One. Go."

*

Chapter 12

Tom Souza had his team moving downhill towards the QRF team at the first sound of gunfire. He'd brought them to a stop once Cain had reported in. There was still one Kaerin out there somewhere, and Cain had been certain his team had only engaged one. A single Kaerin had managed to take out the entire team, killing two and incapacitating the other half. The QRF helo had moved back in to retrieve Cain and his other wounded man, and was only now spinning up to fly them out. Retrieving the bodies of the fallen from the jumbled timber would have to wait. He watched through his field glasses from a position several hundred feet above the saddle where Cain had been hit, trying to determine where he'd be if he was trying to escape.

If he was smart, the Kaerin would have used his partner's engagement as cover to break contact and move away. It would have made sense given what they'd done over the last few days. The enemy had seemed focused on just moving as fast as possible and avoiding contact. Something had changed, though; they'd stopped running and turned to fight.

"QRF Helo—Ground Actual, if your wounded allow, give me a FLIR pass on your way out. Between your position and mine. We are just a few degrees off your nose, to your left, about a mile away, three hundred feet above you on the hillside."

"Copy Actual, wait one."

It was less than a minute before the helicopter crew came back to him as the Black Hawk was lifting off. "Ground Actual—Helo; patients are stable. Fuel status will allow us one pass, over."

"Copy, thank you." He'd take what he could get.

The Black Hawk climbed straight up and seemed to hover for a moment at an altitude almost equal to his own, even as it hung several hundred feet above the windblown saddle of ground between his hill and the next. He knew it would take a moment before the temperature-sensitive sensors in the bird's nose reset against the ground's ambient temperature. The FLIR camera worked a lot better at night; right now, every rock on this hillside, exposed to the bright sun, would be radiating as much heat back to the sensors as a human body.

He had his team spread out in a rough line with Dom on his left and farthest downhill. Grant Ballard was to his immediate right, uphill from his own position, with Hans anchoring the high end of the line. They'd all taken a knee and a breather as they watched the helo slowly beat its way towards them. Guns were up, and everybody had their heads on a swivel. He was as thankful for the breather as he knew his team was.

Early on, it was always the uphill tracks that people bitched about. On the move, at a near-constant pace over several days, it was the downhill portions of their chase that had become dangerous. Brittany had been giving him a hard time over the few pounds he had put on in the six months they'd been on Eden. That extra weight was now well and gone; he couldn't begin to imagine the calories he'd burned over the last four days. He'd had to retighten his belt the day before.

"Actual—QRF Helo."

"Go Helo."

"Hillside looks clean. We have your team, five signatures in a line."

Tom's heart nearly stopped. "Confirm count Helo, five heat signatures."

"Copy—and confirmed, five personnel. We are bingo fuel and returning to base."

"Copy all." He glanced off his left shoulder. He could see the back of Dom's head aligned with his rifle, slowly panning back and forth.

There couldn't be anyone to the left of Dom, not unless they could fly. The hillside dropped off sharply ten feet past Dom.

He switched to his tactical channel. "No one move; no one react. Tango is close and in line with us. Hans, I'm guessing past your position, somewhere above you."

Somebody, he hoped it was Hans, squelched back a single time.

"Dom, stay put, reorient slowly. I want you to cover uphill past Hans' position."

Hans was already focused uphill by the time Tom had sent his warning. During the flyover, he'd thought he'd heard something, but the noise from the Black Hawk had washed over it. He'd gone prone at the edge of a tree trunk and was scanning the ground above him.

It was a bare patch of skin, thirty yards away, that caught his eye: a forearm glowing white alongside the dark outline of what looked like a rifle. The Kaerin was standing behind a tree, and from the angle, appeared to be focused downhill from his own position. There was no way to be certain. The warrior's face and body weren't visible; he had just the forearm and half a rifle as proof there was somebody there.

"Target acquired," he whispered. "Standing behind a tree, thirty yards uphill of me, behind our line. I have no shot."

"Everyone hold." Hans's respect for Tom Souza went up another notch. The guy was a leader; he'd already known that. But right now, Souza's calm had likely already saved a life, probably his own. "Dom, find him."

Hans continued to watch the Kaerin through his scope, his own finger welded to his trigger. If the enemy so much as moved, he was going to throw enough lead downrange to throw off any shot the Kaerin thought he had. So far, the visible arm and rifle hadn't so much as twitched.

"Hans, do you have cover?"

He ever so slowly moved his left hand off his rifle and sent back a single pulse for an affirmative.

"I want you to light him up on my 'go.' Grant, you hit the ground when he fires. Dom—be ready to tag him. Shoot to kill."

Hans sighted in on the patch of forearm he could see. It wasn't an easy shot, even at this close range. He had to believe, hit or miss, the Kaerin would get spotted by Dom.

"Go."

Hans fired a single shot and thought he hit the Kaerin's rifle, given the way it jerked back. His thumb hit the fire selector, and he let loose two bursts against the tree. He was about to fire again when a deeper boom from Dom's sniper rifle punctuated the rolling echoes of his own shots.

"Target down." Dom's voice sounded like a shout in his ear after all the whispering.

They all stood over the Kaerin's body, which had taken Dom's single shot to the chest. The Kaerin warrior didn't look any different to Tom than the men next to him. They never did at this stage.

"What's this in his hand?" Grant pried open the warrior's hand that was clutching a small ceramic vial.

"Collect it, all of it," Tom ordered. "Our aircar is waiting on a fuel drop, and then we'll go join Stant'ala's chase."

"Any word from them, sir?" Grant asked.

"Nothing since last night."

*

Hanlas watched his three pursuers work their way down the same ridgeline he had taken earlier. He couldn't fault their tracking abilities, but as his enemy broke out onto the rock escarpment above the stream, they had stopped, and he had gotten his first good look at them.

There was a Jema leading them. There could be no mistake. The idea of the Shareki enemy that so threatened his people being led by a Jema was beyond strange. The two Shareki warriors looked played out. He would have smiled at the weakness of the one he watched empty his stomach on the rocks, but he had done the same himself, twice, the previous day. The Jema, though, appeared to be no worse for wear. He knew that could not be the case. These last days would have been trying for anything on two legs.

The Jema warrior walked to the edge of the cliff and looked out at the hills beyond, the same hills where he now sat watching back through the Shareki field glasses. The Jema took in the ravine below him and then slowly lifted his head in his direction. A momentary chill passed through him as he imagined the Jema was looking directly at him, but he knew that to be impossible.

He was grateful for the short rest his pursuers took. His legs needed to do the same after climbing for the last three hours. He kept an eye out for others until the Jema moved off down the ridge alone, leaving the other two where they were, stretched out on the rocks. He knew what he had to do. As much as it hurt to admit, the Jema was the threat here, not the Shareki. There was not the smallest part of him that could imagine running from a Jema. He had three hours, perhaps less, before the Jema reached this spot.

*

Stant'ala ignored the burning in his legs. He had thought his thigh was fully healed from where a Kaerin had planted a knife in it nearly half a year ago. The last few days had disabused him of that notion. The Edenite doctor had told him there would always be scar tissue under the skin that might give him trouble. It hadn't seemed credible to him at the time. Scars were something worn for all to see. The tearing of something under the skin was very believable at the moment, and he imagined he could hear the damaged muscle rubbing against something with every step as he continued to plow uphill.

The Kaerin's trail couldn't be missed through the carpet of leaves and needles from the thick forest around him. His quarry wasn't taking the time to worry about his trail. He had been able to follow it without issue and even observed where the Kaerin had gutted a forest veet during his climb. The small pile of guts had just begun turning sticky. His trail was less than an hour cold.

He stayed on one knee, breathing deeply. He removed one of the miraculous energy bars from his pouch and nearly inhaled it. He had refilled the water bag on his back at the creek and took a long drink from the flexible hose stretching from it. He could afford to take a moment. He was closing in on his prey; he could feel it. There was nothing on this world or any other that would stop him.

He heard the snap of a rifle before he realized he had been hit. He was falling by the time the pain in his leg reached his brain. He could hear feet beating through the ground cover as he fought through the pain and rolled over, trying to get his rifle out from under him. He gave up and went for the knife at his hip as the footsteps behind him slowed. A boot slammed down on his forearm, pinning his knife hand to the ground as a knee crashed onto his spine.

"Jema scum!" He heard the Kaerin's long sword whisper out of its sheath. His failure hurt far more than the hole in his thigh as he waited for whatever came next. The point of the Kaerin's long sword paused for just a moment before it plunged through his upper knife arm, pinning him to the ground. The Kaerin gripped his tail of hair and wrenched his head back until he was forced to see his enemy.

"No honor for you under my sword, Jema. I've heard how the Shareki care for their fallen. If you live, I think this chase ends. You will know your defeat."

"Best kill me now," he tried. "We know where you are going. I'll be there waiting for you."

"The Shareki will need to train a new dog. Your running days are over." A knife appeared in the Kaerin's hand for just a moment. He felt the Kaerin's weight on his back shift before a sharp pain dragged deep across the back of his calf, just above the top of his boot. He felt the muscle in his lower leg constrict in an explosion of pain as the muscle rolled up into a ball behind his knee. He started to scream, but something hammered into the back of his head that put an end to everything.

Hanlas stood, wanting to scream in frustration at the necessity of having to leave the Jema filth alive. He retrieved his long sword, flipped the man over, and grabbed at what looked like some device hanging from the man's vest. After the Shareki map device, he wasn't taking any chances, and he smashed the thing against a tree until it came apart. He had watched as the Jema had eaten and was delighted to see a bag full of whatever it was in the strange shiny wrappers. He took the food and the ingenious water pouch and slung it over his back before adding the Jema's vest with his extra ammo pouches. They felt different, and on inspection he could see they were longer, with a heavier bullet than what his own gun fired. The Jema's rifle, though, looked identical to his own. He ended up leaving his rifle and taking all the Jema's gear before bending over and binding the Jema's wounds with strips he cut from the man's leggings. It wouldn't do to let the dog live only to have him bleed out.

He ate one of the strange Shareki biscuits as he set off again upwards. He had stopped being hungry a day ago and was almost surprised at the wave of energy that rushed through him. He was aiming for the rocks he had seen stretching along the top of the ridgeline. Without the Jema, there was no way they would track him there. He had time.

*

Chapter 13

Kirkton Base, Chandra

Kyle took one last look at the surprisingly high-quality photo that the recon satellite had provided. A week had passed since the attack on the Kaerin fort in what he considered Portugal. Since then, the photo-recon satellite had been providing images of cities and forts across Chandra. The satellite and its rocket booster had been built on Eden and then translated to a position five hundred miles above Chandra. It had arrived with what Jensen referred to as its "system" velocity, the speed with which Eden and Chandra orbited the sun. Its vector upon arrival even included the speed with which the solar system—either one, Eden's or Chandra's—orbited the center of their respective Milky Way galaxies. That was all well and good as a starting point, but none of that velocity was relative to Chandra's own gravity well. For the briefest moment, it hung in space, not moving relative to Chandra itself until the planet's gravity started pulling it in.

It had picked up speed slowly, until the attached truck-sized rocket sled oriented the satellite at an oblique angle to the planet and fired its rockets. Over the next eighteen hours, the rocket fired numerous times until the satellite fell into a "low-Chandra" polar orbit moving at over 17,000 mph. The rocket's angular burns effectively converted the increasing velocity into angular momentum that balanced out the planet's gravity. The process was continued until a stable orbit was achieved.

The planet's own gravity had done much of the work of acceleration that was usually accomplished with the massive rockets required to lift a payload off a planet's surface. Jensen had been justifiably proud in explaining it to him, saying the energy expended on the launch was roughly 1/800th of what it would have taken to launch the satellite from the surface of Chandra. That was IF they had such a launch capability on Chandra; they didn't.

Kyle cared far less about the required Newtonian dance than he did about the quality of the photos, which was far better than he had expected. He'd been shocked to see the scope of the Kaerin installations across the planet. The satellite took nine hours to "cross" the entire planet, and it would be weeks if not months before they had indexed enough of the data to build up a comprehensive map of Chandra and the world the Kaerin had built. For the moment, they just needed landing zones for the *Door Knocker*, and he had the next one in front of him.

"You're sure?" Jake was across the table, looking at the same photo upside down. "It's a hell of a lot bigger than the fort in Portugal."

That was an understatement. They were looking at a very large city on the southern bank of the Gulf of Izmir. On Earth, the Turkish city of Izmir sat at the landward end of the massive gulf. The Kaerin city, to include its adjacent fort and naval base, was situated twenty miles further west. Sitting just offshore from the city were a series of large islands that looked to be under cultivation, with no infrastructure beyond some storage silos and a few barnlike structures.

"It is," Kyle agreed.

"Tell me I don't have to go swimming."

"Not a chance." Kyle dropped a finger on the island nearest the city and fort. "We land here with three howitzers, and fire up the fort and naval base. If they want to get at us, they have to come by water, and we'll put out Javelin teams at water's edge to dissuade them." He looked up at Jake. "We'll be taking a lot more bodies this time, just in case."

147

They didn't know what kind of analysis the Kaerin had done over their previous mortar attack in Portugal, but the 155mm SPGs (self-propelled guns) would introduce a whole new world of hurt to the Kaerin. One that every slave living in the adjoining city would see and feel.

Jake was nodding slowly to himself, his finger coming to rest on the airfield on the mainland. "Don't forget they've got airplanes . . . nothing I'd want to strap my ass to, but those big biplane bomber transport things could make a mess of the *Door Knocker*, and I don't think we'd survive an extended stay if it takes damage. We have room for a jump jet on the deck."

"Not with the SPGs." He'd already checked. "Besides, I want to keep those in our back pocket for a moment. Every time we come in contact with them, I want it to be a shock to their system."

Jake snorted to himself. "And everyone thinks *I'm* the evil bastard."

"That's why the numbers for this trip. Just to be safe, I want to bring one of the Air Defense platoons. Their SAMs should keep us safe."

"One of? We have more than one?"

Kyle smiled to himself and gave Jake a nod. "Point; I was being optimistic. I'm loading the one platoon that's actually practice fired the Stingers. If we get a leaker or a kamikaze, the *Door Knocker* has four mini guns, and its own AA missiles for point defense."

Jake gave him a slow nod that seemed to say 'OK.' "Did Jensen give you any idea how much damage that thing can take, and still get my ass home?"

"You want me to lie? Make you feel good about it?"

"Don't bother; I think I knew before I asked."

"I want to be in and back out in less than an hour. The SPGs will roll off, stay close, and then roll back on. Then we disappear."

"They can't stay on the deck and fire?"

"I already asked." Kyle shook his head. "'Not if you want to get home'. . . Jensen's words."

Jake looked back at him for a long moment. "OK, in and out. We can do this."

Kyle smiled and reached behind him for another photo. "We get back here, swap batteries, rearm the SPGs, and wait for nightfall at the next target sight. Then we go again, right here."

Jake looked at the river that cut through the center of the recon photo. "What river is that?"

"You'd call it the Danube. We're going to hit this fort here, downstream from their capital."

"OK . . .?"

Kyle pulled out the large map they had of Europe and spread it out on the table. "Look, everyplace they know we've been, has been within spitting distance of ocean. To include you and Audy last year. And we've always hit their ships while we were there. We're getting ready to do that again in Turkey. I don't want to get them thinking we are focusing on their naval capability, or that we are somehow limited to littoral operations, especially when . . ."

"When our next real target is a big naval base," Jake finished for him.

"You're smarter than people give you credit for."

"What people?"

Kyle ignored Jake's question. "This second target, call it Bratislava if you want; it's in the same general area. If we start a big-enough fire, they might see the glow in Kaerus itself, which sits in the same place that Vienna does on Earth. That alone would be a win as far as I'm concerned."

"There won't be any doubt left that we are getting around via translation."

"I know, but I want them hyperaware that we can go anywhere, anytime we want. We need a deterrent, maybe now more than before."

Jake knew what he was talking about. They'd lost track of one of the Kaerin they'd been pursuing on Eden. They'd almost lost Stant'ala in the process. They knew where the Kaerin was going, and they had five, maybe six months to find him before the Kaerin gates opened again. If they didn't find the Kaerin and stop him, the next Kaerin attack on Eden would likely translate into the middle of New Seattle or Baltimore.

"You think these assclowns understand the concept of deterrence?" Jake was shaking his head, answering is own question.

"Culturally? Hell no. I mean, how could they? They've been running the planet for a millennium and haven't had a challenger. Any clan steps out of line, and the Kaerin hammer falls. They've never been on the receiving end of that kind of threat."

"Until now." Jake was grinning.

"Until now," Kyle agreed. "I've got to believe whoever is leading them has to have the ability to see what they face. If not, he's going to need to be taught."

Kaerus, Chandra

It was well into the night, and the city of Kaerus was at rest. The city's residents were, for the most part, ignorant of the shadows hanging over all of them. Lord Noka S'kaeda stood at his balcony window, looking out at the lights of his city. The city his family had built and fortified to become the center of Kaerin power on Chandra. Noka looked on darkened windows and envied the occupants for their ability to sleep.

"How many ships could they have?" Gasto called his attention back to the room behind him. His friend was looking back at him, waving the hours old report of the second Shareki attack in the last ten day.

The first attack had occurred in the former Jema lands, and had been limited to the shelling of the Kaerin fort at Lucit. He'd initially considered that the Jema had somehow made it back to their homeland after their foray against Lord Madral's Holding, half a year ago. The most recent attack, the one Gasto had just read the report of, had occurred the night before, eight days after the attack on Lucit. The Kaerin fort and largest naval base at the eastern end of the Middle Sea, outside the city of Pagasta, had been savaged by devastating cannon fire. The one ship that had tried to land a force on the island from which the attack had been launched, had been sunk by some sort of rocket launched from the shore of the island.

Gasto Bre'jana was the singular Kaerin lord that Noka S'kaeda trusted above all others. Their two families had been allies in the power struggles within the High Council for centuries. His friend still didn't quite grasp or understand what had happened.

"And how did those ships sail the length of the Middle Sea without being seen?" Gasto was angry enough that he still wasn't thinking clearly. "From Lucit to Pagasta? The Taram Forts at the Straight could not have have missed the force capable of doing this."

"You are right, of course. I don't believe there were any ships."

Gasto's head came around on him in a flash. "What are you saying?"

He watched the realization play out slowly on his friend's face. The shock on Gasto's round face was replaced by something he would not have credited, if he did not have the same fear eating at him.

"The spring gate closed a ten-day ago." Gasto's characteristic stubbornness was missing in the tone of his voice.

He nodded in agreement. His entire long-term plan for waging this struggle revolved around the twice-annual gate activations that would allow them access to the Shareki world. "*Our* gates closed, Gasto. Theirs clearly have not. Like you, I find it impossible to believe the same force that struck Lucit somehow sailed the length of the Middle Sea, under Taram's guns in the straights, all the way to Pagasta without being seen."

"Then the Shareki's gates must have deposited two separate forces that need to be destroyed. They will not be able to hide forever."

"Your search for the force that attacked Lucit found nothing." He looked down his nose at his friend. "I have hounded you over that fact. I think I owe you an apology." He walked over to his desk, poured them both a cup of wine, and handed one over. "The force that hit Pagasta disappeared as well." He waved at the sheaf of papers on Gasto's knee. "I had it removed from the report, but the island from which they fired their cannon was swarming with our High Bloods and a war fist's worth of Kayseri by this morning." He sat back down across from Gasto and waved a hand in front of his face. "Nothing but footprints and tracks in the dirt. They were gone."

"Could they have airboats that could carry such weapons?"

"At this point, it would not surprise me," he answered with a shake of his head. "But the island was under close observation during the attack; it was easy to see where they were. They did not leave by water; no enemy ships were seen and nothing was seen or heard in the air except our two airboats that were blown from the sky by yet more rockets."

"That wasn't in the report either . . ."

"I don't want our flyers thinking they can be swatted from the sky like insects."

Gasto drained his cup of wine and then gave it a frown. "Do you have anything stronger close by?"

He waved at his desk behind him. "It did not help."

"Could they somehow bring a gate with them?" Gasto asked from behind him. His friend was grasping for the same answers he had earlier in the day, when the long-talker had first delivered the report from Pagasta. "The Universe knows they have some incredible machines."

"An artificial gate?" He half turned around in his chair. He had been worried that the Shareki had somehow accessed existing natural gates on Chandra that remained unknown to them. "One that is constructed, you mean?"

"Talk to Tima," Gasto explained as he came back around to his chair. "He has long thought the gate that sent us here from Kaerus Prime was a device, not a natural gate."

"I have never read that." He pulled his head back in shock. "I consider myself an expert of the old records, many of which only a sitting prelate has access to."

"It is nothing he has read. I challenged him over it," Gasto explained after taking a sip of the grain-spirit. "It's a theory he has long held. I got the impression that among the Gemendi, it is somewhat of an accepted fact. After all, our own Gemendi utilize devices they have constructed to hold our gates open, and to direct them."

That was true enough. It was still a huge leap to think that a gate could be created at will. "I had been thinking they had knowledge that enabled them to find natural gates like the one that exists in the caverns beneath our feet."

"Perhaps they do." Gasto almost laughed as he held up his cup in mock salute. His friend paused before drinking. "No!" Gasto gave his head a shake. "That would presuppose they happened to locate gates that somehow naturally existed, adjacent to or within the range of their cannon, to our forts. Twice!"

"Three times." Noka held up his own glass in salute. "Do not forget that they just seemed to disappear from Ran'dor after destroying Madral's fort there."

"Right." Gasto took a sip. "So, three times, then. The Universe may be laughing at our pain right now, but I refuse to believe it would take us in the ass that deeply. You need to talk to Tima; it has to be something they have constructed."

"I wish I could find fault in your reasoning. If you're correct, Gasto . . . it would change everything."

"How do we play this with the council? And by we"—Gasto tilted his head—"you know I mean you. Pagasta is within Lord Oont'tal's Holding; he will use this."

As would I, if I were other than the prelate and wanted the honor. It was no secret Lord Oont'tal had long coveted his medallion. A small part of him wished he or anyone else was wearing it now. "I've removed that option from him. I intend to issue a writ, putting the Kaerin formally under arms."

In concept, the council would go from a room full of cutthroats vying for power, to Kaerin lords united against a common enemy. As prelate, he would go from first among equals to the military commander of all Kaerin. It was authority a prelate hadn't held in nearly eight hundred years. For good reason; the last prelate had held onto that authority for far too long after Chandra had been subjugated. The other Kaerin Lords had been less than understanding.

Gasto looked back at him for a long moment and then seemed to relent to the facts that were staring them in the face. "In the short term, I think it will help quell the challenges. Long term . . ."

He knew the risks. It was all he'd thought about for the last day. In the end, honor dictated he do the right thing. If the threat was as dire as he believed it to be, did he have a choice? If the Kaerin did not survive this challenge, what difference would it make who was prelate?

"I'm aware of the consequences, old friend."

"You have already told them of the threat. When you describe what we believe this enemy may be able to do, in terms of their gates . . . no one should be able to make the argument that your writ is unwarranted. Though. . . some will play the aggrieved party in that they were not warned earlier."

Gasto held up a hand and stopped his reply. "Convince them that we thought this was the Jema alone who were somehow returning." Gasto laughed to himself. "I admit, I maintained that hope myself, until a few minutes ago. We had no reason to believe it was the Shareki themselves until this latest attack. Correctly speaking, we still don't know for certain that this is not the Jema, using Shareki weapons and Shareki gates."

"Which is even more threatening! How many other subject tribes could be armed with such?"

"Exactly," Gasto agreed. "Use it. It speaks to the true threat, and adds to the foundation of your writ."

"Call in the full council—all the houses. As soon as they can gather."

"Minor as well?"

"All of them, Gasto. I'm done trying to wage this struggle in the dark with just the people I can trust."

Gasto stood up slowly and slammed back his drink. "No time like the present."

He looked up as the door to his suites opened of their own accord before Gasto reached them. There were very few who had the authority to do that, and the reasons for doing so was a very short list.

"Prelate, Lord Bre'jana, my apologies." Bastelta Land'asta bowed his head quickly.

"What has happened?" he asked.

"Report from Meldona, Prelate. They are under attack. Our base is under attack."

*

Chapter 14

Meldona, Chandra (30 miles downriver from Kaerus)

"Come on! Move it!" Kyle watched as Jake leaned into the cab of the SPG, from the top of the stepladder running up the front tire's wheel well. "Straight off! It's a wheat field, for fuck's sake. There's nothing to hit." The Jema behind the wheel took him at his word and gunned the diesel engine of the massive, three-axle wheeled truck. The program had access to the designs of any number of modern weapon systems that had been active or on the drawing board as of 2031 on Earth. With the nano-plants' ability to reproduce just about anything, they'd gone for simplicity in the case of the SPG. None of them had seen the need for an armored, slow-moving tracked vehicle. They'd settled on reproducing the Swedish 6x6 wheeled Archer SPG.

With the gun down in its travel position, the six-wheeled Archer looked like a militarized version of a tractor trailer pulling a flatbed with a large metal shed sitting at the back. The twenty-six-foot barrel was hidden, nestled into its cradle along the spine of the truck; it wouldn't pop up and deploy until the truck had planted its recoil spades into the Kaerin wheat field.

"All clear." Carlos's voice intoned in his ear. They'd launched two drones the second the *Door Knocker* had translated in. "Something that looks like a farmstead, and a dorm area about two miles north of us; a few lights on. Nothing moving between us and the target."

The target, lying eight miles away, appeared from the sat photos to be a good-sized military fort with an adjacent vehicle park and airfield. Audy had taken one look at the photos and commented that whatever Kaerin lord controlled the fort, he was much more powerful than Lord Norj'ala, who "owned" most of the Iberian Peninsula and therefore had exercised dominion over the Jema. Not that they needed more incentive, but if tonight's target belonged to some important Kaerin lord, so much the better.

The attack in Turkey the evening before had been a success, but only because they'd been on an island. The defending forces had responded far more quickly than they would have liked. Two paddle wheelers packed with troops had already been headed to the island by the time the Javelin team had reached the shore and readied their weapons. The first paddle wheeler had exploded with a secondary bloom that had lit up the entire harbor fronting the Kaerin city. The second one had its pilothouse removed by a Javelin and had been allowed to limp back to the shore.

This evening was already moving more smoothly. It had to; there was nothing separating them from the base they were attacking except flat terrain networked with cultivated fields and graveled roads. Each of the Archers carried twenty-one 155 mm rounds, and they'd start rolling back to the *Door Knocker* as soon as those internal magazines were depleted. Time was of the essence. Given the distance from the target, the Kaerin might have more trouble locating them, but there was no natural barrier stopping them from rolling out in force once they did.

"Copy," he answered Carlos, who along with Lupe was controlling the drones. "Get an eyeball on the target; be ready to adjust fire."

"Four minutes flight time," Carlos replied.

He turned and looked up towards Carlos. The drone launchers had been welded to the roof of the pilothouse. Carlos waved at him, and he flashed a thumbs-up in response. They didn't have GPS, and wouldn't until the communication network was up and in place. The initial shots would use old terrain maps produced on Earth, with the Kaerin infrastructure drawn in from the satellite photos. The data links between the Archers themselves was fully active, and the artillery crews housed within what he wanted to call the sleeper unit of a tractor trailer could coordinate and link their fire commands across the three-vehicle battery. He'd been more than impressed with the mixed Jema/Edenite artillery crews the night before. The training they'd been put through on Eden had paid off nicely.

He flipped down an NVD monocle over his right eye and watched as the first Archer dropped its recoil spades into the spring wheat field and backed up a foot, sinking them deep. The barrel housing opened, and the gun barrel lifted into the sky even as the second Archer pulled alongside. It all happened without a single crew member having to leave the fire control unit.

He'd selected the fort's vehicle park as their first target. Unless the Kaerin were a lot different than any other military he'd ever fought, they were going to care a lot more about their gear than their conscript army. Audy had reinforced this; he felt if this lord followed the same patterns as the Jema's former master, the fort likely held two sections, one dedicated to the Kaerin High Bloods and the other to the local subject war host.

They weren't going to discriminate between the two, not yet. Not because they didn't want to; they just didn't have the intel to know which Kaerin lord controlled which territory or which subject tribe or clan lived where. That kind of knowledge was kept from the Jema, and they had little to add beyond who they had fought and where. Subject hosts were often transported great distances by ships or marched to do battle in lands they didn't recognize.

Kyle realized Audy had come to stand behind him and was watching the Archer's deployment like he was. The final Archer was positioning its barrel, and they were still waiting on their eye in the sky.

"Your team ready?"

"Ready and loaded." Audy pointed at the three JLTVs; the Joint

Light Tactical Vehicles were nearly ubiquitous in every military on Earth. They'd evolved out of the Humvee and were heavy enough to be configured with a wide range of armament. Eden was producing the things as fast as they could. They formed, for the time being, the backbone of the ground force they were putting together. Two of these had SAWs mounted in the turret, and one had a quartet of Air Defense missiles hanging off of either side of it roof mounted turret.

The *Door Knocker* had teeth of its own, to include an Air Defense SAM system, the multi-barreled mini guns, and a radar, but Audy's response team could play defense a lot farther away. If the Kaerin came out to play, he wanted that fight to be as far as possible from their ride home.

"Did you hear Carlos?" Kyle asked Audy. "There's a farm two miles away."

"I did," Audy replied. "I wish to drive over and make contact. The Kaerin do not farm, of that I am certain. We may learn something of value."

"Go," he agreed. Local intelligence was the one gaping hole that was proving the hardest to fill. He had some ideas on that score, but was awaiting Colonel Pretty's approval. "Just one vehicle, and be careful, Audy. Please."

"Of course." Audy reached back and stroked the Kaerin long sword's pommel above his right shoulder. "I will be in no danger."

"Target area in sight, continuing to move closer. Ready to direct fire." Carlos's voice broke into their conversation.

He slapped Audy on the shoulder and turned to face the self-propelled guns as Carlos spoke again. "Fire spotting round when ready."

"Gun One, spotting round ready, target grid A," the fire control team in the first truck responded. Kyle, as well as everyone else standing outside on the deck of the barge, covered their ears as the call for fire commands continued. He smiled to himself as he watched Jake hop down off the tractor of the first gun and began walking back to the *Door Knocker*'s ramp with fingers planted in both ears. The noise-canceling ability of their earbuds were good, but as the first round fired, he was thankful he'd covered his ears as well.

"Shot, over."

"Shot, out," Carlos replied. Kyle knew the commands were only pro forma. Carlos, the "forward observer," was standing in the *Door Knocker*'s pilothouse two hundred yards from the SPGs themselves. He could see, hear, and feel the actual shots, but that wouldn't always be the case. Practice made perfect. The fire control computers in the SPGs were using the measured barometric pressure, altitude, ambient temperature, barrel temperature, wind speed, and a handful of other inputs to direct the shot, and once the first gun was on target, the data would be instantly shared with the other two guns. All that technical wizardry did nothing to detract from the thrill of watching a gun that size fire a shell weighing over a hundred pounds.

"I hate cannon cockers!" Jake came running up the ramp towards him with a big smile on his face.

"Tell it to somebody who believes you," Kyle shook his head. There was no better friend to a soldier than artillery, so long as it was friendly. If it wasn't, there was no worse place to be than on the receiving end.

"Was that Audy I saw take off?"

He had time to nod in response. "Splash, over." The command coming from the gun that had fired the spotting shot let them know the round should be impacting in the next few seconds.

"Splash, out," Carlos intoned.

The vehicle park was a big target, sitting between the fort itself and the airstrip. He'd have been surprised if they were off target.

"Good shot, Battery—fire for effect," Carlos ordered a few seconds later.

The two SPGs yet to fire had their targeting information relayed from the first gun. The three guns fired within a split second of one another. Then again, and again as the auto-loaders at the base of the guns took over. It took fewer than three minutes for the Archers to fire the twenty-one rounds they each carried onboard. By the time the guns fell silent, Kyle's face felt like there were ants crawling on it, or he'd just walked through a cobweb. The concussive shocks from the guns literally shook loose skin. Enemy or not, he didn't want to imagine what those at the receiving end were dealing with.

"Two large secondary explosions," Carlos intoned in his ears. "Multiple structures and dozens of vehicles destroyed. Airstrip looks to be operable, a few hangars burning." The destruction wasn't over; there were still rounds falling.

"Carlos, start bringing the drone back. We're just delivering a message this evening."

He turned to Jake. "Audy is trying to make local contact at the farm up the road. He's two minutes away and will be last to load with the other JLTVs. Let's get the guns back onboard."

*

"Wait with the vehicle," Audy ordered.

The EDF soldier who had driven his JLTV looked back at him like he was crazy. "Sir? Are you sure about this?"

"There will be no Kaerin here, Corporal." Audy popped the door and climbed down from the passenger side of the vehicle. He saw several heads at backlit windows pull back as he looked up at the dormitory windows. He had lived in a building much like this, if far more run-down, for much of his life. Two floors' worth of bedrooms above a common eating and storage area.

The nearby cannon fire would have woken them. Whoever these subjects were, they'd be scared. He walked through the door into the common area and noted a fire burning in the hearth. He thought the room empty until he saw a woman through the half wall that separated the seating area from the kitchen. She saw him at the same moment, gave a squeal of surprise, and dropped the pot she'd been holding.

"Woman! I wish to speak to whoever supervises this farm."

The woman froze before coming to terms with the fact there was a

Kaerin High Blood standing before her and offered a bow of her head.

"Now." He tried to take the edge out of his voice, but being anything other than a Kaerin in her eyes would probably just confuse her. "I am in a hurry."

She bowed again without a word and rushed past him down the hall leading to the bedrooms.

A middle-aged man, already dressed in his work overalls, walked slowly into the room and offered a formal bow. His messenger stood a few feet behind the man, kneading her hands together.

"Leave us." Audy pointed a finger at the woman and then the hallway behind her.

The farm supervisor turned his head and said something he could not hear. The woman moved back down the hall, where a door slammed a moment later.

"What is your name and position?"

"I am Har'mot, my Lord. The Krathik of this farm."

"These others here, they are your family?"

"Many of them, yes."

"What clan are you? And what Kaerin lord holds these lands?"

"My Lord?" The man's face lost color, and he started to shake his head in confusion.

"I am not a Kaerin, Har'mot." He smiled and pointed a thumb at the sword hanging over his shoulder. "I took this from a Kaerin I killed. The guns you have heard are our guns; we have attacked the nearby Kaerin fort. The Kaerin will want to erase any witnesses of their defeat here. You and your people are in great danger. What clan are you? Who owns these lands?"

"Lord Noka holds the land. We are Jehavian. We are loyal subjects to . . ."

"Yes, yes, I know." Audy realized he had just rolled his eyes. A habit he had picked up from his friends. "I'm sure you are loyal to the people holding your chains." He stopped what he was about to say. "Lord Noka? The Kaerin prelate?" The prelate of the Hatwa Gemendi,

Cal'as's father, had provided that detail to Jake in Legrasi.

"Lord Noka S'kaeda." The farmer bowed his head at just the mention of the name. He knew he wasn't going to break a lifetime of conditioning this evening. He had to rely on fear.

"Your Kaerin lord will raze this farm and kill everyone on it within a day for the simple fact you heard our guns. You have a choice, Har'mot - you and your people will come with us and live free lives, or you will fall under their blades, after being questioned."

"Who are you?"

"You don't have time for that answer. It's enough for you to know that my people used to live as slaves to the Kaerin as well."

"We can't leave, they would . . ."

"They are going to kill you, Har'mot. Come with us and live. How many are you?"

"Twenty-three hands, four small children not yet working."

"Are any of those children yours?"

"Yes." The man nodded and wrung his own hands together. "Three are my grandchildren."

"If you wish them to live, gather everyone up; we are leaving now. You will not need to bring anything."

"Audy! We don't have time for this." Kyle had listened to Audy's request, wanting to just say no. He could hear the decision that Audy had already made in his friend's voice.

"We have time, if you send the other two JLTVs and the ATV buggies. We can do this in one trip."

"Carlos? Where are they?" Kyle asked. Carlos and Jake were listening in and were probably cursing out Audy as well.

"The last look I had, they were massing but hadn't moved. Drone is out of range now; I don't have a visual. They do have an airplane up; radar shows it to be circling the target area, spiraling out. They're looking for us."

"Shit." Kyle ran forward and signaled and screamed into the radio until the last of the Archers stopped, before it began to roll up the barge's ramp where it would block in the ATVs. "Jake, you and Lupe take the two ATVs and the other two JLTVs. Head to the farm. Grab his refugees. Put them on the roof if you have to; you get one trip."

He watched as Jake ran for one of the ATVs, small four-seater, dune-buggy-looking, battery-powered four-wheeler parked under the wing of the pilothouse. Lupe was pounding down the outer stairs of the pilothouse. "Drive dark, Jake. They've got air up looking for us." Carlos or someone else in the pilothouse killed the floodlights illuminating the *Door Knocker*'s expansive deck as he spoke. He kicked himself mentally; he should have already done that. He was already thinking that he needed Jensen's team to install IR beacons and lights over the *Door Knocker*. Lit up like they had been, they probably looked like a strip mall sitting in a wheat field from a distance.

The wheel tracks left through the wheat field by Audy's JLTV were easy to follow. Jake stayed between the twin furrows that cut through the field until he came up on the end of the corrugates and the edge of the planting. He had to slow to a crawl as he eased the ATV over the small irrigation ditch that formed the border between cultivation and a dirt road beyond. He took a moment to glance behind him to make certain Lupe and the other two JLTVs were following close behind. The JLTVs' tires were big enough that they didn't even slow at the small ditch. Once on the dirt road, he mashed the accelerator pedal, and although disappointed in the anemic whine of the electric motor, the ATV accelerated like a rocket.

He power-slid through a curve in the road and was considering slowing down when figures in the middle of the road appeared out of nowhere. He put the vehicle into a hard slide and watched in slow motion as three soldiers dove to either side to avoid being run over. He slid to a stop and hopped out to check on them.

"Hey! You guys good?"

"Yeah, I think so." He recognized Audy's driver as the man propped up on his knees and answering while brushing the mud from his weapon.

"What the hell are you doing out here?"

"Audy sent us back on foot, to make room."

"How many of these folks are there?"

"About two dozen." Another soldier sat up, the front of his uniform caked in mud.

Jake did some quick math and shook his head, looking at the two JLTVs stacked on the road behind him. The Air Defense rig was bringing up the rear. He pinched the mic on his collar and started waving his arms. "You, driving the JLTV! Yeah, you! The one I'm waving at. Un-ass your team and send them back on foot with these three. Be sure they run. They don't want to be left here. SAM truck, keep your team whole and eyes on the sky for any aircraft."

He could see a single lamp hanging on a pole in the distance, marking the location of the farm. Audy was waiting for them in the farmyard, in front of what looked to him to be a very run-down two-story motel, sans the neon signs or algae-filled swimming pool. The graveled yard was lined with bizarre-looking contraptions that he took as Chandrian farm equipment; the miserable looking people cringing behind Audy probably had to pull them through their fields by hand. The gathered group started backing up as the vehicles all rolled to a stop.

"Stay in your vehicles," he radioed as he climbed out of the ATV. "These folks are scared shitless."

"Audy, what the hell?"

"I called an audible. These people are all dead if they stay."

He was about to say something about them being in the middle of a war when a toddler being held tight by an older sister started wailing. *Fuck* . . .

"Load them up, Audy. Cram them in; put some adults on top of the two JLTVs, not the SAM truck. If they need to fire a missile, it'll cook anybody close."

He listened to Audy explain what needed to happen, and still the crowd didn't move. They were all looking at the strange vehicles and the massive JLTVs looming in front of them. He stepped forward and pulled his handgun. He fired straight up three times as fast as he could pull the trigger.

"Move! We are trying to save you!"

The farmers started to move. He holstered his weapon and clapped Audy on the shoulder. "If you want to scare them, scare them." He hit his radio. "You guys un-ass and get these people loaded. Pack them in. Kids and women on laps—it's going to be tight."

The vehicles made a tight circle within the farmyard and started back the way they'd come. Jake looked over at the elderly woman sitting in the seat next to him and the two children she held on her lap. The woman stared back at him with her mouth hanging open in shock or fright; probably both, he figured.

"You will be safe with us." The vehicle was so heavily loaded, with three people sitting in the back seats and two more men kneeling on the back and hanging onto the roll bar, that the ATV no longer skipped or bounced but plowed through the field with a sluicing sound under its tires.

The woman didn't answer; her face didn't even register she'd heard him. Under further inspection, she wasn't as old as he'd guessed. In the ghost glow of his night vision, he guessed she was probably in her forties, but could have easily passed for sixty.

"Why is your face green?" one of the young girls on the woman's lap asked him.

It took him a moment to realize what the girl meant. The green backlight cast by his monocle lit up half his face.

He managed to smile. "It's so I can see at night."

The old woman *was* listening. She let out a gasp, dropped a hand over the young girl's face, and pulled her head into her bosom.

The *Door Knocker* came into sight, looking like a beached ghost whale in the distance. He could just make out the figures of the runners he'd sent back, outlined in front of its hull, as Carlos's voice broke in over the radio.

"Jake, Audy, hold position. Aircraft approaching, we are going weapons-free on SAMs." He slowed to a stop and cringed at the feeling of the ATV sinking into the wet soil.

"What is happening?" one of the men clinging to the roll bar at the back almost shouted.

"Quiet!" he shouted as he hopped out and looked behind him to make certain the other vehicles had stopped as well. He heard the rumble of the aircraft's engines. The Kaerin aircraft they'd managed to identify so far, came in two basic varieties. One was a small single-wing craft not much larger than a Cessna, that they'd labeled scouts. They weren't certain if the things even carried weapons. It made sense; it wasn't like the Kaerin had a need for fighter planes. The other model was a massive four-engine biplane that seemed fit to serve as a transport or a bomber. The Jema, who were used to seeing F-35s and even the light attack prop jobs Eden was now turning out, dismissed the Kaerin bombers as nothing more than psychological weapons meant to frighten subjects.

What he heard was definitely multi-engined. It was less a drone of props and more a staccato rumble of engines that reminded him of a pack of Harleys on a country highway. Psychological weapon or not, it wouldn't take much to damage the *Door Knocker*'s field emitters and effectively strand them here. He was scanning the sky above him and hadn't seen anything when one of the farmers hopped off the back of the ATV and grabbed him by his sleeve.

"The High Bloods have airboats! We must flee."

He jerked his arm free and rounded on the man just as the dark wheat field exploded into daylight. Jake cringed for just a moment until the telltale SWOOSH of a SAM being fired reached him. He turned in time to catch the infrared surface-to-air-missile lance upward off the stern of the *Door Knocker*. A second SAM left its launch rails a moment later. The glow of its exhaust was lost soon after launch. Four seconds later, fire bloomed in the sky, and they all looked up to see a large biplane snap in half. The two halves were alight with burning fuel as they tumbled and fell a lot more slowly than Jake would have imagined.

A second explosion in the heavens, miles away, popped with brief burst of light as the second SAM exploded after expending its fuel. The two pieces of the Kaerin bomber crashed to the ground several fields over.

Jake turned to the farmer, who was standing there with his mouth hanging open. He gave the man a soft punch on the shoulder. "And we have SAMs. We don't run."

"Scope is clear," Carlos's voice announced in his ear.

Jake looked down at the ATV's wheels, sunk into the mud past the axle.

"You two, off! You're going to have to push us out." He didn't doubt these hayseeds were more familiar with mud than they were with Air Defense.

*

Chapter 15

Meldona Garrison, Chandra

"How many impacts?" Noka's eyes swiveled to the fort's second in command. He and Gasto had arrived at the Meldona garrison with the sunrise, to discover Kareel Gral'ast, the man who had served the S'kaeda family and commanded this garrison for twenty years, had been killed.

"Lord, we have counted over forty here or at the airfield. There are more within the Jehavian garrison. There were some that obviously fell short, and one was seen to land in the river."

It was small comfort to see that these Shareki weapons weren't perfect. Perfection clearly wasn't needed. He stared down into the deep crater formed by one of the enemy shells. The front end of a transport truck lay upside down and burnt black at the bottom of the wide hole. The leg of the driver, burned down to blackened bone, hung out of the open door.

"These were not the worst, my Lord. Towards the end of the bombardment, many of the shells exploded in the air, spraying pieces of themselves in a wide arc. Our warriors were out in the open and mustering as ordered when they began to fall." The garrison's leader shook his head. "They were devastating, my Lord. I faltered, I recalled the order to muster, and I ordered the garrison to take cover until the bombardment was over."

Noka could see that the order had saved countless warriors' lives. The dead were still being collected for identification. It was going to be a difficult process in many cases. He watched as two warriors, shirts wrapped around their faces, carried yet another burnt corpse towards a growing pile in the distance. The acrid chemical smell of the munitions used had mixed with the stench of burning flesh. It was not something he had ever expected to experience, not standing in the middle of one of his own garrisons. These were High Blood warriors who had died. *His* warriors. They had never even seen the enemy that had killed them. The young bastelta, in his mind, had acted appropriately.

"I was told we lost the airboat that spotted the enemy."

"Yes, Lord. The fuel reserves at the airfield were destroyed. We had only one airboat fueled. It was one of our transports with the new long-talker installed. They reported spotting the enemy on what they referred to as a large ship, with a flat deck. We lost all contact with them in the middle of their transmission."

"The enemy was on the river?"

"No, Lord, they were nine kamarks to the north, in a grain field. There is no sign of them now. Just large wheel tracks in the mud. Our airboat, the remains of it, was found nearly two kamarks to the south of that position. I have an arm of warriors combing the area for anything that may be useful."

"A ship? In a field?" Gasto Bre'jana had listened in silence to the conversation and now broke in.

"Lord." The fort's new commander ignored Gasto and spoke directly to him. "I can only relay what the pilot reported."

"I would expect nothing else, Bastelta. Get yourself cleaned up and into a new uniform. You are now Kareel . . ."

"Est'ana, my Lord. Pola Est'ana."

Est'ana was a good name. This warrior had an ancestor of the same name who had been among the original marooned on Chandra. "Kareel Pola Est'ana, you now command this garrison in my name. I want you to write a full report of what occurred. I am particularly interested in what you think could have been done in advance to protect this base, had you known of the threat. I want your honest opinion, Kareel. This was the third garrison in the last ten days to be attacked in such a manner. It cannot be allowed to continue."

"My Lord, who did this?"

"An enemy not of this world, Kareel Est'ana. Keep that to yourself for the time being. There will be a muster in the coming days. The Kaerin are going under arms once again."

The young Kareel straightened his shoulders and slammed a fist against his heart. "Meldona will be ready, my Lord."

He looked over at Gasto as his officer limped away towards where a small group of bastelta and tearks waited on their new commander. "You know our history, Gasto; have we ever had siege cannon that could fire nine kamarks?"

"The biggest guns we ever constructed were used against the Barsatian clan. That was four hundred years ago, mind you. They were said to have ranged out to five kamarks but were so dangerous that they killed as many of us as they did the enemy. If I remember what I read, the barrels tended to burst."

This day was not starting off well.

"There *is* a small blessing in this attack." Gasto was rubbing his nose in thought.

"Enlighten me, please."

"Lord Oont'tal will not be able to claim you withheld notification of the enemy in order to weaken his forces." Gasto waved slowly at the scene of cratered ground interspersed with twisted metal, burned-out buildings, and dead warriors. "Not after this."

"Small blessing, indeed." He acknowledged the logic. In Oont'tal's boots, it was the argument he would have used. "Part of me hopes he challenges my writ openly. We need to be under one banner for this, one way or another."

*

171

Island of Landing, Chandra

Kaerin Gemendi were no different from other men in that they liked to talk. The simple fact they were all on an island, surrounded by subjects who would never leave, meant that they spoke far more freely than they would have otherwise. Whatever had occurred during the Kaerin council session in faraway Kaerus the week before, was now the *only* thing the Kaerin Gemendi seemed to be focused on. Within a few days of that council session, Amona, A'tor, and Breda knew far more about the "enemy" the Kaerin still referred to as Shareki.

Amona knew the Kaerin's 'Shareki' label was not going to change. He had to admit, there was a certain optimism and attitude conveyed in the name "Shareki." That said, the "soon to be conquered" had seemed to be able to strike with impunity against the Kaerin, at least so far.

"What did your Lord Tima have to say?" Breda whispered, almost speaking into his cup.

Amona pulled his head back. "He must have forgotten to hand over his notes from the Kaerin Council meeting to me." He shook his head in disgust at the thought and took a drink of his wine. "I learned nothing from him that he didn't announce to the whole island. He does seem pleased, though, satisfied with this new direction."

Breda opened up both hands to either side of his cup and nodded once. "You see? You did learn something useful."

There was no denying that the research into the ancient Kaerin past was taking a back seat to developing tools and weapons that could be produced and used now. Lord Tima had announced *that* fundamental change before the three of them had even begun to pick up snippets of conversation among the Kaerin Gemendi. The Gemendi rumor mill was now very much aware of the Shareki being active on Chandra. The High Bloods themselves were now apparently "under arms." To their subjects, the three of them included, it was a distinction that held little meaning. When had the Kaerin not been under arms?

A'tor laid a hand on the tabletop between them. "Barrisimo's team has not ceased its work on the Kaerin power systems."

Amona knew this as well. The ancient Kaerin power modules, in Lord Tima's words, "would alter the landscape of battle forever." The Gemendi-led effort to that end was not going to let up because the Kaerin wanted new ships, guns, and airboats. A'tor', as part of Barrisimo's team, had not had his day-to-day work altered. He was one of the very few on the island who could say that.

Amona regarded Breda, who had cause to be in a worse mood than usual. The man's plans for destroying the pavilion and the research facilities were just a dream until they figured out how to charge the ancient power cells. Now that dream had been snatched from the man. "Have they told you yet when you are leaving?"

"They have not bothered to tell us." Breda was staring at the tabletop as he spoke. "My team thinks they will wait until the manufactory we are supporting is ready for us. I am to help design and build the steam plant powering the new style forges." Breda lifted his cup and grinned at them. "After that, I will probably be shoveling fire rock to keep the generators fed." The Jehavian took a stiff drink of the wine. "Glory awaits, eh?"

Amona shook his head. "No shoveling for you, Breda. They will move you and your team to another site as soon as your work is complete. I have seen the expansion plans for the new steel manufactories. They are quite extensive."

"I would rather shovel fire rock."

"It is an opportunity, Breda." A'tor leaned forward. "If you can make contact with other Hijala . . ."

Breda laughed bitterly in his cup. "Maybe I can find another Barrisimo."

"Not all of us have forgotten our oaths." Amona could feel himself getting angry as well.

"I know . . ." Breda held up a hand, clearly working hard to stop himself from saying anything more. "I know. You two will be alone here. It may be far easier to kill the old man, than hope you will be able to use any discovery he makes against the High Bloods. I can do it before I am shipped off to who knows where."

"No," Amona said firmly. "If it needs to be done, we will do it."

"We will," A'tor agreed.

"Junidor, by the way," Amona added. "That is where your team has been assigned. I've seen the orders."

"And where on the prelate's silver-plated ass is that?" Breda fired back.

"I have no idea." Amona shrugged. The Kaerin would kill any subject found in possession of a map, any map; it had been that way for centuries. "Just that it is in the holding of a Lord Atan'tal. It is not a name I recognize."

"I know it." A'tor sat back in his seat and smiled at them as he waited for a server to pass by their table. "Atan'tal's lands border Lord Madral's Holding to the west, from the Pike all the way to the Gray Ocean. Madral and Atan'tal are rivals. Their ancestors fought over the Pike long ago. House Atan'tal won."

"How do you know this?" Amona asked.

"I *was* the prelate of the Hatwa Gemendi," A'tor explained.

"Yes," Breda hissed, "and you bowed and scraped there, just like you do here."

"True enough." A'tor shook his head. "Do you want to hear what I know or not?"

"Apologies." Breda waved a hand over his head. "Of course I do."

"Lord Madral's estate was just outside of my city," A'tor began. "In my duties, I attended a few meetings there and caught glimpses of the maps on the walls. I think Junidor is a port city for Atan'tal. It is on the mainland facing the Gray Channel. There's another city on the north side of the Channel. It's within his holding as well."

Breda regarded both of them. "The north? Sounds fucking cold."

A'tor smiled and lifted his own cup. "At least you'll see some rain again."

Breda turned back to him. "Did the orders you saw, say when we were to leave?"

"Tomorrow afternoon," Amona replied and offered him an encouraging smile. "At least your horizon will change." He was more than a little jealous of Breda's reassignment.

"Thanks, old man." Breda lifted his cup. "I will keep that in mind when they hand me my shovel."

*

Kirkton Base, Chandra

Kyle, Audy, Jeff, and Jake were the last to arrive, having just flown in from the training fields around Dumfries. They hadn't bothered to change or even wash up. They'd be going right back as soon as the meeting was over. The joint Jema/Edenite EDF was getting ready to roll south, and there was far more to do than there was time in the day.

Kyle spotted Elisabeth straight off. She was standing between Hank Pretty and Jomra. He had to smile when she grinned and mouthed the word "Surprise" at him. Doc Jensen, Tom Souza, and Kemi'sfrota rounded out the party that had translated in from Eden for the meeting. Souza's being there was a good sign. He'd been requesting the man's presence here on Chandra for two weeks.

"How go the preparations?" Hank asked as the four of them filled in the far side of the table.

"We are ready to march," Audy responded quickly.

Kyle knew Audy was anxious. He was channeling the enthusiasm of the EDF on Chandra, which reminded Kyle of a pressure cooker about to pop. If they didn't let some steam off soon, they were going to start taking it out on each other.

"We'll be ready," he added in what he hoped Audy would take as agreement.

"We should have left a week ago," Jake interjected.

"Every day of training we get, the better." Jeff added his two cents.

Hank Pretty looked at the four of them and shook his head slowly. "I love it when my officers are in sync." Hank remained standing on the other side of the table, grinning at them. "Sit down.

"We've been waiting on a few bottlenecks that are coming into focus. First, our fledgling Navy. We've got a ship operational on both coasts now, and will have a second finished here at Kirkton Base by the time of the assault on Portsmouth. Second, we wanted to see the results of your hit-and-run strikes. Doctor Jensen has a presentation that we'll get to in a moment. Third, we needed the Creight willing and able to be our coast watchers. I've read your reports; their training in that regard has been going well. But, according to Elisabeth, who has been spending a great deal of time with those on Eden, their willingness has been flagging. Which brings us to number four. Elisabeth?"

Elisabeth gave him a smile and then turned to her stepbrother. "Jake, if you're going to do it, now's the time to marry that girl."

Kyle held back his laughter and leaned closer to Jake. "Take one for the team."

"Hey! I'm ready," Jake crowed. "She seemed good with waiting."

"She was probably being sincere," Elisabeth said. "The more time I spend with her, the more I'm sure of it. That said, Rai'nor? And more specifically Mat'isa? They aren't fans of taking the betrothal on faith. Rai'nor and Arsolis have been spending a lot of time together, especially since Lupe and Tama's wedding. Arsolis is . . . well, he's being Arsolis."

"Which sounds a lot like asshole for a reason." Jake looked around at the table and then at Elisabeth. "Sorry . . ."

"I wouldn't have put it that way," Elisabeth started up again. "But it fits. Mat'isa is operating under the belief that our people will wish to or be required to marry into *all* the subject clans we come across on Chandra. She's picking this up from Arsolis, I think, by way of Rai'nor. Rai'nor listens to her, and they know Jake is one of the highest-ranking eligible bachelors we have . . ." Elisabeth didn't even try to hide her glee. "They want their bite of that particular apple . . . now."

"Now?" Jake asked.

"Why wait?" Jeff dropped his fist onto the tabletop. "Not like it's the first side of beef we've given them."

Jake gave Elisabeth a nod after the laughter died down. "Fine, I'll do it."

"Tomorrow afternoon?" Elisabeth smiled. "She and her family came with me. Their ceremony doesn't involve anything more than you two grabbing hands in front of witnesses."

"You're enjoying this, aren't you?" Jake was squinting at his step sister.

Elisabeth leaned forward across the table towards her brother. "Like you wouldn't believe."

"All right," Hank announced and then looked down at Jake. "Jake. Do you want this? If we have to, we can always bring volunteers from Eden to watch the coasts behind us. Joking aside, no one is asking you to do this against your will."

"No need, sir. I'm good."

Kyle couldn't miss the excitement on Jake's face, even if he did look like he needed to hit something.

"OK," Pretty addressed the room. "That brings us to where I think we are ready, but your lightning strikes last week might have provided an opportunity we need to look at. Dave, you're up."

Doc Jensen thumbed a remote, and the projector in the back of the room clicked on. Kyle mentally groaned. He wanted to comment that yet another world was about to be destroyed by one of the most insidious practices that humankind had ever inflicted upon itself; the PowerPoint presentation. He took a deep breath and glanced at his wife, who was rubbing her hands together, still smiling maliciously across the table at Jake.

"First off," Jensen began. "If you've been reading the recon reports I've been sending, some of this is going to be old news. The Kaerin pulled all their lords into their capital last week, two days after your last strike. As you can see from these photos of the airfields around Kaerus, it looks like every Kaerin with a big transport plane flew into town for a powwow. We picked up some of the radio traffic related to this high-level summoning, or . . . whatever it was, in advance.

"We still haven't broken out the radio code they are using, but we are getting very close. Having an event like this to correlate to the radio traffic we did intercept has helped."

"How do these people manage to have secure codes?" Jeff asked. "I mean, they are basically using ham radios? Shitty ones."

"You just answered your own question," Jensen explained. "Our intercept gear is the same stuff you were using in the military on Earth a few years ago. It's designed to capture digitalized packets of RF or VHF data from modern and semi-modern radios or cell towers—not shortwave signals being relayed from station to station. Worse, the code being used is language-based, not math-based. Until we can feed our computers a better sample from the dictionary they happen to be using, it's a slower process than you would think, but we are making progress."

"The radio book we captured on Gotland did not suffice?" Audy asked.

"It was a logbook," Jensen responded. "It did help, but it wasn't a codebook. We understand from your own former Gemendi that they produce new codebooks every year along with scheduled frequency changes. Which brings up what I think is the most interesting thing we've discovered about their communications—there's more than one code being used. Very different coding, different frequencies and schedules. It could be the Gemendi have some sort of, I don't know, call it an "admin channel"—or there could be factions within the Kaerin leadership."

"That's a leap, David," Elisabeth pointed out.

"It's the long jump," Jake blurted out.

"Possibly," Jensen relented. "But each time we've detected the signal, it's been broadcast from Kaerus or the same two sources we haven't been able to pin down yet—one from what we'd label southern

Italy, the other somewhere to the east. The way shortwave bounces off the ionosphere, the direction of a signal is a lot easier to determine than its point of origination."

"Whatever it is," Hank interjected. "Wherever we go now, whether by foot, boat, or *Door Knocker*, we'll be leaving presents behind. The doc's team has disguised some stay-behind antennas that will relay up to our communications birds once that network is complete and operational. We'll carpet this world with them if we have to, and I'm confident we'll break their codes. We don't have a choice. It's been easygoing so far. We've been operating without them knowing where we are. That is going to change very soon, and I don't have to tell you the numbers we'll be up against. We will need every advantage we can get."

"Amen," Jake pronounced.

"When will our communications satellites be operational?" Kyle hid his own grin and changed the subject. Hank was staring down at Jake, shaking his head in exasperation. Jake could get under Colonel Pretty's skin better than anyone.

Jensen gave a huge smile. "It's working right now. In terms of longitude, west to east between the Canary Islands and the Gulf of Oman, it's working as of this morning. We are ready to turn it over to you. That swath of coverage required over four hundred individual satellites in low earth, polar orbits. Each satellite is on any given station for about twelve minutes before the next bird in line takes over. We've another eleven hundred to orbit and tie in before we'll have global coverage."

"This is the advantage that will weigh more heavily than all others," Jomra announced. "They will ready their forces; they will build additional ships and airboats. They will call the subject clans under their banners. But this"—Jomra pointed at Jensen—"the ability to see what they are doing and to coordinate our forces. It is an advantage they will not be able to imagine, nor match."

"It's also an advantage that we need to be selective in demonstrating," Hank countered.

"Coventry . . ." Kyle threw in.

Hank gave him a nod. "Kyle refers to one of our wars in the past, where our side had broken the codes and was listening to the communication of the enemy. We learned of a large enemy attack on a location called Coventry. Hundreds of enemy bombers were going to attack the site. The leadership at the time did not allow the military to act as if they had early warning of the attack."

"What happened to this place?" Kemi asked.

"It was on this island, on Earth," Hank explained. "The enemy bombed it and remained ignorant of our capability to listen to their communications. They would have changed their codes. We maintained the advantage that we employed to great effect elsewhere at a later date."

"You are not suggesting that we sacrifice our forces?" Jomra asked.

"No." Hank shook his head. "We are so outnumbered that preserving our people will be the top priority, always. I'm only saying that we can't be apparent in our use of this advantage. We need to wait until the advantage of using it is so overwhelming that it's worth the risk."

"I understand." Jomra nodded. "Though I believe this situation will come much sooner than you think. As I have said many times, once they know we are on this island, they will do everything to destroy us here."

Hank smiled back at Jomra. "We're counting on it."

"The Jema will be ready."

"No one doubts that," Hank responded. "Hopefully, we won't be the Kaerin's only concern." He waved at the screen as Jensen advanced the frame to a new photo.

The image was of a military garrison nestled outside a small city. It reminded Kyle instantly of Lucit in size and form, but was clearly a different setting. Both the garrison and the city had been burning heavily when the satellite took the photo.

"This is just outside of what we would label Sevastopol on the Crimean Peninsula." Jensen walked over to the map of the world on the wall and pointed at the peninsula jutting out into the Black Sea, for the sake of Jomra and Kemi. "We don't have any data yet as to which Kaerin lord controls the area or which indigenous people live there. What I can say for certain is that both the Kaerin garrison and the local city looked to have been attacked.

"Given the Kaerin's traditional methods, I think we can rule out the regular warfare between the clans. Jomra tells me the fighting was never held near cities or Kaerin forts. Which makes perfect sense if the goal is to cull subject populations and preserve the infrastructure. This was clearly something different."

"We think the townsfolk might have attacked the fort," Hank broke in.

"And lost," Jensen added. "Badly. You can see one wall of the fort looks to be damaged, and parts of it are burning in the shot. The entire town looks to have been fired; parts of it are leveled. And yes, in case you were wondering, this dark oval patch is a mass grave."

"Isolated incident?" Kyle asked.

Jensen nodded back at him. "As far as we know. Understand; I've got a team of fifty volunteers doing on-the-job training in analyzing these satellite recon shots. The one person I have training them used to be a meteorologist. It's a slow process to get good at." Jensen pointed at the screen. "This is the only location we've noted where something like this occurred. What made it of interest is that it's close enough to your attack in Turkey that we thought word of it might have spread somehow to the local subjects."

"Did this attack occur while the Kaerin lords were meeting in Kaerus?" Audy asked.

"It did," Jensen answered. "Whatever this was, we are sure of the timing."

"It might be important," Jomra said. "Audrin'ochal remembers, as do I, how closely we followed the comings and goings of Lord Norj'ala. His absences were often followed by the Jema marching to battle at his behest. Perhaps the people living in this place saw their lord's absence as an opportunity."

"It's possible," Hank allowed. "We've used intelligence like these photos for a long time. One thing we've learned is that it's dangerous to derive intent behind what we see in a photo. That explanation would make sense, but there are others as well."

"A knowable, unknowable," Jeff added.

"What does that mean?" Audy asked.

"Nothing." Jake laughed and grinned back at Hank. "You'd have to be a professional bureaucrat to even think in those terms."

Hank ignored the comment with a roll of his eyes and then turned to Jomra. He pointed at the screen. "Given this event, on the off-chance it was some sort of organic uprising by the locals, I'd very much like to order the *Door Knocker* there. Send a message that we saw it, and are willing to do what it takes to support whoever attacked the Kaerin garrison."

"The fighting looks to be over." Jake jerked his chin at the screen. "Who exactly are we doing this for?"

Pretty smiled in understanding at Jake's point. "Call it payback if you want; or because there's a chance some of the townsfolk survived, and would be there to watch as we rain artillery on the Kaerin. It would be more than worth it to send that message to the locals and the Kaerin. Don't you agree?"

"OK. When do we leave?" Jake asked.

"You're otherwise engaged, Jake . . . literally. You've got allied liaison duties requiring your personal presence. The point I'm trying to make is we could do this, and it may even make sense to do it." Hank turned to Jomra, who nodded in what Kyle took as understanding.

"But you will not send the land ship there," Jomra concluded. "The Kaerin would know we have the ability to see everything they do, even if they could not imagine you have drones in space."

"As much as I want to send that message," Hank agreed, "now is not the time."

"How many people were in that town?" Elisabeth asked quietly.

Jensen let out a long breath. "It's just an estimate, but we think somewhere between ten and fifteen thousand."

"We are going to see numbers a lot bigger than that before this is over," Hank added. "We can hope the Kaerin themselves attack us, but I don't think we can count on that. Until they break their own chains, and for as long as they march under the Kaerin banners, we'll be fighting the locals as well. I know we all wish that weren't the case."

"There are exceptions to that," Jomra deadpanned.

Hank nodded. "I'm sure we'll see the Strema again."

"The Jema have been fortunate of late," Kemi'sfrota added with a smile. "In battle, and more so in our friends. May our luck hold."

"When do *we* march south?" Audy asked. "It is a long walk to the Jema Channel from here."

"The Jema Channel?" Jake smiled. "I like the sound of that."

"I'm sure we all do," Hank added. "But the name won't mean anything until the Kaerin start calling it that."

"When?" Jomra pressed.

"Three days. We have a wedding to pull off." Hank smiled down at Jake. "And I have another mission for the *Door Knocker* that is ready to launch as soon as Kyle and Tom can get back to Whidbey Island, where's she's parked."

Hank turned to him. "Kyle, I'm giving the *Door Knocker* to Tom and his team. They'll be our QRF when we assault Portsmouth, so get him dialed in."

"Permission to come aboard?" Tom gave him a big smile.

"Most definitely," Kyle responded, and then turned on Doc Jensen. "Speaking of which, we should be turning those things out as fast as we can. It's like having an amphibious assault ship that can operate on land, and you don't have to deal with sailors waiting to get there."

"We're working on it," Jensen replied. "We can't just snap one into existence. The *Door Knocker* started out as a construction barge that we converted. We had one." Jensen held up a finger and wagged it back and forth at him. "The next models will be purpose built and have more capability. The critical word there is 'built.' It's going to take some time."

"Back to the present." Hank rapped his knuckles on the table. "Tom's assault force is loaded and waiting on the *Door Knocker*, along with your artillery at Whidbey Island." He glanced around the room at all of them, taking extra time to look at Audy, Kemi'sfrota, and Elisabeth. "I apologize for spoiling the reunion."

"Hey," Jake blurted out. "I'm getting married for the cause; the least they can do is delay a conjugal visit."

*

Chapter 16

Balearic Islands, Chandra

The foghorn atop the flying bridge of the *Door Knocker* gave two quick blasts. Two minutes from translation; Kyle and Tom Souza stood at the edge of the deck of the barge, watching the rest of their team go through their own final prep. Kyle's stay on Eden was going to last only as long as it had taken to get geared up and onboard the barge. Kyle smiled and nudged Tom with his elbow as he watched Hans Van Slyke stuff his mouth with half a pack of gum in preparation for the translation.

"That isn't going to end well," he said, laughing quietly. The secondary effects that hit most people upon translation were psychosomatic. Hans was doing what he could to counteract the taste of having eaten a bug that he'd come to expect. It wasn't going to work. He'd seen other "bug eaters" try to get ahead of the bitter taste. He felt no need or desire to tell his friend that the wad of gum in his mouth was going to be a mouthful of bug on arrival.

"I'm an ear-popper," Tom explained. "I've been told I'm lucky."

"You are." Kyle nodded. "One of the Creight chieftains thought he had ants crawling all over him. If it had lasted much longer, we probably would have had to dart him. I'd heard some Jema describe that one, but it was the first time I'd seen it."

Tom pointed with his chin at the Carlisle brothers, standing to the side of Hans and Domenik. "You're in for a treat. Danny has a bad case of space spiders."

"Space spiders?"

"Consider the source." Tom laughed. "The two of them think they've worked out a solution. I told them they could try it . . . once."

"Do I want to know?"

"No explanation will be needed."

"I get a headache," Kyle answered. "They don't last long at all, maybe thirty seconds. But they're real enough." He couldn't laugh too hard at Han's attempt with the gum. He'd tried loading up on aspirin and caffeine in advance of a translation, but his brain hadn't been fooled one iota.

The foghorn atop the flying bridge gave its final one-minute warning blast. The setting seemed surreal; he could see the dark blue water of Puget Sound in the distance. Kyle could smell the heavy salt air of the ocean, and their "ship" was standing on its stout "legs" in the middle of a graveled parking lot. This was as close to water as the barge was going to get for now. The term "land yacht" had never been more accurate.

The first leg of their travels on Chandra this evening should be a cakewalk. Tom had shared the satellite photo of their target island with him. The small island of Cabrera lay just south of what would have been Mallorca on Earth. The desert island on Chandra didn't even have so much as a dirt road visible. They were going to pop in, deploy two collection antennas, test the satellite communication link with Kirkton, and pop back to Whidbey on Eden. After a quick change-out of batteries, they'd go to Greece for another fire mission. All of it in the Mediterranean, designed to keep the Kaerin focused well south of their real target in Portsmouth. If all went well, he could be back in Kirkton for a late breakfast.

"What is so funny?" Hans had noticed him watching.

"Nothing." He waved. "You're so damned big, Dom just disappeared behind you for a moment." He looked over at Tom. "A very small part of me wants to warn him."

Tom looked back at him like he had three heads. Kyle smiled to himself; Souza was going to be a good fit with the knuckle draggers.

"How *are* our two cowboys working out?"

"Naturals," Tom answered immediately. "Both of them are going to be solid. If we had an advanced course like Ranger School, I'd send them now before they pick up bad habits. If this was old Earth Army, I'd bet good money they'd both pick up a third stripe . . . repeatedly to be sure."

"I don't doubt that," he answered as he glanced at the two cowboys. Josh was pulling on a boxing glove that had magically appeared out of his pack. "What the hell is he doing?"

"Danny's solution to the space spiders," Tom explained. They both laughed as Danny took a stance opposite Josh that looked like a sumo wrestler getting ready to charge across the ring. Danny slapped his own face once and gave Josh a nod. The younger of the two cocked back his gloved fist and waited as the loud electronic beep started counting off the final five seconds prior to translation. Everyone on deck was watching the two brothers; many were shouting wagers when the world disappeared.

Eden's Pacific Northwest late-afternoon skies were replaced with pitch black as the lights lining the deck of the *Door Knocker* were the first thing his brain latched on to. He was already facing the Carlisles and watched as Josh gave a grunt that he heard over the rolling echo that accompanied their arrival. The haymaker landed with a loud *poompf*. Danny's head snapped to the side hard enough that it spun him around on one foot before he went down, landing on his ass. Everyone was quiet, waiting for the frantic screams and scratching to start.

Danny rubbed at his face for a moment and then looked down at his arms in his lap. A second later, he looked up at his brother with a huge grin.

Josh stepped in closer and pulled his fist back. "No spiders?"

"Holy shit! It worked!" Danny yelled. "No spiders . . . am I genius or what?!"

Kyle was torn between wanting to laugh and trying to come to terms with what he was seeing. The program's doctors had given up trying to find a solution to the psychosomatic symptoms. Evidently, the doctors hadn't considered punching people in the face. A loud gagging sound drew his attention as Hans raced to the railing, bowling through people standing in his way. He'd just made it when he heaved his guts out.

He looked over at Tom, whose look of surprise equaled his own. "I usually hate writing SOPs," Tom managed as he pointed at Danny and Josh. "They might actually have something here."

Kyle agreed, and then caught himself grinning. "There's no hurry, Tom. I think you should probably collect some more data on the . . . on the solution."

Tom started laughing as he moved off, clapping soldiers on the back and giving orders. "Alright, drop the ramps! And deploy the ATVs." Kyle watched Tom direct the straightforward deployment in appreciation. Although this first leg was a simple sensor drop-off on a deserted island, Tom didn't miss anything. He could sit back and watch someone else take responsibility. He listened in on the radar reports coming in from the bridge above and behind him; there was nothing in the air around them, but there was a lot of ship traffic south of them.

He grabbed his own radio and looked up at the flying bridge. Augustine Reverte had enjoyed his trip to Idaho last year so much, the physicist had jumped at the chance to command the *Door Knocker*. He had his own small team of engineers aboard, monitoring the systems that would get them back home. "August, this is Kyle. Are you recording the take from the radar?"

"Affirmative," August radioed back. "We have recorded everything from each trip. We are tracking eleven contacts. All but one look to be on a course to or from the port that would be Algiers on Earth."

"We call it Algiers here too," he reminded the scientist.

"The closest one is nearly forty miles away. We are on a hill; the radar has an excellent line of sight. Should I have pushed that contact to you? Our SOP currently calls for alerting of surface contacts within twelve miles."

He smiled to himself. He'd rattled the scientist, and he almost felt bad. "Not at all, your team is doing a great job. I was just wondering about the radar logs. Have you made contact with Kirkton yet?" The *Door Knocker* had its own sat-phone capability, and he wanted that tested before he placed a call with the handset clipped to his belt.

"Establishing contact now, do you want the call relayed to you?"

"Negative, just let me know if it works."

"Affirmative. Drone perimeter established; we are all alone."

Kyle could no longer hear the electric whine of the ATVs' motors as they raced across the island. The only sound was the thumping of boots behind him on the thick steel deck of the barge.

"Two-way comms established with Kirkton Base, sir."

"Give them our regards, August." He lifted the sat-phone off his belt and dialed the number that Jensen had preloaded for him.

The call was picked up immediately. "You called!" Elisabeth sounded genuinely excited.

"Hi, babe. Guess where I am?"

"Jake told me you were going to Ibiza. How's the nightlife?"

"Quiet as a mouse. Sorry about running off as soon as you got here. We should be back by lunch at the latest."

"I know the drill, Kyle. You warned me."

"I can't wait to see you and Sophie. How is she?"

"Hungry! As always. That's why I was awake. I suppose I could be really cliché and ask you to swing by the store on your way home and grab some formula."

"Given that the nearest store to me is on a different planet, but very much on my way home, not very cliché at all."

"Good point." Elisabeth laughed. "In that case, I know it will get you here later, but your mom pulled together a care package for me and Sophie. It's in my apartment."

He couldn't help but laugh. "It shouldn't be a problem. I'll see you in a few hours—go get some sleep."

"I will . . . Kyle?"

"Yeah?"

"I know how tired you are. I could see it in your eyes during that meeting. This *will* end."

"I know it will," he managed. As usual, Elisabeth saw straight through him. "There's just a long way to go."

"Remember what you told Jomra a couple of months ago. 'We just need to start the fire, let the Chandrians win their own freedom.'"

"I know," he answered out of reflex. The problem was, the wood they had to work with was wet—soaked through and worm-rotted.

"Come home and get some sleep."

"Sleep? I haven't seen you in three weeks. You should be resting up."

"Well . . . some sleep anyway." Elisabeth laughed. "Your daughter would probably like to see you as well."

He could hear Tom shouting behind him and getting closer. "I should go. I love you."

"Love you, too."

Twenty minutes later, the ATVs were both back onboard, and the ramp was coming up when the real excitement started.

Kyle was standing next to Tom within the circle encompassing Danny and Josh. Behind them, the rest of the assault force, the Archer gun crews, and even a few of *Door Knocker*'s permanent technical team had gathered on the deck between the back of SPGs and the bridge structure.

Josh clapped his brother on the shoulder. "Just trust me, will ya? We're going to make bank!"

Josh raised his arms over his head. "Bidding starts at two bottle chits back at Kirkton. Who wants to punch my brother? Do I hear two chits?"

Tom put two fingers between his lips and delivered a sharp whistle that stopped the clamoring. "I don't care who hits him. You've got thirty seconds to decide and then we're leaving."

Kyle leaned down and smiled at Danny, who was a little put off at the level of excitement punching him had engendered.

"Two chits," a Jema shouted.

"I'll pay three!" Domenik almost pushed Josh to the side and reached for the glove. The look on Dom's face was one of pure excitement.

"You are going to slap me!" Han's hand clapped down on Dom's shoulder and pulled him back into the crowd.

"I have three chits!" someone else shouted from near the back, just before several shouts of "four" were heard. Kyle winked at Tom and unholstered his sidearm. He fired one shot into the air, stilling the commotion.

"Commander's prerogative," he yelled. "I'm doing this for the science. I'll even throw in a bottle of Earth single malt."

"Done!" Josh yelled and handed him the boxing glove.

The crowd dispersed a little, giving him some room as Danny looked around in panic. "Uhhh . . . sir? Isn't there a rule against officers hitting enlisted?"

"Eden Defense Protocol one dash four, para two," Kyle announced as he pulled on the heavy boxing glove. "Due to extenuating circumstances in the pursuit of knowledge related to the effects of portal travel." He looked over at Tom for support. "Do I have that regulation correct, Captain?"

"Actually, I think it's paragraph three." Tom nodded without missing a beat. "You are well within your rights."

"You heard him!" Josh clapped his brother on the shoulder. "Paragraph three, cowboy up!"

Kyle hoped the smile on his face looked as malicious as it felt as the electronic beep started the final countdown.

"Just for the pursuit of science? Right, sir?"

He winked back at Danny in response. "If it makes you feel better, yeah."

An instant and a different universe later, the *Door Knocker* arrived back on Eden. Kyle stepped into the punch and drove the boxing glove into Danny Carlisle's face. Danny had braced himself and was ready for the blow, and to his credit didn't flinch. Even through the glove, it felt like he'd punched a very solid stone wall. The "wall" in this case did go down, but Kyle had felt the impact all the way up his arm and into his shoulder.

The gathered crew of the *Door Knocker* gave a shout of applause when Danny, still sitting on his ass and shaking his head, looked up slowly and wiped away the trace of blood leaking out of his nose, with a big smile. He raised a thumb over his head. "No spiders!"

"I'll be damned." Tom was shaking his head in amazement. "I suppose I will need to write this up now."

"Leave that to me." Kyle laughed and threw the boxing glove back at Josh. He led Tom a few feet away by the elbow. "That was one hard head," he whispered. "Hard enough that this is my first translation without the ghost headache."

"Huh . . ." Tom smiled. "Maybe it doesn't take as much . . . what? Pain or stimulus as we thought."

Kyle smiled to himself. "We might want some more data just to be sure."

"Absolutely," Tom agreed. "It seems to be good for morale too."

Tom stepped forward. "All right, listen up," he shouted. "Everybody back onboard in three hours. We'll leave as soon as the batteries are switched out. This next one is a fire mission. Figure out who's going to punch Danny well in advance. No screwing around for this next hop. We'll be landing within sight of a large city and a Kaerin garrison. Every one of you will have your heads on tight, or you'll be back at Fort Appalachia whittling on your favorite piece of wood. For now, I want team leads on me."

Kyle noted Tom's men immediately sobered up. The former SF captain had done a great job with his unit. The SPG crews were the same ones he'd already worked with, and this time they'd land with GPS target coordinates preprogrammed into their fire-control computers. He'd go along for the ride and stay out of the way.

He was about to head for the bridge and a cup of coffee when he spotted Dom and Hans making for the rolling gantry that a forklift was pushing up alongside the *Door Knocker*. Without floating alongside a dock or dropping the ramp, there was no quick way to get off the barge. The gantry had a set of internal stairs that led to the ground. He walked over to his two old friends.

"Hans, did Dom slapping you prevent your 'bug mouth'?"

"It did." Hans rubbed the reddened side of his face. "No nasty bug taste. . . I'm not sure if it was worth it."

"Was to me." Dom laughed.

"Try it again on this next hop; I don't think you have to do it very hard." He told them about his lack of a headache, just from having delivered a punch.

Hans looked disappointed. "A couple of the Jema were going to combine their chits with ours. We were going to make certain I was the next to punch him."

Kyle grinned and shook his head at his giant friend. "No need to mess with what's working. I'm certainly not going to tell him. Just don't knock him out; we'll be landing hot."

Hans's laughter sounded like a braying mule. "Understood."

*

Olympic Peninsula, Eden—Kirkton Base, Chandra

The morning had started like any other for Jeremy and the rest of his training platoon, which had lost three people in the first ten days. There'd been one torqued knee from a bad fall during the first run. They all learned the old adage that moving downhill, under a load and exhausted, was harder than going uphill. Dyal Barigai, one of his platoon mates, had been pulled from training three days ago because of his IT networking skills, and sent directly to Kirkton Base.

The last recruit they had lost was a "noob" recruit. The "noob" label had been slowly working its way out of the lexicon, as the most recent arrivals from Earth had now been on Eden for almost two years. Alan Biggs had worn the label like a chip on his shoulder and dropped out on his own. The twenty-six-year-old had been either too good, too smart, or too much of an asshole to "put up" with the training.

Jeremy didn't get that. Once he'd come to terms with the fact that the sergeants and Jema tearks were only interested in keeping them alive, the being yelled at and the daily "Jema stick" beatdown sessions were easier to put up with.

He'd been excused from the morning run and told to report to the training sergeant in the admin building. He was fairly certain he wasn't in trouble. The month-long training course was almost half over, and he'd been doing well. Well enough that he was wondering if he should just stick with the infantry. In the meantime, he was on a mission to learn the sergeant's name, beyond "Sergeant."

"Ocheltree, you never mentioned that you were part of the pilot auxiliary during the Strema fight." He'd been looking for the right office when the all-too-familiar voice stopped him in the doorway of a small office.

He came to attention. "No, Sergeant. I didn't think it was important, Sergeant."

The man smiled back at him as he was caught looking at the nameplate on the door. Black electrical tape covered whatever came after "Sergeant." He wasn't going to win any bets today.

"Oh, it wouldn't have mattered at all. But it does now. You and three other pilot trainees have just had your training certs punched. You are now Private Ocheltree, on your way to lieutenant once you pass whatever they've got going for flight school in Caledonia."

"Sergeant?"

"You're done here, Ocheltree. You would have passed with flying colors. We can usually tell by day three. You're founder stock; we haven't had one of you fail or drop yet."

"Just like that?"

"Exactly like that." The sergeant stood up from behind his desk and extended his hand. The sergeant suddenly seemed like a different person.

"Sergeant, since I'm leaving, can I . . ."

"How much is the pool up to?"

"Over fifty drink chits, Sergeant."

"We usually reward the best recruit at the end, and you *were* in the running. I'll tell you if you can keep a secret."

"Can do, Sergeant."

"Lassiter. Sergeant Roger Lassiter," he said, offering a smile. "Kyle Lassiter's dad. I served my time years ago as a junior officer in the US Army Airborne. Somebody thinks I can still train."

"I won't say a word, Sergeant. Is it really Sergeant?"

"Not really, but 'captain' just doesn't carry the same punch as sergeant when you're a recruit. I wish you the best of luck, Mr. Ocheltree."

"You as well, sir."

Two hours later, Jeremy walked out of the translation chamber at Kirkton Base into a mass of Chandrians he assumed were the local Creight he'd read about.

"Jeremy!"

He looked around until he spotted Callie Hurd's warm smile. He recognized his fellow pilot from the auxiliary even without the long blonde hair she'd previously sported.

"They got you too?" He walked up and gave her a quick hug. She was a year or two older than him, and he'd been too gutless to ask her out when they'd been flying supplies together during the Strema fight.

"I got orders last night," she said. "I've been up north teaching some of these locals how to fly aircars."

"The Creight? No shit?"

"Scariest thing I have ever done. Not natural pilots or passengers."

"Were you waiting for me? Or do we have the same orders?"

"Yes." She smiled back at him. "On both counts. Dee is around here somewhere, looking for something or someone to eat. Girl goes through boyfriends like a stack of pancakes. We are still waiting for one more, a Finn from Wisconsin, or New Wisconsin, I guess. Name's Arti, Art, something like that. But he's not joining us till tomorrow."

"You know where we're headed?"

"New Castle." Callie nodded absently. "Some captain wearing a Navy uniform said she'd be back for us after dinner and fly us across to the East Coast. I haven't seen her since." She gave him a warm smile. "What do you want to see first?"

"They pulled me out of basic training." He grinned. "Anything that won't get me yelled at sounds really good."

She slipped her arm into his and smiled up at him. "I know just the place you can buy me a drink. There's a big wedding here tomorrow, and the Creight have already started. Dee is probably way ahead of us."

"Sounds good," he managed, doing his best to act as if he had a beautiful girl hanging on his arm all the time.

"Jeremy? Have you gotten taller?"

This was going to be so much better than basic training.

*

Chapter 17

Dumfries, Chandra

Sophie was lying against Kyle's chest, sleeping through her uncle Jake's wedding. The Creight contingent on the bride's side seemed to consist of Dere'dala's entire tribe. Although "side" was a euphemism that didn't seem to apply in the open-air ceremony. Everyone had just gathered in a giant donut of flesh as they struggled to watch the ceremony taking place in the middle of it. In terms of a wedding, it wasn't anything an Edenite bride would have dreamed of.

The Creight had discovered the kegs of beer delivered from Eden for the reception and were already drunk. Their spears were festooned with white owl feathers, and those warriors who had made it through the weeklong basic training course had shown up with their newly issued assault rifles proudly slung on their backs.

Creight children were running around the outside of the circle of witnesses, hyped up on sugar from the tables that had been set with all manner of food. The racket they made was a constant din that went ignored by their parents, who made no move to rein them in. The disapproving looks coming from some of the Edenites, in particular his mother-in-law and Jake's former stepmother, didn't even get noticed.

Kyle stood with Elisabeth at the inner rim of the gathered crowd, ten feet from Jake and Dere'dala. He watched as the bride tied their hands together with some sort of flowering vine. Once she was finished, Dere'dala raised their bound hands over her head and led Jake in a slow circle around the inside of the donut hole. Kyle smiled at the amused look on Jake's face and bent down towards his own wife.

"Any of this strike you as surreal?"

Elisabeth smiled without taking her eyes off the couple. "Jake has a wife . . . it doesn't get any stranger than that."

He'd been referring to the different planet, the heavily armed crowd, and the fact that the bride came from a feral band of Bronze Age escaped slaves who were almost to a man or woman, drunk. He had to admit, none of that was any stranger than Jake actually deciding on one woman.

"The rings!" Jake called out and waved him forward.

Kyle handed off Sophie and walked into the center of the circle. Jake had made the determination that because Kyle had been in command of the *Door Knocker* for a couple of missions, it made him a ship's captain and therefore qualified him to officiate a wedding. Who was he to argue? New world, new rules; besides, the bride had her best knife tied to her calf in a scabbard.

He handed over the rings to Jake. "Promise me you'll do this right at some point."

Jake nodded to Dere'dala and replied in Chandrian, "According to her traditions, we're already married."

"We are." Dere'dala smiled and looked at the simple gold band with a small diamond being held by Jake. "But that is a very nice ring."

"We'll get you a much better one, I promise." Jake turned back to him and gave him a nod. "Do it."

"Do you, Dere'dala, take Jake as your handfast?"

She looked back at him like he was slow. "I have done so."

OK . . . "Do you, Jake Bullock, take Dere'dala as your wife?"

"I do." Jake smiled, slipped the ring on his bride's finger, and showed her where he was supposed to wear his.

"I now pronounce you man and wife. You may . . ."

Jake and Dere'dala were already kissing, and he was suddenly the world's most obvious third wheel. The gathered Creight didn't know what to make of the applause from the Jema and Edenites, and decided to let out some sort of warbling war cry. His work done, he backed away as unobtrusively as possible. The strange, quick wedding ceremony was in keeping with their courtship, which had started with the gifting of some cattle.

Elisabeth gave him a knowing look. "Alright, maybe a little surreal."

"You think?"

Junidor, Southern Coast of the "Jema Channel," Chandra

It had taken less than half an hour upon arrival at the windswept harbor of Junidor for Breda to start missing the prison that the Isle of Landing had been. Nine days on a paddle wheeler around the edge of a continent, staying within sight of land all the way. He had seen a hundred shorelines that had looked more inviting than the harbor fortress of Junidor. On the Isle of Landing, Gemendi, even a lowly Jehavian like himself, had been valued for the knowledge they held in their heads. Here, nothing seemed to have any value outside of labor.

This place was truly at the ass end of the world. Even the sunshine, when it managed to break through the low-hanging clouds, seemed weak. Breda had been there three days before he realized that the wind had not let up once. Junidor was more of a Kaerin garrison than the city he'd been expecting. A massive walled complex, encompassing a large and very busy harbor at the mouth of a wide river flowing north from the interior, was the only distinguishing feature.

His only glimpse at the tree-filled landscape south of them was limited to the morning and evening march between the walls of the garrison and the newly constructed steel manufactory. The steel mill that his team was responsible for powering.

If he needed a reminder that he was less a Gemendi and more a subject, the armed warriors escorting his team during the twice-daily marches sufficed. Reinforcing the concept were the straw pallets they slept on in a hastily constructed barracks. The clapboard building had been thrown together for his team's use by Lord Atan'tal's local subjects, the Junata. The building leaked during rain, and seemed to moan in anguish with the unending wind that blew in from the channel.

He'd never seen a people as miserable as the Junata. They went about their assigned tasks with bowed heads and with hardly a word for one another. The High Blood warriors guarding them seemed to take pleasure from driving them to exhaustion, and were ever quick to proclaim that freedom awaited the slaves.

"You stupid, miserable wretches!" The High Blood warrior watching his team work was a tall, broad-shouldered old man named Lert'rana. The High Blood knew as little about steam power generation as Breda knew about the retirement age of Kaerin warriors. It seemed to him that Lert'rana had to have reached the age when Kaerin did whatever they did, after a lifetime of making others miserable. The elder Kaerin had no concern for the Junata work party for which he was assigned to watch.

"You should all go for a swim tonight! Water's warming up." Lert'rana's laugh sounded like a hand bellows with holes in it. The four Junata who had unlocked and removed the side panel from the firebox's side, stood staring at each other for a moment before bending over to pick up the dropped cast-iron panel and moving it aside.

During his first morning head count, after arrival, they had all heard that two Junata had tried to "swim the river" during the night. He had quickly learned that swimming the river was a slightly more optimistic form of suicide than heading out to a sure death in the channel. The other side of the river was as fully controlled by Lord Atan'tal and his High Bloods as this side was. Some Junata were willing to do anything to escape Junidor. Many skipped the interim manhunt and tortuous death the far side of the river represented and "went for a swim" in the channel instead.

"What are you waiting for?" It took him a moment to realize Lert'rana was speaking to him.

"We will have to pull the panel on the other side as well." He dipped his head slightly. "My Lord." His entire life, it had been "yes, Lord," "my Lord," but he had never lived with the ever-present and unspoken threat he could see in Lert'rana's eyes. This warrior didn't care if he was a Gemendi. Breda briefly wondered if most other subjects lived this way and he had somehow lived a sheltered life. He had never worked directly for High Bloods. In Kaerus, he'd always been assigned to other subject Gemendi. Before being shipped off to the island, he had four Jehavian Gemendi above him, and a Kaerin Gemendi overseeing them all. He had been miserable, but his contact with High Blood warriors had been limited.

"You said you needed to get inside; it is open." Lert'rana pointed out the simple logic involved. Breda could feel the residual heat radiating off the thick cast-iron firebox. Lert'rana needed to come closer to the firebox to appreciate the problem.

"My Lord, it will have to cool down a great deal before I can go inside to make my inspection. It will cool much more quickly with both panels removed. You could bake bread in there still."

"Send one of them." Lert'rana pointed at the four Junata workmen. "How long would they have to stay inside?"

As much as he wanted to suggest that the High Blood stick his own head in the firebox, the looks from the four Junata seemed to indicate the comment would probably result in one of them cooking alive.

"Longer than he would live, my Lord."

"You are certain?"

The Kaerin was dead serious, and from the looks on the faces of the Junata, they knew it. "My Lord, I will have to inspect the heat exchange coils and exhaust ports myself. It is not something I can teach them."

"How long?"

"Four or five hours, my Lord," he answered. "I will have them shovel the ash and fire rock residue out. It will further speed the cooling."

Lert'rana took a menacing step towards him. "See that you do. There's no point in you Gemendi fucks building more of these if you cannot keep the first one running."

He watched Lert'rana amble off in search of someone else to threaten before turning to the Junata. "Get the other panel off, and grab that long-handled shovel for the ash pile." He pulled his heavy work gloves off his belt and handed them over to the Junata who seemed to be the leader of the party. "Whoever is on the shovel will need these. If we were not working for an idiot, I would wait until tomorrow." The man took the gloves and touched them to his forehead in appreciation before offering him a slight bow.

"Don't bow to me, Junata. I am as much a slave as you are."

The Junata regarded him for a moment as if he had trouble believing him. "Be careful of that one." The man's eyes darted across the cavernous mill floor in the direction the Kaerin had taken. "He does not like being denied his entertainment."

"What is your name?"

"I am Zat'arno."

"My name is Breda, Gemendi Breda, if the Kaerin are about. Are all of Lord Atan'tal's holdings like this?"

Zat'arno shrugged his massive shoulders. "I do not know. My grandparents were sent here long ago."

A work camp; Junidor suddenly made more sense to him. He had heard of such camps, of course, but he had been raised within Lord S'kaeda's holding. The four-story apartment building that he had grown up in had been overcrowded and poorly heated, but it was technically speaking within the city of Kaerus itself. There, infractions against Kaerin rules usually meant being sent to the Jehavian host as a soldier, which as far as he was concerned was just a different form of prison. In the event of a serious offense, the guilty were simply executed.

"Other cities are different." The youngest member of Zat'arno's work party spoke up, a teenager with hair the color of a setting sun.

"When Lord Atan'tal needs more hands here or across the channel at Irinas, they collect us from our cities to the south. My family was sent here half a year ago. My parents and sisters were taken across the channel. It is said life is better there than here."

Zat'arno cuffed the young man on the back of the head. "That is shit! You are *here,* Meego. Quit dreaming of elsewhere, or take yourself for a swim. It's the same everywhere. We work—they eat."

Breda regarded his fellow prisoners. He could tell Zat'arno was trying to protect the young man. The only thing that separated him from their plight was the fact that he had some technical skill. He hoped Amona had spoken truly; half a year here—and then with luck they would send him somewhere else.

The firebox had cooled enough to allow him inside by the time they had finished their simple lunch. The meal had been delivered to them by Junata women pulling heavy cook carts like two-legged oxen. The meal had consisted of a thick piece of bread and a bowl of fish stew. His stomach was still deciding whether or not he could keep the meal down. The heat inside the firebox, radiating from the thick cast-iron walls and the water-filled boiler tank above his head, was not helping.

The water with which he had doused himself and his head wrapping with, was quickly evaporating in the heat. He struggled to hold the lensed lantern over his head as he inspected the canted roof of the firebox. He spotted the problem in an instant. To either side of the boiler, a thick, gummy tar coated the exhaust vents. One side looked completely blocked. Whoever had been operating this steam plant was lucky not to have destroyed the brand-new building in which the plant sat.

He crawled back out the bottom, headfirst into the arms of the Junata who caught and pulled him the rest of the way out before standing him upright.

"Did you identify the problem?" Lert'rana was waiting for him.

"I did," he managed before sucking in a breath of cool, clean air. "My Lord, I checked the operating logs on this steam plant before we started. It ran for five days before it was shut down?"

"If that is what the log shows." Lert'rana nodded back at him. "Then it is so."

"Where is the fire rock stored?" He directed the question at Zat'arno, already tired of having to kiss Kaerin ass.

"In the shed outside; I can show you."

He looked up at the Kaerin. "My Lord, may I show you what the problem is?"

"The problem"—the warrior nodded towards the boiler—"is not within the machine?" The Kaerin seemed relieved as if it were no longer his issue.

Prelate's balls! The man was thick. He no longer wondered how a High Blood would find himself here at the ass end of the world, guarding slaves. Lert'rana was probably challenged by his current duties.

"My Lord, I need to speak with your Gemendi. This is a technical matter, and until we resolve the issue with the fire rock, this will keep happening." He pointed up at the boiler.

Vad'as, the ranking Kaerin Gemendi of Junidor, seemed to be a decent sort, at least so far. More in keeping with the type of Kaerin he was accustomed to on Landing. Vad'as's specialty was shipbuilding, but he understood cause and effect as well as Breda did.

"This will not do." The Kaerin held the two clumps of fire rock he'd brought with him to Vad'as's workshop. "I have warned the administrator in Irinas that the fire rock he was sending was of two qualities."

"My Lord," Breda started carefully; there was no manner of man pricklier than a Kaerin Gemendi who felt the need to put a subject Gemendi in his place. "It is an issue with tight tolerances arising from the design of the new steam generators. They are far more efficient, but they require the harder, higher-quality fire rock to function well, or at all, for any matter of time."

"I have seen the reports of the new steel mills designed on

Landing." The old Gemendi nodded to himself. "They have managed to design a crucible heated with flowed impetus rather than direct heat, but it requires the generators you are installing to function, does it not?"

Breda managed to swallow his professional pride. He'd been a member of that team on Landing. "It does at that, my Lord."

"Do you know your way around a mine?" Vad'as dropped the fire rock into his waste bin and looked up at him.

"No, my Lord. But I am very familiar with the different grades of fire rock. I have trained and worked with steam since leaving the Jehavian host."

"Jehavian, eh? Well, I suppose this place is something of a disappointment after Kaerus or your time on Landing?"

"I serve, my Lord."

"Good!" Vad'as pounded a knuckle on his desk. "I will send you to Irinas, temporarily. I will have a writ for you shortly that you can present to my counterpart there. It will be up to him how he wishes to proceed. You may be needed to explain to him the importance of your team's generators to the new-style steel mills. Which is why I am sending you. He wants the new steel as badly as I do."

"If I may ask, my Lord? How far is the journey?"

"Across the channel?" Vad'as pointed out his office window overlooking the harbor. "Half a day, even less coming back this time of year. We will have you back here assembling your generators shortly."

Wonderful... "If I could ask another question, my Lord. There are sources of high-quality fire rock south of here. Which would not require bringing it by ship."

Vad'as regarded him for a moment in what might have been annoyance. "Those deposits lay just south of Lord Atan'tal's holding and are being utilized elsewhere. In any event, there is no more efficient way to transport bulk goods than by ship, Jehavian," the boatbuilder answered with obvious pride. Vad'as reminded him in a strange way of

Barrisimo, without the posturing. They were of an age, yet the Kaerin didn't seem to have a need to express his superiority in every statement. He was a Kaerin - it was assumed.

"I understand, my Lord."

"Wait outside; I will have your writ shortly."

Dismissed, he took another glance out the window from the hallway outside the Gemendi's office. The whitecaps atop the very cold-looking gray water of the channel made it appear as if the ocean had stripes. It seemed the ass end of the world was a bit farther north yet.

*

Chapter 18

South of Newcastle, Chandra

They'd fallen into the habit of gathering around a camp at the end of the day's march. The combined forces of the Jema and the EDF were slowly making their way south in a line that stretched from the Irish Sea on the west coast to the North Sea on the east. They had just over forty thousand soldiers, divided into five small "divisions" with which to take on a planet's worth of Kaerin and the Janissary hosts they controlled. New recruits were joining them at a rate of about five hundred a week from the four training camps on Eden. The newcomers manned the reserves, and followed behind. They were the primary labor being used to build the two packed gravel roads and bridges across innumerable streams and rivers as they marched southwards from Dumfries and New Castle respectively.

Their line of advance was far from solid, and the farther they marched south, the more territory they had to cover. The area between the divisions and out in front of the line was "filled" with Hyrika's scouts, utilizing aircars, mountain bikes, and at times helicopters to make certain they spotted the Kaerin before the reverse happened. The satellite photos had been helpful but far from perfect. They'd caught sight of the Kaerin's annual hunting parties setting out from the complex at Portsmouth on the first day of the march, but clouds had prevented the satellite from "seeing" anything useful since. At least on the ground; two Kaerin paddle wheelers were being tracked as they slowly made their way up the west coast.

"Makes sense." Carlos flicked the edge of the photo. "These assclowns move up the coast and put a force ashore, block any Creight still in the south while the warriors on foot drive north towards them."

"Been that way every year." Hank nodded in agreement. "At least according to Rai'nor's people."

The whine of an aircar landing behind them stopped Kyle's reply.

"Think that's Jake?" Jeff asked.

"Should be." Kyle grinned. "You think he remembers why we're here?"

"He will remember," Audy said slowly. "I imagine he could not wait to return to us."

Carlos barked a laugh. "Jema honeymoons must be a lot different than mine was."

"I just realized how that sounded." Audy raised both hands in surrender. "I only meant that Jake truly seems to enjoy fighting, although he does complain a great deal."

"Bitches nonstop," Hank Pretty interjected.

"Yes," Audy agreed, "but you know what I mean. He is like a Jema in this. He enjoys the struggle . . . he always says one must 'embrace the suck.'"

Kyle just smiled as everyone laughed. He knew what Audy was trying to say, and could agree with it on the surface. Deeper than that, he knew Audy couldn't have been more wrong. Jake was just very good at compartmentalizing what was at hand, keeping it away from everything else. He prayed that Jake, now married and having somebody to worry about, could still manage to set real life aside and operate in the here and now. Through the years, the inability to do that had killed more of his brothers in arms than anything else.

"My last bottle of Audy's jasaka says he took her fishing," Jeff announced, tapping at the bulge in his thigh pocket.

"Seriously?" Rob Nagy sat up. "I admit I don't know him as well as the rest of you, but I was at the wedding. I saw his wife . . . I will take that bet."

Audy's jasaka distillery was doing a booming business back on Eden. So far, he had failed miserably in getting a case of the powerful whisky through the logistics logjam at Kirkton and to them at the front lines.

"You brought a bottle with you?" Audy asked in surprise and with a slice of pride.

Jeff smiled and patted the bottle. "My rifle's never been so clean."

Jake entered the circle of light thrown out by the campfire and dropped his duffel bag, staring at all of them with a look of disgust. "If I knew you broke dicks were going to march so slow, I'd have extended my shore leave."

Everybody stood to shake his hand or slap him on the back before letting Jake find a log to sit on. "How was the honeymoon?" Carlos asked. "You get any rest?"

"Slept like a baby." Jake grinned with a smile that stretched across his face.

"Where'd you end up going?" Kyle asked. Jake had somehow convinced the portal engineer at Kirkton to not to divulge where on Eden they'd gone. He'd assumed Jake had threatened the technician with a slow and painful death, because the guy hadn't said a word in the face of attempted bribery.

"Hawaii." Jake grinned. "I know it sounds like a cliché, but it was beautiful; no long plane ride, no golf courses, no traffic, no tourists. The people at the settlement there delivered us by boat to a small island with a beachside bungalow they'd built. We pretty much had the place to ourselves. Dala even learned to swim . . . sort of. Elisabeth knew where we were. She managed to have the phone booth sent from Kirkton to come get us."

"Well, welcome back," Pretty announced. "We've been placing bets on whether or not married life was going to ruin you."

Audy raised his hand. "I was confident you would return to us unchanged."

"Not me." Jeff grinned. "Look at him; he's going soft already. He has that 'I've got a doll waiting for me at home' look."

Jake grinned back at Jeff in challenge. "My doll will be joining up with Hyrika's scouts as soon as she helps get her people moved into position. Don't you go worrying your tiny West Coast, academy brain. I'm back."

Here we go, Kyle thought. The East Coast-West Coast thing with the SEALS was almost as bad as it was for the Marines. Jake appeared to be fine.

Jake shook his head. "As for ruining me, I think I created a monster. The girl likes to fish as much as I do."

Jake looked momentarily confused as the circle broke up in laughter, but he shrugged it off just as fast. "I do have some bad news," he added seriously. "Maybe you've already heard . . ."

"Sir Geoff?" Kyle had been expecting it. They all had. Before setting out southward four days ago, he'd managed to get back to Eden and have a very short, almost one-sided conversation with the man he credited with saving his life in every way that mattered.

Jake's head dipped once. "He slipped into a coma this afternoon."

Kyle knew the old man was gone. He'd been very clear that he didn't "want to be maintained like some potted plant." He glanced over at Hank, who had been as close to Sir Geoff as he had and for far longer.

"Jeff," Hank asked, "maybe we can put that bottle to good use and offer up a toast to Sir Geoff?"

The personal loss aside, they were going to miss Sir Geoff in more ways than he could count. His wisdom and experience would have been invaluable when the time came to navigate the massive power vacuum that Chandra would be left with, when, not if, they broke the Kaerin's hold on the planet. Right now, he wished his friend's soul the peace that he had sought his entire life.

He listened to everyone tell a favorite story or some recollection involving Sir Geoff. When the bottle reached him last, he'd been considering retelling the story of his surreal initial interview with Sir

Geoff in the Nanotech Headquarters. Now, it seemed like a lifetime ago.

Kyle almost started laughing to himself. "I'll never forget the first real advice he gave me," Kyle began. "It was just three words: 'Don't fuck up.' He of course made it sound as if he were sharing some sort of secret arcane wisdom he'd picked up during his years. I think it was just the simple fact that he truly understood it usually comes down to doing the right thing, regardless of the cost." Kyle lifted the bottle. "To Sir Geoff!"

*

Over the North Sea, Chandra

"OK, good to see you weren't exaggerating." Captain Harper signed something at the bottom of her clipboard and dropped it at her feet. "Climb to two thousand feet, circle around, and take us back to the dock."

"Is that it, ma'am? Or is it still sir?"

"I'm Navy, Jeremy. It's just Captain."

The brand-new aircraft climbed quickly. Modeled after the venerable Cessna Amphibian Caravan he'd learned to fly around the Puget Sound on Eden, it had been updated with a modern avionics suite that was going to take longer to get used to than the controls. When Captain Harper had told them they'd be flying recon over the North Sea, he'd assumed, with more than a little fear, that they'd be in aircars. Could it be done? Sure. Was it a good idea? In comparison to a real-life airplane, not at all.

"And yes, I just need to check you out on landing, but it's evident you have some solid experience with fixed wing. We don't plan on you doing any dogfighting."

"Captain? Were you old world Navy?"

"Uh, no. My husband and I used to operate a small fishing fleet out of Stonington Maine. I guess that counts enough for me to command the *Constitution* out here. He has the *Independence* at Kirkton."

"A fishing fleet?"

"Relax, pilot trainee Ocheltree. I have some people onboard the Constitution to run the stuff that goes bang. I hadn't seen or heard of most of the stuff on my ship when I first got it, but they needed captains who know the water, just like I need pilots who can spot for me."

"Got it, and can do." He hoped he hadn't offended her with the fishing fleet comment.

"You'll fly with a copilot/radio operator in this seat, and two spotters in the back. One of whom will be a techie trained up on the ASM, Air-to-Surface Missile you'll be carrying for the missions. They've rigged it for infrared and optical targeting. You've got some decent standoff range, so no dive-bombing. Your job is to fly safely and bring them all back, understood?"

"Yes, Captain."

"OK." Harper pointed out the window. "The tide's coming in hard, and there's usually a standing wave that develops about a mile downstream from the dock where the river flow and tide really fight each other. Set up your landing from inland, well inside the dock. That wave is usually a couple of feet high and would make a mess of this airplane."

That it would; a wave like that would probably rip the pontoons right off the undercarriage as it flipped the airplane into a face-plant. Water was much less forgiving than people usually thought. "Where did you learn to fly, Captain?"

"Spotting for the fishing fleet." She smiled. "Same way I met my husband. Jack liked being out with the boats. When we met, I was captaining my dad's old trawler. Once we got married and had kids at home, I learned to fly and spotted for the fleet. Did some off-season work for the Fisheries Department."

He nodded absently as he started a gradual looping turn that took them over the concrete plant. Just to the south of the growing hole in the ground overhung with rock dust, he could make out the cut in the trees, formed by the newly constructed east road stretching into the woods and chasing the EDF on its way south. He knew there was a "west" road as well; it started in Dumfries and went south along the opposite coast. He had a lot of friends in the EDF, and within a couple of weeks, his basic training mates would be joining them.

"Wish you were with the Army?"

Jeremy shook his head. "Until recently, I'd only wanted to fly. Now, I'm not so sure."

"Not the excitement you expected?"

"It's not that, Captain." He shook his head as he lined up the approach, checked his glide slope, and extended the flaps. "I just meant . . . during basic, I was kind of surprised how much I liked it."

"We'll be turning out aircraft a lot faster than we will pilots, Jeremy. In fact, we already are. You and your friends will start training up on the new ground attack planes at the airfield during your down time. Two days on working for me, two days off. Your off days will be spent at the airfield—sorry."

"That's great news, ma'am! I mean Captain."

Harper smiled at him and then pointed out the window at the approaching river's surface.

Jeremy grinned. He'd gotten his pilot's license when he was thirteen. Admittedly, on Eden, that meant your parents said you could fly. He knew how to fly, and the Tyne, upriver from their riverside base, was smooth as glass. This was cake. He couldn't wait to tell Callie that they'd be getting to fly the new Wolverines. Sure, they weren't the F-35s sitting on the tarmac back at Kirkton, but the turboprop attack planes looked like they'd be fun to fly, and they carried enough ordnance that he knew he'd be doing his part in the fight.

The landing went smooth enough that Harper reached for her clipboard before the pontoons fully settled in the water. "You're a natural pilot, Ocheltree. Something tells me you've got as many hours in the air as I do, and I'm old enough to be your mom and then some."

"We were founders, Captain. I was steering aircars in my dad's lap about the same time I was learning to ride a bike."

"Well, it shows. Bring us dockside. I hope your friends are all as good as you."

"I know Callie and Dee from before; they are both good pilots. I'm sure Arto is as well." Callie was every bit as good as he was. Her founder family had settled in Alaska, and she'd grown up flying puddle jumpers similar to the Caravan. Dee was technically just as good if not as instinctual. He had no idea about Arto Harjala. The Finn had only arrived this very morning, and he hadn't flown with him.

"You will conduct their check flight. Make certain you document any deficiencies and work up a training plan to fix them."

"Ma'am? I mean Captain?"

"Jeremy, you're a better pilot than I am and come with some very strong recommendations. I'm not sure what you did during the Strema war, but Dom Majeski seems to think you walk on water, and he doesn't strike me as somebody to blow smoke. I want you to check flight the rest of them this afternoon. Make sure you bring the airplane and all of them back."

"But . . ."

Captain Harper grimaced. "No 'buts,' Jeremy. I've got a ship that sails out tonight, and I can't spend the day in the air, confirming what your personnel files already say. Callie Hurd is in command of the New Castle recon wing, but you are senior pilot and responsible for check flighting all of them, including Miss Hurd. They are not your friends right now. Are we clear on that? You won't be flying around looking for tuna feeding."

"Clear, Captain."

*

River Trent, Chandra

"Well, I suppose that's one way to do it." Derrick Mills didn't sound impressed as he watched a small band of Creight wade into and then float across the River Trent on logs being pulled to the north shore of the river, by tribesman who could evidently swim. The Creight carried everything they owned and their few children as they went. "Seriously inefficient."

Carlos lifted his eye away from his rifle's scope, from which he'd been watching the scene unfold, and looked up at Mills. He'd been hearing for months how smart Mills was. He didn't care if the guy was some sort of brainiac or not; comments like that made him wonder how Mills had ever been in the Special Forces, as an officer no less. The bone-thin black guy from Silicon Valley seemed way too cerebral to have ever been a soldier, of any kind.

"Not like they can carry boats with them," Carlos responded. "They've probably been using those same logs for a generation."

"No doubt," Mills answered. "Though I was referring to their whole nomadic culture in a land of plenty."

"Oh." Carlos grunted, and pointed south along the direction his barrel was lying. "Don't forget the part about a land full of assholes that hunt them for sport." They were sitting along a line of low hills overlooking the river below them. On Earth, they'd be somewhere just west of Nottingham. The old Earth maps were becoming less important as they actually built roads, not mention to mention forts and cities. Mills's map of Caledonia was filling in quickly as he oversaw the construction of the two roads being built north of them and the supply depots that kept the advance fed and fueled.

"Fair point." Mills popped up on one knee.

Carlo pointed at the river. "Will this place do?"

"I think so." Mills nodded. "Raised solid ground on either side to sink the foundations; wide—shallows below. The permanent bridge won't be up until the army needs it coming back north, but I'll make sure you guys keep your feet dry moving south. You want to name it? I'm running out of names."

"Tangos," Carlos said.

"You can do better than that! How about Carlos Crossing?"

Carlos reached out, grabbed Mills's arm, and slowly pulled him back to the ground. "Kaerin in the far tree line."

"Oh shit, they see us?"

Carlos's eye was glued to his scope. "They're staying in cover, just watching the Creight."

"You'd think they'd hit them in the river, in the open."

"My guess is they have some sort of big party planned farther north, closer to the blocking force they're going to try to put ashore behind us."

His sat-phone vibrated at his waist. "Grab that for me," he said as he continued to try and get a head count on the Kaerin through his scope. He'd counted twenty so far, but figured there were many more stacked behind them within the thick, dark forest. The Kaerin looked to be standing down; they'd probably been bird-dogging this group for some time. The river crossing had slowed the Creight and brought them close. These Kaerin clearly weren't going to be satisfied with this small band of Creight that looked to be three or four families in size.

"Mills here." Carlos listened in on the conversation as he started paying attention to the terrain on their own side of the river. They'd come to do some advance scouting for a bridge site; he was now planning an ambush. He knew it was Hyrika or one of her people on the phone; the Jema scouts must have spotted the same group as he had.

"We see them too," he heard Derrick say. "Hang on; I'll ask."

He knew what the question was. "We'll hit them here. Tell Hyrika to bring up her assault team and let them know this group of Creight will be moving through her people's lines in the next few minutes. Recommend having Rai'nor's people intercept them in a couple hours."

Carlos listened to Derrick's side of the call as he continued to count; he was up to thirty-two.

"Thirty minutes." Derrick put the phone down between them. "We going to have that long?"

"They don't look to be in any hurry." No sooner had he finished speaking when movement on the far side of the river's floodplain caught his eye. Two rifle- and sword-bearing Kaerin had emerged from the forest's edge and were walking towards the river. The last of the Creight, two old women and an old man, had just entered the water and climbed aboard the log. A solitary young Creight warrior was in the water swimming alongside the log, having guided it back across to the last passengers.

"Shit," Derrick let out. "They aren't going to make it."

"Easy," Carlos breathed, focusing through his scope on the two Kaerin. One of them was carrying what looked to be a burlap bag. The bag was rounded and stained dark by whatever it contained. *Fuck . . .* "This is theater."

Carlos reached out and put a hand atop Derrick's rifle. "If we have to, I'll do it. I'm suppressed."

"I think that's a head in the bag . . ."

"I know." Carlos watched as the bag-carrying Kaerin pulled out what looked to be a young girl's head with a fistful of long hair. The High Blood warriors held it aloft as they continued forward. Whether it was simply the appearance of two Kaerin warriors or the fact one of them was holding up a head of a child they recognized, one of the Creight women already shore began screaming.

The Creight log had just reached the shore beneath them, and the young warrior still in the water did his best to get the elders out of the river and moving into the forest to join the others who had taken off at a run. The Kaerin swung the decapitated head around his own like a rock in a sling and let it fly out into the river. Carlos watched the High Bloods laugh at the terror their performance had caused.

Carlos couldn't hear the words the warriors shouted across the water, but his imagination filled in as he watched for any sign that the Kaerin were going to unsling their rifles. They seemed content to just laugh as the Creight were put to flight once again and disappeared into the forest. One of the Kaerin warriors walked forward to the river's edge and took a moment to piss in the river as he yelled across the water. Whatever he said, his fellow High Blood thought it was hilarious.

"I'm going to enjoy this," Mills said, looking down the barrel of his own gun next to him. "Payback Crossing, it's a good name."

"Just when I start thinking you're some sort of geek, you're ready to get some."

"I am a geek, for fuck's sake." Mills gave his head a sharp shake. "A super geek, who really hates bullies."

"I hear that," Carlos said and patted the side of his rifle. "We've come to the right place."

*

Chapter 19

River Tyne, Chandra

The Kaerin emerged from the wood line in twos and threes; the scouts, Carlos guessed, as they were followed by the rest of the Kaerin hunting party several minutes later. They moved without any formation and kept coming at a sedate walk. They'd waited over an hour since the Creight had gone ahead and didn't seem to be in a particular hurry, or, as the voice in the back of his head shouted, they'd been waiting for the rest of their group.

There were over a hundred Kaerin warriors down there, filling the grassy flood plain between the far bank of the river and the forest behind them. They seemed content to walk to the river's edge and stop, clearly waiting for something.

"More coming through the forest." A Jema's voice over the tactical radio buzzed in his ear. Since arriving, Hyrika had put a squad's worth of her Jema across the river a mile upstream. The squad had slowly worked its way back downstream and were now hidden in the far woods flanking the Kaerin to the west.

"Wonderful," he said to no one in particular.

"More for us," a familiar voice whispered behind him. It was Kyle, with Audy in tow.

"This ambush is attracting all the best people." Carlos laughed quietly to himself.

"Not just you." Kyle "swam" on his elbows until he was next to him. "Jeff and Jake are about forty-five miles west of you; they've pushed a little farther south and have spotted another company-sized force. We'll deal with this bunch and then move to them."

"They spot any radios yet?" Carlos asked. He'd been carefully checking and hadn't seen anything resembling the Strema long-talkers they were familiar with. They had to take out these hunting parties and clear the way to Portsmouth without alerting the Kaerin base.

"Nothing yet. You?"

"Nothing but their packs so far. This group coming up behind them could be the baggage train."

"You want to hit them as they start to cross?" Audy asked.

"That's the plan," Carlos said. "One of them lost something in the river. They're going to need help looking for it."

"Do I want to know?" Kyle asked.

Carlos shook his head. "No."

They'd moved downhill, closer to the water's edge while they'd waited for Hyrika's assault force to move to them. Set back into the trees, they were now close enough that they could hear a burst of laughter or the occasional shouted order from the Kaerin milling across the river.

Across the floodplain behind the Kaerin, the forest erupted with shouts as a large group emerged, carrying two large rowboats atop their shoulders. It wasn't more High Bloods carrying the boats and loaded down with supplies. Whoever they were, the three dozen "porters" were guarded by only two Kaerin warriors. Things just got a lot more complicated.

"Shit, we got friendlies in the middle of them." Derrick gave voice to what they were all thinking.

"They are not friendlies," Audy said. "As long as the Kaerin stand, they will fight us. The survivors would probably run back the way they came, to report to Portsmouth."

"Whatever they do," Carlos interrupted, "they'll cross last?"

"Of that, I am sure," Audy answered.

"Alright, we wait until most of the shitbags get across," Carlos said. "Then we light them up. We can let the locals figure out what they are going to do with the river between us and them."

Someone among the Kaerin shouted an order, and the boats came across the grassy banks in a rush. At the edge of the river, the warriors themselves took over. Flipped the boats into the water, and pushed off with eight men paddling each. The entire evolution looked far too well practiced to give any of them any comfort.

"Hold fire until I shoot," Carlos ordered over the radio. Everyone was on the same channel. "If these are scouts, if they come into the woods before the rest cross, we'll take them out. Otherwise, we will hold until the entire party is across. Avoid the civilians if able."

Kyle tapped him on the shoulder and pointed across the river. "There, by that fallen tree, at the root ball. A red sash around his waist."

"Got him," Carlos intoned. The Kaerin stood on the shore, surrounded by other warriors who seemed to be waiting on him to say something. He'd found his first target.

"Come on guys, be stupid, be lazy," Derrick whispered next to him.

The boats unloaded and pushed back across immediately with just a single paddler left for the return trip. The dozen warriors put ashore and quickly spread out into a line fifty yards wide along the river's edge. Without a sound, the Kaerin scouts started across the narrow strip of grass that separated the river from the thickly wooded slope that concealed them.

Shit . . .

"These are not Strema," Audy pointed out needlessly in a whisper from somewhere behind him.

Carlos pushed his mic. "Silenced weapons only. Wait until they're in the woods and out of sight from the river."

They watched the Kaerin come on. Carlos had lost sight of most of them as they neared the woods, but had no problem watching the two Kaerin directly in front of their position. The enemy scouts were moving far too fast to be concerned. They weren't really looking; they were just performing as they'd been trained. Checking out the far bank before the rest of the assholes crossed over. They still thought they were hunting Creight.

Audy had moved silently off to his right as Kyle had slid backwards. A moment later, he could see Kyle off to his left, shielded by a tree. Kyle and Audy both fired within seconds of each other. The sounds of the actions working on their suppressed handguns seemed loud to him, but he'd been expecting it. Carlos doubted if the noise of the bodies crashing to the ground around him could be heard across the water, but he bent back to his scope to be certain.

The boats had just returned to the opposite shore, but their next loads were just standing there, waiting for a signal from the far shore or an order to proceed from the red-sashed Kaerin, who was suddenly staring across the river with what looked like concern. These guys actually knew what they were doing.

"Prepare to engage," Carlos ordered as he pulled his rifle in close. "Don't let any of them make it back to the woods."

He sighted in on the head of the Kaerin he guessed was the bastelta leading them and let out his breath in one long, slow push. "Payback" was only 220 yards away. The boom of his rifle shattered the calm of the pastoral setting. The three SAWs that Hyrika's team had covering their stretch of river opened up. Their new squad automatic weapon used the same 6.5mm Creedmoor ammunition that their assault rifles used. With less recoil than their "old" SAWs using the 7.62 x 51mm the program had initially started with, the new models were deadly accurate. The machine guns opened up alongside nearly forty rifles and sent a wall of lead across the river.

More than half of the Kaerin had been standing at the water's edge with no cover. They went down as if an invisible hand had swept through them. Others hit the ground and started firing back, but the flat floodplain they held offered almost no cover. Carlos searched through the scope slowly, watching for a Kaerin who looked to be giving orders. He didn't see any and settled on a head sticking up over the top edge of a fallen tree. He spotted another, swimming backwards on his belly through the grass. He put that round lengthwise through the Kaerin's torso.

Several Kaerin rounds hissed by overhead, as others smacked heavily into the trees around them, but the volume of return fire was already dropping off. Their surprise had been complete. He swiveled his sight picture to take in the civilian porters huddled in the grass, twenty yards from the water's edge. A Kaerin, down on one knee, waved his sword over them, and pointed across the river. Several of the "locals" stood, hunched over, and started towards the river with nothing but their short swords in hand.

Carlos put a round through the sword-waving Kaerin's chest even as the machine-gun fire from the SAWs stitched through the two porters driving the rest back to the ground. A small group of Kaerin were angling back towards the woods, stopping to turn, working the bolts on their rifles and firing as they moved. They weren't just "running." It was as good an effort of tactical retreat as their shitty terrain allowed for, but it wasn't going to work. They had much too far to go without cover, with far too many guns firing down at them from covered elevation.

He dropped the Kaerin who had managed to run the farthest with one round in the middle of his back. A second later, one of the SAWs focused in on the group and effectively stopped them cold. No sooner had he spotted two Kaerin firing into the woods away from them, when they were spun around and dropped by Hyrika's squad that she'd put across the river.

Their own fire diminished quickly and then fell off to single shots ranging out from either side of him. Their ambush was out of targets. Carlos kept his head down to his scope, looking for movement, as he heard Kyle order Hyrika to get a drone up to look for runners. The only people alive across the river seemed to be the small group of porters who huddled together at the base of a solitary willow tree and

Hyrika's own people, far back in the woods on the right flank.

Audy ordered half of the assault team forward as the other half remained in place covering them. The four-man teams carried inflatable boats down to the water's edge and went in without stopping. Carlos hunted for a target through his scope, looking for any movement that would indicate somebody was still able to fight on the other side. The boats were vulnerable, and everyone knew it. Two men paddled, as two soldiers in front lay prone on the sides of the inflatables, their rifles trained across the river.

The attack came from the last place he expected. Three of the porters stood with a yell and bolted towards the river, with their short swords pumping in time with their strides. He caught the shouts of warning from the Jema in the inflatables. One of them opened up and let out a three-round burst over their heads to try and dissuade them. They never knew if the warning shots would have worked. Half a dozen assault rifles opened up from the woods to either side of him. A single attacker almost made it to the edge of the river's embankment. His bullet-riddled body fell over the two-foot drop and rolled to a stop just as the first inflatable made it ashore.

"It could not be helped," Audy intoned from behind him.

Carlos knew that. That didn't make him feel any better. These poor assholes had been "owned" for so long, they were like loyal dogs. They weren't all civilians; many of them, like Cal'as or Arsolis of the Hatwa, had served in their local subject militia. They were veterans in some respect; their first reaction would be to fight. The shouts to the remaining porters from the Jema on the far shore were getting better results. The surviving "subjects," maybe a dozen of them in total, stood up with their empty hands held over their heads.

Hyrika's team across the river came in from the tree line and went to work. Carlos looked over at Kyle as they both pointedly ignored the flashes from the Jema blades putting Kaerin out of their misery. Kyle just nodded at him in unspoken agreement and then came up on one knee, holding his radio, looking as tired as he felt.

"Alright, let's get everybody across. Look for any Kaerin maps, radios, anything of interest. As soon as we've policed this area, the aircars will come and get the assault team. We have another ambush to set to the west."

*

Five hours later, and forty miles to the west, Bastelta Krod'as didn't know he was leading his two arms of warriors towards the "joint" of an L-shaped firing line. It was almost time to stop and camp for the night. He had used this meadow to camp overnight in years past. There was a spring with fresh water on the far side.

This was the sixth year he had commanded a hunt. Something was different this season that he was struggling to put a name to. It was true, they had a band of Creight on the run, perhaps a day ahead of them. But it was a small tribe; they had yet to catch the trail of a group large enough that it might actually provide some challenge or experience for his warriors. They had yet to come across any sign that they were getting close to such a clan. And this was the western march. The eastern march was riddled with numerous marshes and even more rivers than he faced here. The Creight weren't entirely stupid; they preferred the western march for the same reason as they made their annual escape to the mountains in the north.

It was as if the primitives had started north earlier this season. Something was afoot; he was sure of it. Kareel Ist'arno had gathered him and all of the bastelta leading the hunt before they had departed Irinas. Their commander had wished them good fortune, and told them there would be news for them upon their return. Some of the rumors coming out of Kaerus were so wild he had trouble believing them, but they all seemed to say the Kaerin were preparing for war. Hunting Creight was poor preparation, but he was going to be certain that nothing happened here to jeopardize his role in the coming fight. He would press harder tomorrow; slip the leashes on his scouts and let them press further out in advance of his line of march.

He called his tearks to him with an upraised arm, and started shouting orders to pull up for the day, and make camp. Bastelta Krod'as never knew that other hunters had been waiting for the same signal. He never heard the shot that killed him and remained unaware of the destruction being rained down on his men.

*

Chapter 20

Irinas, Chandra

Irinas, Lord Atan'tal's outpost on the north shore of the Grey Channel, was not the bleak harbor town Breda had expected. It was far larger than Junidor, both the garrison and its surrounding town. The city's heavy stone walls were topped with timber hoarding and occupied the middle of three broad peninsulas that looked like fingers jutting out into the harbor towards a large island that protected the port city from the rough water of the channel. The island, Irinas Ka, was so large, he'd mistaken its coastline for that of Irinas proper as his ship had approached in the early morning light.

The nature of Irinas was different from Junidor as well. Less a work camp and more the typical Kaerin garrison city he was used to. The fort and the city were surrounded by walls on the landward approaches, but the wide gates stood open, and the Junata who labored here seemed to go back and forth on their business without the guards and supervision that had been so prevalent in Junidor. Along the kamarks of waterfront, much of the developed area gave rise to defensive towers spaced regularly. Most of them looked to be in poor repair and sitting unused. The entire complex had the look of a garrison sited and constructed for war, but which had over time, become more commercial with the absence of conflict.

The narrow streets and buildings in the area of the main harbor were of more recent construction than the walls or defensive towers. As he walked, trying to regain his sense of balance that had failed him so miserably during the channel crossing, he wondered about what A'tor had told him of Lord Atan'tal. At the time, he had dismissed A'tor's "history" lesson as wishful thinking. The story of Lord Atan'tal's ancestors having fought those of Lord Madral's sounded to him like a subject clan daydream of Kaerin fighting Kaerin. Breda had never seen nor heard of such a conflict. At the moment, he was thinking he should not have been so fast to dismiss A'tor.

Despite its current commercial focus, Irinas as a whole had clearly been established and built for war. Whoever had designed the place had clearly been worried about defending against an attack from land and sea—no one other than another Kaerin lord could have even attempted such a thing.

It had taken him an hour to find the Kaerin Gemendi Esro, to whom he'd been ordered to report. He had been stopped twice in the street; the writ he carried from Gemendi Vad'as had been examined both times before being sent on his way. The first time with a dismissive grunt. The second time, the grunt had been accompanied with a jerked chin in the direction of Esro's Gemendi complex.

Within seconds of meeting Gemendi Esro, Breda realized the man possessed none of the decency with which he had credited Gemendi Vad'as. Upon reading the writ, the man had balled it into his fist and thrown it across the room into the fire. Lucky for him, Esro's anger had been directed towards the "thrice cursed degenerates" operating the fire-rock mine in someplace the Kaerin Gemendi had labeled Sverat. Just as Vad'as had warned, Gemendi Esro was impatient for the high-quality steel promised by the new steel mill in Junidor.

"I'll send a message ahead of you to Sverat," Esro had announced, red-faced, marching over to his desk. "I will make certain they understand the importance of separating the grades of fire rock. Upon arrival, you will show this writ to the bastelta commanding the garrison there. He will make certain my directions have been followed. You"—

Esro looked up from the writ he was writing with a cold glare—"will make certain the fire rock destined for Junidor is of the quality Vad'as requires. The writ will authorize you for an immediate return to Junidor on the first available rock transport that sails from Sverat. Should you discover an issue that you cannot resolve, you will be authorized to return here. For your sake, the issue had best be resolved there. I do not wish to see you again."

Within the hour, entrusted with a new writ from Esro, Breda had found himself riding atop a supply wagon on the road leading north out of Irinas towards the fire rock mine at Sverat. Wherever on the prelate's backside that was. The Junata driving the six-horse team hauling the lead supply wagon had not said a word to him since admitting that he was indeed the leader of the three-wagon convoy bound for Sverat. The wagon master was at a loss with a passenger who was clearly not a Kaerin, but held a Kaerin writ and therefore the lives of his caravan team in his hands.

Three hours into the ride, Breda was getting tired of looking at the seemingly endless square kamarks of cultivated fields, pastures and the occasional cluster of farmsteads they crawled past. At this rate, he could get off and walk as fast as the heavily loaded wagons creaked along the packed gravel road.

"How much further?"

The old man stiffened and answered quickly, as if he had been waiting for a question. "Further? You mean until we stop for the night?"

Breda checked the position of the sun, which still hung a couple of hours above the horizon. *Shit* . . . "How much further to the mines, to Sverat?"

The driver looked at him strangely. "It is a hundred fifty kamarks by the road's path. If the road's been repaired from the spring washouts, we should be there by the end of the fifth day."

"Five days?"

"If our luck holds." The man nodded. "My writ is to haul thirty kamarks a day, and I will, roads allowing."

Breda almost caught himself smiling. It appeared the ass end of the world was far larger than he'd guessed. Impatient or not, sitting on this wagon was a lot better than working in Junidor under the glare of High Blood prison guards. He went on all fours, across the top of the crates of supplies, until he was able to drop down on the bench next to the driver. He may as well try to learn something about this land. It appeared he was going to have the time.

"What's your name, friend?"

*

"Cal'as? What do you think?" Jeff, the Edenite officer the Jema called the "Black Jema" for reasons that had nothing to do with the man's dark skin, turned his head and asked his opinion.

Cal'as Bendera had told himself a thousand times over the last six months to stop questioning the Edenites and their strange ways of doing just about everything. That included, without doubt, why a commander should ask the opinion of someone who held no rank; namely him. Cal'as's education and adjustment since being "given" to the Edenites as a hostage by his own father had, at times, been painful. Jake, whom he still privately thought of as "Jackass," especially after learning what the word meant, had delivered the first lesson in the form of an embarrassingly quick defeat after he'd challenged the man to a fight.

Several Jema tearks had over the ensuing months had made a point to demonstrate to him, painfully, what they thought of the qualitative difference between a young un-blooded Hatwa warrior and a Jema; any Jema for that matter. He had slowly learned and come to realize just how "fucked up," as the Edenites often said, his world truly was. He had gone from worshipping the Kaerin as a Hatwa subject, to hating them with a passion that he would not have believed he was capable of, in a very short time. Three days earlier, the ambush on two arms' worth of Kaerin High Bloods had tied that particular knot for him. The Kaerin were not special; they bled and had died just as easily as any man. And his new brothers and sisters in arms had made it seem easy.

"You want my opinion?" He was almost ashamed at the surprise he heard in his own voice.

"I do." Jeff was tapping a can of the noxious tobacco many of the Edenite soldiers and Jema chewed against the knuckles of his other hand. "I know these aren't your people, but if we were in Hatwa lands." Jeff pointed at the road far below them. "What would you make of that?"

"Oh." He nodded to himself. "I would say it was a supply caravan for a garrison or destined for warriors in the field for training."

"Why not just farmers hauling shit to town, or from town for that matter?" It was Jake who asked the question. Cal'as had long learned that everything "Jakas'" said was loaded with what his friend Lupe Flores had called cynicism. He was not certain he recognized it all the time, but he knew it made him angry. Everything Jake said to him, seemed meant to anger him.

Cal'as pointed down the hill at the three wagons slowly making their way through a series of long switchbacks. "There is no High Blood escort," he answered. "Which means whoever they are, the local Kaerin trust them to carry out their writ, their orders. Those large crates in the wagon are Kaerin supply crates; they get used again and again until they fall apart. Anything of importance to the Kaerin goes in such a crate. Everyone, at any port, knows that nothing gets moved until every High Blood crate has shipped. The Hatwa, or whoever these . . . subjects are, would not be moving them, if not for the Kaerin."

"Bird-dog them?" It was Jake again; this time, he directed the question at Jeff. "They're moving slow. We could just let them pass— your call, though."

"Why don't we put the drone out?" Lupe suggested. "Follow the road ahead of them, see where it goes."

"Satellite hasn't seen shit out that way, Wales, right?" Jeff lifted the binoculars and panned to the west.

"Satellite hasn't seen shit anywhere south of Kirkton for a week,"

Jake responded. "Doesn't mean anything."

Lupe had explained to him what a satellite was and how it worked. Cal'as had learned to believe these strange people when they referred to some technological marvel that he could not imagine. His first glimpse of a satellite photo had been truly shocking.

"Point," Jeff allowed.

"We could just go down and ask?" Jake smiled. "Burn the supplies, send them packing? Maybe they have some roughage in the wagon. Fucking MREs . . . I'm so stoved up, I'm almost afraid to eat." Jeff and Lupe laughed at the apparent joke while Cal'as was left trying to make sense of the rapid-fire exchange in English.

Jeff looked down the hill into the wooded valley with his binoculars again. In the distance, the wagon train had inched itself behind a turn in the road, and only one wagon was still visible. "Be dark soon," he announced and turned to Jake. "Take a team down there and intercept them. Lupe, get your drone up. Follow the road and figure out where they are going. Hopefully, it's not so far that we have an answer before you're ready. Stay up on the radio; I'll do the same."

"Copy," Jake said and slapped him on the shoulder. "Cal'as, you're with me. We may need a cultural liaison."

"A what?"

Jake stuck his hand in front of his face and moved it in a jawing motion. "Somebody to talk to them."

"Oh, I thought 'intercept them' meant to attack them."

"It could," Jake responded as he moved away. He turned his head over his shoulder, and smiled. "In fact, it probably does, but you're the closest thing we have to a Creight at the moment. Come on."

"I am not a Creight," Cal'as barked before thinking. He had learned to accept the good-natured insults with which his new colleagues seemed to communicate. With Lupe's help, he was even learning to "hold his own" to some degree. The fact that Jake saw him as equal to a Creight was going too far.

"That's *not* what he meant, Cal," Lupe explained quickly.

Jake came to a sudden stop and slowly turned back around. "It's exactly what I meant," he said. "We've been turning over the locals we've come across to Rai'nor's people. You've seen it." Jake gave him a slight nod, daring him to interrupt. "They've done a great job at it, but they are too far behind us right now. I thought it was a job you could do better than I could."

Jake took two quick steps towards him until his eyes were inches from his own. "My wife is Creight," Jake said quietly. "Are you somehow better than they are? Because the way I see it, their ancestors had the balls to escape, and your people are still slaves."

"I . . . apologize." Cal'as had learned that word early on. "That is not what I meant."

Jake nodded sharply and then winked at him before slapping him on the shoulder. "Well, alright then! I'm glad to hear it. Now, let's go."

Cal'as looked back at Lupe, who was smiling and offering a wave goodbye. "Have fun."

Cal'as shook his head and realized his streak of a ten-day without "stepping in it," as Lupe called it, had just ended. *Just keep your mouth shut, keep your mouth shut . . .*

*

At least the scenery was changing, Breda temporized. The hills were getting bigger, and their road was suddenly "above" the dark shadows of the lowland forest they had been traveling through these last days. The surrounding trees were slowly thinning out and going over to pine. He had spotted bare, rocky hilltops ahead before the wagon caravan had stopped for the night. His companions no longer feared him, and seemed willing enough to engage him in conversation, as long as the discussion didn't waver from the three pillars of approved intellectual debate made up of weather, horses, and 'One Ear' - the dog that seemed to belong to all three of the drivers.

Which wagon the mangled and scarred mutt chose to "run with" during a given leg of the journey was a constant source of wagering and entertainment for the drivers. Breda had given up after the second day, trying to get anything useful out of his companions. And now, at the end of the fourth day, he could not wait to reach their destination, if only for the prospect of someone to talk to. He held out his last morsel of bread towards the dog. It was coated with the thick gravy of the road stew these laborers seemed to live on. One Ear did not move; even the dog seemed to classify him as cargo.

"Made good time up the hill today," Eg'as, the leader of the caravan, announced to all of them. The other two wagon masters nodded slowly in agreement. Breda watched Brugest for a sign that the conversation would continue, but the enormous Junata thought better of it and went on eating. He had learned early on not to expect anything from Sesh. The eldest of the trio just leaned down and patted One Ear's head as if to say their good time had been due to the dog.

The mutt's head popped up in a flash as it let out a low warning growl. They all watched as it moved on stiff legs to the edge of the light cast by their fire. The dog's head move from side to side as if it could not decide where the bad smells were coming from.

"Wolves?" Brugest asked in general.

"Been years since I've seen them." Eg'as stood slowly and dipped his torch into the fire. One Ear barked twice and shot off into the darkness. Eg'as followed much more slowly, looking back at the three of them still around the fire. "Sesh, ready a rock." Breda had been impressed with the old man's skill with a sling. He had managed to keep the road stew furnished with fresh rabbit. The harsh barking started up again, farther into the darkness than he'd imagined the little dog had gone, only to cease with a suddenness that set his nerves on edge.

"One Ear! Where are you?" Eg'as bellowed. "Come back!" The circle of light thrown out by Eg'as's torch moved farther out into the darkness; the torch itself was hidden behind one of the wagons. A noise in the gravel behind Breda brought him to his feet as he spun around. Three black-suited, helmeted figures appeared out of the darkness.

Guns that looked too short to be rifles were held to their shoulders. Breda found himself focused on the one aimed at his head even as he puzzled over the black smudges of what looked like fire rock dust that covered the men's faces.

One of the strange soldiers spoke calmly in a language he did not understand. A moment later, the three warriors moved as one towards them, as if some unspoken order had propelled them. His brain took a moment to catch up. The strange uniforms and rifles, the language . . .

"It's you! You are the Free People!"

One of the soldiers motioned him and the other two wagon drivers back down to their logs and came closer, the barrel of the strange rifle pointed at his head. "I am Jema," the soldier said and then cracked a smile. "And yes, we are free."

"But you know of the Free People? The others?" He realized he sounded frantic.

"What do you know about us?" a voice asked as three more black-suited warriors appeared out of the darkness from between the wagons. They were pushing Eg'as out in front of them. The warrior who had spoken carried One Ear in one arm. The dog was eating something out of the man's hand.

The man had said "us." Free People, here! Standing in front of him. "My name is Breda. I am a Gemendi from . . ."

"What's a Gemendi doing riding around on a supply wagon?" The warrior was not even looking at him as he rubbed the dog's ears.

He was surprised for a moment that the warrior seemed to know what a Gemendi was. "It is a long story. I was—"

"Yeah, hold it there, Slick . . . I don't care." The man spoke in Chandrian, which made the word "Slick" all the stranger. "I'm guessing you are in charge here. Right now, I just want to know where these wagons are going."

"To Sverat," Breda answered. "To the fire rock mines, but you do not understand! I am -"

"Going to be late," the man cut him off again and sat the dog down.

"How many Kaerin warriors are at this mine?"

"I do not know. I have never been there." He pointed at Eg'as. "This is their road; they will know. I was directed there, under a Kaerin writ." The tall warrior, who seemed to be the leader, regarded him for a moment before looking over at one of his companions.

The leader pointed at him with his chin. "You take Gabby here, and figure out who he is. Play nice." Again, the mixture of Chandrian language and the strange words threw him.

"You three." The leader looked over the wagon drivers, who were back on their appointed logs around the fire. The leader swiveled his gun until it was pointing at the dog. "Who is waiting for you at the mines? And how many? Start talking, or One Ear is going to need a new name."

The warrior who had been directed to speak to him pulled him off towards the wagons, followed by another.

Ten minutes later, Jake was on one knee, rubbing One Ear's belly as he waited for Jeff's aircar to settle onto the road atop the IR chem-flares he'd thrown out. He looked back at the fire and smiled at the looks of fear and amazement on the faces of the wagon drivers as the 'magical' vehicle came out of the sky and landed amid a swirl of dust. The locals had revealed that they were "Junata," and a minute into their interrogation, Jake had reached the conclusion that their dog should have been in charge. But they had shared what they did know. There were "many hundreds" of Junata miners at Sverat, and perhaps twenty Kaerin warriors overseeing them.

He was of the opinion that the force they were leading south should just bypass the outpost, or maybe let Kirkton deliver a team by boat to deal with the Kaerin at the mine. He was more concerned that their aerial scouting and satellite photos had missed the installation and couldn't help but wonder if there were others they didn't know about. Their prisoners had been adamant and consistent that Sverat was the only other place on Irinas, outside of the garrison city itself and the sprawling farmland around it that held Kaerin.

Irinas . . . he liked the names Caledonia and Portsmouth a lot better. More to the point, so did the Jema. If they pulled this off, it would probably be the first Kaerin place name of any significance that would get a permanent name change.

Jeff gave the mutt a strange look as he approached. "What is it with you and dogs?"

"They're good judges of character."

"Recognize their own, more like," Jeff muttered, glancing over at Junata being guarded by the rest of the team. "How'd we miss a freaking coal mine?"

"Don't know." Jake shrugged. "Shitty weather is my guess; could be the people we've got looking at the satellite take."

"I pushed it up to Kyle and Colonel Pretty. They said they'd be back to me within the hour." Jeff added a boot rub to One Ear's belly. "Kyle and Audy hit another hunting party this afternoon, and Nagy's group had their first contact on the east coast this morning."

"How many does that make?"

"Five total," Jeff answered. "Six if you count the small group Hyrika's team dealt with. That group we fired up was the largest by far. Going by ten-day-old sat photos, we've dealt with most of the hunters we saw leaving Portsmouth."

"The Kaerin call it Irinas," Jake said. "Same name they have for the whole island."

Jeff shook his head. "Just me? Or is it like the Kaerin ran out of names for shit or something."

They both looked over as Cal'as came running up out of the darkness. In the dim glow from the aircar's cabin light, the young Hatwa looked excited.

"Be nice," Jeff said under his breath.

Jake was still staring at his fellow SEAL in disgust when Cal'as reached them.

"You aren't going to believe this." Cal'as was almost having trouble keeping both his feet on the ground.

"Report," Jake commanded.

Cal'as seemed to check himself and reconsider what he'd been about to say. "The Gemendi, Breda, does not know anything about the coal mine, but he is certain there is a radio there. A message was sent to the mine from Irinas, I mean Portsmouth. He is expected there."

"That changes things." Jeff shared a look with him. "A radio; they'll want us to deal with it."

"No doubt," Jake agreed. They would take any measure possible to make certain Portsmouth didn't know they were coming. Jake watched Jeff walk back to the aircar to update Hank and Kyle and looked over at Cal'as. The Hatwa looked like he was about to explode.

"I'm thinking you had something else you wanted to say."

"The Gemendi, he is from Landing! The island the Kaerin sent my father to. He knows my father!"

Jake had met Cal'as' father, A'tor. He'd liked the elder Hatwa a lot more than the son. There had been a time when he'd thought that meeting had gotten A'tor Bendera killed. If what the little rat-faced Gemendi was saying was true, he could understand the kid's excitement. "What in the hell is this guy doing here? I thought Landing was in the Mediterranean somewhere."

"He says he is here to check on the fire rock for steel mills. He keeps saying that he must talk to one of our Gemendi. That he has information for them and for them alone."

Gemendi? The closest thing they had to a caste of science geeks was Doc Jensen and his people. That said, any high schooler from Eden was going to know as much "science" as any Chandrian subject, Gemendi or not. "You believe him?" Jake asked. "I mean about your father?"

"I do. I gave him my first name, and he recognized it. He already knew the rest. My father had told *him* about me, the Jema, and your people."

That explained the Gemendi's Free People question he'd overheard during the capture.

Jake looked at Cal'as and nodded. He'd been purposely hard on the kid. The son of a Hatwa Gemendi prelate, Cal'as had grown up worshipping the Kaerin. As a warrior in the Hatwa host, he'd adopted a lot of that arrogance. Trying to knock that bullshit out of Cal'as had been almost fun at times. "Do you know what you just did well?"

"I only did what you told me to do. I was . . . nice."

"Not what I meant." Jake shook his head. "You gave us the most important information to our tactical situation here, on this road in the middle of the night, first. That's improvement."

"But his story about my father and Landing? He may know where it is."

"Probably even more important in the long run, but right here, right now?"

"The radio tower at the coal mine?"

"Exactly. Jeff is reporting it up the chain. If we can do something about your father, we will. But first, your new friend has an appointment at the coal mine that he's going to keep."

"You trust him then?" Cal'as jerked his head back in surprise.

"Hell no!" Jake slapped Cal'as on the shoulder. "That's why I'm sure we'll be going with him. Go and keep him talking. Tell him I'm a Gemendi and will be over to talk to him in a moment."

"You? A Gemendi?"

Jake took a deep breath. He almost replied that he'd managed a C minus in high school chemistry, which qualified him as a fucking rocket scientist on this planet. But the kid was already confused. "Cal'as . . ."

The Hatwa checked whatever he was about to say and nodded once. "Right, will do."

*

Chapter 21

Sverat Mines, Caledonia, Chandra

Jake looked over at Breda as their lead wagon approached the closed timber gate of the coal mine. He didn't know what to make of the angry little Gemendi. If the wiry little Jehavian's unending diatribe was taken at face value, the man was firmly on their side. Breda hadn't stopped talking about how he wanted to kill every last Kaerin on the planet since they'd set out for the daylong journey to the mine. No doubted if anyone could fake that much hate. The subject Gemendi acted as if the idea to rid Chandra of the Kaerin had been his idea. Breda hadn't stopped talking, almost levitating in his seat with excitement about what he thought should be done. Jake thought some of it actually made some sense, and he'd placed a call to Doc Jensen and Hank Pretty.

During the call, Jensen had been very clear that if anything happened to Breda before he had a chance to talk to him, the doc would live to make Jake's life miserable. That conversation had occurred while they were underway. Breda, next to him, in the middle of the bench between him and the wagon master, had looked at the sat-phone with a fascination bordering on reverence. Even if they didn't understand the language, they could hear the other voice coming through the speaker. Eg'as, their escort, had almost begun crying in fright at the sight. Breda, once he had gotten over his surprise, seemed to take the idea of the long-distance communication in stride.

Jake had been wholly unsuccessful in trying to put the local Junata at ease with the explanation that the phone was just a tool. Breda had stepped in and done a passable job of explaining who these strange warriors were, and what their presence could mean to all of the Junata and the people of the entire world. Jake had listened in, confirming what Breda had already told him and Cal'as. Breda truly did seem to know of them, and it was all tied to Cal'as's father and this place called Landing.

One thing Jake had been successful in explaining to the Junata wagon masters was what would happen to them if they failed to do exactly as instructed. He'd demonstrated a hand grenade thrown from the wagon, down the hill off the road as they had first set off in the morning. Eg'as and the other two Junata drivers had been duly impressed by the explosion. He'd then explained that they'd each be sitting on one of the grenades as they rode through the gates. As their lead wagon rolled to a stop in front of Sverat's gates, he looked past Breda to their driver. Eg'as seemed to be taking the threat for real as he waved in greeting to the two Junata guards.

"Eg'as! You are a welcome sight for hungry bellies. Who are all these people?" The Junata guards carried the characteristic short sword at their waists and looked friendly enough. Jake let his eyes travel along the rough outer "wall" made up of piled scree and loose rock, looking for some Kaerin bastard with a long sword but didn't see anyone. No one would label the piles of rock a proper wall. One could climb it on all fours, and it might have explained why they'd missed seeing this place.

"This one," Eg'as answered, jerking his thumb at Breda. "Is a Gemendi from Irinas; he has a writ to speak to the High Bloods. The others are a new team of drivers we are showing the road to."

"They going to take your job? What will you be doing if you're not keeping us fed?" The lead guard shouted over his shoulder as he walked back towards the gate and began unlatching the short loop of cable holding it closed.

Eg'as looked over at him, eyes wide, looking for an answer. Jake was at a loss and nudged Breda with his knee. "Depends on my discussions with the High Bloods," Breda belted out. The guard, if he was listening at all, didn't seem to care. He pulled the narrow gate open and walked its arc across the road in front of them without comment.

"Just stop in front of the warehouse; we'll get you some hands to help with the unloading."

"Where do I find the bastelta? Or is it a teark here?" Breda asked as they rolled past.

"Bastelta Welt'as," the guard responded. "He will be taking his meal, or getting ready to. I would let him finish if I were you."

Jake was listening to the conversation, but his attention was focused on his compad lying on the floorboard between his feet. Lupe had just launched his small drone from where he waited behind them on the road. It was circling high over the interior of the fort. Lupe had pushed the image to him, and Jake was doing his best to get a mental picture of what awaited them within the settlement without being obvious about it.

There were four buildings all in a line at the edge of the rocky escarpment dropping to the waters of the Bristol Channel below. There was a stone-lined path and a coal chute that led down to the single wharf on the water, where a single ship was tied up. What he'd call a radio shack was located in the middle of the line of simple buildings. It was adjacent to a two-story, gray-bricked building that dominated the installation. The building's roofs were all of the same slate-colored rock that made up the erstwhile walls, the surrounding ground, and much of the rocky hillside above them. No wonder they'd missed this place; from the air, it was just a pile of dark slate gray rock.

Jeff and fifty EDF soldiers were piled off the road behind the rearmost wagon, waiting outside the gates. With luck, they wouldn't be needed. Jake took one glance at the wide-open area at the base of the hill overlooking the interior of the mine and the Kaerin buildings that made up Sverat. He reached down to his com-pad and placed a finger on the area he selected, depositing a single yellow dot on the image. He noticed Breda watching him, his eyes as big as saucers as he pushed the transmit button.

The image with the yellow carat was transmitted by the satcom link to Kirkton, a little more than two hundred miles to the north. Colonel Pretty was waiting for it and used a compad to convert the image and its marker to coordinates. The colonel handed the device off to one of Jensen's technical staff, who stepped into the portal bound for Eden.

"What will happen there?" Breda whispered.

"Magic," Jake answered and pointed at the interior of the settlement as they rolled through the gate. "Keep your eyes out for any Kaerin." Eg'as had already told them the Junata miners lived, ate, and slept in chambers they'd mined out of the hillside. The small contingent of Kaerin warriors were the only ones here who rated actual buildings, windows, and roofs. All the structures were fair game, and they'd arrived at dinnertime. The only figures he could see moving in the distance were clearly the local labor force, milling around the outside of dark mine entrances cut into the hillside. He bent his head to the mic on his collar and caught a whiff of Eg'as from the man's coat that he'd borrowed. He swallowed his gag reflex. "Targeting sent, incoming."

"What is happening?" Breda asked.

He looked up and saw Eg'as looking at him as well. He glanced down at the timer on his compad. He'd sent the targeting data eleven seconds ago; they'd figured it would take less than a minute for delivery.

Ignoring the question, he reached across the Gemendi and slapped Eg'as on the leg. "Stop here."

"I was told to go to the warehouse."

Jake reached behind him and pulled his rifle from where he'd hidden it. "Stop the fucking wagon, or I'll shoot your horses." He stood up and waved at the two other drivers to pull up next to them. The old Junata, Sesh, did as he was bid, but Cal'as in the rearmost wagon with the big Junata, Brugest, had to jam his handgun into the man's gut to get him moving.

"Kaerin." Breda was pulling on his sleeve. He turned around, followed the Gemendi's gaze, and spotted the sole Kaerin across the yard. The High Blood seemed to have appeared from the edge of seaside cliffs. Must be the head of the staircase down to the water, he guessed. The Kaerin warrior had seen something he didn't like and broke into a run towards them as he began pulling the heavy rifle off his back. The man was over two hundred yards away as Jake fell back into his seat and brought his own rifle up, aiming over the heads of the horses. He fired once, and the Kaerin spun around and went down.

The horses jolted hard at the shot, knocking Jake back against the cargo before Eg'as was able to stand on the brake and hold the wagon in place. The Kaerin had almost crawled to his own rifle before Jake managed to get stabilized and put two more rounds into him.

Eg'as let out a cry in anguish, and hurled himself off the wagon, whimpering.

"Eg'as!" Breda shouted.

"Let him go." Jake grabbed up his compad and leaped down from his own end of the bench as the wagon inched forward to the sound of squeaking wood on wood. At least Eg'as had left the brake on. "Come on, now!" He waved the Gemendi off the wagon. If the horses didn't like his gunshot, they were going to go apeshit when—

KRAK-Whoom!!

The pressure wave caused by the sudden appearance of the *Door Knocker* could be seen flying outward across the mine's yard from four hundred yards away. It picked up a wall of dust and washed over them like a sudden thirty-mile-an-hour wind.

"Hibit! Tha!" Breda shouted something in Chandrian that he didn't recognize, but the delivery and tone seemed appropriate to the moment. He dragged the Gemendi to the rear of the wagon, aware that the horses were doing their best to jump out of their traces.

"Help me!" he yelled as he pulled on the heavy crate at the rear of their wagon. They'd both just gotten a good grip on the crate's rope handles when the crazed horses did the rest and pulled the wagon away with a loud popping sound. They both nearly lost their toes as the oven-sized crate smashed to the ground. The wagon flew forward about ten feet and stopped. A quick glance under the wagon and Jake saw the horses were gone; running full out, less their load towards the cliffs overlooking the water.

"Get behind it!" he screamed at Breda. "Stay down!" He'd just taken a knee himself when a handful of Kaerin spilled out of the largest structure and pulled up, looking at the massive steel barge parked three hundred yards away from them.

The *Door Knocker* had four miniguns, two to a side. Situated as it was, the barge could only bring two of them to bear. Modeled after the venerable M134, but improved with all sorts of stabilization, the two six-barreled, electrically driven Gatling guns opened up on the Kacrin buildings. Each one was capable of firing up to six thousand 7.62mm rounds a minute. The deafening *BRRRRRRRRR* of their firing sounded more like the world's biggest chain saw than a weapon. The Kaerin warriors, standing in front of their buildings, had just brought their rifles up when they were converted to chunky paint.

Jake looked away from the carnage in time to catch the distinct pop-up of a Javelin launch from the stern of the ship. The missile was clearly visible as it nosed over, picked up speed, and streaked across the yard, slamming into the radio shack. The explosion was just punctuation amid the constant scream of the miniguns as they chewed through the brick buildings, first destroying the facing walls and anyone behind them, and then far walls as the rock roofing began collapsing. Jake kept his head up looking for Kaerin, but did a double take at the sight of Breda laughing hysterically next to him with tears rolling down his face.

Tom Souza's assault team aboard the *Door Knocker* were rolling as soon as the bow ramp crashed to the ground. Two JLTVs with SAWs mounted on rooftop turrets were rolling toward them. The lead vehicle opened up on something or someone they'd seen move near the cliff's edge. A second missile whooshed across the yard and smashed into what remained of the largest of the buildings just as the miniguns fell silent.

Looking over his gun resting atop the crate, he saw the scene was dominated by two pillars of rising smoke and dust from the missile explosions. The other Kaerin structures were reduced to piles of rubble, with a layer of slate from their roofs lying on top. He heard a muffled cry from Breda kneeling next to him, and his first thought was that the Gemendi had probably freaked out just like the wagon driver had. Glancing down, he couldn't help but smile. Breda's face was streaked with tears as he pounded on the crate in laughter.

"You liked that?"

"It is. . . a good beginning," Breda gasped between breaths and wiped at his eyes. "I had not believed what was said of you." One of the JLTVs roared past them, headed in the direction of the cliffs overlooking the wharf below. The little Gemendi was so excited, he half stood as if he was going to follow.

Jake yanked him back to the ground even as he reached for the mic on his collar. "Jeff, there was movement coming up from the water; can you get eyes on?"

"We're moving." Jeff's voice sounded as if he were running. "The drone picked up a few Kaerin down there; we think they are accounted for." If it had been the figures Jake had seen at the lip of the drop-off, they were more than accounted for. The JLTVs' SAWs had made certain of that.

"Why this?" The Gemendi was pulling on his sleeve.

"Because I don't want to get shot." He swatted the man's hand away as he scanned back and forth across the reduced buildings, looking for any movement.

"No! I mean why here? If you want to hurt the Kaerin, this place is nothing." Breda's tone came across as that of somebody who was used to being the smartest guy in the room. And for all Jake knew, maybe the guy was. He looked down to the side and shook his head. "Baby steps," he answered with a grin.

"What does that mean?"

"Right now, it means stay still and be quiet until we secure the area.

He stared at the Jehavian, who was close to his own age. "In general, it means we have our reasons that you don't have a need to know." He'd half expected, and maybe wanted, to offend the guy a little a bit. He just wanted to secure this place and get on with moving to Portsmouth, and that meant unloading the Gemendi on Jensen or other people with the time to answer the man's endless questions.

Breda nodded in what looked to Jake to be acceptance. "You need to understand I may be of more assistance if I know what it is you are trying to accomplish here."

Jake bit down on what he wanted to say and stood up as several of the EDF soldiers caught up to them after coming through the gate on foot. He waved them on to the piles of rubble that had been the Kaerin buildings and looked back down at the diminutive Gemendi. "Right now, it's keeping all of us alive. That means you will stay right here. If I have to, I'll shoot you in the leg."

Sometime around midnight, Jensen came to them, via an aircar. The *Door Knocker* had departed for Eden an hour earlier with another, though far less powerful, shock wave. The noise, however, was something next level. The air rushing to fill the vacuum its translation had created was, if anything, louder than it had been on arrival.

Jensen walked up to him from where he'd been chatting with Breda and Cal'as. Jake had been watching Rai'nor's people, who had arrived with Jensen to deal with the Junata miners. As a group, the miners were too scared to cause any trouble, but they seemed far less pleased that their Kaerin lords had been killed than Jake thought they should be.

"Is there any local on this planet that likes you?" Jensen was smiling as he spoke.

"Besides the one that married me, you mean? What!? Is that little rat-bastard complaining about me?"

Jensen smiled back at him. "Did you threaten to shoot him?"

"Probably just a language issue." Jake shrugged. "I suppose he could have taken it that way."

"Uh-huh . . ." Jensen glanced back at where Breda was standing with Cal'as. "I've just had a few questions answered, and if it checks out . . . your new friend might be even more important than he thinks he is."

"That would be saying something."

"I'll be taking him back to Kirkton with me, and probably on to Eden. We've got a lot of questions for him. You did good, Jake."

"Thank Cal'as." He nodded in the direction of the two Chandrians. They both looked to be giving him the stink eye. "He was the one who figured out who the guy was."

"At any rate, thanks for not shooting him."

"Team player, big picture guy, that's me."

Jensen gave his head a slow shake with eyes closed. "Riiiight."

*

Chapter 22

Kirkton Base, Chandra

"Sorry to pull you away." Hank looked up at him from the map table as he came through the door of one of the countless Quonset huts that defined Kirkton.

Kyle waved off the apology. He knew Hank was the last person in the world to jog his elbow if it wasn't needed. He and Audy had ambushed another Kaerin hunting party that afternoon, a company-sized group of warriors, supported by a platoon-sized element of local Junata acting as mules hauling their gear. The fight itself had been textbook; the Kaerin party had been both outnumbered and surprised. The EDF had still lost one of their own from a friendly fire incident and taken a couple of serious casualties from the return fire the Kaerin had been able to mount.

"It's alright," he answered, as he accepted a cup of coffee from one of the aides Hank had running around the place.

"The good news is the weather cleared over Portsmouth in time with the satellite passage." Pretty pointed back down at the map table. "We got some fantastic shots of the whole area. The bad news . . ."

"We see something we don't like?" Kyle approached the table. The map beneath was entirely covered with recon photos.

"Isle of Wight," Pretty began. "We thought it was all laid out for agriculture; we'd actually had a previous view of the River Medina here, that we had thought would have held any large military base on the island. It's the biggest inlet by far, splits the island right down the middle, deep enough for anchorage, and it's where people had settled it on Earth."

"But?" Kyle could tell where this was going. The Isle of Wight wasn't a rock with a lighthouse on it. It was over twenty miles wide, and twelve miles north to south. It sat just off the coast of Portsmouth like a fat guard dog.

"But . . ." Pretty rotated one of the photos and pushed it across the table at him. "These newest photos show a sizeable naval base and garrison fort, three and a half miles to the southeast of the Medina's mouth, here at Wooton Creek. There's even what looks to be a small airfield supporting the garrison. Obviously, the *Door Knocker* can't be in two places at once when we hit Portsmouth."

"And our ships . . ." Kyle could see the issue clearly. Wooton Creek was five miles away from the waterfront of Portsmouth/Irinas, and they would be able to see what was happening there, as well as respond.

"Will be otherwise engaged," Pretty finished the thought for him. "You know as well as I do how busy the portals on Eden are going to be just supporting the attack on Portsmouth; you and Jensen wrote that plan. If we steal a slot in the portal schedule, we could translate a force to the island and tie up the garrison, but I'd feel a lot better about that if we had knocked out their radio tower in advance."

Pretty's finger dropped to a spot on the photo. "This large building here, just downhill from their airfield, that's a radio tower. When we take Portsmouth, we are going to need as much time as we can buy to dig in and prepare for what they'll send across the channel at us. If this Kaerin force on the island manages to get a message out during the attack, we'll lose those days of confusion where they're just wondering why Portsmouth doesn't answer the phone."

"Pathfinder mission." He nodded to himself. "In advance of the attack and take out the radio."

"Which is why I pulled you in." Hank rubbed at the space between his eyes. "Jensen's little GPS toys are wonderful, but until he can figure why the portal targeting is slightly off, we need to mark the targets." Hank might not be marching southward with the EDF, but Kyle was willing to bet the soldiers were better rested than their commander was. "Can Audy handle your division?" Hank asked.

"No problem there." He was staring at the photo. Kaerin agriculture practices had developed more in line with what he thought of as a European model of a central village surrounded by cultivation, versus the American model of independent farmsteads. It no doubt made it easier to control their captive labor force. It would make an approach to the garrison possible from a number of directions.

"If we portal in, we risk being heard. The translation would wake most of the island." Kyle looked up at Hank, who was nodding in agreement.

"I don't want to risk putting a ship down there in advance of the attack," Hank added. "Even one of Arsolis's hulks, and it would be a long shot getting him down there before the flag goes up anyway." Hank rubbed at his nose and pointed back down at the photo; "unless you can convince me otherwise, I think insertion by a Black Hawk or an Osprey carries the same risk of discovery, if not more, than using the portal. You can pick your team, but I need to keep Audy with your division for the attack. Same with Jeff, Jake, and Rob Nagy; I need them where they are."

"Fuck me." Kyle shook his head. He knew what the only remaining option was. "We've never actually tested the idea."

"I know." Hank nodded. "It's your call. If you don't want to try it, we can try inserting an aircar. You would be at the bleeding edge of its range until the ground forces move farther south, and we've already lost one to the winds over the Irish Sea. The channel won't be much better. It goes without saying, I can't afford to lose you. If it makes you feel any better, Jake and Audy are riding into Portsmouth on a wagon through the front gates."

He knew what his two friends were risking and couldn't let them have all the fun. Jake would never let him hear the end of it. His remaining option for getting to the Isle of Wight didn't scare him nearly as much as the thought of his next conversation with Carlos. "We'll give it a go."

"At least it's something you've done before," Hank added, doing his best to make light of the mission. "How different can it be?"

"We are through! You hear me?!" Carlos growled. "This is some crazy, fucked up, hillbilly bullshit!"

Kyle craned his neck with some difficulty and smiled back at Carlos, his face a few feet away on the cold stainless-steel floor of the portal chamber in New Seattle. The helmeted and goggle-wearing faces of Domenik and Hans lay at crazy angles to them both enjoying Carlos's misgivings. They were all similarly laid out on their stomachs in a tight circle on the floor, lying atop equipment bags strapped to their bodies, their necks twisted, enjoying Carlos's show.

"Relax, Marine." Kyle hoped Carlos could see him smiling. "We've all done this before."

"From an airplane, *bendejo*! This is no *bueno*."

"Translation in five, four," the portal chamber's electronic voice continued, unaware of and uncaring over the terror of the occupants within. Kyle's Spanish wasn't good enough to follow Carlos's mutterings, but he picked up on the words "*Espirito Santos*" in there and figured it was a prayer. Which sounded like a really good idea about now. None of them had done "this" before. No one had.

"Two, one . . ."

It was pitch-black over the Isle of Wight, and at an altitude of ten thousand feet, the sound of their translation would hopefully be taken as distant thunder among the clouds. He was certain that Carlos's screams wouldn't reach the ground. They'd translated in with zero velocity. For the briefest moment, he'd been weightless and had hung there in the total black without the slightest indication of direction or orientation. The painful popping of his ears and the cold air were welcome as they seemed to give his mind something to hang on to.

They had none of the wind resistance a paratrooper used to feel their way through the sky, none of the speed of an airplane you usually started with. Most importantly, no one had been stupid enough to try this before, and they had zero institutional knowledge to operate on. They'd just appeared—then started to fall. Vertigo overwhelmed him as his stomach flipped even faster than the rest of him did.

They'd started on their bellies, in formation, hoping that they could stay there as they fell, but that had been wishful thinking. Instead, they tumbled every which way in the pitch-black night. It took about three seconds for their free fall to pick up enough speed that the pressure of the air-resistance against his body could be converted to some sense of direction by his disoriented brain.

By the time Kyle had managed to come out of his tumble, his NODs had adjusted their electronic irises, and he spotted two blotchy figures relatively close by, their IR beacons showing clearly. One, he knew was Hans just due to the size of the figure. He flashed an upturned thumb and got a response from both as he spotted the fourth member of his team below them. The light green ghost image came out of a tuck and managed to go flat, belly down for the ride in. So far, so good. He checked his altimeter and it read "7.5," seventy-five hundred feet to go.

"Everybody good to go?" he asked loudly over the sound of the air rushing past. One issue no one had bothered to fix yet was the noise-canceling ability of their earbuds and mics; they still didn't work for shit in free fall.

"Three, good," Hans answered after waiting an appropriate time for Carlos's response.

"Four, good," Dom answered immediately.

"Carlos?"

"You better hope my chute doesn't open."

Fair enough, Kyle thought. "Popping at three K." He scanned the ground, which looked identical to the pitch-black sky except for the occasional individual light scattered here and there. Miles to the north, the lights of the Kaerin base at Wooton Creek were visible, as was the broader though dimmer glow from the more distant Portsmouth, across the small channel separating the Isle of Wight from the mainland.

"OK, on my mark, Dom, you're up first."

"Ready."

Kyle's eyes were glued to the glowing altimeter on his wrist. "Now," he yelled. They'd all pulled into a fairly level plane respective to one another. In the view from his night vision, Dom was jerked up and out of their small formation. The moment his chute deployed, Hans disappeared as well and Carlos right after. Kyle waited only long enough to confirm that Carlos's chute was open before setting his jaw and pulling his own chute.

Once he'd stabilized and was riding his "wing," he popped an IR chem light attached to the bundle of gear strapped between his legs and hit the release on the equipment. He let the cord play out through his gloves, until the slack went out of it and he could feel the tension from its weight in his harness. He looked up above him and could see the rest of his team having already done the same. They could now follow him in. He adjusted his path slightly towards the large dark spot in the earth which should, if his orientation was correct, be planted fields several miles south of their target.

Kyle prayed for a soft, empty, level field—preferably something nice, like clover or hay; free of rocks, trees, ditches, rivers, snakes, gopher holes, and two-legged bad guys who had scared the shit out of him every time he'd jumped at night. He didn't like heights, not at all. Every jump he'd made in his life had been accompanied by prayer and had been an act of sheer willpower. Nothing could have gotten him to admit it beforehand, but Carlos was right; this was "no *bueno*."

*

Over the North Sea, Chandra

Jeremy had a feeling; today was the day. They'd spotted the two large Kaerin paddle wheelers on radar in the late afternoon of the previous day, just as the enemy vessels had turned out of the North Sea and started up the Humber Estuary. Creight coast watchers and even an EDF detachment had been detailed to watch the ships from land. Everyone had thought the Kaerin warriors aboard were going to be off-loaded, but the ships had only anchored for the night. The same EDF contingent had reported an hour ago that the Kaerin ships were heading back out to sea. The new assumption was that the Kaerin would try for the River Wear or perhaps the Tyne.

The E.N. *Constitution*, under Captain Harper, was waiting for them on the North Sea. Jeremy was waiting as well, ten thousand feet overhead. The drone from the Caravan's powerful 850-horsepower engine was a comforting sound as he cruised slowly in a broad circle at a sedate 160 mph.

"Air One—*Constitution*, we have surface contacts twelve miles due east of Scarborough Bay. We are fourteen miles north of them and moving to intercept. Request your time on station."

Jeremy looked over at Dee, who was sharing the cockpit with him. She had the map laid on her lap. "Plenty of fuel," he said. "Tell them we've got two hours to play with."

"That's only thirty miles from us." Dee nodded. "We can be there long before the boat can."

"It's a ship," he countered with a smile. "And we only have one missile. We're clean up, Dee. And only if needed. Tell them we will stay out of visual range until we are ordered in."

"*Constitution*—Air One." He listened to Dee's communication, aware that his two passengers in the back were hanging in the narrow cockpit door. "Fuel status is green, two plus hours. We are approaching area and will stay out of visual range of enemy. You should have visual on us in a couple of minutes."

"Copy Air One, be advised. Stay below enemy visual horizon. This is our surprise."

He shared a look with Dee, who rolled her eyes. "Copy *Constitution*." Dee slammed the mic back into its holder. "By the way, and in case you didn't hear, don't get spotted by the Kaerin."

"Navy," said a voice from behind him as he put the plane into a shallow dive. Carl Doherty was their weapons officer and looked old enough to be a grandfather to either him or Dee. Carl had supposedly been the guy who had figured out how to jury-rig the Eden-produced version of the Maverick AGM (air-to-ground missile) to aircars during the war with the Strema. He operated the weapons station mounted to the bulkhead behind Jeremy's seat and was in sole control of the naval strike version of the same missile turned out by the nano-plants on Eden. "The sailors are probably scared shitless that they might have to ask for our help."

"Let me guess?" Dee asked over the crew channel. "You must have been in the Army."

"Army? Godless heathens, all of them. I did three years in the Air Force after high school, paid for most of my college while your parents were still learning to read."

"Air Force?" Dee almost turned around in her seat. "So, you've done something like this before?"

Carl smiled back at the young copilot and shook his head. "Closest I ever got to an airplane in the Air Force was picking up cigarette butts off a runway or changing the light bulbs in the pilot's briefing room. This is new to me as well."

"Oh . . ."

Carl took a moment to enjoy the surprised worry on the young girl's face. "Relax. I spent thirty years working on missiles and avionics for just about every defense contractor we had." Carl shrugged. "Or have. I suppose they're still there. Don't worry, this will work."

*

E.N. *Constitution*

"I hope this works." Captain Amelia Harper was sitting in "her" chair next to the young man driving the ship, looking at the two blips on her surface radar. The *Constitution* had closed to within seven miles of the two massive paddle wheelers. She'd studied up as much as time allowed on old naval databases. The closest Earth analogues to the seagoing Kaerin paddle wheelers were among the first steam-powered warships produced on Earth, around the time of the Crimean War. The Kaerin versions resembled the four-hundred-foot behemoths that had been used to lay down the first transatlantic telegraph cables following the US Civil War.

"Captain?"

"Just praying that we get in range and launch before they can get radio messages out."

"We're not sure they even have radios, Captain." Kent Bower had been recruited by the Eden Navy from the fishing fleet working out of Astoria on Eden. He wasn't any more experienced in a naval position than she was, but his boat-handling skills with the eighty-five-foot patrol boat were superb.

"I think it's safer to assume that they do, don't you?"

"Yes, ma'am."

Her pilothouse reminded her more of her high school computer lab than one of the trawlers she was comfortable with. The front glacis was sloped ballistic glass to give her a fantastic view of the relatively calm, for once, North Sea. Three high-backed chairs sat in a row surrounded by computer monitors. She'd spent a solid portion of her life in and around ships, but it had taken her weeks to get familiar with the controls and readouts that she'd never seen before.

She glanced at the "Weapons Status" screen above her left knee—that was new to her. Cod and tuna didn't require anti-ship missiles. Laser lock and terminal guidance weren't terms that she'd ever heard of five months ago. At the moment, they were foremost in her mind.

"Weapons." She didn't have to raise her voice: the weapons officer, Sanjay Pratha, sat on the far side of Ensign Bower. The pilothouse was well insulated from the two massive marine diesels pushing them through the water at a leisurely 20 knots. "Activate laser designator, targets are twenty degrees to starboard."

"Aye, Captain, target acquisition is now active."

"Open her up, Ensign Bower. Bring us up to thirty knots."

She reached for the radio, which was the one piece of equipment on the bridge that she hadn't needed to be trained on. "Air One, *Constitution*. We are starting attack run on target. Do you have visual on target?"

"*Constitution*, Air One. Negative visual on target. We have visual on *Constitution*, and smoke from targets. Maintaining distance."

"Copy Air One, be ready to move in when you see our launch. We'll be counting on you for . . ."

"PSR, Captain," Ensign Bower spoke up next to her.

That's right—post strike reconnaissance, she knew that. "Counting on you to let us know how we did. Be ready to engage if needed. You are weapons free after our launch."

She listened to the read-back of her orders even as the lookout on the flying bridge above the conn reported in over the PA. "I've got two black smoke trails. Thirty degrees to starboard."

She could see them as well. They were there with a suddenness that surprised her. "Swing to port, Mr. Bower. Loop us in; I want two clear broadsides to look at. Just like we practiced. Kick it in the ass."

"Aye, Captain."

The whine of the diesel turbines could be felt through the deck plating as the ship came up out of the water on its planes and actually rode a little smoother than it had a moment ago. She glanced at their own speed as the gauge ticked past 40 knots and kept climbing.

"All hands, man weapon stations. Target bearing off starboard bow, we will be turning in." She prayed the two 25mm chain guns wouldn't be needed.

It took longer than she thought it would until she could see the two ships without her binoculars.

"Captain, we have laser lock on both targets." Ensign Pratha at the weapons station had said his job was easier than a lot of computer games he'd played growing up. The "kid" was almost grinning.

"Range?"

"Four and a half miles—closing."

The *Constitution*'s anti-ship missiles were an improved version, modeled after something called the Griffin. That had meant nothing to her during the training. She knew they followed a laser beam to the target, and they had a five-mile range. There were better missiles coming, fire-and-forget jobs that had their own radar guidance, but that was waiting on bigger ships.

"Two missiles per target, Weapons Free."

"Firing."

Jeremy watched as the *Constitution* fired its four missiles in quick succession. The ship was moving so fast below him, the smoke blooms from the missile launches left behind a trail of what looked like four massive cotton balls being towed on a line behind the ship.

"Hold this altitude," Doherty spoke over the plane's crew channel.

He glanced at his altimeter: twenty-five hundred feet. He added throttle. There wasn't any point in trying to stay hidden at this point. He left the *Constitution* well behind and flew on towards the target.

"Approach the ships on the same line as the missiles." Doherty was in command of his airplane at the moment, and there was something comforting in that. "Watch them go in."

"I can't see them."

"You won't." Doherty sounded far too calm for someone who hadn't done this before. "Watch the targets. Five or six seconds more."

He "saw," sort of, the first missile strike on the Kaerin vessel closest to him. He definitely saw it exit out the other side of the wooden-hulled vessel and explode twenty or thirty yards past the target.

"Holy shit!" he yelled. "It went right through it."

The second missile did the same thing, managing to explode just as it exited. Jeremy had no trouble seeing the splatter of ship wood fly out in all directions.

"They are exploding too late."

"I warned them about the fuses," Doherty growled.

The third missile passed clean through the second ship directly amid ship and didn't explode at all. Jeremy was still tracking it as it plunged into the waves and exploded half a mile past the ship.

The last missile hit something solid. The back half of the second Kaerin vessel erupted with a gout of black boiling smoke laced with fire at its core. "That's a hit!"

The rear half of the ship looked like some prehistoric sea creature had leaped out of the water and taken a bite out of it. Forward of that, fires were burning. Wood might not detonate a missile very easily, but it did burn. Jeremy ignored the figures he could see jumping off the ship and others pointing upward at him and raising their rifles. One paddle wheel was still turning as the crippled vessel turned its bow towards land.

"I've got a lock." Doherty's voice overrode the report he was about to make. "Point us directly at the undamaged ship."

He only had to adjust his controls slightly. "Done."

"Firing."

There was a metallic click, and they all felt the big Cessna lurch as it was suddenly free of the six-hundred-pound Maverick missile it had been carrying underneath its fuselage between the two pontoon floats. Jeremy knew Doherty had a bird's-eye view from the missile itself by way of his launch control system. He was relegated to watching its flight path through the windscreen. For a moment, he wondered if the missile was going to overfly the target. It suddenly dropped out of its graceful arc and powered down directly at the relatively undamaged paddle wheeler.

The explosion obscured the ship from view for nearly five seconds until he had flown onward enough to give him a clear broadside view. The explosion had erased most of the wooden ship from the pilothouse aft down to the waterline, and still managed to punch a massive hole through the bottom of the ship. Jeremy was looking at a large, smoking raft of wreckage still somehow attached to its bow. A moment later, what remained of the vessel rolled over. Of the bodies he could see in the water around the ship, very few were moving.

"*Constitution*—Air One. One ship destroyed; the southernmost ship is still afloat. One paddle wheel in operation. It looks to be listing. Missiles hit, but did not explode. I say again, did not explode."

"Copy, Air One." Amelia spoke into the mic as she held her field glasses up to her face. "We saw that. Moving in to finish second vessel. Stay on orbit." *Finish the second vessel?* She'd sounded so clinical. She swallowed hard to fight the gorge rising from her stomach at what she was about to do.

"Get us in close, Mr. Bower. Weapons Free, take out anything that looks like a radio mast, and then punch holes in her at the waterline."

"Looks to be a lot of survivors, Captain."

No, there didn't, she told herself. The water temperature was just above 40 degrees Fahrenheit this time of year, and they were ten or eleven miles from the nearest shore. Some of those Kaerin warriors might be lucky enough to cling to wreckage long enough to make it to shore somewhere. If they did, it would be somebody else's problem. She wasn't about to order her people to strafe survivors or to put the same crew at risk bringing survivors onboard. Her job was to kill their ship; she would do that.

She forced herself to watch as the 25mm chain guns cut through the wooden hull like scissors on paper. Water pressure against the hull did the rest as she saw the gray-green water rush inward through numerous rents. One enemy gun crew was on deck, trying to bring the barrel of their cannon in line with the strange-looking, relatively tiny ship shooting at them. She watched their entire gun carriage slide backwards with the list of the ship. The Kaerin warriors managed to scramble out of the way in time to avoid being crushed.

The explosion of the enemy's boilers caught her by surprise. It opened up the back end of the paddle wheeler almost halfway to the pilothouse. Within moments, the nose of the Kaerin's ship was 20 degrees out of the water as it was being pulled down by the stern. Wooden ships did indeed sink, especially when they were full of iron and seawater. They'd told her that during training. Part of her hadn't believed it.

"Cease fire." She turned back to look at her command crew. "Did we see any spike on the shortwave scanner?"

"Nothing, Captain," Ensign Pratha related. "Nothing that looked like an antenna on this target. Unknown if the other ship carried a radio."

"Very good. Ship's yours, Mr. Bower. Get us home; make sure to call off our eye in the sky."

*

Chapter 23

North of Portsmouth, Chandra

Hank was happy for once, to be driven, or in this case flown, by an aide. He could pay attention to what he was seeing as the aircar followed a graveled road built by the Junata for their Kaerin overlords. All roads in England, or Caledonia as the Jema referred to it, led to Portsmouth/Irinas. The EDF's advance had reached its stepping-off point and was quickly recombining at three points, forming an arc north of their target. His compad map showed the rally points as the towns of Owlesbury, Petersfield, and Heyshott, three English towns that didn't exist on Chandra. They had labeled the three forces West, North, and East Groups respectively.

The Kaerin hunting parties had been dealt with, and the entire northernmost swath of the agricultural belt surrounding Portsmouth was now behind them and under control. The Junata farmers they had bypassed weren't presenting a security problem. What he liked to think of as his civilian "hearts and minds" team was made up of Edenite civilians, Creight, and a few Jema women. Some of the latter had reported for duty with infants strapped to their chests or in strollers while they carried assault rifles. The civilians were doing everything they could to reassure the Junata that the strange warriors who had marched through their farms were headed to Portsmouth to fight Kaerin.

"We've had more than a few Junata who have asked to join the fight," Hank said to Jomra. They were overflying a farming village. He could see several pickup trucks, an airtruck, and most importantly a white flag flying over the largest building in the small settlement. The flag let them know the settlement was in friendly hands.

"It is a good sign," Jomra answered. "I caution you though." Jomra pulled his own gaze back from the window and turned to face him in the back seat of the aircar. "The Junata in the city, those under the eyes of the Kaerin, will not share that attitude. They will fight us until there are no more Kaerin to drive them."

"If we weren't relying on surprise, and if the Junata could read, we'd do a leaflet drop. Let them know who we are and what we are trying to do."

"If?" Jomra smiled. "Your people use this word a lot, but I have never seen you engage in this Edenite habit of . . . pretending things were different?"

"We call it wishful thinking." Hank smiled. "It's a disease, Jomra. I've seen firsthand what wishful thinking does at the strategic level. My country's political leaders on Earth let it define their stance towards the rest of the world for half a century. If they were here, they'd be trying to convince us that Kaerin don't deserve the war we are waging on them."

"I am pleased those Terrans are not here." Jomra smiled.

"Me too." Hank nodded and pointed out the front of the aircar. "What about the Kaerin civilians?" He held up a hand to stop what he knew Jomra was going to say. "I know all their men are under arms, and the retirees are what we would call reservists, but what about their women? Their children? It's a Kaerin city we are going to attack. We'd both be engaged in wishful thinking to assume they won't fight. If they are anything like your Jema women . . ."

"We had no contact with Kaerin women." Jomra shrugged. "I do not know if they will fight. Elisabeth believes they will not, at least not in an organized fashion."

"I read her analysis." Hank nodded. "I guess I'm asking whether you agree with it?" He wasn't at all surprised that Jomra had read the report as well. The man devoured everything he could get his hands on. Elisabeth had looked at the limited data they had collected from their contact with the Hatwa, Creight, and the recently "rescued" Jehavian farmers. Elisabeth believed the dominant Kaerin social structure had been imprinted, or hammered more like, in his opinion, onto the indigenous Chandrian cultures. And so far, with all the clans they'd had contact with, the women worked and raised children. The men served in the subject host and fought. As in so many ways, the Jema were the exception, not the rule. Cultural genocide would do that to a people.

"Her conclusions make sense to me, but as your people often say, the proof is in the pudding." Jomra grunted to himself. "I was surprised to learn that saying makes no sense to you people either, yet you use it."

Hank nodded in agreement. "Whatever it means, you used it correctly."

Jomra shook his head. "As to the other half of your question, we do not make war on children, even Kaerin children."

"Your people have never attacked a city." Hank shook his head in response. "For that matter, none of the EDF outside of a few veterans have either. Trust me on this; it's a special kind of hell. If it goes on long enough, some of the guns pointing back at us will have kids behind them. The biggest danger is what it will do to our own people."

"You are not doubting our commitment?"

Hank wanted to laugh at that. But Jomra was fully in his formal mode of speech, and it would have been out of place. "The Jema's commitment is something we could never doubt. We are with you in this, to the end. I don't have a doubt we will take Portsmouth, Jomra. The question I have is; when it comes time to make a decision that will affect the broader war on the Kaerin, will you be willing to trust me if my decision looks like mercy?"

"Mercy? For the Kaerin?"

"You know the word 'contingency'?"

"Planning for a wide range of outcomes?" Jomra's eyebrow went up in an arch. "We have done this, yes?"

"We have." Hank nodded. "But this morning, I thought of a possible opportunity that may present itself." Hank shook his head. "It will look like mercy, and it sure as hell will feel like it to us. But trust me, if I go in that direction, for the Kaerin it will be a knife between their ribs."

"That sounds . . . better," Jomra acknowledged, after a long pause in which he was worried whether Jomra would dig in his heels. "The Jema have never had to worry about anything that we could not see past our rifle sights. We are learning what we can about strategy. Until then, we have no alternative but to trust you."

"It is not a trust we will abuse."

Jomra gave a solemn nod. "As the Jema's leader, I never dreamed I would be in a position to trust another people again. I am thankful I can do so without misgivings."

Their aircar was approaching the outskirts of the North Group's encampment. There was no town here as his compad map said there should be, just a small group of Junata farm buildings, and a lot of planted fields surrounded by forested hilltops that had never been cleared for cultivation. Most of the twenty thousand soldiers of the North Group and their vehicles were hidden under the trees.

Jomra barked a short laugh and sat forward, signaling that he was dispensing with formality. "Speaking of trust, Audrin'ochal trusts that Jake's plan to map the enemy city will work."

Hank was confused for a moment. He knew Audy and Jake were riding wagons into the city in the company of the Jehavian Gemendi they'd co-opted. They were going to try and geo-tag target sites before riding back out to join the EDF for the assault.

"Jake had told me, it was Audy's plan."

Jomra just looked back at him for a moment in confusion and then barked another laugh. "I think those two trust each other more than they do the two of us."

*

"This plan of yours better work," Jake muttered before hopping down off the wagon.

"My plan?" Audy took half a step towards him, whispering. "You said we needed to survey the city."

Jake nodded in response and clapped Audy on the shoulder. "And you came up with a good plan; at least it better be."

Breda stepped between them and hissed in Chandrian, "You two must stop speaking that . . . other tongue." It had taken some doing to convince Hank and particularly Doc Jensen to allow Breda to accompany them. But the Kaerin writ the little Gemendi carried was the golden hall pass they needed to wander the city. Without it, Audy and Breda had assured Jake they would be stopped. The best thing that would happen then, was that they would be ordered to report to a work crew; the worst was that they'd be questioned. Nothing good would come of that.

The Kaerin guards at the gate hadn't even looked at the empty wagon as it had rolled through the city gates on the northern edge of the city. They were just one in a double line of similar wagons going in both directions. If the Kaerin suspected they were about to be attacked, they hid it very well.

Audy had parked the wagon in a marshaling yard adjacent to some warehouses. The entire area was full of Junata laborers and wagons in the process of being loaded or unloaded. Breda had recognized it as where Eg'as had started from. The Gemendi hadn't known the first thing about driving horses, and had taken offense at Jake's assumption that he should. It had fallen on Audy to drive the borrowed wagon and horses from where the rest of their West Group contingent waited, ten miles northwest of the city.

"Ai there, you are the one that went out to Sverat, with Eg'as?" A tall Junata shouted with an air of authority as he pushed his way through the crowd. "Was there trouble with the road?"

"No trouble," Breda said confidently. "The High Bloods at Sverat needed the wagons for a few days; he will be late returning."

The Junata shook his head in what might have been disgust but seemed to accept the answer. The man's lean face scrunched up in confusion. "Wait! . . . how is it that you have returned. I had not expected Eg'as for another two days. Did you fly?"

"Actually, I did," Breda answered truthfully. Jake and Audy exchanged a look of shock with each other behind the little Gemendi. Breda reached into his belt and withdrew his Kaerin writ, and shoved it up under the nose of the Junata. "The High Bloods put us on horses and escorted us back to a farm where they ordered us to bring this wagon in. Leave it here; we will be back shortly for it."

The Junata's eyes had gotten big at the sight of the writ. "Can I at least move it out of the way?"

"Just make certain it is not blocked in." Breda sounded to Jake, like somebody who was used to bossing people around."

The yard master jerked his head once in acknowledgement. It was clear he wasn't used to taking orders from anyone outside a High Blood in *his* cargo yard. "It will be waiting for you over there." The man pointed to a warehouse with closed doors.

"See that it is." Breda tapped the writ against the man's chest. "Or the High Blood that wrote this, will know why." Jake smiled as the Junata jerked back as if the writ were electrified and started shouting orders at somebody to move the wagon.

"I've got to get me one of those," Jake said in Chandrian, eyeing the writ as Breda prominently displayed it hanging off his belt.

"It will not work if we get stopped by a High Blood," Audy pointed out.

Jake had a small GPS transceiver bandaged to his shoulder under his tunic, with a wire running down his sleeve to a button in his left hand. He'd pushed it as they rode through the gate. He planned on geo-tagging a lot more before they got the hell out of this city. He clapped a hand on Breda's shoulder and gave it a friendly squeeze. "Don't get stopped by a High Blood."

"See that pile of rolled-up carpets?" Breda pointed to where they were being unloaded. "We are going to walk over there, and you two are going to throw one over your shoulders. Do not say a word. Just do it. I'll handle the Junata."

Jake glanced over at Audy in question. Audy rolled his eyes and then nodded. "I believe I understand what he is thinking. We will be beasts of burden; he is the one with the writ. It will give us a . . . story to sell as we make our way through the city."

Jake eyed the heavy-looking carpet. "Not all it's going to give us."

"Seriously?!," Jake growled three hours later. His end of the carpet had been on his right shoulder the entire time. He wasn't sure if his neck would ever be able to hold his head straight again. "You're sure this is the most direct route to the Citadel?" He was convinced Breda had been taking the long way through the city to each of the targets he had given the little man. First, he had him walk them along a section of the northern wall, then they'd cut through the center of the city to the waterfront, and Jake had mashed the button on the GPS marker next to each building that looked like it was full of Kaerin. Which was most of them - there were High Bloods everywhere.

Not one of them had bothered to stop them. All they saw were two slaves carrying a load between them, led by somebody who must have looked like he knew where he was going. They'd made a wide circle around the fortified building that looked to be the headquarters or something important for the naval forces centered around the docks.

Breda slowed a step and looked around him before speaking. "I am NOT sure," he almost yelled. "This is my second time in this cursed place, and the first time lasted half a day. I am not from here, you ungrateful, thick-headed . . . giant."

Jake smiled to himself. He'd recognized straight away that Breda had some serious attitudinal flavor; they all had. Jake put it down to a bad case of the Napoleon complex; the Gemendi might never have heard of Napoleon but he couldn't have been more than five feet four in the boots he wore. He found that he kind of liked the disagreeable runt. As far as Jake was concerned, the fact that Breda was uncomfortable walking around the Kaerin city was a good sign.

Jake let the insult go. "Don't get your panties twisted up, little man. You're doing good. Just get us past the front walls of the Garrison's Citadel, and then head back to the main gate."

"What does the word 'panties' mean?"

"Jake . . ." Audy growled a warning behind him. Jake wanted to turn and look back, but oh yeah, he had a hundred pounds of carpet on his shoulder, and he couldn't move his head.

"I will explain it later," Jake wheezed. "Just get us there."

"Why are we doing this?" Breda's tone changed to something a little more respectful. "What does this walking in circles accomplish?"

"I promise, when we attack, you'll see."

"You will allow me to fight?" Breda's tone changed to something that sounded like chastisement to him. "David Jensen said you must return me to him when we are finished here."

"You want to stay with us, you can stay. We don't really listen to our Gemendi here." Jake offered him a big smile. "They worry too much."

*

"Where the hell are they going?" Doc Jensen sat hunched over his laptop, ignoring Hank and Jomra looking over his shoulder. He been integrating Jake's geo-tag markers and overlaying them onto the digital map he'd produced using the satellite images. Getting the *Door Knocker* where it needed to go did not require the very precise targeting "other" applications did. The GPS system they'd built into their nascent satellite network used geographic data taken from Earth, by way of Eden. Those worlds' geography were nearly identical. Anyone looking at a map of Chandra could have been forgiven for assuming it was an identical match as well. The computer program running the GPS program said it wasn't, and it had been driving him crazy.

It had taken him two days of coffee-fueled calculations and searching lines of code in the GPS software until he'd figured it out. The forty-three feet of deviation from where things on Chandra should be and where they actually were had a very simple explanation. The continents weren't where they were supposed to be. Throughout the eons of tectonic drift, Chandra's Atlantic Ocean had somehow grown slightly faster than the analogues on Earth and Eden had; forty-three feet faster.

Jensen was willing to bet the Pacific was slightly smaller on Chandra as well. Once they'd completed the satellite network over Asia and the Pacific, he could put that to the test. Right now, the GPS markers that Jake and Audy were putting down were recalibrating the network for pinpoint targeting.

"Their signal looks to be headed in the direction of the Citadel," Jomra pointed out. "Why do they not go across the central square? It is much more direct."

"Jake's probably stopping along that waterfront to ask how the fishing is." Hank motioned to the laptop. "Any geo-tag from Kyle and his team?"

"Nothing yet, I have their signal." Jensen manipulated the laptop until the image changed to the Isle of Wight. "They haven't moved since the sun came up. You want to risk calling them?"

"Not yet." Hank shook his head. Kyle's GPS transceiver had him just on the outskirts of the Kaerin air field at Wooton Creek. "He's probably waiting for nightfall. Son of a bitch! I hate sitting here staring at maps."

"We are all waiting for nightfall," Jomra announced.

*

Chapter 24

Isle of Wight, Chandra

No plan survives contact with the enemy. The old adage always turned up. He'd never been on an "op" where it hadn't. Kyle and his team had buried their parachutes in the middle of the field they'd landed in and made it cross-country to the outskirts of the Wooton Creek base before sunrise. There, they'd quickly discovered that the base's radio tower was on top of, not adjacent to as the satellite image had seemed to show, the large building lying in between the small harbor and the base's airfield.

Worse, the bottom floor of the building was the barracks where between a hundred and 150 Kaerin warriors slept. But not all of them; there had been more than a dozen warriors patrolling the perimeter in pairs throughout the night. It was too soon to risk discovery. The goal was to take out Wooton Creek's radio tower at the same time the radio tower across the straight in Portsmouth was destroyed. Anything else risked a message getting out. Their goal was to surgically remove Kaerin control of Portsmouth without anybody being the wiser for as long as possible.

"We are going to create a diversion that should let us get the drone in place." Kyle spoke into his phone. Dom was next to him in one of the muddy drainage ditches that spider-webbed the area adjacent to the landing strip. Carlos and Hans were in the next ditch over, keeping an eye on their target.

"We are shooting for twenty-two hundred hours local. When they react, we'll use the drone to deliver the GPS transceiver and mark the target building. Once you have that target data. Give us two minutes to clear and then start the music."

"Copy all," Hank came back. "Doc Jensen left for Seattle an hour ago to get everything ready at the portals. Will your diversion be visible from Portsmouth?"

He knew Hank was worried that Portsmouth's radio could report something happening on Wooten just as easily as the reverse. He looked up at Dom, who was nodding in an emphatic "yes."

"Affirmative," he answered. "You'll be able to see it as well. Recommend you start the attack on Portsmouth with our diversion. These guys here are going to be too busy to get on their radio. We'll ground the airplanes here, and the Navy should be able to bottle up this shitty little marina. We do not see an immediate need to portal in an assault force to this location during the attack. They'll be left here watching across the water with their dicks in hand."

"Understood," Hank replied. "Just make certain you get your asses out of there before we deliver our presents." *No shit*, Kyle thought. He almost said it out loud, but Hank had been exactly where he was now, enough to know how this worked. "Once you send all clear from your exfil site," Hank continued, "we'll extract you by aircar, and you can join the party here."

"Sounds like a plan."

"Godspeed, Kyle."

He hung up and looked at Dom, who had a hand placed against his ear, listening to their tactical radio.

"Carlos has eyes on two Kaerin, walking out past the end of the runway. He says they are carrying shotguns."

"Shotguns?"

Dom shrugged. "He said they look like they are going hunting."

He turned his radio back on and checked his watch. It was 1820 hours. "Carlos? The two hunters? Are they wearing their uniforms?"

"I have served under worse bastelta than Per'tala," Teark Aleen'as answered the recently transferred Dadus Gos'san. "And a few who were better," he admitted. Gos'san had transferred from the mainland and been assigned to his fist a ten-day past. The dadus had asked his advice on how to "handle" Bastelta Per'tala. He knew the real reason for Gos'san's worry; the man had been in for nine years. If he was not selected for teark by his tenth year, Gos'san would remain a dadus until he retired in another fifteen. Teark Per'tala held Gos'san's future in his hands. The last thing he wanted to share his evening hunt with was a dadus full of worry and complaints. Still, he was the man's teark. It fell to him to set Gos'san straight.

Gos'san stopped for a moment and looked back over his shoulder towards the garrison at the far end of the runway. "I am starting to wonder what I could have done to offend him. I have not failed in any tasking."

Aleen'as gave his head a shake, beginning to understand why Gos'san was still a dadus. "You think he does not know you have begun your tenth year? He will push you. More, he will make certain I push you. The bastelta will be wanting to know if you have talents that have been overlooked, or if he just needs to back the decision of your last bastelta."

"May not matter what he thinks." Gos'san flashed him a knowing smile that told Aleen'as the troublesome dadus was not listening to him. "The rumors around Tellas have us getting ready for something big," Gos'san continued. "There might be more teark positions opening up."

Those rumors had reached Irinas as well. Kareel Ist'arno had briefed all the bastelta in Irinas nearly two ten-days past and word had filtered down amongst the tearks. Something was in the offing, but there had not been anything other than rumors since. Some of those rumors did not warrant serious attention. Chandra was being invaded by another world? Personally, he thought that was as believable as the one that said ghosts of the Jema had returned.

"If you think Per'tala would name you ahead of other deserving warriors just because you are in your tenth year, you don't deserve the rank."

"That is not what I meant."

Yes, it was. Aleen'as himself, had been promoted from dadus to teark in his sixth year; and that had been ten years ago. He had seen it all. If there was one thing he had learned to smell over the years, it was warriors whose ambitions far outmatched their judgment and abilities. Gos'san, he decided then and there, fell squarely into that bucket. He was already wondering which finger to assign Gos'san to, knowing it would probably be a disservice to the four Dadu Gos'san would have authority over. "Give it time," he advised. "It will happen, or it will not. We all serve."

"We all serve," Gos'san responded out of reflex and marched along the edge of the field. "I appreciate you speaking to me in confidence."

"You are in my fist," Aleen'as answered, already wondering if he could somehow convince a fellow teark to trade Gos'san for another troublemaker. He was certain Gos'san was the type who was going to be an even bigger problem when he did not get promoted. The kind of problem that ate away at the fist. "Besides, I truly thought we would have scared up a hen or two by now. They nest out in here in the grass along the ditches."

"My bad luck continues," Gos'san whined.

"There is no such thing as bad luck in my fist," Aleen'as said proudly. "See that grass moving up ahead?"

Head shots weren't advised unless you were in close and had the time in a tactical sense to aim carefully; or, just for argument's sake, you wanted to wear the uniforms attached to the aforementioned heads. Carlos and Hans fired their suppressed rifles almost simultaneously. A flight of some kind of partridge burst out of the tall ditch-grass behind them.

Carlos jerked around at the frenzied wing beats and then let out a long breath. "Must have been what they were hunting."

They belly-crawled forward through the thigh-high grass until they were adjacent to the two Kaerin bodies and began stripping their uniforms off. "You ever wonder who they are?" Hans asked, coming up on one knee. "I mean, are these two cooks? Infantry? Maybe they were buddies or second cousins or something."

Carlos stopped what he was doing and just looked back at Hans over the two bodies. "No, not ever."

"Me? I'm always curious," Hans admitted.

"That doesn't make it harder for you?"

Hans pursed his lips and thought about it for a moment before giving his head the slightest shake. "No, never."

"You're a lucky man, Hans."

*

"I still would have preferred you on overwatch." Kyle looked over at Carlos, dressed as he was in Kaerin High Blood fashion, long sword and all. Everything but their boots was courtesy of the two Kaerin hunters. If there was something to worry about, they both carried Kaerin shotguns and not the large-bore elephant guns carried by every other High Blood they'd observed.

Carlos thumbed his tunic. "Well, seeing how Dom's a midget and Hans's a freaking wall, you didn't have a choice. We'll be all right; they can both shoot."

Kyle nodded in agreement. Carlos saying someone else could shoot was high praise. They walked out into the open at the midway point of the short grass runway and turned towards the airplanes parked at the garrison end of the runway. Nothing to see here; just two Kaerin returning late from a hunt, empty-handed. Except that wasn't exactly true.

"Radio check." Kyle had his radio channel open. If something happened, he needed Hans and Dom to know it.

"Five by five," Dom's voice came back in his ear. "We have you in sight. And tell Carlos that I am the tallest person in my family. I'm one point seven meters."

"Use whatever system you want." Carlos laughed. "You're still short."

"Heads up," Kyle hissed. He'd just seen two Kaerin step onto the runway ahead of them, near where three large biplanes sat parked. The half-moon hanging in the sky shone brightly for the first time in what seemed like two weeks. The one night they could do with total darkness, and the weather had cleared. "We've got incoming," Kyle whispered. He didn't think the guards had spotted them yet.

"We see them," Dom responded. "Give the word."

"We've got them," Kyle answered. "Just let us know if another patrol pops up."

Dom responded with a single click.

"Straight at them," Kyle whispered.

"Yep," Carlos agreed. "If your shitty Chandrian manages to fool them, I'm betting my beautiful Chicano skin won't."

"We'll drop them before that," Kyle agreed, touching his chest where his suppressed 9mm was strapped on just below his sternum. The Kaerin tunic seemed almost tailor-made to make reaching for a concealed weapon possible. In no way did he think his Chandrian would fool a native, not for long at any rate. Besides, this was a relatively small detachment. Everyone probably knew or at least recognized everyone else. Two unfamiliar faces were going to raise questions before there was any chance for conversation.

"Can we just let them come to us?" Carlos asked. "These pants are eating my *juevos*."

Kyle couldn't disagree. The lower half of the Kaerin uniform was a heavy blend of wool and cotton, with what had to have been horsehair or maybe barbwire woven in. Chafing didn't begin to describe the discomfort. He adjusted the pocket-covered pants with a grunt of his own. He couldn't imagine marching far in these things.

"Just means we'll have to drag them farther."

"Good point . . ." Carlos agreed. "When you come up with high-level shit like that, I can understand why you were an officer. Portaling into midair? At night? Not so much."

"Not going to let that go, are you?"

"Nope."

"Teark Aleen'as?" The Kaerin on the right stopped twenty feet away. There was a submissive tone overriding the question that told Kyle and Carlos everything they needed to know. The Kaerin guards on patrol duty reported to the Kaerin teark whose uniform one of them was wearing. Kyle figured these guys knew their teark had gone hunting and now he was back, looking "different."

He just nodded in response, his hand already reaching for his 9mm. He was aware peripherally of Carlos doing the same. The two Kaerin fell against each other as they collapsed on their way to the ground and landed hard. Too hard; one of the guards must have had their finger on a trigger. The long rifle, its barrel pointing back towards the airplanes, fired—and shot a four-foot-long lance of fire and hot gas out the barrel.

"Shit!" Kyle muttered and ran forward, pulling the rifle away and stripping the ammunition bandolier from the nearest Kaerin.

"Head shot," Carlos diagnosed calmly as he hefted the Kaerin rifle that had fired and looked down at his victim. "Fingers are still twitching. You get that sometimes when the base of the brain remains whole," Carlos recited in a flat monotone, sounding like a doctor telling a patient the strep throat test had come back positive.

Kyle wished he didn't already know that particular fact, but he did. He knew Carlos wasn't trying to impart information; his friend was doing what he needed to do in order to shift emotional gears; observing as a third person, clinical and detached.

"No need to hide bodies," Kyle said as he removed the two remote-controlled charges he carried. "You ready? I'll take the plane on the left and the fuel tank. You get the other two planes."

Carlos fitted his own borrowed bandolier and removed the fist-sized charges of plastic explosive from his thigh pockets.

"Dom? Any movement?"

"A lot of heads came up," Dom reported in his ear. "Looks like you've got a single pair of guards headed your way up the hill from the barracks building. If you hurry, you can get to the planes ahead of them."

"Ready." Carlos came to his feet and slung the Kaerin rifle across his back for show, just like the swords they carried.

They took off at a run towards the planes sitting less than a hundred yards away. Shit! Surprise was their biggest ally, and the first real shot fired in this war had been delivered by a Kaerin whose brain hadn't realized he was already dead.

They split up, each taking a side of the runway where the biplanes were parked. Without knowing if the four engine planes were fueled or not, Kyle placed the first charge on the lip of the inboard engine. They only needed to disable the planes; the fuel tank sitting thirty yards away would be the signal rocket for the rest of the EDF across the narrow straight to begin their attack.

Kyle ducked underneath the big plane and watched as Carlos moved to his second plane. "Carlos, make for the fuel tank when you're done." He came up on his feet, already tired of lugging the extraneous Kaerin rifle around, and sprinted for the fuel tank. The Kaerin patrol coming up the hill from the garrison didn't have far to go and would be showing up any second.

He made it just in time. Carlos almost made it, but a shout from out of the darkness to their left had them both moving around the backside of the fuel tank. Kyle was certain of two things; the Kaerin couldn't see them right now, and behind a fuel tank was not a good place to hide.

Carlos tapped him on the shoulder. When he turned around, Carlos was holding up the detonator for his two charges.

"Dom, you guys have a shot on the patrol?"

"Negative, airplane in the way."

Kyle was looking at Carlos as he spoke into the radio. "When we blow the charges, you two hightail it directly to the exfil site. You won't be able to cover us down at the garrison. We're going to try and blend in." Carlos grinned back at him and held up his detonator.

Kyle pulled his handgun and inched farther around the backside of the tank. The fumes coming off the ground around him reminded him more of diesel than the high-octane kerosene smell of most airport aprons he was familiar with. He placed his last charge as high up on the tank as he could reach and then looked back at Carlos, motioning that they should go in opposite directions around the tank.

He waited just long enough for Carlos to make ready. "Blow it."

The two charges on the airplanes across the runway cracked almost simultaneously, shattering the pleasant evening. Kyle moved as fast as he could, hugging the steel tank. The two Kaerin guards, turned towards the burning planes, were outlined clearly. He dropped the one on the right with two shots in the middle of the back and had just switched targets and fired once when Carlos's shots landed.

"They're all coming your way," Dom yelled into his ear. "You've got about a minute to hide."

"Copy," Kyle shouted back. "You guys get moving. We'll be there as soon as we can." Kyle waved at Carlos and set off down the trail towards the barracks building, which was suddenly lit up by a yard light of some sort. They were close enough they could hear the shouted orders coming up the hill towards them.

He didn't want to push their luck. He angled off the road and plowed through the bushes lining either side of the road. An unseen limb nearly took his eye out and cut along his cheekbone. He slowed and went to the ground, lying on his belly as Carlos crashed through the underbrush and behind him.

"You going to wait until the crowd gathers?" Carlos breathed heavily next to him.

"Yep."

They didn't have to wait long. Two or three dozen Kaerin, half of them not even wearing shirts, surged by them on the road up to the landing field. They couldn't see the burning airplanes, but the glow from the fires gave them a good look at the Kaerin who had been rousted from their barracks. Kyle thought their response time was impressive.

Kyle waited a few more seconds and then mashed his thumb down on his detonator. The airplane he'd rigged went first, followed a moment later by the fuel tank. For a brief second, the night became brighter than day, and they both instinctively went flat. A half second later, the shock wave and sound of the raging bloom of fire rising overhead washed over them. Kyle glanced up and grinned. That fireball would easily be visible across the strait.

"OK, launch that sucker. Clock's ticking." Kyle looked over at Carlos, who held the small quad copter drone in one hand, looking straight up into the overhead tree cover.

"I need to get it out on the road, too much canopy here to launch it."

"Screw that." Kyle pulled on his sleeve and pointed farther into the bushes. "We go downhill, there's a stream right here running down the hill; canopy should open up above it."

*

Chapter 25

Hank would have seen the bloom of the explosion on the northern coast of the Isle of Wight even if he hadn't been watching for it; from his position atop a small hill two short miles north of Portsmouth's walls, it looked like the flash of a massive camera bulb that lit up the otherwise dark horizon. Which meant the Kaerin within the Portsmouth, along the waterfront or higher up within the central Citadel, could have seen it just as easily. He lifted his sat-phone, already linked to the portal room in Kirkton. His command to start the show had worlds to travel, but it wouldn't take long. "Drop now."

Ten seconds later, standing within the control room of New Seattle's portal room, David Jensen heard the telltale boom of someone's transit arrival outside the building. It could only be the courier from Kirkton they'd been waiting for. They'd set this process up and practiced it for the last week. One member of the courier team was waiting outside with a radio on the same channel as the one on the console in front of him.

"Drop now." The voice came through loud and clear.

Jensen took a look at the monitor showing the contents of the portal chamber and pressed the button. Four five-hundred-pound iron bombs, placed in each corner of the chamber, winked out of existence, at least on Eden. He'd sent them to Chandra, a thousand feet above their intended target, the radio tower atop the central Citadel in the center of Portsmouth.

He confirmed the portal doors were coming open; his team were already wheeling in the next load of bombs, this one 'only' two five-hundred-pounders. He picked up his compad and sent the "go" signal to the *Door Knocker*, ready and waiting on Whidbey Island. Eden's four other portal sites, at Whidbey Island, Japan, Northern Italy, and New Santiago in Chile, would get the same message. They all had bomb loads to deliver to preselected targets courtesy of Jake, Audy, and the Gemendi Breda. He watched the team of technicians working steadily to remove the bombs from their wheeled carriages as he waited on the next arrival from Chandra.

Ninety seconds was the best they'd been able to do in cycling the doors up, bringing a load in, getting the bombs off the carts onto the floor, and waiting for the door to seal. He checked his watch; it had been over three minutes and still no signal on the coordinates for the radio tower on the Isle of Wight.

"What's taking them so long?" Dr. Creighton, the English physicist, asked from the chair in front of the monitors. "Should we go to our next set of coords?"

"No," Jensen fired back. He'd been wondering the exact thing. He didn't need Creighton second-guessing him.

The now familiar boom of a translation arrival reached them through the walls of the building. His compad lit up a few seconds later with the coordinates collected by the satellite network over Chandra. The network of mini-sats had detected the signal from the transceiver emplaced by Kyle and his team. He handed his compad to Creighton, and watched him input the numbers, trying to convince himself that Kyle had enough time to get clear. He figured twenty to thirty seconds for the satellite network to pick up the signal and download the coords to Kirkton. The tech there would have spent a minute verifying the target coordinates against the original GPS settings from Eden and Earth, and a few seconds more handing off a compad to a portal courier and activating Kirkton's chamber.

Once on Eden, the transfer to his compad had occurred at the speed of e-mail. Creighton took about twenty seconds to enter the target location. David did the rough addition in his head, easy for someone who could speak math, and came to the conclusion that Kyle had better have been running ever since he'd emplaced the beacon two plus minutes ago. He pushed the button activating the portal. A brief flash of light was the only evidence that the bombs had been there a second ago.

"What was the range of that quad copter drone they had us rig up?" Creighton again.

"About a klick," he said, before remembering that this very room was probably the closest Creighton had ever been to being shot at. "Call it a thousand meters, but they would have made sure to get closer than that." He was a physicist; if there was one thing he was familiar with, it was the look on another math guy's face when he was doing calculations in his head, on the fly. He was watching as Creighton's eyebrows went up either in shock or appreciation.

"I'm sure they found cover."

*

Kyle and Carlos had started moving through the thick underbrush the second Carlos had sat the small drone down on the roof of the barracks building next to the antenna's base. If they'd run, they would have been seen or heard by the Kaerin who had filled the area between the target building and the burning airfield.

They both saw the hole in the ground at the same time and jumped in. There could have been punji sticks or poisonous snakes in the bottom of the muddy hole, and they wouldn't have hesitated. An oak tree had lost a battle with the wind some time ago and been ripped out of the ground, leaving a hole overhung by its massive root ball. Kyle landed hard on his side; Carlos crashed into his shoulder as they instinctively transformed themselves into the absolute smallest possible versions of themselves.

"Cover!" Kyle yelled out of ingrained training.

"No shit!" Carlos yelled back, followed by laughter muffled by the dirt pressed against his face.

How long had it been since they'd activated the GPS beacon? Kyle wondered if they should have kept moving a little while longer, when the world behind his eyelids went bright pink for a split second as the two five-hundred-pound bombs impacted the top of the barracks building at Wooten Creek. They had good cover from the fragmentation radius of the bombs; it was the blast radius and the shock wave racing up the hill that tried to pick them up and pull them from their hole. It passed over them in a flash that felt like something was trying to pull his brains out his nose and ears. It was followed a moment later by a sighing gush of wind that raced inward to fill the pressure void created by the explosion.

He lay there for a moment, telling himself that he was alive. He was pretty sure he'd pissed himself. He lifted his head slowly, making certain the bones in his neck were still whole. "You good?"

Carlos rolled slowly onto his back and looked over at him, his mud-caked face looking ghostlike in the view from his NOD monocle. "I'm too old for this shit."

"You and me both," Kyle agreed.

"You guys alright? Kyle? Carlos? Come back . . ." Dom's voice was ringing in his ear.

"We're good. Do you have eyes on the target?"

"Target destroyed," Dom reported. "You guys get moving. Stay in the trees until you get to the midpoint of the runway; then you should be clear to move to where we were set up. Every Kaerin we can see, which isn't very many, is headed back down to the harbor."

Kyle sat up, realizing that there was six inches of foul-smelling rainwater in the bottom of the hole. So, he hadn't pissed himself.

"Come on, Carlos. We just started a war."

"Yay . . . us," Carlos moaned.

*

Portsmouth

As the commander of Irinas, Kareel Glas Ist'arno had made it a point to walk the walls of the Citadel every evening. From the walls of the fortified keep at the center of the city, he could see, as he often thought, "both sides of his writ." He could look inward at the Citadel and see the High Bloods he commanded in Lord Atan'tal's name. He could look out over the city, and further out past the city walls to the square kamarks of productive manufactories and farms that produced the wealth that Lord Atan'tal's council reminded him "guaranteed his continued command of Irinas."

Two sides to his writ indeed. He was a Kareel now, and old enough to have lost the naïveté of a young warrior. It was the production of places like Irinas that enabled Lord Atan'tal to rule and maintain his seat on the prelate's High Council in Kaerus. For the last ten years, squeezing every bit of production from this place had been his primary task. But in the last two moons, that had begun to change. Lord Atan'tal was suddenly concerned regarding the readiness of his High Bloods. Something had happened, somewhere. The Kaerin were preparing for war, that much was for certain. The question was, against whom? Answers had been promised; he'd been ordered to fly down to Atan'tal's seat at Tellas in a ten-day for a gathering of garrison commanders.

Tellas was the jewel of the west. The city with the large estates, broad avenues, and lighted towers was where he wanted to be, not stuck out here on this rain-soaked island driving Junata slaves. A seat at Lord Atan'tal's conference table and an estate to call his own had been his lifelong ambition, and war was the quickest way to get there. Privately, he worried he had done his job too well. He came to a stop and stood between two merlons of the wall and looked down over the city and the fleet of fishing vessels filling Irinas's harbor. How much wealth had he pulled from this place? From the Junata? Could Atan'tal afford to send him to war?

What he took for lightning above the island of Irinas Ka caught his attention as the outline of the island was backlit by a glow that did not dissipate. Suddenly, there was a mushroom-shaped cloud of fire rising against the horizon across the five kamarks of water separating the Irinas waterfront from its guardian island. Then the rolling boom of sound reached his ears. It was not loud; it would not be given the distance. It was not lightning either.

He turned to yell for a messenger and spotted a warrior already running towards him along the top of the wall. "Get to the long-talker!" he shouted, the second the man was in earshot. "Find out what has happened on Irinas Ka!" There was a fuel tank at the landing field there; he could not imagine what else there could have exploded. An accident like this was not what he needed right now.

He watched the warrior bound down the steps two at a time before sprinting across the wide courtyard to the stone keep. The warrior had just disappeared inside through the torch- lined archway when Ist'arno's world flashed white. He was blown off his feet like a leaf in the wind and slammed into the battlement wall. The sound and heat from the explosion washed over him as he impacted the shoulder-high merlon. Something cracked loudly in his rib cage, and slammed into his arm before he slid down the inside of the battlement to the wall walk. The pain in his chest and back kept him conscious enough to see the towers of the keep collapsing in on themselves underneath a roiling black cloud made visible in the night sky by the fire within.

He choked and gagged on a mouthful of blood as he sucked in a hot lungful of air. Retching, he squeezed his rib cage and managed to push himself to his feet using the wall as support. Two flashes of light cracked ahead and behind him at either end of the long wall. An instant later, he felt the opposing explosions pulse through his body, driving him back to his knees. Something buzzed past his head like a bullet as he felt the wall shudder beneath him. Twenty strides wide at the base, five at the top; he had the strangest thought that such a thing could not move and remain standing.

Everything in sight within the Citadel, not made of stone, was on fire. The fires provided more than enough light that he could see the massive breach in the northwest corner of the Citadel's walls. Ahead of him, the corner tower was gone, and the walls nearly a hundred strides in either direction were a pile of rubble. Getting to his feet was an exercise of sheer will. His broken ribs threatened to impale him from the inside with each breath, and he was aware of the warm blood sheeting down one side of his face and dripping off his jawline.

Behind him, the southwest tower was gone as well, as was much of the southern wall. The remains of the western wall, upon which he stood, ran to a pile of rubble in either direction. The stone of the interior keep looked like a pile of children's blocks; in places, the rubble was piled nearly as high as his place on the wall. In the middle were craters void of nearly everything.

His first coherent thought was wondering who could have done this and how. His second thought was more of a hope; it seemed to have stopped. He let the wall hold him in place as he looked out over Irinas and the dark waters of the straight. The fire at the garrison on Irinas Ka was still burning. Whatever had happened out on the island was no accident. It had simply been hit first. He had to report . . . Lord Atan'tal must be alerted. The long-talkers! Of course! Irinas Ka had a long-talker just as the Citadel had. Whoever had done this had destroyed their ability to communicate with the mainland. Which meant this was not over. Someone was coming to take Irinas from him.

A large boom, sounding more like thunder than another explosion, rolled across the city from the north and overrode the ringing in his ears. He turned to face inland, his eyes immediately going to strange lights flashing atop the beacon hill overlooking the city five kamarks to north. He had a small detachment on duty there. Twenty warriors who kept eyes on the boat and cart traffic flowing in and out of Irinas. The flashes lighting the top of the hill seemed far too rapid to be gunfire, but at least there was not another explosion. The hill tower was too far away to worry about. His immediate concern was how he was going to get off his remaining section of wall and organize his warriors.

An explosion rocked the waterfront, and he cringed like a fighter having been hit too many times to know where the next strike would land. The naval station and the adjoining powder cache went up with a bright cloud of fire that lit the entire city as it climbed, standing out against the dark water of the bay like a living fist. Seconds later, the eastern barracks at the base of the city's walls was hit, followed by another series of explosions that spun him back around to the north. The northern gate and the city walls for three hundred strides in either direction seemed to shatter and take flight as if they had been packed with powder and set alight.

He stood staring in shock until a smoking, melon-sized piece of the city's walls hit the battlement wall in front of him, having been tossed nearly a kamark through the air. He did not see the massive explosion behind him out on the island. He was focused on the alien-looking flying machine that had just appeared over the space of the destroyed city walls. The craft seemed to hang in the air without moving, it's spinning wings pulling the smoke and dust from the air in a strange pattern. The craft's nose dropped and it picked up speed moving out over the city. He lost sight of it for a moment and could hear the rifles of his warriors in the city firing at it, as the strange sound of its wings, a rapid drumbeat, came closer.

The craft appeared suddenly just over the edge of the Citadel's still-standing northern wall. Rifle fire from a hummingbird gun erupted out of the side of the craft, and he could see the figures of men inside the craft's open door, sweeping his warriors off the northern wall. The fire lasted just a few seconds as he watched the craft turn slowly and fly over the remains of the Citadel towards him. He had lost his rifle somewhere, but he still had his handgun, a gift from Lord Atan'tal himself when he'd been promoted. His broken right arm did not want to work, but he managed to draw the weapon with his left.

"The central keep and radio tower are destroyed." Jiro Heyashi spoke into his mic, continuing his report as he maneuvered the Black Hawk within the airspace over the rubble of the citadel. He spotted another guard who looked to be the sole survivor on the remaining section of the Citadel's western wall. The poor bastard wasn't going anywhere; that section of wall was a teetering orphan. But the Kaerin guard didn't seem to want to wait for it to fall.

"Target, west wall," Jiro reported.

"I see him," the voice from the door gunner answered a moment before she opened up with a short, accurate burst from the SAW.

Jiro added collective and rose straight up over the city, focused on the output from the forward looking infrared (FLIR) camera mounted to the underside of the helicopter's nose. There were so many fires throughout the city that the image washed out, and he had to adjust the spectral gain to focus on people, more specifically the groups he could see coming together. This fight wasn't over by a long shot, but at least with the radios down, the EDF would have some privacy.

"Company to battalion-sized groups of warriors gathering near the central square and near the waterfront," he reported.

"OK, Eyeball," Colonel Pretty came back. "Get out over the straight and watch for leakers by boat. Navy, are you on station?"

"Columbia on station," a woman's voice answered. "No surface contacts to seaward."

"Independence on station, radar is clear, and we have Wooton Creek covered as well."

"My regards to the Navy," Hank came back. "Eyeball, you are in command over the water. Send the Navy where you need them."

"Affirmative," Jiro responded as he moved out over the city, much of it still intact and standing out all the more for the areas that were burning.

Chapter 26

"I did that! That was me!" Breda was jumping from foot to foot as he watched the blooms of fire and shock waves tear portions of Portsmouth's walls apart. They were just off the main road leading into the city, in a darkened camp that stretched nearly a mile in both directions.

Jake squinted at the outburst in confusion and shook his head. He'd already explained to Breda, in very broad terms, how the bombs were being "dropped" from a universe away. *That*, the annoying Gemendi seemed to grasp. How Breda figured he was due the credit was beyond him. Nonetheless, it was still refreshing to come across a Chandrian who was actively seeking to "get some" against the Kaerin when most of them cowered at the name High Blood. Besides the Jema, he corrected himself. The Jema took the "let's get some" mentality to a whole new level.

"Yeah, that was all you, killer. You are going to stay here with Colonel Pretty." He pointed at Hank, who was on the horn with Jiro, already airborne. "And do you see that large, angry man there?" Jake pointed at the Jema, "Jo-Jo," whose real name was Joose'cel'jo'as or some weird shit that the Jema didn't even try to use. Jo-Jo was Jomra's one-man honor guard and took his job very seriously.

"He has orders to gag you if you can't keep quiet and let the colonel and Jomra do their thing. He *will* shoot you in the leg if you try to follow us. Do you understand? Doc Jensen wanted you back on Eden, but I figured you deserved to watch the show. Don't make me regret the decision."

Breda glanced up at Jo-Jo, who stared back at him and placed a single finger up against his lips. Jo-Jo was a big teddy bear, unless he was fighting. It had cost Jake a bottle of Audy's jasaka to seal this deal, and Jo-Jo seemed onboard.

"I understand. I will not get in the way."

"You are a strange man," Audy said in English, standing next to him. "You like him?"

"Annoying little bastard." Jake nodded. "But yeah, he's alright. Like an angry mascot."

"Jake! Audy!" Hank yelled. "Get your guys rolling! *Door Knocker* has secured their hill and off loaded their artillery. They are standing ready with fire support. Let them reduce any strongpoints that get set up. Herd 'em like we planned. Nagy will breach the east wall; Jeff's on the west. You have the ball, and everybody goes in together." He and Audy scrambled to the JLTV that sat waiting for them; a line of the vehicles stretched out in either direction, backed by their main force that would follow in trucks and on foot.

"Guys!" Hank shouted again. "No fucking sword charges or forlorn hopes. We've got a world to go up against. We'll need every one of you."

Jake flicked Hank his standard, lazy "no shit, I'm in a hurry" salute and climbed into the armored truck. He knew Hank's last was meant for Jomra and more specifically Audy, who would be in a position to hold the leash on the Jema once inside the city. He yelled his own order before slamming his door: "Get Kyle back here."

Audy was looking at him across the cavernous cab of the vehicle with one eyebrow cocked up in complaint. "Hank still worries that the Jema will draw their swords and charge Kaerin rifles?"

Jake reached deep into his bag and flashed Audy the best look of confusion he could muster. "What do you mean?"

Audy just stared back at him in silence, that freaking eyebrow dropping back to rest and then slowly climbing again until it looked like a middle finger standing almost vertical over his eyeball.

"Yeah," Jake admitted. "Maybe a little bit."

Audy shook his head and reached for the radio mic on the dashboard as the JLTV fired to life. "All units will stay inside their vehicles until ordered to dismount. Remote weapons stations only until ordered otherwise." Each of the JLTVs, whether equipped with a SAW, a 30mm chain gun, or a few that carried surface-to-air or ground attack missiles, had the ability to operate the weapons from a control station inside the vehicle.

Audy slammed the mic back into its cradle as Jake slipped the vehicle into gear and began rolling forward. "Feel better?"

"Hey, nobody likes a wild-ass charge more than I do."

Audy flashed a grin. "It would be glorious, though, would it not?"

Nope, not at all. Jake held his tongue. You could only train the Jema up so much. At their heart, they were always going to be a little bent when it came time to do battle. He laid both forearms atop the steering wheel and pointed out the window at the wide-open gate of the city. "We're charging!"

Tom Souza dropped the binoculars against his chest and thumbed his mic. "Alright, the main attack is rolling. Be ready for any calls for fire." He was talking to the artillery unit the *Door Knocker* had already off-loaded atop what their maps had labeled Portsdown Hill. It was only about three hundred feet higher than Portsmouth itself, but on the flat coastal plain, it provided a wonderful view down into the burning city just over four miles away. Come sunup, the artillery would be able to see and correct their own fire.

Four Archer mobile artillery units were spread out in an arc on the hill, behind two companies of EDF infantry who were still digging in after neutralizing the small force of Kaerin they'd surprised upon arrival. The squad-sized Kaerin guard force hadn't stood a chance against the *Door Knocker*'s guns, but they had stood their ground and returned fire against the steel behemoth that had snapped into existence on top of them.

It was time to get the *Door Knocker* back to Eden and embark his assault force. "Ground Force, be advised. We are transiting out in thirty seconds; plug your ears." Tom reached into his pocket and slipped the finger cuff that the techies had come up with over his index finger. Upon transiting, the 9-volt battery powered capacitor would step up the voltage and deliver a painful but short-lasting shock. Upon arrival at their current location, the "pain inducer" had worked as advertised, and he hadn't suffered his usual painful ear-popping syndrome.

He looked over at the small security detail still onboard. Danny Carlisle had a tissue crammed up one nostril to stop the bleeding *his* pain inducer had caused. Corporal Tay'asta had forked over a month's worth of drink chits to the Carlisles for the "honor" of punching Danny in the face and preventing a return of the space spiders.

"You boys ready?"

"Ready, sir." Josh Carlisle nodded back at him and slapped a hand down on his brother's shoulder. "Technician Ross has the honors."

He recognized Ross as one of the radar/radio operators who normally would have been in the pilothouse during a translation. The technician didn't look like he'd ever thrown a punch in his life, but the look of excitement on his face was unmistakable.

"Danny? You still good with this?"

"Yeth, thir." Danny was mouth breathing and flashed him a thumbs-up. "Beaths the spiders all day long, thir."

He couldn't help but smile; morale *was* important. The loud electronic beep countdown started. He silently wished the artillery good shooting. The *Door Knocker*'s next trip to Chandra was going to be a lot different.

*

Kyle instinctively cringed as Carlos's rifle barked once from the woods in front of him. It was simultaneously comforting to know Carlos had him covered, while imagining that whoever Carlos had just shot had been targeting the middle of his own back as he ran for the next tree line in the dark. Night vision for the win, he thought, as he jumped the small ditch at the edge of the planted field and ran deeper into the woods. He spotted Carlos's frame separating itself from the dark trunk of a tree and pulled up.

"I think that's the last of them, for now." Carlos's voice in his ear sounded like he was talking through a wall. Their proximity to the bombs Doc Jensen had 'dropped' had given his head a good rattle, and his hearing still wasn't right. The former Marine sniper had made him wait for nearly five minutes, lying flat in that field before giving him the all clear to run the last thirty yards to the tree line. "They've got decent tactics," Carlos continued. "That last asshole just ran out of patience. They can't see for shit in the dark though."

For now were the words Kyle focused on. "Dom? Hans? Any news from our ride?" The other two members of his team were three hundred yards farther south of them, waiting on them at the edge of the next field over.

"Inbound," Dom answered. "ETA five minutes."

"We've left a trail of bread crumbs, breaking contact," he said. Bread crumbs being the Kaerin corpses strung out in a line behind them, leading all the way back to the airfield. The Kaerin had reacted quickly to the destruction of their barracks at Wooton creek. The enemy that he had half expected to stand around looking at the smoking hole that had been their barracks, had immediately sent squad-sized teams out looking for whoever had attacked them. He could hear Audy's voice in his head, "These are Kaerin, not Strema."

Their current issue was a result of the fact that the Kaerin were firmly entrenched in Napoleonic-era tactics; they couldn't imagine long-range fires from over-the-horizon artillery, let alone an aerial bombardment that used a quantum bridge to deliver ordnance from a world away. He had no doubt the Kaerin would get a decent picture of their capabilities very quickly. But for now, the Kaerin had been attacked; therefore, the attackers had to be close. This time, they just happened to be right.

That last thing he wanted to do was lead whoever was following that trail of bodies to their exfil site. It was already far too close for comfort. Kyle glanced up at Carlos's shadowed face as he spoke into the radio. "We'll hold here until you have our ride in sight; you two can cover our approach if needed." Carlos was nodding in agreement with him.

"Copy that." Dom signed off with a single squelch.

"Sounds like we're missing a party in Portsmouth," Carlos whispered. They could both see the flashes of explosions reflected off the low-hanging clouds to the north of them.

"I still can't hear for shit," Kyle admitted. Occasionally, he'd get the echo of what sounded like a shotgun going off a few miles away.

"Arty." Carlos socked his head. "Sounds like one five five; the *Door Knocker* must have made its delivery."

"At least Jake and Audy are calling for fire," he said. "I'm still worried we are going to get caught up in house-to-house bullshit."

"Your ears ringing? Or you just can't hear?" Carlos stepped closer and tilted his head back by gripping his helmet and taking a look at his ears. "You aren't leaking."

"They're ringing; it'll pass."

Carlos clapped him on the shoulder. "That's as close to a five-hundred-pounder I've ever been. Not something I want to do again. Then again, I'm a Marine. We're smart that way—teachable."

"Yeah, that's what you always hear about Marines . . . you're all rocket scientists."

"You really think the city will get down to house to house?" Carlos ignored the insult and lifted his rifle to slowly sweep the field behind them.

"No, we'll raze the place street by street before we let ourselves get caught up in that bullshit."

"Amen, brother," Carlos intoned.

*

"Here they come!" somebody shouted over the command channel. Jake wanted to scream back that numbers and a fucking direction would have been nice. So far, the EDF had followed orders well, but there was far too much empty chatter coming across the tactical channel which every one of their forty JLTVs sat on. They'd pushed through the destroyed gates and set up a crescent-shaped perimeter stretching inward from the city's north wall. Close to the gate, many of the roads were nearly impassable due to pieces of barrel-sized stones from the destroyed wall. They'd still managed to push in and set up a secure pocket for the unarmored infantry to enter the city behind them.

For the moment, the Kaerin seemed satisfied with pulling their forces together near the waterfront. Resistance had been piecemeal; single Kaerin warriors who had somehow survived the bombardment of the wall's defensive towers had needed to be swept off the remining sections of the outer wall. An occasional burst from one of the JLTV's weapon's stations had been the only indication that the Kaerin were going to fight. Until now . . .

"Get me a fucking direction, link the drone feed, or stay off the air."

Audy slapped him on the shoulder, and passed him a compad. "Junata, in force. Two streets over to the west."

At least somebody was using the drones they'd lofted to good effect. He took one look at the massed Junata, rifles and short swords held aloft, looking more like an angry mob than a real threat.

"Shit . . ." he whispered and glanced down at his tactical map on the console between their seats. Each of their armored vehicles had a GPS transponder, and at least the blue-force tracker seemed to be performing well.

"PR Truck," he mashed on the command channel. "Move to truck eleven, ASAP. Get on your bullhorn—tell them they will not be harmed if they lay down their weapons. Trucks eleven and fourteen, be ready to lay down a carpet of gas on that intersection in front of you. Everybody stays buttoned up."

They had one JLTV designated as a "public relations" vehicle. The techies had mounted a set of loudspeakers on its front hood, below the firing line of the SAW mounted on its remote turret. It was capable of sending more than one message.

"Is it normal they'd send the Junata first?" He asked Audy as he backed their vehicle up a few feet and cranked on the wheel before attempting to squeeze past another JLTV and a stone building that had partially collapsed. Jake regarded the two stunned-looking EDF soldiers sitting and staring back at him from the cab of the other vehicle, as he tried to squeeze the ten-ton vehicle past their front bumper. "It's OK, assholes! No, don't bother backing up. I got this."

"You are getting upset." Audy regarded Jake and shook his head.

"I don't want to have to kill a bunch of innocent people."

"Understandable. And for the hundredth time," Audy raised his voice. "They are not innocent, Jake. They are part of what the Kaerin have built—they are like the janissary armies I've read about in your history. And to answer your question: yes, it is normal for the Kaerin to use subject hosts first. Why would Kaerin sacrifice their own to test your fire?"

"Yeah, what was I thinking?" Jake drove over, rather than around, a field of loose brick carpeting the cobblestone road. He took a moment's perverse pleasure in the rough ride he was giving Audy and his four mounted infantry in the back. "For the hundredth time, you do realize how royally fucked up this planet is, right?"

"Is that not why we are here? Some crazy asshole once told me, 'A good dog does not hunt only in warm weather.'"

"What the fu . . .?" Jake stopped himself and looked over at Audy. The man's smile broke him. He knew the Jema weren't any happier about what they would have to do on Chandra than he was. Nobody understood the task ahead of them better than the Jema seated across from him.

"Alright, point made. Just don't be throwing my Cajun wisdom back at me. Pisses me off . . ."

"No one wants that." Audy gave a short laugh before his attention was diverted to the compad he was holding. "Shit!"

"What?"

"They fired too early," Audy began.

Audy held the compad slaved to the drone over the target intersection in the space between them. Thick clouds of billowing smoke were sprouting from a couple of dozen tear gas cannisters. The leading edge of the Junata wave were now just becoming visible as they made their way up the road from the waterfront.

"Son of a bitch!" Jake slammed on his brakes and looked down at the blue force tracker. The Junata were human; they weren't going to fight their way through a cloud of tear gas, nor would they get in range of the PR speakers before their eyes, noses, throats, and lungs went tits up.

"Trucks eight and nine, stay on your current road, and move up two blocks and cover the intersection from the east and west." It was his fault; he knew that. His order to "prepare to lay down the gas" had been a little too broad for the overexcited EDF troops in truck eleven or fourteen—for either of them, he guessed as he glanced again at the drone image and realized how many tear gas cannisters were now scattered across the wide intersection, releasing their noxious contents.

"Just once, one freaking time, things could maybe go as planned." Jake was half talking to himself, half shaking his head at Audy.

"The gas will not stop them." Audy was a paragon of calm. Far too calm for Jake. The only time he'd seen Audy get really excited about something, was when his friend was running a Kaerin through with his sword. "Their families even now are under the Kaerin guns. They will continue their attack."

Jake wondered for a split second if Audy had gone through the tear gas demo and gas mask practice that they put the EDF through and just as quickly dismissed the question. Of course, he had. Audy had probably been the first Jema to suck in a lungful of the gas and throw up.

He pulled to a stop next to truck eleven and resisted the urge to bitch them out for firing the tear gas—what was done was done. There was enough moonlight that he could see the gas barrier. It was thick enough that he couldn't see shit behind it. The IR view screen showed blobs of heat images coming through the cloud; a lot of those blobs were on the ground but picking themselves up. A handful of Junata appeared out of the swirling front edge of the gas cloud and immediately went to one knee and fired.

"Hold fire!" he yelled into the radio. Heavy slugs hammered into the light armor of the JLTV. One round smacked into the ballistic glass of their windshield between them. The shot left a golf-ball-sized white "bruise" on the glass. Jake's mind went back to his first briefing on bullet-resistant armor; there was an ocean's difference between bulletproof, which didn't really exist, and what they had between them and the nearly .50 caliber rifles carried by the Junata and Kaerin.

"Truck eleven," he ordered. "Illumination flares."

The image of the Junata emerging from the edge of the gas barrier tore at him under the light of the overhead flares. A single Junata warrior went to his knees after firing and doubled over, retching from the effects of the tear gas. Jake watched as the warrior's hands opened the breech of his rifle, pulled a round from his bandolier, and slammed it home. The Junata took a moment to wipe at his face, trying to clear it of the thick mucus and tears which were pouring out of his nose and eyes. The warrior came up on one knee and fired again, as more of the enemy emerged from the swirl of smoke and fired the moment the armored vehicles at the far edge of the intersection came into view.

He could hear the PR truck blasting its message into the air. It might as well have been playing music for all the effect it was having. The Junata did not stop; they stumbled, weaved, and fell like drunks emerging from the gas. But they did not stop. It was a slow-motion version of the first Strema charge he'd witnessed. There was only one way they were going to stop.

"Jake . . ."

"I know . . ." Jake lifted the mic. "All trucks fire."

Kaerin scout Dadus Cag'ista had been sent forward with the Junata to observe and report back. He'd followed the sacrificial Junata at the tail end of their loose formation and left it as they went over the canal bridge. He went to the third-story roof of a subject tenement building and watched as the strange hand-bomb-looking objects were shot out from the armored vehicles with which the enemy had attacked the city. He could not imagine why the invaders, with the power to destroy the Citadel and the city's walls with such ease, would choose to hide behind a smoke screen.

Then the smell of the smoke cloud reached him, and he understood immediately what had nearly stopped the Junata attack. He covered his mouth with his tunic and watched through watering eyes as the Junata stumbled their way forward through the thick cloud beneath him. He was lying prone, watching over the edge of the building, when the armored vehicles opened up. The strange-looking machines atop their vehicles were hummingbird guns, which shot so fast they looked to be shooting beams of light that he easily tracked back to their source. He counted only five vehicles firing, from three different points across the intersection. Looking down into the mass of Junata, the three hundred warriors were too blind and stunned by the gas to attack effectively.

He did not wait to see what the enemy did next. The moment those deadly guns ceased firing, he moved. Bastelta Reka would need to hear of this gas, of the guns he was sure his Kaerin brethren had already heard. He paused to take one more look over the edge of the building through burning eyes that covered his face in tears. It felt as though someone pushed him. He was dead before his body hit the pavement below.

Jake ignored what he'd just done and focused on the drone image in his lap. Friendly sniper fire boomed again from one of the buildings behind him. There'd been reports of observers, probably Kaerin, watching from buildings on the far side of the intersection. The Kaerin forces were still coming together at the wide plaza between the waterfront and a line of brick buildings at the southern edge of the city overlooking the water. There looked to be four or five thousand

Kaerin, with nearly that many Junata coming together at that point.

"East Force, push forward until you can take the main Kaerin force under fire," he ordered. "Jeff, hold your team back on your side of the Citadel; we want them going that direction. North Force, roll south four blocks. Hold at this side, the north side of the canal. Be ready to roll straight south when East Force engages." He dropped the compad on the middle console and looked over at Audy.

"We'll give them one way to go. They'll have to fall back to the Citadel."

Audy shook his head. "I know the plan; it will not work. We should be ready to support Rob Nagy. Once he puts the Kaerin under fire, they will attack him in force. They will not seek the path of least resistance."

"You're probably right." Jake nodded and held up his sat-phone between them. "If that happens, we'll make them wish they'd moved."

Chapter 27

"Tell me where you want us?" Kyle was yelling into the aircar's radio. Jeremy Ocheltree had come and retrieved them from the Isle of Wight with an aircar that was dangerously overloaded. The combined weight of his team, which included Hans's 280 pounds, had the aircar's turbo fans red-lined as it screamed across the narrow straight towards Portsmouth. Between the fires burning in the city and the light beginning to eat its way skyward on the eastern horizon, they had a good view of the Kaerin force that was digging in at the first line of buildings from the city's waterfront.

The Kaerin fortifications were partially obscured by a rough line of roiling white smoke from their rifle fire. It instantly brought back memories of Strema firing lines. He knew it was the shitty powder they used in their cartridges, but at the moment, it was serving them well as the smoke went a long way in obscuring their position.

"Welcome back!" Jake's voice filled the cockpit. "Stay up high, with the light; they've managed to take out our two drones in the last few minutes."

Kyle started to order their pilot upward, but Ocheltree had overheard and was already climbing. "Where do you want us?"

"Put down in the city north of our lines." Jake's voice sounded like he'd been in a fight all night. "Nagy has their attention to the east, and they've sent two massed charges north towards us so far. Jeff is holding position behind the Citadel. They are not retreating to the west as we hoped."

Kyle could see that in an instant. The western end of the Kaerin line was inactive. The enemy wasn't acting like any force they'd ever been up against. The Kaerin had the enemy in sight, and they weren't going to move, regardless of the fact they were being shredded. He could see a carpet of bodies, probably Junata, leading from their lines to the east and north. From their height, the dead looked like debris deposited by a high tide that had washed into the city from the waterfront.

"Is there space for the *Door Knocker* behind them?" Jake yelled.

Probably, he thought, but there was a shitload of enemy down there. Enough that the crazy assholes would probably try and swarm the barge. "Not yet," he shouted. "Call for artillery. Enemy have reduced most of the buildings fronting the water for cover and firing positions. Light them up. We are inbound to you."

"Copy."

"They are just going to sit there and be killed?" Dom asked them all. "Why don't they maneuver?"

"They aren't human," Carlos yelled back. "Not really. They may look like us, but they aren't human."

*

"We have played with these fools long enough." Junior Kareel Jen'gast had long thought that he deserved command of Lord Atan'tal's host on Irinas. In his opinion, Kareel Ist'arno had been too focused on the island's commerce and production. Deserved or not, he had command now and was missing his commander's experience. No one had seen Ist'arno since the attack's first wave of explosions that had reduced the city's defensive walls, destroyed the Citadel, and allowed the enemy, whoever they were, in.

He turned to his cadre of surviving bastelta. "We will drive to the east with all remaining Junata, and one war hand of High Bloods. I ask for two of you, to command that diversion."

Every one of the twenty-three surviving bastelta that he had managed to gather saluted with a fist against their chest—volunteering, in spite of the horrific weapons arrayed against them. He nodded in approval. "You all honor your blood. Ben'sho, Tar'nast, you are both now Kareel by my order. Drive your attack home all the way to the eastern wall. I will lead our forces to the north. Go!"

He did not expect them to succeed; the weapons atop the enemy's vehicles put out a hail storm of lead that had stopped the previous attacks in that direction. The area to the east of wharfs lacked the cover the city's center would provide his force. Worse yet, were the small bomblets that were launched from the enemy's vehicles in numbers that had shredded the Junata they had directed towards the enemy.

He turned to the remaining bastelta, who stood ready and looking to him for leadership. If they were to be defeated here, his highest remaining writ was to give these warriors a death the Kaerin would set to a poem. "We will attack up every street. Remember, stealth . . . above all else. Move slow; utilize building interiors to move as best you can. I have put fingers in the tunnels with explosives, and we will attack their vehicles from beneath. Time your own final rush to the attacks on their vehicles. Those charges will explode as they are emplaced. Wait for the one in front of you before assaulting."

He looked across at Norj'asta; they had both served as the highest-ranking bastelta under Kareel Istan'arno for years. When he'd been promoted over Norj'asta, to Junior Kareel, his former friend had remained quiet. A trend that had continued for the last year.

"Norj'asta, I would ask that you lead the attack on the surface."

"And where will you be, Kareel Jen'gast?" He could tell from the tone of his old friend's voce that Norj'asta was genuinely curious, not accusing him of cowardice.

He hefted the heavy backpack that had been resting at his feet and pushed an arm through the straps. "I have asked the warriors carrying the explosives to forgo the use of fuses. I will lead the attack in the tunnels and do the same. Remember, get as many warriors, as close as you can, before you push. Wait for us to strike before you rush. Let us open up those vehicles and get to the men inside." *If they are indeed men;*

their weapons are like something out of legend. "Let our blood sing."

The salute they offered was again heartfelt. His fate was decided; they all recognized it was the last salute he would ever receive. He seated his final strap and rushed into the sanitation works building that remained unscathed so far. His fellow sappers had gone on ahead of him, and he would have to rush to catch up to them. He had just entered the building and started down the service tunnel when a tearing sound filled the air outside, growing louder with each second. He ignored the flash of light behind him as the first shell landed outside, along the waterfront. The explosion provided a warm, gentle push in the back that only propelled him faster.

*

Hans got his compad talking to the Blue Force tracker as they circled downward to the streets of Portsmouth, and they landed directly behind Jake's command truck. The first thing Kyle noticed was the carpet of shell casings he stepped on. The SAW atop Jake's truck had been busy. He looked behind them to the north and could see EDF infantry on foot, or in unarmored pickups stretching back several blocks. He hated fighting in a city.

"Jake, we're here. Do you have dismounts up in the buildings overlooking the canal?"

"Affirmative," Jake fired back. "All along the canal. We're coming out."

Jake and Audy both came around to the back of the JLTV. The sound of automatic weapons fire erupted to the east, filling the city. "Welcome to the party," Jake shouted and pointed off to the east. "Nagy just reported another push, mostly Junata."

Jake pointed up at the buildings on either side of them. "You want a truck, or do you want to stay on foot?"

"How long before the artillery starts?" Kyle asked.

"Figured I'd wait until you landed; any second now."

"I'm climbing." Carlos shouted from behind them, waved over his shoulder and headed into the nearest building across the cobblestone street. "Don't pull out and leave me; I'm tired of walking."

Jake smiled at him. "You guys have fun? I've been directing little blue icons."

"They've dug in," Kyle started, and stopped as the loud ripple fire from their artillery barked in rapid succession off to the north.

"Not well enough . . ." Hans shook his head as they listened for the falling rounds. The artillery battery fired again in rapid succession, and then a third time before the high arc of the relatively short-range fire mission brought the first rounds screaming in.

They were nearly a mile from the waterfront, with blocks of buildings and warehouses between them and the target area. The ground still shook with the impact. Blooms of smoke and dirt shot skyward in a line over the tops of the buildings south of the canal. The lightening southern sky was still dark enough that they could see streaks of fire and superheated gases within the clouds.

Kyle spun back to the aircar. Their pilot was standing next to the car, just watching them, and had retracted the roof. He wondered for a moment if the kid remembered him. Jeremy Ocheltree had been the first person he'd met on his first trip to Eden. It seemed a very long time ago. "How much fuel you have?"

"Good to go." The kid flashed him a thumbs-up. "I started at Colonel Pretty's headquarters just outside the city."

"I'm going aloft," he said and looked over at Dom and Hans. "Stay with Carlos and watch Jake's back."

"Stay away from the waterfront," Jake shouted at him. "We think they took our drones out with grapeshot from small cannons. I've got replacements coming up."

Another flight of artillery ripped through the air. "What about our own artillery?" Jeremy croaked.

"It's short range and falling almost straight down," he said, climbing in. "Stay over the central city; we'll be fine."

"You're sure?"

Kyle felt himself grin; the odds of being taken out of the air by their own artillery was beyond remote. "I sure hope so," he answered as he climbed in and slammed his door. "You a religious sort?"

"Yes, sir," Jeremy announced before vaulting over the top of his car door and falling behind the wheel. "Especially lately."

He understood that all too well. "Good man, take us straight up."

As the aircar climbed above the buildings, he waved at Carlos, who had just reached the roof of his building by an interior staircase. Once set up, Carlos would be in a good position for overwatch on the bridge, crossing over the canal in front of Jake's position. He arranged his tactical radio and sat-phone in his lap, ready to use either, and was looking behind them to the north towards Portsdown Hill where the *Door Knocker* had dropped off their artillery battery.

"Sir! There they are!"

The stone-lined canal diverted what had once been a tidal stream cutting across the peninsula which this particular Portsmouth sat on. As it lay, it cut across the city and ran above and parallel to the lower city and waterfront before flowing underneath the eastern wall. The slight arch to the heavy stone bridges crossing the canal at each road prevented a direct line of sight down to the enemy's position. With their altitude, that restriction was gone.

"Jake! You've got the enemy moving up towards you in force. Six or seven blocks down the hill. All of them, it looks like." He swung to Jeremy, aware of a buzzing sound that went over his head. "Check the next streets over and get higher!" A round slammed into the nose of the aircar and put a big hole in the trunk that was located at the front of the vehicle.

Jeremy goosed the turbines, and the aircar dipped its nose and shot towards the enemy. Kyle gripped the door frame and was about to scream that "higher" meant UP! Over the canal, Jeremy turned sharply to the left and banked the aircar. Centrifugal force pushed him into his seat as he imagined they were about to slam into the rapidly approaching building he could no longer see through the car's floorboards. The aircar was nearly on its edge, its six turbofans blasting the upper-story walls of the building as it slid past.

Kyle had the strangest thought, that he shouldn't be screaming like a terrified kid on his first roller coaster as he turned to face his "driver," who was grinning like a madman. He looked back behind them as they leveled out of the turn following the canal and shot skyward. The first things he saw were shutters and slate shingles still falling from where the aircar had blasted them loose. His attention refocused instantly, as he almost screamed again.

There was wooden framed catwalk under the bridge and two Kaerin warriors were in the process of crossing beneath the bridge looking right at him. He almost dropped the radio before he could bring it up. "All units, Kaerin are using tunnels under the roads—I repeat, they are in tunnels beneath you! The tunnels cross the canal on catwalks under the bridges. Infantry, move up and cover any drain or manhole you see."

"Oh shit . . ." Jeremy suddenly looked concerned.

He was about to agree when an explosion erupted two blocks to the east of Jake's position. The back end of a JLTV was launched like a catapult, riding a black, fire-rimmed mushroom cloud that spilled out of the intersection across the canal. They'd been certain that the bridges would support the weight of a JLTV; they hadn't figured on dropping a ten-ton truck on one from thirty feet up. He cringed as the JLTV landed roof first and kept going right through the stone arch until it splashed into the dark water of the canal.

"All vehicles, pull back from the intersection, NOW!" he screamed into the radio as another explosion went off on a street behind them. He imagined a line of drains paralleling the canal at the "bottom" of the upper city, the same line on which they'd deployed the JLTVs. "Get eyes on the drains, grenades!"

He watched several JLTVs pull back far below them. The machine gun mounted atop one of them opened up on a figure climbing out of a manhole thirty yards in front of it. A second later, the figure, the manhole, and the street fifteen yards to a side disappeared, sending a fountain of cobblestones skyward. The ovoid crater destroyed the roadbed all the way back to the canal. When the JLTV's front end collapsed into the hole, it was met by the canal water rushing in to meet it. That was one tunnel that was definitely out of commission.

The telltale white billows from the Kaerin long rifles erupted all along the south edge of the canal. A moment later, the rippled sounds of the enemy fire reached them eight hundred feet above. The JLTVs responded in kind, as did the infantry stuffed into the buildings on the northern edge of the canal. Mortars landed in a thick pattern across the canal, on streets, rooftops, and amid the enemy as the automatic 40mm grenade launchers begin lobbing their terrible little payloads. Within seconds, a block-wide strip of Kaerin real estate lining the south edge of the canal was obscured by hundreds of grenade explosions. The tracer rounds from the SAWs and the 25mm automatic cannons atop the JLTVs were aimed via infrared and unleashed hell across the canal.

Kyle was watching closely and could just make out another flight of the small grenades being shot across into the abattoir. They had the enemy by the nose—it was time to kick them in the ass. "Artillery, immediate cease fire. Confirm!"

It was five seconds later before the battery answered with a confirmation. "Last shot out, no fire, repeat, no fire." He forced himself to count to twenty slowly after the last shot impacted the waterfront before reaching for the sat-phone. "Calling Room Service, repeat, calling Room Service now."

*

"You rotten . . . DICK!" Danny Carlisle yelled over the echoing recoil of the *Door Knocker*'s translation into Portsmouth's open wharf area.

Josh looked back at his older brother, who was holding up his hand, the middle finger fully extended with the "shocker" Captain Souza had given him.

"So, the shocky thing? It worked?"

"Yeah, it fucking worked!" Danny yelled. "And I didn't have to get punched in the face either." Danny extended his arm until the middle finger was inches from his face. "How long have you known about this?!"

"Long enough to collect over seven hundred drink chits," he fired back. "We'll never have to buy another drink again." Josh could see the wheels turning behind his brother's eyes.

"How many?"

"You heard me, over seven hundred."

"Alright! Listen up." Captain Souza's voice came in over the radio and assaulted their eardrums. "The ramp's coming down. As we planned, vehicles stay in pairs; everybody stays buttoned up unless ordered to dismount by me or higher. We extend in teams down the wharf before turning into the city and pushing north to the canal. Unless we hear different, forces north of the canal are friendly. No friendlies between here and the canal. Weapons Free."

Their vehicle was one half of the second pair stacked behind the ramp. They couldn't see anything beyond the rear door of the JLTV parked in front of them. Fifteen JLTVs, loaded for bear, were stacked bumper to bumper, three to a line down the length of the barge. Danny looked out his driver's-side window and could see the barge's gun crews racing to their mini-guns. He knew mortar teams were waiting for them to clear off the deck. The sounds of gunfire, lots of it, and explosions going off like giant microwave popcorn killed what he'd wanted to say about an equitable split of the drink chits.

"Gun up?"

"Gun station, and grenade launcher up, video and tracking up," Josh reported back. "Safeties on until we roll free."

The armored truck in front of him inched forward until it suddenly pulled away and shot down the ramp. He did the same and followed the first pair until it turned left at the first road leading north from the docks. He caught a glimpse of the Kaerin troops massed up the road and stacked tight for the next two blocks, just as the lead pair of JLTVs turned up their appointed road and opened fire. Each pair of JLTVs, just like his own team, had one .50 caliber machine gun, and one 30mm chain gun.

He looked over at Josh just as several rifle rounds smacked into the side of their vehicle as they drove past. "Did you see that?"

"Holy shit, that's a lot of bad guys." Their own truck, carrying the remote .50 caliber weapons stations on top, also had a UAV launch system.

"Launch the drone now, before it gets shot to shit."

"Launching," Josh confirmed and then picked up his radio, linked to the guys already on the ground to the north of them. "UAV launched, controls set for channel 4 Bravo, repeat 4 Bravo. Confirm handoff."

Josh turned to his brother. "I think we're going to be too busy to control that thing."

"No shit, brother." Danny slowed slightly to go around the collapsed edge of a building as he turned left up their designated street.

"Confirming handoff, we have the drone." Somebody's disembodied voice came over the radio. He barely heard it as the cab of their vehicle suddenly sounded like they were in a broken music box as slugs hammered into it.

"Firing!" Josh yelled as the machine gun opened up above them, drowning out any other sound, until their sister vehicle opened up with its 30mm chain gun into the ranks of Kaerin who were suddenly faced with an enemy in front and behind them. The Kaerin stacked in the streets were chewed up as the enemy tried to flow away into the buildings and around corners of cross streets to avoid the devastating volume of fire. Hundreds of them had too far to go to relative safety and were mowed down. It seemed to take forever as they were forced to watch, hunched over the steering wheel, staring past impact scars in the thick ballistic shield front window as men were torn apart by their fire. Thirty seconds later, the 30mm cannon next to them ceased fire, and he could hear their own machine gun again.

"Cease fire," he yelled on the truck's internal circuit. "For the love of God! Cease fire." Danny fought down the need to retch as he could see the blood making its way down the road towards them along the gutters.

It was three or four minutes of relative silence, broken by Josh taking control of the remote weapons station from his seat and firing short bursts at Kaerin appearing in windows above the street. The vehicles that had turned up the streets after they had, were still firing, but even that seemed to be dropping off as the Kaerin sought cover or died.

"All right, stay in your lanes, and back out slowly," Captain Souza ordered over the radio. "Pull back to the wharfs, keep weapons and noses front. Team leads confirm when movement complete. *Door Knocker*'s heavy mortar teams are standing by for the all clear."

His team's road, where it met the intersection, was partly blocked by a collapsed building, so Danny had to wait until his partner JLTV backed through the gap before he could follow. His attention on his "rearview" camera was shattered when Josh opened up with the machine gun again. He looked up in time to see half a dozen Kaerin who had decided to attack them over the windrows of their dead compatriots. The enemy went down in a line as Josh tracked the remote weapons station across their front.

"Stupid assholes . . ." Josh muttered.

He swallowed the nasty bile in the back of his throat and focused on his backup camera.

*

"What now?" Jeremy Ocheltree looked a little green in the gills. Kyle understood all too well. He'd had to look away from the drone feed loitering high over the Kaerin's position. At this point, he didn't care if it was bravery or some shard of the Kaerin's societal makeup; he was convinced they were insane. He'd personally called in AC130 gunships in his past life. The level of destruction the flying gunships delivered was legend; and wholly impersonal, almost clinical compared to the scene below him.

After the artillery salvo, and probably because of it, the Kaerin hadn't reacted to the *Door Knocker*'s arrival. They hadn't recognized the sonic boom for what it was. Tom Souza's assault force had moved into their rear, approached and gutted them along the entire backside of the Kaerin assault. Even now, the *Door Knocker*'s heavy mortars were joining those thrown by Jake's and Audy's troops. They'd given up on trying to drive the Kaerin anywhere; they seemed intent on dying right where they were, and Jeff's force had moved in to seal off the western perimeter. Rob Nagy's force was dug in, inside the eastern wall. The Kaerin had nowhere to go.

The first heavy mortar attack had lasted twenty minutes, reducing the buildings in the central city to so much rubble that even from low altitude, some of the former streets were barely discernable. The JLTVs from the *Door Knocker* had moved in twice during lulls in the mortar barrages. Led by the PA system extolling them to surrender and guarantees of their safety. Both times, the remaining Kaerin had thrown themselves at the vehicles as if they were glad to have an enemy they could see and come to grips with. There were far fewer of them by then, and they'd died even more quickly.

"I have no earthly idea," he admitted. "I'd like to bring in some armored bulldozers and just scrape that part of the city clean."

"The roadbuilding crews have bulldozers," Jeremy pointed out. "They're not armored or anything, but I know the road is within sixty or seventy miles of the city. I just flew over them yesterday."

As good as the idea sounded to him, he knew it was just wishful thinking. "How are we for fuel?"

Jeremy glanced at his dashboard. "About five minutes from hitting the reserve."

"OK, get us back to Colonel Pretty's headquarters."

*

Chapter 28

"We've got the countryside locked up," Pretty reported. "We moved the reserves up, and they've done a great job managing to corral the Junata at the outlying farms." He smiled to himself. "It certainly didn't hurt that the locals all thought we were Kaerin as we rolled or flew in. They were more than aware of what was happening in the city, but were clueless as to the whos or whats. We've made contact and explained the situation to over seventeen thousand of them so far. I wish I had something similar to report from the city."

Pretty unrolled a map of Portsmouth or Irinas over the top of the table. "We're confident they're in the tunnel systems. Warriors pop up in the ruins every few hours to die. We have them very much contained, and control the tunnel entrances on their perimeter. We have no idea what the mix of warriors and dependents are. Given what we witnessed firsthand and Jomra's insight, we are certain the Junata host is . . . gone."

"We've had one contingent of Kaerin women and children exit the tunnels under Jeff's position in the west. Just under three hundred women and half that many kids. We're holding them within the courtyard of the Citadel."

"At least they're capable of surrendering." Rob Nagy sounded hopeful.

Hank sucked on his bottom lip and shook his head. "Yeah . . . I thought so too. They didn't surrender. They thought they were escaping, and Jeff let them come through before moving in. Those that figured out what was happening went back down the hole as fast as they could. Elisabeth and Kemi'sfrota are talking to them now."

*

"I would rather you give me my blade back." The Kaerin matron spoke quietly, as if she was worried someone would see her speaking to a non-Kaerin, to someone who should be a subject. "I would slit the throats of these children myself, before I see them taken prisoner by the likes of you."

Elisabeth had always considered herself an intellectual. Not from any sense of superiority or ego, it was just how she was wired. She approached situations intellectually. When it was needed, she could leave her emotions at the door. Kyle called it her "doctor mode." At the moment, her education, training, and experience were failing her. She wanted nothing so much as to slap the look of disgust off the face of the Kaerin woman standing in front of them. Kemi'sfrota had yet to say a word to the woman.

"You are not prisoners," Elisabeth tried again. "None of your warriors who lay down their arms will be kept as prisoners. You will all be allowed to depart across the channel in your own ships."

"Allowed?" the woman hissed, looking between the two of them and shaking her head. "No warrior worth his own blood would lay down his arms."

"I agree," Kemi agreed with a grin, and dropped a hand to her own blade. "Our warriors defeated yours in a single night and day. Even now, those that remain hide themselves—in holes, like scared prey. If they wish, your warriors will be allowed to fulfill their honor. We will kill them all." Kemi snapped her fingers loudly in the woman's face. "This easily. Nothing you say or do will change that simple fact. The fate of the Kaerin women and children will be decided by you, not us. It is not our mercy we offer, but our own honor that would see you live. We have no room for mercy where Kaerin are concerned."

Elisabeth was so out of her element that she just listened to Kemi with a straight face. She'd read of cultures like this; Spartans and Athenians came to mind, as did the Jews at Masada against the Romans. The hate radiating off the Kaerin grandmother was palpable and was matched by Kemi's cold Jema determination.

Kemi had touched a nerve in the older woman, and Elisabeth decided to reach out and pinch it. "It will be one thing in the end," she added. "Our warriors are growing bored. The choice is yours." Kemi flashed her a look of approval and nodded in agreement.

"I would need to return and speak to our warriors." The Kaerin woman looked back in the direction of the leveled city.

"Of course," Elisabeth answered. "Know this - all Junata who survived are expected to be released as well."

"There are none," the Kaerin answered without concern. "Your warriors slew them."

"I was speaking of their women and children."

The Kaerin matron got a confused look on her face as if she did not understand what was being said. "Their warriors fell in defeat. Their whores and spawn paid for their defeat."

Kemi had warned her that the Junata civilians had likely all been killed. She hadn't believed it, or rather, she'd hoped that Kemi's prediction had been colored by what the Kaerin had done to the Jema.

"What are you saying . . . ?"

"It's done." Kemi grabbed her by the arm and turned her in place, away from the Kaerin. If Elisabeth had been wearing the gun that Kyle had given her, she would have used it.

"Go with these warriors," Kemi ordered the Kaerin woman and signaled to a squad of EDF soldiers. "They will see you back to your hole. You have an hour to return to us here. Tell your warriors that after you are safe with your children, they will be allowed to present themselves for battle. Now go."

Elisabeth was aware that Kemi was looking at her. The anger she felt was like nothing she had ever experienced and tinged with a feeling of nausea that wouldn't let go. "How could they . . . just kill them?"

"With no more thought than you give swatting a mosquito." Kemi grabbed her gently by the shoulders. "I have worried about this moment: when your people see for the first time what they are capable of."

"It's not like we didn't believe you, Kemi."

"That is not what I meant." Kemi gave her a sad smile. "We Jema have enough hate to see this through. A piece of our soul is forever gone because of it. I would rather this not happen to you and your people."

*

"This is fucked up." Carlos gave voice to what Kyle was sure they were all thinking.

Kyle doubted if any of them disagreed. He certainly had nothing to say that better described what he was seeing.

"I was there when Audy and Jomra explained what would happen," Jake added. "Jomra said, if we took them prisoner, and put them on a boat, they'd just throw themselves overboard. If they happened to make it to the mainland, they'd be shamed and flayed alive by their own people for allowing themselves to be captured."

"Like samurai," Jiro said and looked around at the rest of them. "Old school."

Old school or not, the Kaerin had left the sewers beneath the rubble and were assembling in a tight formation as if standing for inspection. Many of them were wounded and could barely stand. Those who could, carried the bodies of those who had died from their wounds, dropping them in loose piles with no more care than if their former brothers-in-arms were luggage.

"More than I thought there'd be," Kyle noted.

"Getting close to four hundred of them." Lupe was down on one knee at the edge of their group, just watching, clearly counting.

"After what they've done . . ." Jeff paused and put a dip in. "Part of me wishes there were more of them."

Kyle understood that sentiment as well. After word had percolated that the Kaerin had slaughtered over two thousand Junata women and children, no one had an issue treating them as war criminals. Hank had planned on keeping them prisoner, until the Kaerin on the mainland figured out what had happened to their garrison. Hank's 'mercy' would have released the defeated Kaerin back into the ranks of those across the channel. The Kaerin warriors themselves had refused that offer, just as Jomra had said they would.

If the surviving Kaerin believed their sentence gave them some semblance of honor, so much the better, Kyle thought. The most important outcome was that they'd come out of their holes, and the EDF could get on with securing this place. The Kaerin women and children, nearly two thousand of them, were being held within the remaining walls of the Kaerin Citadel and being well looked after. The Kaerin warriors had been willing to allow their dependents to be returned to the mainland.

The procession of dead men walking ended, and the Kaerin formation was as complete as it was going to get. Five JLTVs were arranged in a rough arc facing the Kaerin, who stood quietly in front of a city block's worth of stone walls that had somehow survived the mortar bombardment. Several of the Kacrin women had requested to be present and were even now standing under guard behind the vehicles arrayed against their husbands or sons.

The Jema had mounted black eagle flags on all the vehicles' front grills. These Kaerin would know without a doubt who was doing this to them. Jomra and Audy had both been insistent that their Edenite allies should play no part in what they deemed a necessary evil. Even from their safe distance, Kyle and the rest of them could tell that it was Jomra who climbed down out of the truck and walked directly out towards the Kaerin.

"I really wish he wouldn't do that." Kyle shook his head, wondering how many of those Kaerin considered trying to take a Jema with them.

Jomra stopped between two trucks and shouted something across the forty yards that separated him from his people's former masters and executioners. There was no time for a reply before he raised a single fist and slashed his arm down. Kyle's body betrayed him, and he gave a start as the machine guns opened up. This fucked-up world and the Kaerin had demanded a price be paid for the lives of two thousand Kaerin women and children. Kyle was certain his people and the Jema had just paid their share. Not in lives lost, but in terms of what this enemy had forced them to do.

*

Elisabeth waited patiently for the bulldozer to rumble past, pushing another pile of rubble out to sea. Over the last week, the stone and brick that had made up the Kaerin city of Irinas had slowly become the new breakwater that stretched out into the harbor's water. Even now, she could see the road taking shape atop that wide strip of stone rubble. The city of Irinas was being scraped down to its foundations, and the Jema were already in the process of rebuilding it as Portsmouth. Much of that construction had a distinctive defensive nature; she'd seen an airplane from New Castle or Kirkton land at the new airfield that morning. The Creight and Junata were helping, and she felt that particular aspect of their foray on Chandra was going as well as could be expected.

She paused at the solitary gate of the Kaerin Citadel that was still standing. The whole edifice was going to be taken down once its current occupants were situated. The two EDF guards touched their foreheads, and she bowed her head in acknowledgement. The entire EDF had picked up Jema habits, and she was and always would be the wife of Kyle. The man who had offered the Jema a gift that could never be repaid.

"Bit of a dustup this morning, ma'am," the Edenite soldier reported.

"How serious?" She'd been half expecting something. The Kaerin women had been getting surly over the last couple of days.

"Several of the young boys attacked those working in the mess hall.

They were dealt with." It was a Jema soldier who answered. This one had a face like stone.

The look on her own face must have betrayed her. "They were . . ." The Jema looked over at his Edenite companion for help.

"We had to cuff a couple of them upside the head, ma'am. They went away wearing it like a badge of honor. Nobody was hurt."

Elisabeth had no doubt the Kaerin boys had been put up to it by their mothers. From what she'd been able to observe so far, Kaerin "motherhood" was basically meant to prepare their boys for a life under arms, and their daughters for lives as broodmares. It was a system she understood from a clinical viewpoint. The system supported their culture, and warfare was the only occupation among the Kaerin. Earth's history had dozens of analogues of the same basic cultural practice in its distant past.

Nar'sa was the only name the Kaerin women's leader had offered. Every day, Elisabeth had visited to check on their welfare, and each visit had been greeted with nothing but open hostility and a bare minimum of words. Elisabeth watched Nar'sa being escorted across the makeshift camp that had been set up in the stone courtyard, by a pair of soldiers who looked like they'd rather be anywhere else than guarding prisoners. She hoped today would be different.

"Good morning, Nar'sa," she started. "Your transport has been arranged. You will all be leaving this evening aboard four of your own ships that we have repaired in the harbor. This time tomorrow, we will have you across the channel and back with your own people."

"You will release us? As you said?" The Kaerin woman acted as if she didn't *want* to believe it.

"We have never intended otherwise. As I have explained, we were only waiting for your people on the mainland to discover what has happened here. Three of their airboats flew over the city yesterday. We allowed one of them to return with what they saw here. I have no doubt the news that his city is gone and all of Irinas is being held by the Jema and the Edenites will come as a shock to your Lord Atan'tal."

"You are one of these Edenites? Your warriors were the ones that did this."

Elisabeth smiled and bowed her head slightly. It was the first time the woman had bothered asking her anything beyond the daily "when are we to be released?" "I am an Edenite. I caution you, do not make the mistake of thinking that the Jema are our subjects. We and the Jema are as one. We are of one mind when it comes to freeing Chandra."

"Who are you people to decide anything for this world?"

"Wrong question, Nar'sa." She shook her head slowly. "Who are the Kaerin to enslave a world?"

"We are the Kaerin!"

She gave a slight laugh. "Yes, you are . . . and you've seen with your own eyes how little that means to us." She turned her back on the woman and took a step away before turning back. "Take a message to your leaders for me. Before this is over, their own wives and mothers will have to make the same bargain you did."

Kyle was waiting for her outside the Citadel's ruined walls. "How'd it go?"

"Pretty sure I made an enemy for life."

Kyle shrugged and held out both hands. "Welcome to my world. She's pissed off, then?"

"I guarantee that woman won't have to be tortured or given heartspeak to tell the truth to whoever asks."

"Good." Kyle nodded. "We want them pissed off."

"They are." Elisabeth smiled and took her husband's offered arm. "Better yet, they're pissed off because they are scared and worried. They as a people have very little experience in dealing with either of those emotions." Elisabeth smiled up at him. "It's so much better than . . . just angry."

"You scare me when you are like this."

She gave his hand a squeeze. "Around that woman, how I feel . . . scares me." She could tell from Kyle's face that he understood and could have said "welcome to my world" again. Instead, he just squeezed her hand back. She worried what this place, what they would have to do, was going to do to them. Especially to Kyle and the others she cared about. She wouldn't waste another second wondering if it needed doing.

An hour earlier, across the scraped stone foundations of the same city, another Edenite came to a decision, looking down at where Kaerin blood had soaked into and stained the stone. Daryl Ocheltree had stood helpless and watched while the Jema had executed hundreds of Kaerin warriors in cold blood. They'd all watched; Colonel Pretty and every officer of the EDF had stood by in silence as the Jema had carried out the first step of what promised to be many in their blood feud with the Kaerin. Eden had marched in step with them. In his mind's eye, he'd taken a step as well.

He had cause to get back to Kirkton: he was in charge of arranging another supply caravan from the supply yard there to Portsmouth. The railway track was already being laid southward, but it would be months before it reached the south of England. He had no expectation of seeing it completed.

Upon arrival, the atmosphere around Kirkton Base was one of celebration. A week had passed since they'd taken Portsmouth, and most of the Jema not already there were headed in that direction or toward points along the coast where bases were being set up to guard against what they all assumed would be the Kaerin counterattack. He even saw a few of the Junata in Kirkton, recognizable by the heavy-duty work clothes the Kaerin had allowed them.

The Junata were already a step ahead of the Creight in their ability to adapt to the new world their neighbors had arrived with. In another month, they'd be wearing Edenite clothes and would be indiscernible from an Edenite until they spoke. It was bad enough that his own people were fighting a war not their own. The process of uprooting and destroying indigenous cultures had already started. A day past, he'd seen a company's worth of Junata recruits start training under Jema tearks in Portsmouth.

The argument that somehow all Chandrians deserved to be out from under Kaerin control was to him, at best, a manifestation of the cultural exceptionalism that so many of his fellow Edenites seemed to espouse. The Jema shared the attitude as well, if for a different reason. That same sense of superiority was one of the reasons he'd left Earth in the first place. Now his own people were exporting the idea here and were actively roping in others to fight and die needlessly. After all, if the subject people of Chandra had it so bad, there were surely more than enough of them to overthrow the Kaerin themselves.

He added himself to a portal delivery headed back to New Seattle. Two dozen EDF soldiers were headed for Eden, and he fell in with them. They were both Jema and Edenites, still full of swagger from their victory. Most of the soldiers wore the strange- looking patch on their shoulders that designated them as "Door Knockers." He'd heard rumors of another portal mission in the offing, yet another attack that would demand Kaerin retaliation. The soldier's excitement as they joked with one another struck him as being in poor taste. The cycle of violence that had started with the murder of his own family all those years ago was now a full-scale war, and no one seemed interested in knowing whether or not the enemy "wanted" the war.

He considered grabbing an airtaxi and swinging out to Lake Washington to see Cynthia. As much as he wanted to explain to his wife what he was about to do, and why, he knew she'd try and stop him. He knew she'd probably succeed. He prayed the letter he'd left for her and the kids, and especially Jeremy, would make them understand. He stayed with the soldiers and hopped aboard the airbus that was taking them out to Whidbey Island.

No one at Whidbey gave him a second look. As a logs officer, he'd passed through here half a dozen times in the last month alone. He left the soldiers when they broke off as a group and headed towards the large facility that had been built to support the *Door Knocker's* operations. Next to it, looking like a semi-organized scrap heap, was another portal assault ship already under construction. Large cranes hovered over the steel carcass as an army of hard-hatted welders put the thing together.

He went the opposite direction, towards a series of large buildings adjacent to the island's nano-production facility. Many of the large prefab buildings were warehouses, where the consumables for and the products from the nano-plant were stored. At the far end sat a large, squat concrete edifice built around and atop the portal chamber.

He carried a large duffle bag with him, full of supplies he might need in the event his targeting was off. The bag, as much as his uniform, got him through the outer door without so much as a second glance from the young man standing his post.

"Special delivery for Colonel Pretty." He patted the bag. "From Dr. Jensen."

"Yes, sir." The young corporal held the door open for him.

The portal control team recognized him and waved at him through the window of the heavy steel door that separated the control room from the large anteroom situated above the portal room itself.

"Where to, Captain Ocheltree?" The voice coming through the intercom speaker was friendly, and he wished he could remember the name attached to the young face on the other side of the glass.

He pushed the talk button. "I've got a one-off in terms of location. Special delivery from Dr. Jensen to some of Colonel Pretty's people on the ground." He held up the orders he'd typed himself that morning.

He hoped the paper hid the breath of relief he let out when the door buzzed open.

He hefted the duffle bag. "Some updated aerial maps and fresh batteries for a recon team that we inserted by helo a few days ago." He handed over the orders. "It's a bit of a secret, that we have people there on the ground."

The technician with the orders in hand kicked off and shot backwards across the room in his wheeled chair. "Coords are coords," he replied, looking down at the numbers and inputting them into the computer. "But the field generators were aligned for New Castle; it'll take a minute to recalibrate."

"Not a problem," he answered, smiling down at the younger technician he recognized from the portal operations at Kirkton Base.

"Seems kinda boring after the loads of bombs we sent." The young man smiled at him. "Were you there when those puppies hit?"

"I was," he admitted. "Outside the city, of course, but I saw you guys take out whole sections of the wall and the defensive towers. Very precise, impressive."

"Wish I could have seen that," the young man replied.

"Like I said," the older technician at the computer console crowed. "Coordinates are coordinates; the portal doesn't care. We just watched them wheel in the bombs, waited for them to get out of the chamber, and pushed the button. Same thing in Seattle, Italy, Japan, and Chile— we just sent them where we were told to."

"Still," Daryl admitted. "A lot safer than having to fly over a target and drop the things." The comment brought to mind Jeremy. His son would have been one of those pilots who would have had to drop the bombs. The portal's use had saved Jeremy from having to live with that act. Now, if he was successful, the portal could end the war.

"OK, coords are set," the older technician commented. "It'll be a few minutes before she's ready." Only then did the technician *really* look at the orders. Daryl looked over the technician's shoulder at the portal setup. He'd watched enough portal translations from control rooms on Eden and Chandra both, to know how the process worked. It needed someone with access to the computer to input the coordinates. After that, it was just a matter of waiting for a series of green lights as the coordinates were fed to the field generators.

"These coordinates are in . . . Central Europe?" The technician's eyebrows scrunched up in confusion, and he wandered over to a monitor set into the surface of the console panel. "Hell, this is just outside the Kaerin capital."

Daryl was relieved his coordinate calculations were correct, but he had already pulled his gun and leveled it at the technician by the time the man spun around to face him. The technician's hand shot out across the panel, reaching for something he didn't get to. Daryl pulled the trigger and shot the technician in the leg. The man spun out of his chair to the floor, screaming in pain. He pivoted towards the younger man behind him and waved him away from the door. "See to him."

"What are you doing?!" the man he'd just shot yelled. His leg was bleeding heavily, the blood pooling quickly around him. Daryl realized that he'd hit the man's femoral artery. Nothing else would explain blood loss like that.

"Use your belt!" he screamed at the younger technician. "Put a tourniquet on his leg." He made sure that was happening as he pulled out a pair of handcuffs and glanced down at the console. The last indicator light for the field emitters surrounding the chamber below flashed green. Once the tourniquet was on, and the two men were handcuffed to a thick electrical conduit pipe running down the far wall, he tossed an envelope down on the console and set the portal for a thirty-second delay.

"Don't do this, Captain." Seers; he remembered the young man's name at that moment.

"Someone has to." He double-checked the settings and pushed the timer's button. He scooped up the technician's radio on the way out the door. He raced out of the control booth and down the wide ramp that led to the portal. The steel doors were just starting to close as he approached.

"All units, medical emergency in portal control room." He didn't wait for a response and tossed the radio back the way he'd come. He made it to the middle of the chamber as the vault doors shut with an audible hiss and loud click. A few seconds later, the electronic countdown started. The letter he'd left explained it all. He'd put a great deal of care and thought into his explanation. He believed they would come to understand. He prayed Jeremy could forgive him.

In an instant, his world flashed out and back into existence. He was standing in the middle of some sort of pasture, near the top of a short hill. A small herd of cattle were running for all they were worth away from him. It was a clear day, and he could see the blue and white peaks of the Alps in the distance. In one of those strange portal moments, he absently wondered what the Kaerin had named those mountains.

He turned and started walking towards a road he could see at the bottom of the hill. There were men on horseback along that road. Some had stopped and were looking in his direction. He noted they wore long swords on their backs. The Kaerin warriors could not have missed his arrival. He kept walking towards them. Not a traitor, he told himself; an envoy.

*

Chapter 29

Isle of Landing, Chandra

Calas wanted to ask why they were going so slow. He was belted into the high-backed chair in the back of the small boat his compatriots called a "RHIB." He knew that was not its correct name, or full name. Like most things from Eden, it took its name from a combination of the first letter of each word of a thing. They called it an acronym, and the whole principal of the naming system just confused the hell out of him. Especially when they decided not to use it. Before they'd started this journey inside a portal room on Eden, Jake had referred to their boat as a "Willard."

The boat had been wheeled into the steel room on an ingenious trailer. The Willard, their equipment, and their small team had translated back to Chandra, to a small cove on the northeast coast of a tiny island that Kyle had called Comino. Their arrival point lay twelve miles or thirteen kamarks from where his father was being held on the Kaerin island of Landing. He had been warned, and had expected the noise which resulted from their arrival. But it was the clap of water against the boat as it rushed in and lifted them on a fountain of water before slamming them back to the roiling surface of the bay that had been truly terrifying.

Jeff had started the RHIB's engine immediately and motored them offshore where they had just sat in the dark, bobbing up and down on the ocean swells for nearly half an hour, waiting for some kind of response that hadn't come. Since then, they'd been headed southeast at a sedate pace, and were off the coast of the island of Landing.

"I thought you said this boat was very fast." Breda, the Jehavian Gemendi whose 'capture' and story had brought them here, was sitting next to him. "Why does the angry Edenite not go faster?"

"I suspect we will move much faster on our return trip," Cal'as answered. He nodded towards where Jeff and Jake stood at the controls. He was certain it was Jeff controlling the craft, but he knew Breda was referring to Jake. "He is not angry; it is just his way."

"I don't think he likes me."

Cal'as smiled more to himself, than in response. "If he did not like you, you would know it." Lupe had said that to him on more than one occasion. "If he didn't trust you, none of us would be here," he added.

Kyle couldn't help but overhear Cal'as. The proud Hatwa warrior had come a long way under Jake's and Jeff's "tough love" tutelage. He couldn't help but think Cal'as's turnaround and ability to contribute was the best harbinger for success that they had on Chandra so far. How many Junata farmers, miners, and laborers, still coming to terms with the reality of their freedom on Caledonia, would be willing to pick up arms against their former masters as Cal'as had done? Hundreds? Perhaps thousands? The scope of their mission here, which in the broadest terms came down to freeing, then recruiting and training the locals, overwhelmed him at times. They would be able to count themselves lucky if Cal'as turned out to be the rule and not the exception.

Even at their distance offshore, it was easy to see the lights and industry of Landing, which Kyle could only think of as Malta. He could not imagine a stranger or more unlikely place to host an industrial revolution, which, true to Breda's word, looked to be well underway. The volume of raw materials and shipping to and from the island that they'd been able to see via satellite photos had confirmed it. All the new Kaerin industry could have been bombed, and probably would be in the near future. What brought them here was Breda's insistence that the Kaerin had access to ancient and very advanced technology. Technology and tools that the Kaerin ancestors had arrived with. David Jensen and even Paul Stephens from his wheelchair were far more worried about that aspect of Landing, than they were concerning the rescue of Cal'as's father and associates for the intel they might provide.

"Scopes clear." Jake's voice in his ear snapped Kyle out of his own head. Jake and Jeff, the two former SEALs, were backlit by the dim glow of the instruments emanating from the central console of the boat. Jeff was piloting the RHIB, while Jake stood next to him, his attention glued to the small maritime radar's monitor. "Several big, slow returns out to sea. Two are inbound. Cargo or transports, I'm guessing."

"Drag the angry elf up here," Jeff called a moment later. "I'm ready to turn into shore."

Kyle could see that as well. Landing's main harbor was in the same location that their Earth-based maps labeled Valetta's main harbor. It was shaped like a giant mouth, with small, jagged spits of land jutting into the sea from both outer edges like teeth. A fat "tongue" of land stuck out in the middle of the harbor. The same geography that had made the place such a formidable fortress throughout Earth's history, and given everybody from the Ottomans to the Nazis a headache, now provided the Kaerin with a natural fortress.

Breda's knowledge of their target had been detailed. The middle peninsula and the massive stone buildings it housed were collectively referred to as "the pavilion," and it included a labyrinth of underground structures and tunnels. They weren't about to motor into the main harbor under the numerous watchtowers. Breda had given them another option.

Kyle had to help Breda undo the clasp of the six-point buckle holding him in his seat. They'd planned their approach with Breda's help, and hopefully, they'd be able to walk into the place. Bending over, he caught a whiff of his Kaerin uniform that the sea breeze had been masking. Taken from a dead High Blood at Portsmouth, it still carried some of the smell from the sewers they'd taken refuge in. His had two .50 caliber bullet holes in the front, matching the exit holes in the back.

"We're ready to approach; go show Jeff where we should land."

Breda gave him a weak nod and came to his feet, fighting to steady himself. "I do not like boats."

"Neither do I." Kyle clapped him on the shoulder.

"There." Breda pointed inland once he'd gotten next to Jeff. "From there, we can walk a short kamark up to the shore road. We should be able to hail a carriage that will take us to the pavilion."

"Should be able to?" Jake spun away from the console, towering over the diminutive Gemendi. "You said there would be carriages."

"There will be," Breda fired back.

Ten minutes later, Kyle was the last of the shore party to jump to shore. Hans, Jake, and Cal'as, all wearing Kaerin uniforms, carrying long swords, and strapped with bags of party favors, were already waiting for him. Breda was dressed just as he had been when they'd found him. Here, Breda was back to being one of the hundreds of subject Gemendi working on the island. They had no choice but to trust the man.

He looked back at Jeff, who would be minding their ride home, with a solitary EDF soldier who had been a fisherman in Astoria a year earlier. "Come back for us?"

"Where else would we go?" Jeff joked and waved as he backed the boat slowly away from the narrow beach.

He turned to the others. "OK, Breda, lead the way."

The Gemendi drew himself up in pride and then wrinkled his nose. "You all smell like . . ."

"Like Kaerin shit!" Jake thumbed his tunic. "We know! They're rentals; now move."

*

It had taken Amona longer than normal to fall asleep. He had been drinking too much wine of late and had decided a week ago to try and limit himself. He had given up that doomed attempt as of a few hours ago at dinner with A'tor. Later, alone at the desk in his airless room, he had polished off nearly a bottle of the stuff on his own. His sleep was fretful enough that when his door opened, spilling in the lantern light from the corridor, his first thought was that he had overslept and Lord Tima had sent warriors to roust him.

He then realized he was dreaming. Breda's face, grinning like the madman he was, hovered over his own. Breda had been sent off the island, to the ends of the earth; he could not be here. A big hand slapped down hard over the bottom half of his face. Breda's maniacal grin came closer.

"I am back, old man," the voice whispered. "I have brought new friends. The Free People are here with me. Do you still want to see a new horizon?"

He was aware of several shadowed faces above Breda's, looking down at him. He was sure he had seen the outlines of sword pommels above their shoulders when the door had been opened. It had to be a trick; Breda would not be here with Kaerin. He was either dreaming, or he was a dead man.

"Mmmmmmphhh pffff."

"Hans, I don't think the guy can breathe."

The strange language confused him further, but the meaty hand came off his face. Breda slapped him then, hard enough to remove any remaining thought he was dreaming.

"These are Free People," Breda explained. "Are you still asleep? Or drunk?"

"I'm not drunk."

Breda smiled at him and nodded, pulling his face back a little. "He is drunk," Breda said.

Amona pushed Breda off him as strong hands at his back helped him sit up. Breda was surrounded by Kaerin. He looked around him and realized the giant behind him had to duck to keep from hitting his head on the stone ceiling.

"What Breda says is true." One of the Kaerin guards knelt in front of him. "We are here to get you off this island and retrieve the device Breda said he helped you hide." Amona was struck by the stench of offal coming off the man even as he digested his strange accent. He pulled his head back in reflex.

"Apologies, these are borrowed uniforms, from Kaerin we had chased into the sewers." The Kaerin or Free Man smiled at him. "Breda has mentioned you want off this island. If that is true, we could use your help."

"Is A'tor Bendera still here?" another voice spoke up from above him.

"Could we light a lantern?" Amona asked, his head swimming. He was certain he was about to retch, and would at least like to find his bucket first. "I think I am going to be sick."

Ten minutes later, they had the old man believing them. Jake had given him a "stay awake" pill and forced some water on him. Breda hadn't stopped answering Amona's questions, and Kyle waited only until he was certain the old guy wasn't going to dime them out.

"The reunion can wait." Kyle clapped his hands. "The two of you will go with Cal'as and Jake. Retrieve Cal'as's father first, then go get this battery. How long will that take you?"

"About half of one of your hours." Breda pulled up his sleeve and showed the Edenite watch he was wearing. "Less, if we do not encounter a patrol on the stairs down to the bottom level."

"OK," Kyle nodded. "Come straight back here when you have them. We will meet you here and go out together."

"No!" Breda shook his head. "We should make our way to the outer courtyard separately. If we have to come back here, we will have to pass the same guards again."

"He is right," Amona threw in. "After we retrieve the battery, it will make sense if we are seen to be walking towards the work areas through the main pavilion. From there, we can walk straight out to the surface courtyard. Equipment coming back into the subject quarter of the pavilion would get us shot on sight."

Breda nodded in agreement. "He is right; you can trust us."

Kyle glanced over at Jake in question.

"Sounds legit. The little bastard has a hard-on for the Kaerin. He's solid."

"What did he say? Do you understand them?" Amona asked Breda.

"I do not know," Breda answered, looking over at Jake. "They do that when they do not wish to be understood."

"True enough," Jake replied in Chandrian.

"Fine," Kyle announced, switching back to Chandrian himself. "We will go with your plan. Hans and I will go back out the way we came in, and check out the gear you say is in the pavilion. We will meet up there." He slapped at the map Breda had hand drawn in advance of their arrival. "We will go out together."

"Check . . . out?" Amona started.

"Not important." Kyle waved him off and faced Jake and Cal'as. "Don't forget to start dropping presents once you get out of this dormitory area." He hated sending Jake out alone with three Chandrians, soon to be four—if they could find Cal'as's father; but he'd known that it was part of the plan all along. "Quiet as a mouse and head on a swivel, Jake."

"No shit, same to you."

Jake, with Cal'as at his side, followed Breda and the older Gemendi Amona through the warren of tunnels. His sincerest hope was they looked like a couple of assholes escorting two sheep. He still wasn't certain who this Amona was. Breda had been insistent that he wasn't a real Gemendi in a technical sense, but was nonetheless a Gemendi of the highest standing here on this stony rock of an island, "and knew everything." Ten minutes of long corridors hewed through solid rock, lit by shitty filament light bulbs every fifty feet; then two chiseled staircases, one taking them back towards the surface before a second dropped them back down into the depths of the labyrinth. Jake was about to lose his shit. It felt like he was being led to a cell where the High Bloods would gamble on how thin they could slice his skin off.

"Stop," he hissed. "How much further?"

"We are nearly to the subject Gemendi quarters," Amona said, steadying himself against the wall. "You will need to tell the guards at the gate we are to retrieve one of our colleagues."

"Guards? You did not say anything about talking to guards."

"If we speak to them, with you present, it would be suspicious."

"I will speak to them," Cal'as offered.

Jake turned to Cal'as and nodded. "I know you are excited to get your dad back, but you need to play it cool. Play your role, right?"

"I can do this." The young man looked like he meant it. He waved the two Gemendi forward. "Just be sure to warn Cal'as's father before he comes out, I do not want any happy hugs or tears. Right? No excitement!"

"No excitement," Breda agreed, before grabbing Amona by the elbow and leading them onward.

The last curve in the tunnel opened up into a wide circular chamber with two bored- looking Kaerin standing on either side of the single doorway carved through the opposing wall. Two staircases, one going up, the other leading deeper into the maze, stood unguarded on opposite sides of the room.

"These two have to retrieve one of their colleagues." Cal'as flashed a quick salute to the chest, and spoke before either of the two guards could say anything. The guard on the right looked like a very bored "sergeant" if Jake had ever seen one. He didn't see any colorful belt or sash to designate him as a teark, but the man looked the part.

The Kaerin waved to the cut in the wall between them and looked at Amona. "Go."

Breda started forward with Amona, and the other guard's arm shot out and pushed him back. "Does it take both of you?"

Amona ignored the exchange and ducked into the dimly lit corridor beyond. Jake watched Breda bristle but retreat a step in silence.

"What's so important this time of night?" The older guard turned and addressed Jake directly.

"Something in the workshop," Jake answered. "If I heard, I do not think I cared."

The response seemed to go over well enough; the older guard smiled knowingly and gave a nod in understanding but kept looking at him. Jake had his right hand on his hip, inches away from his 9mm strapped to his ass cheek under his tunic.

"I have not seen you before. Where did they bring you in from?"

"Legrasi," he answered quickly. He'd given it some thought, and he was proud the response came so quickly. "The Hatwa lands."

Next to him, Cal'as let out a held breath that sounded a lot like "oh shit" to him. The guard's heads, both of them, pulled back in confusion. He'd clearly said something wrong.

"What do you mean? Hatwa lands! What shit is this?!"

Aware that the conversational phase had reached its conclusion, Jake was already reaching for his gun. "I . . . uh." He was slower than Cal'as. The lad's suppressed 9mm barked twice, echoing loudly in the rock chamber. The guards fell back against the wall as Jake was moving forward. One guard was dead on the spot; the other was struggling to bring a whistle to his mouth. Jake ripped the leather cord that was holding the whistle away and dropped his gun. He finished the guard off with a knife under the ribs.

He holstered his gun and turned to look back at Cal'as and Breda. "What the hell did I say wrong?"

"Hatwa lands?" Cal'as was just shaking his head. "You said 'Hatwa lands'! No Kaerin would ever say that. It is Lord Madral's Holding."

"Good to know." He nodded to himself. "Come on, let's get these bodies out of the lobby."

"Does this not count as excitement?" Breda whispered as he bent over to lend a hand.

They were stuffing the two Kaerin guards into a small closet chamber just inside the subject quarters when Amona and A'tor Bendera came down the narrow hall, moving fast. Jake hadn't seen the Hatwa Gemendi prelate since the night the man had foisted his son off on him, but recognized him immediately. The man was grinning as he came up to him, until he looked past him into the closet where his son was covering up a body.

"What happened?" Amona burst out.

"They started asking questions," Jake answered and grabbed Cal'as and Breda by the backs of their tunics.

He gave Cal'as and his father a moment, long enough to hug and shake arms, but it was time to move. "How long before the guards are missed?" he asked Amona.

Amona was peeking around the edge of the father-and-son embrace into the room with eyes as big as saucers. "Until the next patrol."

"How long?"

"It depends on how long it has been—"

He stopped the man with an upraised hand. "How often do they come by here?" Jake was already tired of herding his wards.

"About twice for every one of your hours." It was Breda who answered. "Unless they have changed their patrol schedules since I was last here."

"They have not," Amona answered, giving Breda a nod.

"OK, get us downstairs to this battery thingy as fast as you can."

He tapped his mic button on his collar. "Kyle, if you can hear me through this rock, father retrieved; we are moving down to the battery."

*

"Say again." Kyle had been surprised the radios worked at all down here. He'd gotten a couple of broken syllables. He looked up at Hans in question.

"Jake, say again," Hans tried with no luck and shrugged. "Too much rock between us."

They'd followed the rough map that Breda had drawn them in advance. Either the Kaerin had managed to move corridors around, or the Gemendi had the sense of direction of a drunk college freshman during rush week. They'd just been wandering until they came out onto a balcony, overlooking a massive chamber whose floor was thirty feet below them. The chamber stretched several hundred yards in both directions. It was lit very poorly by two lines of lights running the length of the chamber, on wires strung at a level with them.

Looking at the rounded walls and smooth domed ceiling, Kyle thought Breda's explanation of the Kaerin having built this place, or having carved it out of the stone, was dead wrong. It looked to him like the leftover void from a translation that had been misdirected into solid rock. The upper gallery they stood on and the one opposite them across the gulf had clearly been built after the fact.

At least they knew where they were now. The pavilion floor below them was full of truly alien-looking equipment arranged in neat rows. None of it looked to have been moved in a very long time. Dark black metal in the form of things that were clearly meant to fly. They were shaped somewhat like thick 3D versions of the paper airplanes he'd made as a kid, albeit with a dark glass cockpit. Next to them were vehicles that he guessed were armored personnel carriers of some sort, or maybe just tanks. They had what looked like gun barrels, long thick tubes running the length of the vehicle along their dorsal spines. The aperture opening on the end of the barrel was no bigger than a pencil. It all looked very advanced, and different enough from what they'd seen so far on Chandra that it sent a chill down his spine.

They knelt behind the base of a stone column and waited until a pair of Kaerin guards disappeared out of sight at the far end of the pavilion. "I don't see a way down from here." Hans pointed across the space in front of them. The multiple staircases they could see leading down to the floor all originated from the gallery opposite them.

"Tie your rope off." He motioned over the edge of the stone

balustrade. "We'll take the quick route. I'll get photos of everything I can." Jensen was going to blow a nut over some of this stuff.

*

He could feel all of them looking at him. Jake lowered his suppressed rifle off his shoulder. He'd just dropped the pair of guards standing watch in front of yet another simple door set into the wall of their corridor.

"What you must consider excitement is starting to scare me." This time it was the old man, Amona, who was the smart ass.

Jake ignored the comment and gestured at the door. "Behind that door, right?"

"Yes. We could have just asked to be let in." Amona spoke up again.

"Faster this way," Cal'as answered before he could. He nodded in approval—the kid was starting to come around.

'Faster' was starting to matter. It had taken them more than thirty minutes to get here. They'd been held up at the top of a flight of stairs, behind two Kaerin guards going the same direction they were. It had taken every ounce of control he had not to take them out. The only reason he hadn't, was that they hadn't passed a doorway to hide the bodies in for several minutes, and he hadn't liked the idea of leaving that kind of bread crumb.

He reached into his open bag and pulled out the first of the detonation charges. "How long will it take you to get the battery?"

"I know exactly where it is," Breda spoke up.

"Alright." He didn't have a choice but to trust the man. "How long from here to the workshop and pavilion?"

"That way." Breda pointed past the two dead guards lying across the three-way intersection from them. "It slopes directly up to the pavilion. Five of your minutes if we are not delayed."

"We will cover you from here. Go get the damned thing."

The three Gemendi hustled across the hallway and dragged the Kaerin guards in after them. He was left standing there with Cal'as.

"Must be good to see your father again?" he asked conversationally after waiting in silence for a few minutes.

"It is, yes. Very much so."

"Might as well dig your rifle out of your bag. We'll be done sneaking as soon as they get back."

Cal'as did as he was ordered but kept the somber look of concern. "What's eating . . . what is bothering you, Cal'as?"

"I do not believe Breda has a freaking clue how long a minute is."

He looked across the corridor and could see shadows of people moving within what Breda had called a storage cellar. He glanced at his watch; it had been nearly three minutes of the five they said it would take to reach the pavilion.

"I think you're onto something there." He hefted the demolition charge and the attached timer. "It's why I've been waiting to set this thing." Jake was about to send Cal'as across to check on them when A'tor and Breda emerged with a canvas bag, sagging heavily between them.

He waved them on ahead up the corridor as he set the timer for twelve minutes and signaled Cal'as to fall in behind them. He placed the charge above his head in the corridor where'd they'd been waiting for the Gemendi and ran to catch up to them.

"Breda, just how long do you think a minute is?"

Breda was clearly struggling with the weight of whatever was in the bag, but he looked back over his shoulder. "A one-hundred count. I have made a quick study of your numbering system; it is based on ten—just as ours is."

"Huh." He shook his head. "I'm not blaming you, but a minute is sixty seconds. Sixty minutes to an hour. How long is it going to take us to get to the pavilion?"

"That makes no sense. Why would your system of timekeeping not be based on your system of counting?"

"Because. . . it just isn't," he answered. "More to the point, how fucking long is it going to take us to get to the pavilion?"

"That *is* a confusing system." A'tor looked across their shared burden at Breda. "I can understand the assumption you made."

"About five minutes. . . more," Amona answered just before Jake was about to shoot one of the Gemendi on principle. He looked over at Cal'as, who was grinning ear to ear.

"Is why I want be soldier—not Gemendi," Cal'as said in broken English.

According to the countdown timer he wore on his wrist, they made it to the top of the ramp without seeing another patrol in exactly four and a half minutes. He'd planted two more charges on the way up from the depths of the place, and Jake stopped them with a hiss when he thought he saw movement far down the pavilion. The hiss meant nothing to the three Gemendi, and they kept right on going until Cal'as translated with something that sounded like a grunt.

He squeezed the mic on his collar. "Kyle, this is Jake—we are in the pavilion. Where are you?"

"Jake, good to hear you. We're here, too, at about the midpoint of the ground floor. We're underneath the wings of one of these fighter-looking things."

"I have eyes on you," Jake said, lowering his rifle and letting out a long breath. He flashed the IR illuminator underneath his barrel in Kyle's direction, down the length of pavilion. "Fuse is burning, seven minutes, ten."

"We see you. Catch up to us, and let's go."

Jake swept the pavilion and the galleries above them with his gun before signaling Cal'as forward. He fell in behind them.

"Was he speaking via a long-talker?" A'tor turned back to ask his son. "It is so small."

Cal'as nodded yes, and shushed his father with a finger to his own lips.

Jake had had just about enough of babysitting techies, from any planet, when Kyle's voice hissed in his ear—"Hold up!"

He got the group stopped behind a Kaerin vehicle of some sort that reminded him of the old-school Marine amphibious assault vehicle, except whatever the Kaerin used the thing for, it clearly didn't need to move. There were no wheels or tracks he could see. He ignored the strange vehicle and pulled his group back behind it; whatever had caused Kyle's alert was coming from the direction they'd been headed.

Breda and A'tor sat the battery down with a bang that echoed through the cavernous gallery. He cringed, and before he could slap either one of them upside the head, there was a shout, and he could hear footsteps running towards them. He brought his gun up and peeked around what he guessed was the front nose of the Kaerin vehicle. Two High Blood warriors were running towards them, between the outer wall and the nearest column of parked equipment.

The Kaerin guards had just passed what he figured to be the midpoint of the pavilion when he watched both take several suppressed rounds in their backs, and crash headlong to the floor. One of the Kaerin long rifles impacted something unseen and discharged with a flash of fire and bloom of smoke in the dim light. He spun on his heels and turned back to his group.

"Stay with me! Keep up! Cal'as, follow and keep an eye behind us."

"But . . ." "Should we not . . ." "They know we are here!" All three of the Gemendi spoke at once, and he swallowed what he wanted to say. Amona wasn't encumbered with the battery, and he was the closest to him, so he settled on grabbing him by a fistful of tunic and hauled him to his feet. "Move! Now!"

Jake moved out, gun up, scanning the gallery balustrades above him to either side as a Kaerin guard somewhere in the distance blew his whistle. It was impossible to determine where the sound came from. Every footfall, and more to the point, every gunshot from a dead Kaerin guard seemed to be amplified as sound bounced between the curved walls and ceiling overhead.

A friendly light winked at him from the gallery floor up ahead, and he angled towards Kyle and Hans, hoping the Gemendi were keeping up with him. He was on top of them a moment later as Hans surged past him and caught the battery, which was about to be dropped again.

"How much time we have?" Kyle asked from behind his own rifle as he scanned for threats in the direction they needed to go.

He glanced at his watch as the rest of their party slid to a stop behind the scary- looking aircraft. "Six minutes and small change." He took a moment to slap another charge to the fuselage of whatever it was they were hiding under.

"Quickest way to the surface! Which way?" Jake turned on the three Gemendi and pointed at Amona. "You! Speak."

"End of the pavilion, go right; the long ramp there leads directly to the surface." Amona was breathing hard but smiling. Jake thought the old guy seemed to be enjoying himself. Breda was shaking his head and holding up his hand. "There will be guards on the ramp!"

"Pretty sure they know somebody's here." Kyle stood and signaled them all up. "Let's go."

"Wait!" Hans was on his knees, stuffing the battery into a pack. "I will carry this thing."

"It is very heavy," A'tor pointed out needlessly.

"Not so heavy," Hans grunted as he got the pack closed and swung it onto his back with one arm. He put his other arm through the strap and cinched the belt tight. "Let's go."

*

Chapter 30

They'd made it far enough up the ramp that they could see the half-moon hanging in the sky, further out past the opening. Shouts behind them, coming from near the bottom of the ramp, froze them in place. Kyle had recognized the words, "Stop now" in the shouted Chandrian; he didn't have to guess what the rest was.

"Keep going! Hans, Cal'as, go with them," Kyle ordered as he turned back to the threat. "Let's take these guys," he called out to Jake, who was already walking backward with his gun up. The Kaerin long swords sticking up over their shoulders were probably the only thing that had prevented them from being lit up so far. From a hundred yards away up the dimly lit ramp, they still looked like Kaerin guards escorting slave labor around.

Kyle unclipped two grenades and got the pins pulled. "Grenades," he grunted as he bowled the one in his left hand down the steep corridor as hard as he could, before pivoting, winding up, and making the best outfield throw he could with his right. Jake went to one knee and started firing before either of the two grenades exploded. A couple of the Kaerin decided not to wait either. Stone chips fell off the ceiling above Kyle's head as the ricochet of the Kaerin round screamed up the tunnel beyond them.

When they exploded, seconds apart, the bowled grenade had managed to go a lot farther than the one he'd thrown. Neither had made it close enough to the Kaerin to do any serious harm, but he hadn't expected them to. He popped a smoke grenade and rolled it towards the enemy as Jake continued to fire in short, controlled three-round bursts.

"Reloading!" Jake yelled just as he got his gun up and started his own fire.

"Charges?!" he shouted, figuring Jake had time to check his timer as he reloaded.

"Twenty-four seconds!" Jake shouted back just before he started firing through the growing wall of orange smoke that was billowing up the corridor towards them.

"OK, back out!" he yelled. Knowing Jake would retreat up his own side of the corridor, before stopping, firing, and allowing him to do the same. They leapfrogged in reverse twice before Jake dropped a High Blood who had braved his way through the barrier of smoke.

"Time's up," Jake shouted as Kyle raced past him up and onto the flat stones of the courtyard on the surface. He felt the vibration of the charges through his feet before the sound of the explosions traveled through the warren below them and made it to the main ramp. Jake joined him a second later and fired a last, unaimed burst down the tunnel just as the volcano erupted.

They were already facing back over the expanse of the pavilion, or at least its surface structures, when a pillar of fire nearly a mile away shot skyward. Night turned to day as the shock wave picked them both up and rolled them across the gravel and flagstone courtyard.

He lost all sense of time, but the next thing Kyle was aware of, as he came to one knee, was a gout of flame and smoke shooting out the entrance they'd just used. He glanced over at Jake and tried to shake the cobwebs out of his head. *Why is Jake doing a push-up?*

"What the hell . . . ?" Jake moaned.

Kyle drew in a deep breath and swallowed what he figured was a tooth before he managed to spit out a couple of small pebbles of gravel. "What'd you do?"

Jake looked back at him as the earth around them began to groan.

They both made it to their feet by the time the collapse of the caverns was underway. Many of the buildings on the surface came apart and crumbled to their foundation, and then kept going as the caverns beneath them gave way. An area the size of a football coliseum dropped in a rolling wave 150 feet downward as the labyrinth below surrendered to the weight above it. At the far end of the collapsed bowl, the pit was on fire and looked like a scene from Dante's *Inferno*.

"Secondaries?" Jake offered up, before hacking out a lungful of dust.

"Ya think?" Kyle made sure he had his weapon and grabbed Jake by the shoulder, as much to keep himself from falling over than to guide. He glanced around for a moment; the lights of the harbor area and in the city behind them were out. The glow of the fires below them cast the remaining skyline in an eerie, flickering orange light. "Let's get out of here."

The rest of their party had made it back to the RHIB and was waiting for them as they half climbed, half fell aboard like a couple of drunks. Jeff hovered over both of them, checking their eyes with a flashlight and shaking his head in concern.

"Idiots . . ."

Kyle was dimly aware of Hans getting him buckled into the high-backed chair behind the boat's center console. *This must be how Sophie feels when we strap her into her stroller.* His consciousness seemed detached from the rest of his body. He could still think clearly, but no part of his body seemed to want to work. He could have sworn he was ten feet above the boat, looking down at the whole scene. As the RHIB accelerated away from the shore, Jeff turned around and started poking and prodding at him and Jake, who sat mumbling in the next seat. Jeff's look of concern softened. He hovered over both them with a huge smile on his face. "The *Door Knocker* will be waiting to retrieve us. . . What the hell did you guys do?"

"Don't know," Jake spoke up. "Secondaries . . . I guess." Whether it was Jake's speech or his hearing, the words sounded slurred.

"No shit." Jeff grinned. "We were way offshore and nearly got hit by a piece of stone the size of a minivan."

"Secondaries . . ." Kyle heard his own voice agreeing, sounding as if he were back in the tunnel. He had the distinct feeling that somebody was still talking; it might have even been him. Some part of his brain decided it had had enough excitement for the night and stopped listening.

*

Lord Tima Bre'jana of Landing had mixed emotions associated with the destruction of the Gemendi Pavilion. Many of those emotions would never, could never be given voice; not if he wished to keep his skin. It was a loss that could not be replaced; no one could deny that. When his airboat touched down outside Kaerus in a few hours' time, he would express his regret at the loss of so much of his people's heritage and the technical marvels that served as symbols of their past. He would accept personal responsibility and take whatever decision flowed forth from the council.

Privately, he saw the destruction as an opportunity to yank his people out of the beliefs that they were invincible and that their salvation lay in the past. In the context of Chandra, the tools their ancestors had arrived with those centuries ago fed the Kaerin sense of superiority, regardless of the fact the equipment could not be used. Not after all these years, and certainly not by today's Kaerin, who could not even determine what powered the weapons. No one ever seemed to stop and ask why their ancestors had possessed such weapons.

Tima had thought of little else in the last day and a half. A people, any people, by his way of thinking, built weapons that would further conquest or prevent the same from happening to them at the hands of others. Weapons were built to meet those two distinct challenges.

Advancements in weapons of war arose to meet and overcome challenges. He only had to think of the new factories turning out weapons that they would use against the Shareki, or the new shipyards that were being built in every harbor across the world. A reaction to a threat; in this case, to build a fleet that would take back Irinas. He was certain their Kaerin ancestors had built the wondrous weapons now trapped under hundreds of spans of collapsed rock to meet a similar threat. The ancestors hadn't been omnipotent; they'd still thought they needed such weapons when they came here. What threat had those ancient weapons been meant to overcome?

He hoped he could convince Lord Noka that the destruction of the pavilion would now force the other Kaerin lords to face the fact that they must adapt, evolve to meet the current threat, and quit relying on an inherited, and as recent events seemed to suggest, an unwarranted sense of superiority.

He would tell his tale to the High Council; relate how he had been blown out of bed the night of the attack. How it had been over before they had realized they were under attack. How a mere handful of the enemy had been seen escaping by boat, wearing Kaerin long swords that had allowed them to access the pavilion. He would relate the stories of the few survivors they had recovered from the ruins; they spoke of a gun battle that had erupted within the caverns before the explosion.

He would tell the truth; and could only hope the men on the council would put aside their personal ambitions and come to the same conclusion he had. In the context of what had already occurred on Irinas, with an enemy now sitting just off their shores, their only hope of success lay in looking forward, and not backward. He tore his eyes away from the curved window of his airboat and glanced at the crate he'd brought with him. Anyone looking at it would think he was arriving with a gift of wine.

The destruction of the pavilion had yielded one surprise with which he was still coming to terms. He had almost given up on his search for ancient records within the chain of sealed and half-forgotten ancient chambers around the periphery of the pavilion. After his first "find" of some helpful technical manuals, crumbling with age, there had been nothing to show for his efforts, for months.

The explosion of the ancient ordnance had shaken the entire peninsula; indeed, some of the new factories kamarks away from the harbor had "felt" the explosion and reported some damage from stone that had rained down on them. The collapse of the pavilion had brought down a false wall within one of the old chambers and revealed the device he had packed away in the crate. The subject workers who had discovered it were now feeding crabs at the bottom of the harbor. The unlucky Kaerin dadus who had been supervising them was now one more body to be "recovered" from the pavilion.

It was the first piece of ancient hardware he had seen for which a technical manual was not required. Its simple purpose and operating instructions were etched into the metal of its surface. This he would not share with the council, not unless Lord Noka ordered it. He was certain that would not happen. In Kaerin fashion, the contents of that crate would either condemn him or save him in Lord Noka's eyes. His family's ties with Noka S'kaeda would not save him. Indeed, his own father was one of the more conservative members of the High Council, and he could not expect any support from that direction.

Tima Bre'jana counted himself among the most learned men among the Kaerin. In the last year, his knowledge base had, constant frustrations aside, been expanded greatly. They had learned of, or rediscovered as the case may be, natural principles and laws they could not have guessed at a year ago. Names had to be created for many of their new fields of study. Regardless, he did not understand how the gates between worlds worked; no Gemendi truly did. Given the story of how his ancestors had been marooned on Chandra, perhaps no Kaerin had ever fully understood those laws. *The story of how they had been marooned* . . .

It was a lie. The device he had found proved that beyond doubt. It was, in the simplest of terms, a beacon. The old Kaerin script etched above the operating instructions labeled it a trans-dimensional marker.

Words that had meant little to him, but whose purpose he had grasped immediately. The device could have allowed the Kaerin home world to locate those who had been marooned.

There was a reason the device had not been used. Any of the reasons he fabricated in his mind reinforced the fact that Kaerin history was far different than what was widely believed. He believed Lord Noka might know the truth, the real truth. Under threat from the Shareki, the always-present danger from the subject clans, Tima did not believe their people could afford anything but the truth. Secondary to that, was a hope his discovery would not see him executed on the spot.

*

His own father had been already been present in Lord Noka's office when Tima requested an audience. It was an unwanted reunion. He had no wish to condemn his father with what he had come to say. There were manners involved, though, and father or not, Gasto Bre'jana sat on the High Council. He had waited for an opening in the small talk to politely ask his father to leave him alone with Lord Noka.

"As glad as I am to see you unharmed, Tima, I wish you had not insisted on an audience with me before the council meeting." Noka S'kaeda wagged a finger at him in admonishment. "Oont'tal might choose to make a point out of it." The look on Lord Noka's face told a different story. The prelate was clearly hoping one of his challengers would make an issue out of this private meeting.

"He has been supportive so far," Tima's father spoke up. "No doubt he will remember this meeting, and bring it up in the future if he has cause."

"I do not doubt that." S'kaeda sat back down behind his desk and regarded father and son Bre'jana.

Tima turned to his father in the chair next to him. "Council member Bre'jana, I apologize. But I must speak to the prelate in private, as my Lordship allows."

S'kaeda himself seemed far more surprised by his announcement than his own father did. "I can appreciate the formality, Tima. I assure you, I share everything with your father."

He remained silent and turned to look at his father. If S'kaeda wished to guarantee the secret he had brought with him remained secret, perhaps his own death would be enough, and his father's life would be spared. "With apologies, Lord Bre'jana. I must insist."

His father held up both hands before standing with a smile on his face. "Plant his seed, feed him, train him, and the next thing you know, he is asking me to leave the room." His father gave him a friendly clap on the shoulder. "As is his right."

He waited for the door to shut behind his father before he looked up at the Kaerin prelate. Noka S'kaeda, the man he had called "Uncle" as a youth, was no more. Sitting behind the desk was the Kaerin prelate and all that entailed, all that risked.

The prelate flashed a smile devoid of warmth. "The guards talk like women in the baths; Lord Oont'tal will not know what to make of this."

"He will never know from my lips." Tima pulled the crate up onto his lap, and unlocked the lid with a key he carried around his neck.

"Did you find something interesting?" The prelate's question didn't hide the formal tone he had adopted.

"More than interesting, my Lord." He pushed the straw packing material away and lifted the device free. It was slightly larger than a lantern. He leaned forward and sat it heavily on the prelate's desk.

S'kaeda's reaction told him everything he needed to know. The curiosity dropped from the prelate's face, replaced with something far more controlled. Unless he was mistaken, Tima was certain Lord S'kaeda had seen such a device before.

"From the old chambers? The ones you have been digging through?"

Tima had not realized his activity on Landing had been so closely monitored. Was it due to a lack of trust or out of concern regarding what he might find? Had found. He bowed his head in acknowledgement. "You recognize the device."

Lord S'kaeda stood up slowly, leaned in, and examined the device before looking up at him. "The ancestors brought two such devices with them when they came through the world gate." Lord S'kaeda tapped the top of it with a knuckle. "This one was thought to have been lost."

"And the other one?"

Lord S'kaeda focused on him in silence as he slowly moved out from behind his desk and came around to the front edge, putting himself between the device and where he sat. The prelate's eyes, cold and devoid of anything Tima recognized, bore into him. In an instant, Lord Noka had gone from being a second father to the Kaerin Prelate Lord S'kaeda. The transformation had been seamless, and for the first time in his life, he truly understood why men so feared Lord S'kaeda.

"Guard!" S'kaeda's shout did not surprise him. He had wondered whether S'kaeda would do the deed himself or order someone else's blade to fall. No one was outside the reach of the prelate's authority, not even one whose father was counted the prelate's closest colleague.

The doors to the office suite opened immediately behind him. He took some pride from the fact he did not flinch or turn in fright. Whatever his fate, everything he was or ever would be flowed from the power that stood before him. He would not bring shame to himself or his father in his last moments.

"Teark Ban'are," S'kaeda called out. "Please advise the council that we will postpone until this afternoon. Lord Tima and I have much to discuss."

"My Lord." The door closed with a soft click behind him.

Lord S'kaeda looked down at him and shook his head. The face of the Kaerin prelate slowly softened back into that of Lord Noka. "I am curious to know whether you would have rather died in ignorance, or learned that everything you have ever been told about our history is a lie."

"The truth, Lord," Tima answered. "I am a warrior, yes. But I have always sought the truth of the world. In that, I suppose I am more like other Gemendi than I care to admit."

Lord Noka smiled at him. "Your thirst for knowledge, or truth as it were, does you credit." Noka gestured over his shoulder. "But you have found a truth here. . . that must remain a secret."

"The subjects that discovered it have been dealt with. No one else alive, outside this room, knows anything of the device. The other device you mentioned? This one's twin? Why was it never used to contact our home world?"

"I learned the truth I'm about to share, upon taking this office." Lord Noka shook his head and touched the medallion around his neck. "From prelate to prelate, the truth has been passed down, going back to a time when the truth was known by many. Known certainly by most of the officer corps that led at the time of our arrival. The warriors that served under them, were told what they needed to know, no different than now. It was my own father who told me the truth when I took this office. It was no less painful for me than I suspect it will be for you."

"We were not marooned here." Tima shrugged. "I have already come to terms with that truth."

"I understand your reasoning, but you are mistaken." Noka went back around to his own side of the massive desk and took his seat slowly. For perhaps the first time, Tima recognized that Lord Noka was the same age as his father, who had always seemed far older.

"There was a mistake made, or something went wrong with the gate. Our arrival here, for better or worse, was not intended. We were supposed to have joined other surviving remnants of our faction on an entirely different world. One that Kaerus had controlled for some time. We were survivors who had retreated following what our side had considered the final battle in a global civil war that had lasted two generations."

"Kaerin factions? This was a war. . . we lost?" Tima knew the answer; victors did not retreat. As much as the secret history of his people intrigued him, it was their current struggle here on Chandra that was pulling at his thoughts. The Kaerin had lost before, and could do so again.

"A war our ancestors certainly thought lost. At any rate, the beacon you found would have only told our mortal enemies where we were." Noka looked up at him in question. "Or would still, if the device were found to still function."

"Its power source is depleted. I confirmed that." He shook his head in frustration. "Same issue with most of the equipment now buried within the pavilion. I believe it would still work if we could power it."

"I have often wondered if they still live." Lord Noka shook his head slowly. "Our enemies on Kaerus, or our ancient brothers-in-arms for what it is worth. It has been so long without any word." Noka jerked a thumb over his shoulder. "In my apartment, there is a small hidden library from that era, reserved for prelates. I have read and reread those writings. It was a time of great danger. They speak of weapons whose power I cannot imagine. I have wondered if they might not have destroyed themselves. If they live, why have they not found us by now? Our old enemies or our own people."

"How many worlds are there?" Tima asked the question out loud.

"The universe knows." Lord Noka tossed a hand in the air. "We've trouble enough with this one, with the people who *have* found us."

"Does this library contain anything that would aid our research efforts?"

"Doubtful; most are personal journals from the early prelates, when the truth of what occurred was still fresh and painful. I will give you access to them in the hopes you can derive something from them."

"How does an entire people forget their history?"

Lord Noka lifted both arms in explanation. "Quite easily, from what I have been able to discern. It has been more than a thousand years since we arrived. Forty some generations have come and gone. The vast majority of those marooned here, were simply warriors with no knowledge of the lost battle, no idea that our faction was retreating. Among the officers who knew? If you tell a story enough times, it is believed. Especially when you tell children, who tell their children, and so on. I'm the sixty-fourth prelate. With good fortune, you will be the sixty-fifth."

Tima didn't know what to say. Being told the truth and allowed to keep living had seemed more than enough a moment ago.

"Don't look so surprised, Tima." Lord Noka smiled at him and waved to the door of his office. "I did not decide to tell you the whole truth a moment ago; I chose my successor. Truthfully, it was a decision I made some time ago. It will be your library at some point. For the moment, I am still prelate and am allowed to break with tradition if circumstances require. And . . . if these days do not constitute an extreme danger to our people, I do not wish to live through those that do."

"I am honored."

"Do not be, Tima." Noka laughed as he stood up. "If I could spare you, I would. If I live to turn this medallion over to you, I believe our current issues will consign *you* to a life of worry that you will be our last prelate."

"We are survivors, Lord. The truth of our history proves that as much as the stories we believe."

"I hope you are right, Tima." Noka gestured to the door of his office. "There is one more thing I need to show you."

The long walk from Noka's private chambers, through hidden corridors and down narrow stairways secreted behind the walls of the prelate's fortress, was disconcerting. He had heard rumors of the secret passages; everyone had. He took Noka's lead and remained quiet, following the Kaerin prelate with only a tiny lantern to light their way. They finally emerged from behind a hidden door into a wider, well-lit stone corridor far beneath the fortress.

"Have to stay quiet in the passageways," Lord Noka announced once the hidden door was shut behind them. "There is nothing separating them from the public areas but a thin wall, but it's enough to allow me to come and go unseen when I need to."

Tima recognized the symbols on the line of doors across the hall. It was the private quarters for the prelate's honor guard. One of the doors was flanked by two guards who were gauging his presence with Lord Noka with unconcealed surprise.

"Lord Tima will have access to the prisoner anytime he wishes," Noka announced as he approached the pair. "Be sure to let your brothers know."

"Prisoner?"

Noka waited until they were let into the apartment and the door shut behind them before responding. Across the room, flanking an interior door, were two more guards. "An Edenite officer." Noka offered him a smile. "I believe his rank is somewhat of a mid-ranking bastelta. He speaks our language passably well, though with an accent that is almost painful to listen to. If he is telling the truth, and I believe he is, he came here on his own, without writ from his superiors. An action, which if I interpreted his protestations correctly, ripped all honor from him in the eyes of his people."

"You have questioned him under knives?"

Noka nodded absently, as the interior door was opened by the guards on the sleeping chamber beyond. A man lay abed, asleep or unconscious, swaddled in fresh bandages that circled his head and torso. Long strips of wrapping concealed wounds on the prisoner's arms and legs as well. In many places, blood was already seeping through to stain them.

"Of course, and heartspeak as well. He certainly believes what he is telling me is the truth. Of that, I am certain. The Gemendi I have looking after him is quite amazed at his powers of recovery. We will be able to continue the questioning soon."

"We?"

"Trust me, Tima. You will learn more from this man in an hour, than in a lifetime of digging through the rubble of your pavilion. I have doubts we will even need to induce him further."

"Why would a man do this?"

Noka shook his head. "I cannot say, but perhaps this universe has not forsaken us yet."

*

Chapter 31

Louisiana Bayou, Eden

The Osprey circled the cleared meadow adjacent to the small farm. In the distance stretched the jungle that hid Stant'ala's prey. Jake referred to the jungle as a "bayou," a word that he understood came from one of the Edenite's other languages. Kyle and Carlos, both asleep in their seats next to him, had referred to it as a "swamp." It was a terrain he had never experienced, and he had asked for their help in tracking his prey; the Kaerin scout who should have killed him. Some words sounded like what they were, and "swamp" sounded accurate as he gazed out the window over the seemingly endless track of islands, bogs, and plant-choked waterways.

Jake leaned forward and slapped his leg. "You sure you are up for this?"

Stant'ala knew there were teams of EDF standing ready to move in should he fail. His need to redeem his honor was secondary to making certain the Kaerin scout did not return to Chandra. He understood all that, and it was to the Edenite's credit, and due to Audrin'ochal's influence with the men next to him, that they would "give him a shot." The EDF had spent a lot of effort in tracking his prey from a distance, using drones that flew high enough that they could not be seen by the Kaerin on the ground. He knew where his prey was hiding. Was he "up for this?"

Twice now, his body had been repaired by the tiny machines the Edenites had injected the Jema. This time, an Edenite doctor had to perform surgery and reattach the muscle and tendon in his leg before the tiny machines could do their work. That had been nearly five months ago, and he had missed the fight to capture Caledonia. He had been stuck in New Seattle's hospital for almost a month, the last half of which and those that followed had been "physical therapy"—which was a very strange name for torture. Gemendi poisoners could learn a thing or two from Edenite physical therapists.

The tiny woman, with a warm smile, soft eyes, and zero compassion for his pain, had made the therapy bearable. After a time, she had made it pleasurable, and she was now going to be his handfast, or wife as she insisted on naming herself. Tara—the name sounded almost Chandrian to him—was less than happy with him at the moment. He had tried to explain that it was his duty to stop the Kaerin who had defeated him; that there was no possibility of him taking a handfast until he completed what he had set out to do.

She had been less than understanding and told him not to bother coming back to her. He did not believe her. He had learned much about the Edenites, and it was widely known they said much, whether in anger or in jest, that they did not mean. That she was angry with him, there was no doubt. On the other edge of the blade, there were things that Edenites would never understand about the Jema. The most important of which, to him, was the fact that an enemy had laughed at him in his moment of defeat, and then allowed him to live with the shame of it. Such a man could not be allowed to go on living and breathing the same air as he did.

For a warrior, death was an ever-present part of life. It was the shadow they all convinced themselves was not there. He knew the shadow followed him. He could recognize the same understanding in the men across the seat from him. Edenites, yes; but they were men whose shadows walked as upright as his own.

He nodded across the cargo hold of the Osprey, stacked with the equipment he would use. The most important of which was something Jake had called a duck boat. He had practiced for days controlling the craft in the calm waters of the large lake outside New Seattle. "I am ready."

*

Following a snack of fresh crawdads that Jake had trapped, the three of them had paddled their own duck boat to within a mile of the Kaerin's campsite on a small island amid the labyrinth of water ways and bayou. Carlos had sat at the bow, scanning with his rifle, as Jake and Kyle paddled though brackish water as black as the night sky around them. The recon drones had confirmed that Stant'ala was just outside the Kaerin's campsite, and they wanted to be close enough to end this should the Jema fail.

Upon leaving the boat, the final hike in, to a point where Carlos had a line of sight to the target, had been pure misery for Kyle. He'd done some training in Louisiana, at Fort Polk, back in the day. There had even been some work with the Peruvian military along the border they shared with Colombia, and of course, his deployment to Indonesia. He had enough experience with swamp of varying flavors to know he hated them all. Sure, there were trees and plants that had figured out how to grow without land, but lots of trees and plants did not equal land. Not even close; and then of course, there were the snakes. Personally, he'd rather be dragged under by one of the gators that Jake had said they were going to eat on the way out, than see another cottonmouth. If he heard Jake explain away the danger of venomous snakes one more time by saying "they're good eatin'," he was going to leave his brother-in-law in the bayou.

When he and Carlos made it to the patch of gooey mud, Jake was waiting for them and holding up a snake he had just killed. It was impossible to tell what kind of snake it was though the lenses of his NODs, but Jake's shit-eating grin was impossible to miss.

"You're an asshole. You do know that?" he whispered as quietly as he could.

"Didn't want you to scream," Jake whispered back and then turned to point across yet another weed-choked waterway. Ghostlike sentinels of cypress were just beginning to be visible, with the false dawn turning the black sky to purple along the horizon.

Carlos edged past both of them in silence and went prone, setting up his rifle.

Kyle wanted Stant'ala to be able to do this himself; they all did. Carlos and his rifle were going to make certain that whatever the Kaerin had learned on Eden, stayed here. It might be a moot point with what Darryl Ocheltree had done, but there was always a chance the traitor had been killed by the first Kaerin who had found him. Kyle knew he wasn't alone in praying that was the case.

The patch of mud that Jake had found was just large enough for the three of them. He and Jake sat down near Carlos's feet, where Jake dropped a ghillie blanket over Carlos before unrolling another and draping it over them.

Underneath the camouflaging shroud, the air felt even thicker than it had a moment before, which was hard to believe. He managed to open a gap in the ghillie netting that was reasonably close to his NOD's lenses, until Jake did the same thing and shifted the whole blanket.

"Asshole . . ."

"Dick . . ." Jake whispered back.

It was easier than one would imagine to laugh in complete silence, but they both did. The release felt good. Jake tapped his leg with a tin of Copenhagen in silence, and he gratefully accepted. It didn't make up for the snake thing, but it was a start. There was nothing for them to do but watch and wait.

*

Hanlas lay atop the pile of relatively dry reeds that had served as a bed for the last two moons, as the river delta came alive around him with the lightening sky. Above his head was a low dome of branches that he had woven together and covered in leaves to keep the worst of the almost daily rain off of him. He did not mind getting wet, especially when it meant he did not have to boil water to drink or walk miles to the only nearby spring that he had found. At any rate, it was impossible to stay dry in this place, but he wanted to keep his captured weapon in good condition.

The day before, like every day before it, he had checked his traps and then returned to his hut to cook whatever he had caught over the smallest fire he could manage. It usually meant cooking the meat in bite-sized pieces, a process that always took far longer, but he was not about to build a large fire. Time was the one thing that he had plenty of, and he had burned every small branch and twig on his tiny island a moon ago.

The larger pieces had gone into constructing the raft that he would use to find the world gate. He had one more moon to wait, before he would paddle into the ghost fog he had been instructed to look for. He had never imagined that he would be doing this alone, and that aspect was the most difficult part of his mission. He rolled over and gave the miraculous water bag he had taken off the Jema a shake. Outside of his map book, it was the most valuable thing he owned. He hoped the Gemendi on Chandra could figure out a way to replicate the almost clear, rubbery material the inner bag was made of. Kaerin warriors would carry a "Hanlas" on their backs, and he would be famous.

He drained the container through the drinking tube. It was a long, hard walk to the spring, and the scaly giant lizards that seemed to congregate around it were always a challenge. Their one redeeming quality was that the meat in their tails would feed him for a ten-day. He sat up slowly and peeked through a gap near the hut's opening. It looked to be a clear day, and it struck him that the birdsong was not what it usually was. It had been so long since he'd seen another human, enemy or not, he assumed there must be one of the big *verdota* close by. He had seen the padded paw prints with finger-long claw marks in the mud during his wanderings, and had heard their screeching growls in the night. It was the one animal he truly feared in this horrible place.

He crawled out of his hut and froze upon coming to his feet. There was a short moment of panic when he thought that his mind had broken, and he was seeing things—or people as the case may be. A Jema warrior, the eagle tattoo standing out on his bare chest, stood next to a tree, so still that he almost looked to be part of it.

"I told you, you should have killed me." The Jema's voice, any voice after so long alone, sounded strange in his ears.

"This is not possible," he heard himself mumble with the voice he used to talk to himself. He forced himself to stand taller and withdrew the knife on his belt. "You should have stayed where I left you."

"You will be left here, Kaerin." The Jema's rifle was leaning up against the same tree he stood next to. It remained there as the Jema flowed into motion, his short slave blade in hand. The Jema moved straight at him, almost running the short distance. The Jema was a slave! The sheer audacity of the attack surprised him enough that his looping strike aimed at the man's neck missed. The Jema dropped into a roll, went under the strike, and came up almost behind him. He felt the first prick of the knife against his kidney a split second before the hammer blow struck as the knife sunk in deeply and slashed its way out.

The pain nearly dropped him, but he spun around on one foot, trying to catch the Jema's head with his other. The Jema caught his leg, pinned it against his own body, and slashed open the inside of his groin with a quick dragging slice. His weak strike with his own knife missed as the Jema danced out of range.

They stood staring at one another in silence as he felt his life pumping out of his body. A strange wind blew in his ears, pulsing with the beating of his emptying heart. He tried to bring his knife up to throw it, but the motion dropped him to his knees.

The Jema threw his own knife. He flinched as it sank into the soft mud in front of his knees. It took his remaining strength and focus to lift his head and look up at the Jema who had killed him. A Jema! In that final moment, he was thankful for being alone. No one would witness his shame. He never felt his face slam into the mud.

*

"Remind me never to get in a knife fight with a Jema." Kyle pulled the binoculars away from his face.

"Holy shit," Jake almost shouted; "and we were worried?" The blanket was still draped over them; the morning's sunlight passing through gave everything a green tint.

"Damn, that's some scary shit." Carlos's voice spoke out loud from in front of them. The former sniper hadn't made a sound in the last five hours. "Check him out!"

Kyle and Jake both raised their binoculars. Stant'ala was looking right at them and waving them over.

"How the hell does he do that?" Jake wondered in admiration as he pulled the blanket off of them.

Kyle blinked at the sudden brightness and pointed out across the swamp. He flashed a grin at Jake. "The same way you can suck the ass end out of a crawdad and call it breakfast, or more to the point, crawl through the swamp to grab the boat and come pick our asses up."

"What do you mean?"

"Practice . . ."

*

A note -

First and foremost, I want to take a moment to thank all my readers. I would be unable to count the number of times a review or a note from a reader helped keep writing in general - and in this series specifically - something I wanted to do, versus something that needed to get done. I hope you have enjoyed reading the story. If you have, please leave a review on Amazon. There's no better way to keep the robot happy which ultimately determines the success of a book or the continuation of a series.

At the time of writing, I'm already hard at work on book #3 in my 'Seasons of Man' series – and book #5 in the 'Eden Chronicles' will be next up. Sign up to follow me at my website www.smanderson-author.com. I will put out a quick e-mail alert when I release a new book - and only that. No one need worry that I'm going to fill up your inbox with musings on how I feel. . . about anything. For those of you interested in following more closely, I hope to add regular new content to my website. No promises, as I haven't done it yet, but it remains on my 'to do' list. I'm also on Facebook, at www.facebook.com/SMAndersonauthor.

I've met a lot of great people doing this and it's a welcome break for me to step out of a story and hear from readers. As always, I try to answer everyone. I have to thank a number of people, but first and foremost is my family who somehow puts up with me. I'd also like to thank Marcia Trahan for her editing, Mihai Costea for his work on the cover and my terrific beta readers who probably saw too much - in terms of how the sausage is made. I'd like to give a special shout out to Todd Anderson (no relation) and Brett G. for their in-depth help. As always, my first readers Matt and Craig were a huge help. These two young men have reminded me that they owe readers in Australia and Scotland a car wash for their reviews. They believe I should get them there asap. COVID-19 travel concerns have their uses.

Best regards, S.M Anderson

Made in the USA
Coppell, TX
16 October 2023

22941205R00203